Praise for *Noah's Wife*

BOOK of the YEAR, ForeWord Review Magazine
Historical Fiction 2009

"Thorne is a terrific storyteller . . . transporting readers to another time and place, while opening a window into the fascinating psychology of her brave and persevering heroine."
—Sena Jeter Naslund, author
Ahab's Wife, New York Times Best Seller

"What a journey! It could be an action thriller, but it is so beautifully written, tender and historically enlightening that it is simply an extraordinary work."
—Dianne Mooney, founder
Southern Living At HOME

". . . a novel of epic sweep, emotional power, and considerable beauty."
—Ron Gholson
The Blount Countian

"Not since Mists of Avalon *or* Ahab's Wife *have I enjoyed such a finely crafted woman's point of view on an oft-told tale."*
—Perle Champion, freelance writer and artist
Alabama Writer's Forum

"Thorne writes with what she has—heart, good sense for story, and an understanding of what makes us humans tick. Noah's Wife looks at our origins in a brand new way. It is more Clan of the Cave Bear *than theological treatise—and that's a whole lot more fun."*
—John Archibald
Birmingham News

*"I LOVE it! I am a teacher who deals with students with various disabilities, emotional and ph*ysical, *and I have a stepson with Asperger's. It is really u*~~...~~ *a historical character portrayed like t*h~~...~~ *completely real for the audience."*

D1041969

Noah's Wife

a novel by
T.K. Thorne

BLACKBURN FORK
PUBLISHING

Author's Note

This book is a work of fiction. Names, characters, places, and incidents are used fictitiously, and any resemblance to actual persons, living or dead, except as noted below, and actual events is entirely coincidental. Some persons named in Biblical text appear as characters and events in the book to give a sense of historical context; however specific incidents are entirely fictitious and should not be considered real or factual.

A glossary of names used in the novel may be found at the back of the book.

Copyright © 2009, 2010, 2011 T.K Thorne
Cover art copyright © 2009 Laura Katz Parenteau
Inside illustrations copyright © 2009 Patricia Martin

Blackburn Fork Publishing
Springville, Alabama, USA
www.blackburnfork.com
ISBN: 978-0-9837878-0-8

Printed in the United States of America
First Edition

For Mother

Who danced to the grocery store music
and taught me to test my wings.

Aknowledgements

A big heartfelt thank you for all the dear souls, both friends and family, who read this manuscript, sometimes more than once—Art, Alecia, Clarence, Barbara, Brenda, Chuc;k, Danny, Deanie, Dianne, Debra, Donna, Dottie, Ellen, Fran, Gladys, Harriet, Irene, Jimsey, Joan, John, Kelly, Khristi, Kristin, Laura, Lee, Paul, Perle, Rick, Roger, Sarah, Sue, Suzanne, Valerie, and Warren. Each of you will always be special to me.

To Irene Latham for the poem that seeded the concept of a story about Noah-and-the-flood from a new perspective. To Dr. Temple Grandin for sharing her research and inspiring personal perspectives about Aspergers in her books. To the marine geologists William Ryan and Walter Pitman for their amazing work documenting and dating the Black Sea flood; and to explorer Robert Ballard for his exciting discoveries beneath the Black Sea. To the Birmingham International Center and the Turkish Cultural Foundation for providing me the opportunity to experience the wonders of that fascinating country.

To Patricia Martin for understanding the pictures in my mind and producing the perfect map and illustration. To Joyce and Joy at Chalet Publishers, my first publishers, a big thank you for the opportunity and support you gave me.

A special thank you to my wonderful friends and family for their support and especially to my sister, Laura, my cheerleader for many years, who is turning out to be a fine editor in spite of herself, and who designed the beautiful book cover. Thanks also to Rodney and Maggie for helping her with technical support.

And to my husband Roger, who has never once complained about all the hours I've spent on the other side of that door. I can't adequately express my thanks for your encouragement, support, and love. You are my rock.

Black
Lake

Cave
of the
Goddess

Ruins

Rock Formations

Na'amah's
Village

Mineral Springs

Anatolia

Na'amah's World
(Ancient Turkey circa 5500 BCE)

Cave of the Goddess

5521 BCE

PROLOGUE

Prologue   5521 BCE

My name, Na'amah, means pleasant or beautiful. I am not always pleasant, but I am beautiful. Perhaps that is why I am trundled atop this beast like a roll of hides for market and surrounded by grim-faced men.

If my captors had bothered to ask me, I would have told them that their prize is of questionable value because my mind is damaged. But they did not, and I lie draped, belly down, across the back of an aurochs, a large black ox with an eel stripe that runs down his spine and a stench worse than a rutting goat. My mouth is parched and swollen with dried blood, and every step the animal takes sends a jolt of pain into my chest. Snatches of ground appear between the cloven hooves—a succession of earth, grass, and rock obscured by the dark tangle of my hair—all I have to measure the growing distance from the life I have known.

Savta, my grandmother, believes a narrow birth passage pinched my head. A skilled midwife, she convinced the Elders that my disfigurement would right itself, and they allowed me to live. Tubal-Cain, my brother, would prefer it otherwise. He claims I tore our mother from inside and killed her. I did not intend to do such a thing, but if I did it, we are even, since she squeezed my head. Well, perhaps not even, as she is dead, and I am not.

The aurochs stumbles and I grunt from the jerk. The tall

man with fiery hair who leads the aurochs looks back at me. My village sees many traders, so the strangeness of these men's dress and speech means they are from a distant land. Where are they taking me?

As much as I hate the days, I dread the nights. The tall man pulls me off when it becomes too dark to travel, and my legs wobble beneath me. It is a chance for food and water, but I am fifteen summers, and I know the intent of men who steal a woman. So far, they have not tried, perhaps because I smell like the aurochs, but when they do, I will fight. I am small, but my teeth are strong and my legs have climbed the hills since I was very young. *My hills.* How I miss my hills.

To distract me from the aches in my body and my heart, I will put together the words of my story. I remember everything. Memories appear as images in my mind. Each word-sound I hear has its own color and shape and fits together with the others in patterns that I can recall, just as I can name every sheep on my hillside.

This story will be truth. I speak only truth, unwise as it may be, since lies distress me. And it will be for my own ears, as my words and manner seem odd to other people. I am more comfortable with animals, who do not expect me to be any way than the way I am.

I will start with the day three summers ago when Savta told me I had a secret.

5524 BCE

PART 1

Chapter One

It was my twelfth summer, and Savta and I sought refuge from the sun in my father's house, which sat on the outer edge of the village, near Deer River. We tied the door skins aside for the breeze. The sounds I knew so well were a comforting presence around me—the brown patter of children's bare feet on ground worn free of grass, women's silvery chatter as they prepared food or sang to the Goddess, the *chip-chip* of stone knapping stone to shape it. I heard those things even through the plaster-mud walls. My hearing was very good.

Savta coaxed thread from the pile of soft, cleaned wool, while I gnawed my lower lip at my clumsy sewing, frustrated with the thin copper needle that seemed determined to prick my fingers. We had dug out cool places to sit in the floor of the house. Savta sat on the edge of her hole so she had a space in which to drop the spindle and let it twist the thread, but I believe she also liked to dig her feet into the cool dirt.

The smell of earth mingled with the sweet odor of cedar chips soaking in heated oil, a soothing smell that sent my mind floating to my favorite place on the hills where I could see Deer River twisting like thread to the north, into the Black Lake. Behind me, clustered mountains rose into the sky, their slopes painted the eternal green of conifers, their tops capped white like old women. Below, grey-brown sheep speckled the grazing slopes.

From my perch, I could watch the Black Lake's moods. Winter winds stirred her surface with such violence that she swallowed any boatman foolish enough to try and fish. That was why her name was "Black," but in summer, she was smooth enough to catch the sun when he melted into her.

"What are you seeing?" Savta asked me. She knew that sometimes I saw images of what I was thinking, and then it took me longer to speak, because I had to translate what I saw into words. Often, this was good, because there were things in my mind that I should not reveal, even to Savta.

"My sheep," I said, as though they belonged to me.

In the distance, a dog barked. The rusty sound identified her as Dawn, the aging bitch whose puppies had supplied our tribe with so many good shepherd dogs, she now wandered the village, fed anywhere she decided to linger. Dawn saved her voice for important announcements, a stranger's arrival or perhaps returning hunters.

Annoyed at my needle's obstinacy, I dropped the sewing into my lap. "Why do I have to learn spinning and cooking? I am too clumsy. I am much better at herding."

"Beauty may tempt a man," Savta said predictably, "but a full stomach and warm blankets keep him. Grown women do not watch sheep. When your blood flows, you must marry and start a family."

This was not the first time I had heard these words. I pouted. "If my father and brother are typical of men, I prefer the sheep as company."

Savta snorted.

"Besides, I practice with my sling almost every day, and Yanner says I have ears as good as the dogs, and he would take me hunting if Hunter Clan did not forbid it."

Yanner was my only friend. We were born two days apart. On evening watches, we shared shepherd duties. Like me, he was beautiful, but his eyes were green as spring grass and his hair the color of honey held to the sun.

"I like Yanner," I said. "Maybe I will marry him. He would

let me watch sheep. His mother can make blankets and cook."
Before Savta could object, I added, "I will take my turn in the
wheat and barley fields too, of course."

"It's not for me to say who you will marry," Savta said, but
her mouth pinched in a funny way that always made me think
she was trying not to smile. Savta rarely smiled. She said she
had too much to do, caring for me, my brother, and father, but
I think it was because she had lost all her children, my mother
the last. I suddenly realized that she would have no other woman
in the house when I married.

"Maybe I will not wed Yanner," I said. "Maybe I will just
stay with you."

Her mouth softened. "You are a special girl, Na'amah." The
phrase had sung in my ears so often, it calmed me, a counter to
Tubal's constant taunts.

I asked my ritual response. "How am I special, Savta?"

This time she surprised me with her answer. "In a secret
way. When your blood flows, I'll explain, but you must never
speak of it."

"Why?"

"Always with the 'why?' I remember when you were a tiny
bit of nothing, you toddled out into a storm to see how the
butterflies dodged the raindrops." She sighed, a peculiar swishing
sound, because one side of her mouth did not work right. "For
once, listen. If anyone learns, you'll be thrown in the pit."

I took a quick breath. Two moon-cycles ago, the Elders had
stripped Nigel, the potter, and cast him into the deep hole in the
center of the village. For days, he called and cried, but no one
could speak to him or give him food or water, because he had
broken tribal law by making a clay Father God image wrong.
Elder Kahor claimed it resulted in a sickness that made a bear
attack his hunters.

My heart beat a faster tempo. "Why would knowing my
secret make the Elders pit me?"

She lowered the weighted stick that twisted the thread
between her fingers, and considered me, the left side of her

mouth drooping lower than it usually did. That meant she was either very sad or thinking hard.

"What wrong have I done?" I asked.

Her stern eyes softened. "Nothing, child. You've done nothing wrong."

"Then why?"

A great sigh. Savta sighed a lot, as if a pain in her needed escape. "Do you know the story of First-Woman?" she asked me.

"I know the pieces I have heard on washday." On washday, the women gathered in the river to wash clothing and to gossip. I did not like washday. People avoided me because I said things they did not expect.

"Our ancestors, First Woman and First Man, lived in the Land of Eden," Savta said, her voice taking on the soft singsong of a Teller, "where mist rose to water the land, and the earth was lush with trees and fruit. Mother Goddess spoke to First Woman in a secret language that First Man could not understand, telling her where to find nuts and seeds and all the earth's bounty."

"Is that why men had to hunt animals?" I asked. "I never heard that part."

"Of course you haven't. You've only heard the man side of the story."

I loved stories, though many of them were not truth. People pretended they were, so sometimes I did too, but I had never seen Mother Goddess or Father God. I did not understand why. Even the wind, which was hard to see, carried leaves in its arms and tickled my ears to proclaim itself. The moon never said, I am a manifestation of Mother Goddess. It just hovered in the night sky. I did not say these things aloud, though it was difficult not to say what I was thinking. Speaking such thoughts would get me thrown into the pit. My mind might be damaged, but I was not stupid.

At that moment, I heard footsteps and raised my knuckle to my lips to warn Savta. My hearing was sharper than anyone I knew. Savta often said I heard too much. The footfalls belonged to Tubal. My older brother's left foot hesitated a bit, a heritage from a snake's bite when he was seven and stepped over a rotten log without looking at the other side. The deeper thud of his stride meant he carried something heavy.

We worked in silence until Tubal entered the hut with a dead fawn draped over his shoulder. He dropped it in a bloody heap before me. "Clean this, Ugly One," he said with a glance at me, striding to the oak barrel to dip his bowl for a draught of beer.

The glazed eyes of the young creature stared at me. A spear wound opened her flesh behind the front shoulder. The smell of blood mixed with the scent of cedar chips. A piece of her ear was torn, an old injury. I wondered if she had already escaped one predator only to fall to another, and if her mother mourned her loss.

"Well done, Grandson," Savta said, "but there's no need to bring a carcass into the house. Hang it in the tree, please."

He took another drink and stared at me with displeasure, his normal habit. "Don't let Ugly One wander off and leave you with the work of dressing it, Savta."

My back stiffened with anger. Tubal used to trick me into leaving my chores, telling me I was supposed to be doing something else. I believed him. I was too young to understand lies, but when Savta explained, Tubal could not fool me again. So, I was not confused when Tubal called me "stupid" or "ugly." I knew he said lies to hurt me.

I was not ugly. When Savta combed my hair, she said it shone like the Black Lake on a moon-full night. She rubbed olive oil into my skin to keep it soft, and Savta always told me that I was not stupid; I was special. I did not speak for the first two summers of my life, even though I understood what people were saying. The rainbow of colors that the sounds made in my mind distracted me. Perhaps that was why Tubal thought I was stupid. At two summers, I started speaking in whole thoughts, so he should have known better.

Now that I was older, I knew what a lie was, and I could tell one if I wanted to, but I did not understand the rules for lying. For example, if a person interrupted what I was doing and asked if she were interrupting, I was supposed to say "no," even though she was. This rule, however, did not always apply. If I interrupted Savta, she told me so and scolded me. This was confusing, so things were simpler if I told truths. It was my habit, like walking the same path to the river to bathe. Changes made me uncomfortable.

I pressed my lips and pretended to study the tear I was mending. The needle's sharp prick brought a whimper to my lips and a bead of bright blood to my finger.

Shaking his head in a gesture that proclaimed my uselessness louder than any comment, Tubal grasped the fawn's legs, swung it over his shoulders, and strode out.

When he was out of hearing, I sucked my finger and returned to our conversation to take my mind from the needle's bite and Tubal's scorn.

"What happened next in the story?" I asked Savta.

She lifted the stick and set it spinning again with a deft twist.

"First Man was jealous," she said. "He bade First Woman to speak to the serpent guarding the Tree, so he could overhear and learn the secret, thinking he could gain the ability to understand Mother Goddess' language."

"Oh." A strange thought that a man would be jealous of a woman. Women bear the pain of childbirth, the discomfort of moon times, and the feeding of babies who pull on their breasts. I did not look forward to any of those things.

"Because of love for First Man, First Woman did so," Savta continued without further prompting, her nimble fingers twisting the strand into a fine, even thread. "But when she spoke to the Serpent of Wisdom, First Man did not learn Mother Goddess' language." She paused. "What he learned was fear.

"So enraged was Father God that he cast them from the land and burned it, so they could not return. The earth in Eden is scorched and no man or beast can live on it."

"That was mean," I said.

Savta snorted. "The gods are the gods."

Her explanation was as difficult to understand as the gods

themselves. I frowned, returning to the part that dealt with me. "So, if Father God and Mother Goddess meant for woman to have this secret, and I am a woman, why should I be pitted for it?"

"Oh child, you have much to learn. The man-story lays the blame of angering Father God on First Woman's back."

"But First Woman did it at First Man's bequest."

"That is our story, passed from First Woman to her daughters to her daughter's daughters. Man's story is that First Woman forced forbidden knowledge from the serpent and that angered Father God."

"How do we know which story is truth, man's story or woman's?" I asked.

Savta looked at me as if she wanted to open my head and pour sense into it. "You are chosen by Mother Goddess. How could you have her gift if her story wasn't true?"

I did not understand why Savta thought Mother Goddess chose me. I had no idea what this secret gift was. I had no unique knowledge of foraging or planting. I was good at watching sheep.

Savta reached over and arranged the wool shawl I was mending. "You must decide yourself where the truth lies but, if you value life, you will keep the secret of Mother Goddess's gift and woman's story. Revealing either could mean death."

I also did not understand why truth should bring punishment, but it seemed linked to Father God's anger at First Man seeking women's secrets or First Woman's willingness to share them.

Savta recognized my frown of confusion and said, "You will understand better when you are older, but if people knew, especially the men, they would fear you."

"Because I would be powerful?" I asked, thinking it would not be a bad thing to have Father afraid of me for a change.

"Because they would fear you'd find the Serpent's Tree again and bring the gods' wrath upon us."

That was not likely. The Tree was somewhere very far to the south in Eden, and why would I go to a land that was a scorched, barren desert? I did not even like to wander far from our village, as I was used to what things looked like here.

The rest I will tell you when your blood flows and not before," Savta said in dismissal, pulling the raw wool with fingers that seemed to know their task without guidance from her eyes or mind. I had to explain everything to my hands, and they still were clumsy.

Chapter Two

My blood would not flow for several more summers, so I had to wait for Savta's promise to tell me why I was special, but I did not care because I met Bennu, a most unusual friend. It was early spring after my thirteenth summer.

The morning of that market day, I watched the other children in the fields just beyond the village playing that they were hunting wild horses. I did not understand the way they played, because they kept changing the rules. I knew from experience that they did not want me to join them. It made me unhappy when I did not know how things were supposed to go, especially when they did something silly or impossible, like having a horse run in a different direction from the herd. I had watched horses many times, and they always ran together.

The fields were bright with sunlight and a clear sky. The horse herd consisted of children and the pigs that rooted in the stubble of the wheat fields, not yet burned for planting. The pigs did not cooperate. They did not understand what they were supposed to do either.

Everyone stopped at mid-day to eat and bring water to the houses around the village square, the responsibility of all the children not on shepherd duty. Yanner helped with my portion, since I was small, and he liked me to see how strong he was. In return, I shared my lunch—bread and mashed chickpeas moistened with olive oil, garlic, and honey.

Later that day, Savta called me in. "Go to market. I need a bundle of this." She held up a dried herb sprig. She did not put it in the basket, because she knew I would remember which one. "Your father and Tubal are not back from the hunt, so bring home a fish for dinner and a jar of the yellow powder I use for healing salves."

I smiled. Father hated fish, so it was a treat for Savta and me. I placed a pouch made of fig leaves for the fish and two clay jars for the powder and herbs in the market basket. I always paid careful attention to what herbs Savta used and in what amounts. Perhaps because at four summers of age, I came near death when Tubal coaxed me into eating a handful of dried mushrooms that Savta thought she had kept out of reach. I was terribly sick for many days and perhaps lived only because of Savta's skill, and the fact that she forced from Tubal what he had done.

Yanner joined me on the way to market. In spite of the heat, he wore a deerskin over his linen under-tunic to show his sincerity at seeking adoption into Hunter Clan. Enticed by the weapons displays, he took my arm and started to drag me toward one. When I hung back, he stopped. "Na'amah, you have that look on your face."

"What look?"

"The ox-stubborn one."

"I do not want to look at weapons."

"Come on, Na'amah, I need to see how other tribes shape their blades and whether they use antler bone or flint.

Yanner's father was a shepherd, but Yanner wanted nothing to do with guarding sheep. All the children took shifts watching the sheep, answering to the adult shepherds who made decisions about which rams to use for breeding and which to castrate. Yanner said my company on the hills was the only thing that kept him from dying of boredom.

"Fine," I replied. "When you are an adult of Hunter Clan, come visit me in the hills. That is where I will be."

"I've never heard of a grown woman becoming a shepherd."

"Yes, you have. You just did," I said. "You go look at weapons.

I want to see what animals are here."

Yanner threw up his arms in disgust. Those of Hunter Clan were scornful of the tending of the earth or even herding, though they did not mind eating goat meat or lamb or bread cakes, and they wore wool or linen beneath the animal skins that gave them status. They kept many of the old ways, except they worshiped only Father God. My own father was of Hunter Clan, as was my brother, which was a good thing, as it kept them away from the house for long periods. Father said it was important not to hunt big game near the settlement or we would not have the meat nearby in lean times.

"Fine," Yanner said with a dark tone of voice that meant it was not fine. I was not confused because it was Yanner, and I had asked him enough times to understand it meant he was not happy, but accepted my decision.

We went our separate ways.

That day, like all market days, people brought goods to sell in the village center, a large, square area. They traded with sheep, goats, raw copper, and turquoise. I fingered the three brightly marked cowrie shells in my pouch. The shells came from the south near the Middle Salt Sea and our tribe accepted them for trade. It took many shells to equal the value of a ewe.

I went first to the west end of the square, to Mother Goddess' temple, where her tapestry hung, and where a little stone image of her watched from the wall's alcove. With some reluctance, I placed one of the cowrie shells next to her. Savta said they went to the Goddess, but I believed Elder Mariah took them on the Goddess' behalf.

From the corner of my eye, I saw that Yanner had managed to temper his enthusiasm for looking at weapons long enough to leave an offering at Father God's temple, which presided on the square's east end, where the oil pot always burned.

The remaining sides of the central square housed workshops where artisans shaped pottery, stone, wood, or copper for tools or pots. They were all open so people could see the work and wares. Village houses, including my father's, formed the outer ring around the square. Beyond the houses, Deer River meandered along its course into the Black Lake.

I stopped to speak with Aunt Adah. She was my father's first wife, so she was not really my aunt, but a wife-sister to my dead mother. She did not live with us. Father had put her out before I was born. Aunt Adah always had a smile for me.

"Greetings, Na'amah," she said, looking up from punching the first indentions into a ball of clay. She swiped at a lock of escaped hair with the back of her hand, leaving a smudge of wet clay on her cheek.

"Greetings, Aunt Adah." My gaze brushed her face for courtesy and then dropped to the pot, watching her deft fingers shape the clay with the same familiarity as Savta spun wool into thread.

"Before you leave," she said, "I want you to take something to Savta." She nodded at a cup with a funny face on it. "If that doesn't make her smile, nothing will."

The cup made me smile. "I will remember."

She gestured toward the square. "Go on then. Have fun."

I turned and stepped into the marvelous smell of roasting mutton seasoned with garlic and leeks that permeated the air, masking the subtle tang of animal urine, dyes, and human sweat. Food, jewelry, pottery, and wools, both raw and dyed, lay on hides or woolen blankets throughout the center square. Strangers came on market day to buy the fine wools that were our tribe's pride.

The pit was covered and no one was in it screaming to get out, which made the day more pleasant. I could not ignore it, as others seemed to do. I also did not like the press and jostle of people or the loud market noises, which jumbled together in a confusion of images and colors, and I always made sure to stuff bits of sheep wool in my ears, which helped.

I did like the animals. Pheasants and ducks shifted and squawked in wooden cages. Boar-pigs grunted, rooting for grubs in their enclosures and, of course, sheep and goats were everywhere, both to sell and to trade. Only rams and ewes, of course. The whole tribe owned the wethers—rams that the shepherds deemed unsuitable for breeding and castrated. Anyone who needed meat could slaughter a wether, but taking someone's ram or ewe earned the thief a life shortened in the pit.

The most interesting animal at the market was a large, beautiful bird like none I had ever seen. It was white like an egret, but with a sharp, overjutting top beak. It's eye had a pink center within a yellow circle. When its owner was not looking, I stepped close to its cage, which was in a choice position near the large, flat stone the Elders stood on to make pronouncements.

When it stretched its wings, I could see that the feathers of one were clipped. Below the crinkly skin of its toes, the long curving nails of one foot grasped a half-eaten fruit. The bird tilted its head and looked right back at me. I was uncomfortable looking at people's faces; it made me anxious. I used to look aside, but learned that looking down was better. Men saw it as a demure gesture and women as submissive, and they treated me more as a normal person. Animals, however, keep their communication simple, so I did not mind looking directly at them.

After a moment, the bird dropped the food and sidled toward me on the cage floor, its talons splayed out for balance. I was not afraid, even though the large beak looked as if it could take a hunk of my flesh. Its mouth opened, exposing a thick tongue that looked like a person's. I leaned my face against the wooden bars.

With great care, the creature reached up and grasped an eyelash between its powerful upper and lower beak, scraping down the length of the lash. I do not know why I did not even flinch. Something about the way it moved told me it meant me no ill, but I jumped back at the owner's shout behind me.

"Idiot! That bird's got an ill temper. You want to lose those pretty long lashes?" He spoke as if his mouth and throat were not comfortable with the sounds of our language. He was a stranger, a foreigner.

"Is that bird for sale?" I asked, though I owned nothing to

trade for it, and the two cowrie shells would hardly be enough for such a creature.

"You don't want that bird," another man commented before the stranger could answer. I did not need to look to recognize my cousin's voice, which undulated like green hills. Jabel owned sheep and cattle that grazed on the hill behind mine.

"Yes I do," I replied, wondering if Jabel would loan me a sheep to buy the bird. It was not likely.

"No, girl," Jabel said, as if he did not know me, "a white animal like that is ill luck. White is the death color."

I knew that, of course, but I did not like him saying it. "Everything dies. Why is that ill luck?"

Jabel shook his head and stroked his short black beard.

"Mind your own business!" the bird seller snapped at him. "This is a rare bird. It belonged to a chieftain of the River-People and came from a land more distant still, a dark place of jungles and people with skin the color of night. Very rare creature, this."

"Yes?" Jabel replied with an arched eyebrow. "Why didn't this chieftain keep it? Bet the bird bit him." He laughed.

At that moment, a large rat scuttled at our feet, burrowing under the stack of cages and followed by several dogs in pursuit. Catching the scent of their prey, the lead dog dug wildly at the ground before the cages. Others jumped around. Even old Dawn had joined the chase, her tail wagging with excitement. I did not think she could see what she was after, but she could still smell.

When the dogs' antics knocked over several cages, including the white bird's, the stranger added to the confusion by waving his arms and shouting. He kicked at the dogs, just missing Dawn. One of the clay jars under my arm slipped from my grip and fell, knocking loose the peg that secured the white bird's cage before shattering on the ground.

Released, the bird took to the air, but the clipped wing forced it to trace awkward circles over us.

"See what you've done!" the stranger accused, railing at Jabel and me.

It did not seem fair that he placed the blame on our backs.

Neither of us had caused the rat to hide there or the dogs to chase it and knock over the cages, so I paid no attention to him. My gaze remained on the white bird, hoping it would make it to freedom, despite its wing. I would not like to live in a cage, and imagined it would not either.

To my surprise, it gave a screech of frustration, dove toward us and landed on my shoulder. Strong talons dug into my flesh, but I tried not to move, amazed at such an exotic creature so close. The bird's fan tail brushed my back between my shoulder baldes.

In the same moment, I realized another man was looking at me. I do not know why, because many people were watching, and I was stunned that the bird had settled on my shoulder, but I felt the man's gaze and turned.

Blue eyes above a large, hooked nose and full lips—I saw all of that, including the scar along the ridge of his jawbone; the wild bramble of hair and beard; the rough weave of the sleeveless linen tunic; the worn ox hide wrapping his feet and calves; and the polished stone pendant hanging on a cord from his neck. I saw many more details, but Savta said it was distracting to relate everything I noticed.

It was distracting to notice everything.

The blue-eyed man was Noah, the boat maker. I knew him more from people's talk than anything else. He lived apart from the village. He approached without taking his gaze from me, or perhaps the bird on my shoulder held his attention. Closer, I saw the stone necklace was a piece of blue-green malachite, a charm that brought health to its wearer.

The seller grabbed my bird—that was how I thought of it, since it had chosen my shoulder of all the shoulders in the village center. It protested with a loud squawk and bit his hand as he stuffed it back into a cage, one even smaller than its original prison. I wrapped my arms around my elbows to deal with the rush of sorrow that filled me.

Swearing in a language I did not understand, the seller sucked on his wound and grabbed a strip of cloth to wrap his hand. "Cursed bird. If it hadn't cost me so much, I'd give it away."

Noah now stood near. He towered above me, but I did not give up my position near the cage. The stink of his body was strong enough to rise above the general odor of animals and men. I decided he lived alone. A wife would have made him bathe in the river.

"Why do you wrinkle your little nose?" he boomed.

I winced at the volume of his voice, and realized he was addressing me. "Because you smell bad," I said, keeping my gaze on the bird, which was using its beak and talons to climb in endless circle over the ceiling and walls of its cramped cage.

There was a long moment of silence, and I sensed tension in Jabel and the bird seller, as though Noah might explode with anger, but Noah broke the silence with a grunt and turned to the seller. "How much?"

The look in the seller's eyes changed at once, the tense pucker at their edges smoothing. He smiled. "Well, I can offer you a bargain, I can."

Conflicting emotions tumbled through me. What did the boat maker want with this bird? Yet anything would be better than it staying with this man. Perhaps Noah would build it a big cage, and I could visit and bring it treats. Birds ate bugs, seeds, and fruit. I could do that . . . if he would let me. I looked up at him and found, to my surprise, his gaze was still on me, not the seller or the bird. His eyes were a piercing blue, yet it was not an unkindly look. I dropped my gaze to his feet, noticing the sturdy stitching in the worn hides. He turned his attention to the seller, who had not stopped relating the bird's praises, claiming it could do about everything, including talk.

"I will buy it," the boat maker said, cutting off the monologue.

The seller sputtered in surprise.

"At half the price you named," Noah continued. He placed in the man's hand an obsidian spearhead that had cost the knapper a full day's work. "I'll bring you a she-goat tomorrow morning to add to this."

"But sir—" the man protested, "it has been an expense

to bring the bird all this way, not to mention the exorbitant purchase price."

"Probably stole it," Jabel grumbled.

The seller flushed crimson. "Absolutely not, I—"

Noah shrugged and knelt on one knee to scratch behind Dawn's ears. "This is my final offer then. You can lug that cage and ill tempered bird around to other villages."

"Yes," Jabel drawled. "The people here, you will find, don't have resources to spend on a fancy bird that wouldn't make a meal in a pot."

The seller looked horrified, as did I. "Surely," he blurted, "you wouldn't consider cooking such a rare creature?"

"Wouldn't waste a stone on a white anything, if you asked me." Jabel gave Noah a wink that the seller couldn't see, but that made me lock my mouth. "Bad luck, such an animal."

"True," Noah said, rising to his feet and turning to leave. "I don't know what I was thinking."

"No!" the seller cried, grabbing Noah's hand. "Sold. The bird's yours and the cage with it."

I blinked, recognizing the familiar scenario of negotiation, but worried about the bird's future. Had Noah and Jabel had been jesting about the pot? I took people's statements plainly, though I understood the concept of joking. I did not like jokes. They were like lies. I laughed when Savta tickled me or when I ran across the fields, because it was a joy to run or jump from a tree. I did not laugh when someone tripped another and he fell, as I had seen Tubal do to younger boys. I did not understand that kind of joke.

Chapter Three

Three days later, after a dinner of goat stew and dates, we heard a rap on our door. Father grumbled in irritation. "Probably Batan's wife again wanting to borrow salt. Tell her to buy her own."

Savta was mending a linen tunic and indicated with a wave that I was to go to the door. I pulled it open, my mouth gaping at the sight of Noah filling the passageway. A fine wool blanket dyed in yellows covered his broad shoulders and a bulge at his side.

"A warm night to you," he said politely.

I could not find the words to respond and settled for a nod, moving aside to allow him entry. He stepped in with a puff of cool, spring air that still bore the stench of smoke from the burned field stubble. That smell always meant several days of hard work in the fields, so a crop could be planted and take root before winds or rain stole away the rich soil and ash. It meant days away from my hills, and so the smell always made me downcast.

I stared at Noah before remembering that I held the door skins in my hand and dropped them.

My father rose at once. Savta started to put aside her yarn, but Noah put out a hand. "No, keep your seat. Don't let my presence disturb your work."

"Have you eaten?" she asked. "We have a full pot of stew."

This was not true, but it did not confuse me, because I knew Savta was being courteous in implying we had plenty of food, so our guest would feel free to eat.

"My thanks, but my belly is full," he said.

Her shoulders relaxed. "Very well, but at least something to drink? Barley beer?"

He nodded. "That would be welcome." He moved from one large foot to another, as if not sure what to do with them. I noticed he smelled better.

"Na'amah," Savta said, startling me out of my trance.

I brought it to him in our best mug, the only one without chips. Savta made fine beer. "Good," he pronounced with a smack of tongue that put a satisfied smile on Savta's weathered face. The slight droop at one end of her mouth made her rare smiles a slanted line.

After awkward talk of boat making and the status of game, Noah finally made his way to the topic he had come to discuss— me.

"Lamech, of the tribe of First Man," he said. "I wish to make a request for your daughter, Na'amah."

My heart sank to my knees. I knew I would marry at some point, but not yet! I did not wish to be trapped, subject to the whims of an old man, for Noah was at least twenty-five summers or more. As a married woman, I would have to give up my job as herder to care for a household. I loved the hills, loved how the sun nested in my hair; the wind whispered secrets in my ears; and the night sky dazzled me with its spread of stars. I knew every one of the stars, `their place in the sky for that season and moon phase, just as I knew all the sheep in my herd, their favorite grazing partners, and whether they preferred the center of the herd or the edges. I could tell at once if one was missing or hurt or if the herd was frightened or merely restless. How could being wife to a man compare with such things?

My father regarded Noah with a keen eye. "I see," he said and his lower jaw tightened, which meant he was not pleased. "I am Hunter Clan," he added, establishing that he had a high status.

Hunters, at least in his mind, were the favorites of Father God.

"I am a wood shaper and a boat maker," Noah said, placing his calloused hands palm up on his knees. In his mouth, these words did not seem a humble comparison to a hunter, but a quiet declaration of who he was. "My father," he continued, "was a direct descendent of First Man through his son, Seth. We are of the same tribe and my ancestry is honorable."

Father's jaw protruded farther, a hopeful sign for me. I wondered if he took offense at Noah's claim of honorable ancestry, as father's side of the family was descended from Cain. Cain's name linked us all to shame when he killed his own brother, Abel. I did not know Noah, but his rough-featured face seemed open, and it would not gain him to anger my father.

"Also," Noah added, as if he might have realized his blunder, "I am well able to care for a woman and children," meaning he had sheep and goats. I knew which ewes were his on the north hills. They were healthy with good coats.

"Boat-making is honorable work," Savta said, her fingers back to her sewing.

My heart leapt. Savta's interference would only solidify my father's stance.

Noah spoke again. "I live apart from the village so I can be near a supply of wood, but my house is sturdy and well made. I know she is young for marriage. I only seek betrothal and will provide a share of my wheat and barley for your family as though you were my own father and grandmother." Before Father could draw a breath to reply, Noah added, "And with this understanding—that I will wait three summers for her and, if at that time, you or she does not wish the marriage to consummate, I will withdraw." He sat back, as if he had recited a long-practiced speech and had no more words left.

Father's jaw twitched. It was an excellent offer, one in which he could profit without risk. Even I was mollified, as he offered an escape after three summers. Still, I was edgy. I did not like change. I knew where everything was in our hut. I knew the paths from here to the river, the pastures and the forest, and the way to the Black Lake. I did not want to be married and live in another place with a stranger.

After a few moments thought, father said, "It is a fair offer."

"A generous offer," Savta said, pulling a thread tight and biting it off with her front teeth. She was proud that she still had several teeth, despite her age.

"Quiet, woman," Father instructed.

"Then I have your blessing?" Noah asked, his body tense as an elk that has scented a wolf . . . or, I amended, a mate. I knew men married women to have their children. Savta rubbing oil into my skin was one thing—she was careful to move slowly and allow me to adjust to her touch—but the thought of Noah scraping his huge, rough hands over my body made me shiver. The older girls' stories often included graphic details, and I had heard the virgin cries of newlywed women. Also, I had no desire for smelly babies to clean and wash who would pull at my nipples.

Father rose and spit into his hand. Noah did the same and they clasped hands in an oath bond. My belly twisted in anxiety.

"I brought my betrothed gifts," Noah said.

Father nodded and Noah turned, looking at me for the first time. "Please accept my gifts, Na'amah." Before I could tell him I did not want anything from him, he produced a bone knife in a deerskin casing. I took it without a word. Then he raised the blanket from the object at his side. I felt like an idiot for not realizing what it must be, but I drew a quick breath. The white bird! It picked up one foot and scratched its head with a claw, one eye on me.

"Mother Goddess," Savta breathed.

Father glared at her. He did not like mention of the Goddess in his house, as he was Hunter Clan and followed only Father God. Savta sniffed and concentrated on her next stitch. She said Father God was useless without the Goddess. What purpose was the bee without nectar? Man had honored the Goddess from the time he realized woman held the power of creation in their bellies. Besides, did not all the animals belong to her? This rejection of the Goddess by Hunter Clan was nonsense and the reason game was scarce. She said these things to me when Father was not around.

Father coughed. "A strange betrothal gift. Not much meat to it."

"He's not for the pot," Noah said quickly. "He's a companion."

"How do you know the bird is a male?" I asked, my fears forgotten for the moment.

"His name is Bennu. The seller claims it is a name for a sky god in bird form. He wasn't clear, but he said Bennu comes from a land far to the south and needs to be protected from cold weather."

I crossed the room and squatted before the cage, not believing my fortune. Bennu was mine and not even Father could protest a betrothal gift.

"Does he make you happy, Na'amah?" Noah asked.

I glanced up at him, unable to alter my beaming smile, despite my fears. He seemed to drink my smile like a thirsty man drinks water. Then he said, "He likes to be up high, so I brought a little something I made." He hesitated. "If I may?" This time he directed his question at Savta, which was appropriate. Women had status over home matters.

Savta nodded, her eyes bright, as though, after such a long life full of knowing what the next day and even the next moment would bring, she welcomed surprises.

Noah left and returned with a wooden structure as tall as my chest though half as wide. It had two sections with doors. Fitted through a hole in its top was a forked branch. Noah had obviously made this for Bennu. He opened the bird's cage door and presented his second and third fingers pressed together as a perch.

Bennu tilted his head and studied the fingers for a moment before wrapping one talon around them, followed by the other. Noah pressed his thumb against them as he drew his hand through the cage door. Bennu fluttered his wings, but did not try to fly, perhaps realizing his talons were anchored. Noah presented him to the branch, releasing his thumb. Bennu bent forward and touched the smoothed wood with his beak. Satisfied, he stepped onto it, turned himself around to face us, fluffed his feathers, and dropped a little dung pellet.

Savta grunted. "It will be your task, Na'amah to keep it clean. One of those in my soup and that thing is out of this house, betrothal or no."

"Yes, Savta," I breathed, afraid now that Father would speak up and negate the whole arrangement.

At that moment, my brother, Tubal, entered, reeking of stale beer. "What's this?" he cried, eying Bennu.

"He is mine," I said, moving between him and Bennu.

Tubal raised a hand to strike me for my insolence, but the hand froze in mid-air as Noah stepped into his view. Noah was a large man. He moved with calm deliberateness between Tubal and me. "I'll not have my betrothed struck by any man save her father." This was right according to Hunter Clan law, not because Lamech was my father, but because he was head of my clan and house. By Hunter Clan law, he would always own my allegiance, even if I married. Savta said it was not like that in other tribes who gave the most honor to Mother Goddess. Then the husband came to the wife's tribe and followed their ways. I wished we were of those tribes.

Tubal's cheek twitched in surprise and agitation, and he blinked reddened eyes. He had the same dark hair and eyes as I, but a sour disposition. "Betrothed?" he said.

"Yes," Noah replied. "By oath agreement."

After a stunned moment, Tubal's laugh scraped my ears, but his hand dropped. "You're a fool, boat maker. Her face has turned your head backwards. Don't you know she's an injured little runt? We should have put her outside when she was born." He swayed.

My toes curled in anxiety. Would Noah snatch away his gift at this news?

Noah looked at my father, who tried to meet his eyes, but found something of interest in the deerskin warming his feet.

"Have you something to say, hunter?" Noah asked. Tension

had returned to his shoulders.

My father cleared his throat. "I thought you knew of her deformity," he said. "Or I would never have agreed."

"What deformity is that?" Noah asked calmly.

"She's different, is all. Says strange things sometimes."

"Ha!" Tubal interrupted. "Different? Yes, my friend, she is different, indeed. Her mind is injured, squeezed at birth. She came out looking like a smashed gourd."

Noah frowned. "Her head looks fine to me. Is she crazed? I've seen no sign of that either."

"She's not crazed," Savta snapped. "Just different, as my son-in-law says. She will make a fine wife."

She did not mention my clumsiness with spinning or cooking, probably intending to increase her efforts to teach me. I sighed.

Noah turned to me. I held my breath, knowing I should keep my gaze down under his scrutiny, but I could not keep them from darting to Bennu, who sat on his branch and regarded us all in silence.

"I will keep your counsel, Tubal-Cain," Noah said, "yet I stand by my oath, which has been given." Bitterness stained his voice. He plainly regretted his hasty bargain. I should have been happy as I watched him leave. I had my white bird, and Noah no longer wanted me, but for some reason, tears leapt to my eyes, though I refused to shed them before Tubal.

Chapter Four

I did not see Noah again for half a moon-cycle. Bennu was the sweetest of creatures. Each morning I cleaned his stand and fed him a nut or greenery from the garden or even a piece of fish. To my delight, he shelled the nuts himself and ate anything I ate, except he did not like garlic. He sat on my shoulder when I spun wool into thread, trying to copy Savta's even work. It took a while before he learned not to try to climb the distaff that held the skein. Sometimes he got bored and would work his way beneath my hair, scratching my neck with his claws or reach into my ears and clean the fine, almost invisible hairs. If he were out of sorts, he would try to climb on top of my head, which I discouraged because it hurt, and I was afraid he would drop a dung pellet on me to let me know it was time to go out and see the world.

At first, I tied a braided piece of yarn to his foot, afraid he would fly away, but he did not try, he only flapped them for exercise. I suppose he knew he would crash or perhaps his previous owner had trained him. He liked treats and I could not get away with eating anything without sharing a piece with him. Sometimes I hid a berry or a nut under a pile of leaves or a stone. He got very clever at uncovering the treat.

After a hand of days, I removed the yarn and took him with me to the hills. Wildflowers covered the fields like colored dyes swirled together. The sheep, who were more sensitive than the goats, acted silly for a few moments at the sight of Bennu on my shoulder, then settled down. I moved carefully under his weight, because my shoulders were full of sores where his talons had drawn blood, gripping me for balance. The other children wanted to pet him and hold him, which I would not allow, afraid they would frighten him. They were unpredictable.

The days were touched with a spring nip and the new grass was thick, so the herds moved slowly, giving me and the dogs little to do. My position was to the east of the herd, where I could catch any wanderers, but more importantly, keep an eye on the forest for predators. The dogs were usually the first to give sign of something wrong, so when Brown Dog froze, alerting toward the trees, I sat up. Sometimes it was nothing more than a fox or rabbit, but this time a large object moved in the trees' shadow.

At first, I thought it might be one of the adult shepherds who traveled from herd to herd to make decisions, such as which rams to mark for breeding. I glanced again at Brown Dog. He would know the shepherds, and he continued to alert to the creature. Too big for a fox or wolf, I first feared a leopard, then as I got a better look, a bear. To my surprise, Bennu shifted on my shoulder and gave a cry that sounded almost like a word. I gave him a quick glance, not believing I had heard right, but Grey Dog joined Brown Dog in a defensive posture, so I stood and loosened my sling.

I was not as good with the weapon as Yanner, who could hit a moving beast with uncanny accuracy, but I had earned my right to guard the herd's east flank. Even I could hit a bear. The question was, would it be enough to dissuade a full-grown bear from its intended prey? Bears were also unpredictable.

Though the beast was still too distant to see clearly, appearing about the size of the little reed boats that floated along the river, I placed a stone in my sling and began a slow swing over my head, hoping the movement would frighten it. Instead, it moved closer. Bennu stayed on my shoulder, as I had taught him. Flying into the whirl of my sling would kill him. With my free hand, I snatched the ram's horn from its place on my hip. As I took a deep breath to blow for help, the creature stepped from the forest shadows, and I saw it was not a bear, but a large man.

Noah.

It must be. No one else in the village was that size. I cast the stone at a sharp angle into the ground nearby. It hit with a *thud*.

Noah climbed the hillside as though he were a bear, sometimes dropping to his hands to clamber up a steeper grade.

When he reached me, sweat flattened the wiry hair over his forehead and he breathed a little deeply, but not like a man unaccustomed to work. For the first time, I wondered what a boat maker did, how he shaped the wood to his design, what kind of strength or skill was required. I realized I knew nothing of this man who was still, in a formal sense, my betrothed. Not that he would want anything to do with me now that he knew of my deformity. That he had not known it was curious, but perhaps due to his isolation from the village.

"Greetings," Noah said between breaths.

I flinched at the loudness of his voice. That was another thing I love about my hills—the quiet.

"Greetings." I returned. "Have you come for a ram or a goat? The goats are further up." I pointed over my left shoulder to the rocky crags above us.

He said nothing for a breath, then laughed. "Neither."

"Then what?" I asked.

"To speak to you." His words had the texture of wood in my mind, wood stripped of bark. In one way, they were simple, but in another, they had worn grooves and whirls.

I stared at him, despite the discomfort it brought me. He stared back. I dropped my gaze. "Do you want Bennu back?" My stomach twisted with the question. Bennu was more than a pet bird. He looked at me with his opaque eyes as if he saw me, right down to the heart of me. It was my right to keep him. He was a bride gift, even if the husband no longer wanted the bride.

Noah towered over me like a bear over a fawn. A child and a man alone on a hill. If he wanted Bennu, there was nothing I could do to stop him. I decided I would fight for him anyway.

Perhaps I could bite Noah's hand when it reached for Bennu and run. Bennu would fly away and follow me.

To my surprise, Noah settled with a grunt on the ground beside me. "My legs are no longer like the memory of my legs," he said.

I scrunched my forehead, hearing his words, but not understanding them.

He saw my expression and smiled. "In my mind, I am young. I once raced up these hills as I imagine you do, laughing and catching my breath for only a moment and then running again. I forgot how steep they are."

"Did you watch the herds then?"

"Oh yes, until I was thirteen summers. My uncle also taught me to work with wood. My father was a fisherman, so when his boat sank, my uncle and I made one. It's been my trade ever since."

"I know how to spin and bake bread," I said and then blushed, lest he think I was trying to win him back. I did not want to be married, I reminded myself, and amended, "But not well."

He plucked a blade of grass and twisted it in rough fingers. His hand alone could encircle half my waist. I looked away, focusing on the herd below me.

"Bennu looks good," Noah said. "His feathers have put on a shine since you've had him. How does it go with him?"

I moved my head closer to my right shoulder, seeking the softness of Bennu's feathers on my cheek, the warmth of his body. Sometimes, when I did this, he would peck in mock anger at me, but now he snuggled closer, sensing my need for his touch. Despite the sores on my shoulder, I would miss the weight of him there, his gentle caresses, his knowing eyes.

"I am pleased for you to keep him," Noah said, "no matter what happens between you and me."

I looked sharply at him, unable to keep from blinking my surprise. The blink released a tear. He intercepted it with a calloused finger as it slid down my face.

Finally, I managed, "Thank you."

We both watched the herd in silence. Crows cawed to each other, staking their territory. Wind bowed grass and autumn flowers. A dog moved from his position down the hill, giving a shake. I did not look directly at Noah, but I saw a lot from the corners of my eyes.

He smiled, his gaze still on the grazing animals. "My first wife liked to talk. She hated the fact that the air was empty, and she kept it filled with words."

"She is dead?"

"Yes, she died in childbirth."

Like my mother, I thought.

"The child was stillborn," he added. "It was our first, a boy. My son."

I heard the old sorrow that roughened his voice like a lightning wound charred deep into a tree.

"I lived," I said.

He looked at me then, and I understood the question in his eyes, wondering how I escaped being put outside the village at birth for the gods' judgment. "Father God looked kindly on you," he said.

"I do not believe in the gods." In the stunned silence, I heard the muffled thud of my heart and saw myself naked in the mud of the pit, banished from the world. What had made me utter such a foolish thing? Even though it was truth, I knew better. If someone asked me if I believed in the gods, I would say "Yes," even though it was a lie. I understood that rule well enough.

Noah did not jump up and throw me over his shoulder to present me to the Elders. He said nothing for several heartbeats, then in a reasonable voice, he asked, "How can you not believe in the gods?" He looked up at the clear sky and then down over the valley below us. "Isn't the wind the breath of Father God and the sun his eye? Isn't the fruit's seed Mother Goddess's promise of life?"

I looked toward the Black Lake shimmering in the sunlight. There was no point in pretending I had not said what I had said. "I do not know where the wind comes from, but when I was young I did not know the origin of my nurse- mother's milk either. It was a magic that appeared when I was hungry and cried, but when I grew older I understood it came from her breast."

"You think we are as children to the world?"

I noticed Noah seemed more comfortable talking alone to me than he had in the crowd at the market or in my father's house. He had adjusted his voice to a quieter tone, although I had not said anything to him about it.

I nodded. "Not understanding something does not mean there is no reason for it. I want to know why everything is, but I do not want to make up the reason just so I can have an answer."

He stared at me again for a long time. "I don't know if I have heard great wisdom or great foolishness."

My toes curled in embarrassment. Not only had I spoken like a teacher to an older person, but a man. No wonder my brother hated me, my father ignored me, and Savta sighed so much.

"I know this," Noah said, without a trace of anger or condemnation in his voice. "Your mind is not damaged that I can see, only different, as your Savta claimed."

I felt such a mixture of things, I was not able to speak— relief that he was not angry and I might escape the pit; fear that he might decide to keep me as his betrothed; fear that he might not. Whenever things got too confusing, I rocked and sang, so I did that. Savta said the Goddess graced my voice in compensation for my other faults. I hugged my knees to my chest, closed my eyes and sang softly, rocking my upper body in rhythm with the tune, a shepherd's song of stars and the stir of sheep in moonlight.

Opening my eyes, I was surprised that Noah still sat beside me, forgetting he was there in my concentration on the song and rocking. I felt better, but he looked bewildered. I tried to explain why it helped me to shut out the world. He nodded slowly, like a man who stood on a bog that might sink beneath him at any moment.

"Why did you buy Bennu?" I asked.

He shrugged. "I don't like to see animals mistreated. His cage was too small."

34

"Why did you ask to marry me?"

He plucked a piece of grass and placed it in the corner of his mouth. "Because you said I stank."

I waited for a more satisfactory answer.

After a moment he said, "Though my wife filled the air with words, they were not all true words." I sensed this was all the explanation he wanted to give.

He sat with me until the moon rose as Mother Goddess. With the brightest of her star-children as companions, she poured blue-gray light onto the hills, just enough to see the white underbellies of the sheep.

Noah left before my relief arrived. Though I was still a child, and he my betrothed, he thought it not seemly to be found alone with me. "I don't want your father to think I violated my agreement to wait for you."

For a long time after he left, I sang and rocked, though I kept my eyes open. It was my responsibility to watch the herd.

Chapter Five

Noah came to the hillside many times after that. Mostly he sat with me when I was alone, but sometimes he came on the night watch when Yanner was with me. We did not talk much then, because Yanner assumed an adult man would prefer to speak with a boy rather than a girl, at least that's what he told me. He did not think much of Noah.

The rains began in late autumn. No one could remember a time when it rained so long and so hard. Day after day. People whispered that Father God was angry, but every story had a different cause for his anger. Our thatched roof collapsed in several places, and I worked all day emptying pots of water, while my father and brother tried to mend it. My head began to ache and I could not stop shivering.

Noah came to help. He was too heavy for the roof, so he took the clay jugs from my arms, guided me to a relatively dry spot, and made me rest. I watched him through the haze that clouded my eyes—back and forth. Savta tried to save our best wool cloth from the water's ravages and the flax strands we had teased out of the stalks, bundling them up in rolls.

When the chills made my teeth spasm and brought blood to my lips, she unrolled two blankets, dumping out their contents, and wrapped me in them. My elbows and knees ached. My skin burned on the outside, but inside I was so cold, it felt like my bones rattled against each other. I faded out of the world and dreamed Noah knelt beside me. I was glad he did not stink anymore. He had told me he bathed every night now. He bent closer and took the malachite from his neck, tying the cord around my neck, so the healing stone would lie against my hot skin.

Then I dreamed the river rose and rose and crept toward us. I dreamed the Black Lake became briny, killing the fish. It swelled and crept toward us, until it lifted our mud and straw house like flotsam, spinning us around and around.

I woke to find myself on the floor in a pool of water.

"Mother Goddess!" Savta cried, throwing her best weaving aside to rush to me, but Noah was already there, scooping me into his brawny arms.

"The river!" I heard my brother cry from the roof. "It's coming!"

"Hurry!" Noah shouted. "We have to get out!"

"I can't leave," Savta cried in anguish. "My weavings, my cloth, my pots—"

"High ground," my father said. "We must get to the hills."

"No time for that!" Noah turned to the door. "The river banks are overflowed, and the ground is too soaked to absorb any more."

Almost too weary to care what happened, I opened my eyes. Water slopped into the house, rising quickly to Noah's knees. Bennu gave a shriek that jerked me from my fog of misery. "Bennu," I croaked. "We have to take him."

"Leave the stupid bird," Tubal snapped. "Maybe he'll figure out how to fly."

"He still cannot fly for long," I protested through cracked and bleeding lips.

Noah waded to Bennu's perch and coaxed him to his shoulder, holding me with one brawny arm. The water was now to his knees and Savta's thighs. Tubal was out the door, carrying whatever goods he deemed of value. Father grabbed Savta and pulled her through the skins that covered our doorway.

Outside, the water pulsed against our house. Wind worked it into wrinkles and then waves. Rain pelted us with the force of tiny stones. Bennu hunched miserably as close to Noah's neck as possible.

Tubal scowled at Noah, who held me against his chest. "Is that the best you could carry out? Better to leave her for the fish and save something of worth."

His words meant nothing to me. I was like the ground, too full of them to absorb any more, but my ear was to Noah's chest and a low growl rumbled there.

"The hills!" Father cried above the wind and rumble of thunder.

"No." Noah shook his head. "You'll never make it through the valley."

"We'll make it," Father said. "We have to."

Noah let go of me with one hand and grasped Savta's thin arm. "The women won't. They come with me." There was no question in his voice, despite the fact that he had no authority over us, other than the oldest authority of all— strength of arm.

Tubal shrugged and turned toward the valley, but Father scowled at Noah. "Where are you going?"

"To the boats," Noah said.

Father placed a hand on Savta's shoulder. "Take my daughter then, but my mother-in-law comes with me."

Of course, who would cook or clean for him? He would have to take another wife, and he was too stingy to give a bride price.

Savta straightened her back and scowled. "With Na'amah ill? Who'll care for her?" She shrugged off his hand. "I go with my daughter's child."

Anger flared in my father's face, but Tubal called to him. "Let them go! We must hurry."

I knew little of our flight through the village; only glimpses remain in my mind, like torn bits of a nightmare. I remember Savta pushing a floating tree branch from us, Bennu squawking, familiar faces twisting in panic, and Noah yelling, "To the boats!"

Animals swam by. I thought I saw Dawn paddling bravely and reached for her, but the water bore her away. More dogs swept by and boar-pigs, even wild creatures—a fox and a deer, eyes whitened with fear. People cried and begged for help. I was too weak even to cling to Noah. At first he held me to his chest then, when he needed an arm to ward off floating debris and pull Savta back when a current threatened to overwhelm her, he slung me over his shoulder. A tiny head bobbed by. I reached after it, but it was gone almost before I realized what I had seen. With a shudder, I vomited into the swirling water. My last thought was a vague relief that no one would have to clean it up.

I woke to a gentle rocking. My eyelids were stuck closed. I moaned. At once, something damp wiped across my face and when it lifted, I could see. Savta's lined face hovered over me, framed in a sky so blue it made me blink. My eyes watered, blurring her features.

"Na'amah," she said and the world was in that word, all her care and loving, all her fears. "Thank you, Mother Goddess," she whispered.

"Thirsty," I managed.

She held a chipped bowl to my lips. The water slid like a cool blessing down my parched throat. Only then, did I smell the stink of tar pitch and realize I was on a boat. A squawk made me look up. Bennu perched on one of the thick ropes that bound the reed bottom. Four other people were on the gently rocking raft—Aunt Adah, the stone knapper and his wife, and Noah.

"What happened?" I asked.

"You've slept for three days and nights," Savta said. "I thought we would lose you." She leaned close to my ear. "Mother Goddess wrapped you in her arms and saved you for her special purpose."

I considered the tightly bound reeds sealed with pitch that separated us from the water beneath us and thought it more likely that Noah's strength and skill in boat making saved us both. "Father?" I asked.

Her face pinched. "We don't know who made it to the hills yet. Many perished. The village is devastated."

I hoped Yanner had survived, but I did not ask. I was too weak to handle it if he had not. "I am hungry."

She worked a small piece of lintel bread from her apron. "I saved this. There was little food. No one thought to bring water, so we drank from the Black Lake and many sickened."

I did not want to think about that and pushed aside the vision of bodies being heaved over the boat's edge. I chewed the bread, despite its moldy taste and struggled to sit up. Bennu made a clucking noise and bent down, grooming a strand of my lank hair. Beyond him, I saw only water and several other boats rocking in the wide water's embrace. The river must have pushed all the boats downstream into the Black Lake.

Noah made his way to my side. Weariness stained the skin around his eyes, but they were still clear and blue as the sky. He nodded at me, approving that I lived.

An odd weight pressed on my neck and I lifted it, recognizing Noah's malachite stone. I had not dreamed that part, then.

I must have looked like a piece of flotsam. My hair hung in dirty strands and my face felt like a dried leaf, but I said, "Do you still want me for wife?"

His brows drew together in puzzlement. "Yes."

It was father's place to set a bride price, but he was not there, and I knew what I wanted. "Then you must build me a house," I said. "A house that can float."

I remembered his laugh. As I leaned back, strength draining from my body like grain through a sieve, my heart lightened at that uncontained, azure sound that was wide as the sky, embracing and challenging the fearsome world.

Chapter Six

I did not like changes. I noticed everything, and when things were out of place, it confused me. But there was so much to do, I had no time to rock and hum to myself, so whenever I could, I shut my eyes and pretended that was what I was doing, instead of hauling water or debris, or gathering the scattered sheep. The goats had stayed together, but the stupid sheep scattered over the hillsides and took many days to find. Our best shepherd dogs survived, having stayed with their charges in the hills, but many hunting and companion dogs living in the village had perished, including old Dawn.

Noah did not forget his promise to me, but he had little time to work on the boat-house, as my brother disdainfully called it. I thought it was an accurate name and used it, which irritated him. Tubal was now head-of-house since my father died trying to cross the flooded valley. The water had spun a piece of timber across Lamech's head, and Tubal could not reach him before the current took him under. I did not grieve much. My father had never given me much attention, but I was sorry Tubal was head-of-house.

It took several moon-cycles to clean what remained of the village. So many of our family and people I knew had not survived, including my nurse-mother. Yanner lost his entire family and moved into a friend's house. Only Aunt Adah, and one of her sons, Jabel, were left of our family.

Much of the herd that survived the storm in the hills was slaughtered to feed us, even the ewes. All the crops and grain stores were ruined. Everyone grew accustomed to a gnawing belly.

Tubal insisted on rebuilding our hut over the old one. The water had melted away the walls and left only a few branches that had supported the mud-clay walls. I liked the thought of living in the same place, but I knew it was as stupid as the sheep that had gotten lost in the storms. What if it rained like that again? I told Savta we should build on a hill or move into Noah's boat-house. Everyone in the village laughed at the idea of such a thing. Tubal had spread it about to ridicule him, but Noah ignored them.

"Go ahead and tell your brother to build on a hill," Savta grumbled, her fingers busy mending Tubal's tunic.

Of course, I did not. Tubal would have only struck me for my trouble and disrespect.

In the moon-cycles following the flood, the Hunters grew stronger in influence because there was no grain, and we depended on their skills. It was a difficult winter. Tubal rose in prominence, becoming the leader of the young men of Hunter Clan. This was a fine thing, for it kept him busy, and I did not have to wait on him the way he demanded when he was home. We also had plenty of meat, because the young huntsmen gave a cut of whatever they killed to our house. Tubal was supposed to distribute what we did not need to the widows and orphans, but I think most of it went to his own friends. I wished he would take a wife, but he seemed content for me and Savta to do all the work.

Hunters may work hard when they were hunting, but when they came home, they sat around like hibernating bears and just ate, drank and slept.

It was a very cold night when Savta woke me. "Get up, Na'amah. I need you."

I tried to snuggle deeper into my furs and murmured something about the water being too deep to go outside, confusing the waking world with a vague dream that dissolved before I could return to it.

"Up," Savta ordered, her words sharp icicles.

This time, reality asserted itself and I sat up, alert now and worried. "What is it? What is wrong?"

"A birthing. I need you."

My eyes widened. Savta never took me to birthings. I was too clumsy and not much help to her, though I was fine with helping sheep or goats give birth. "Where is Adah?" I asked, as I tied the lacings of my foot coverings. My aunt always helped Savta.

"She's gone to visit her cousins. Hurry. Things are not going well."

I hurried, but I was not happy. What if the baby was born with a misshapen head, as I was, or a missing limb? Would I be the one instructed to take it out in the woods and leave it? This worried me.

Savta did not have time for my concerns. I carried the things she needed in her basket and stumbled behind her, still groggy. We crossed the center square, careful to avoid the pit. Father God's oil pot burned brightly, the small flame twisting upward, protected from the worst of the wind by the surrounding walls of the workshops and houses. It provided enough light to see our way, as clouds hazed the moon. Our destination was a house on the far side of the square.

It did not take us long to find the right place. Inside, a girl not much older than I, writhed on the floor. The women around her parted at once to let Savta go to her. My grandmother knelt, feeling the girl's tight, swollen belly, giving her a kind word, and then parting her legs. I stood in the same spot, like a stone embedded in the ground.

I could not see anything for the press of women around the girl, but I heard everything, including her pants and groans of pain that battered me like panicked crows. The room smelled of blood.

"How long has she been like this?" Savta asked.

The older woman to her right rocked back on her heels and dabbed her forehead with a woolen shawl. Her lips were a tight slash across her face, her cheeks pinched in the firelight. "Since the moon rose. We thought it would be an easy birth with no need of you. I've seen many children into the world. Never been a problem with the baby's head already visible, but every time I try to put her on the birthing stones, she screams to wake every ancestor's spirit that walked the land."

"Pain is normal," Savta said. "But being on the stones should be easier on her at this stage than lying down."

The fire, well fed by wood, put out enough heat to pop sweat from my forehead and palms, despite the cold outside. I did not know what to do.

"Na'amah," Savta's sharp voice startled me from my trance. "Come here with my basket."

I moved beside her.

"Bear grease," she snapped.

I reached for the pot and held it while she slathered it on her hands and then carefully worked her way inside the girl I now recognized as Coel. Like all the other girls, she never had much to do with me. I had volunteered to take her herding duty on the day of her wedding.

Coel winced and panted like a dog, while Savta explored the baby's head and then reached deeper. Finally, with a grunt she sat back, scowling.

"What is it?" the woman who had spoken first asked. "What's wrong?"

"The birth cord is wrapped around the baby's neck," Savta said. "If it is born, it will die. If it is not born, the mother will die."

Silence filled the house. I did not need to hear words to know what everyone there was thinking: There had been enough death.

"Is there nothing that can be done?" Coel's mother sobbed. She held the girl's head in her lap. "My poor child!"

Savta sighed, then straightened her back and held her hand out to me. "Na'amah, the knife."

I will hear Coel's screams for the rest of my life.

44

Savta's skill saved the baby, in spite of her prediction, but Coel began to bleed and there was nothing to do to stop it. By dawn, she was dead. Had I caused my mother such pain? I shivered in the room's heat and did not stop, even when we returned home, and I crawled back under my furs. Savta did not chastise me or make me rise to do my chores. She gave me a hot broth that stilled my shivers and eased me into a dreamless sleep.

Savta never took me with her to a birthing again.

Chapter ✦ Seven

When the next spring came in its fullness, I was relieved that it did not rain more than normal. Elder Batan and Elder Kahor pacified Father God with the sacrifice of a first born lamb. Elder Mariah placed the round moon cakes on Mother Goddess' altar. Savta's perfect cakes were likely among them. All the chosen women now gathered in the village center, bringing the special length of thick wool thread each had spun and dyed. Savta chose red, a favorite of the Goddess. I would not be allowed to participate until my blood came, so I stood with others along the walls to watch. The women had moved all of the blankets and market things to make room.

The women faced each other, making a square within the square of the village center. Elder Mariah's voice rose into the silence that settled like soft snow around her. She faced the small Goddess in the temple's alcove. "Today, we honor the Goddess for the fruit of her womb, for the life that comes forth in this season to bring us the harvest in another. We recognize her," she intoned, pointing to the four sacred corners of the square, "as Mother, Virgin, Lover, and Blood-seeker."

As always, I wondered how the Goddess could be all these things at the same time. How could a carving, even in the shape of a woman, be anything more than a piece of stone? It never spoke or moved. How could it be so powerful? I did not understand, but I loved watching the woman weave the tapestry, and I gladly ate the moon cakes Savta made that were not perfect enough to qualify for an offering.

Flute music began, a sweet soaring that danced like blue and green ribbons before my mind's eye. The women on two sides of the square walked toward each other. When they met, they each grasped an end of the other's thread and then backed into their original places. This left them holding two threads, one in each hand. When the flute reached a certain phrase, the woman lifted their arms over their heads. Those on the opposite sides of the living square tied off the ends of their own threads to the waft edges and moved under the canopy, weaving them between the ones held tautly above.

"This is stupid and boring," Yanner declared under his breath.

I glared at him and spoke my first sarcasm. "I am sure it is much more meaningful to roll around in the blood of an animal."

He looked stunned. "That is a secret Hunter rite. How do you know of it?"

With a sniff, I turned back to the ceremony. "Everybody knows that."

"Well, you're not supposed to," Yanner grumbled. "Come on, let's sneak away and play sticks."

"No."

"Yes, come on, Na'amah. I'll let you have first drop."

"I want to watch the weaving."

"Na'amah—"

"No."

"You are so stubborn. You're more stubborn than Gadem's ox."

This was a definite insult, as Gadem's ox was famous for its defiance. Sometimes it gave him as much trouble as a wild aurochs. I punched Yanner on the shoulder with my knuckle, as he had taught me.

"Oww," he protested, but stopped nagging me.

The ceremony continued and, as always, I lost myself in the weaving, absorbed in the details of the yarns' journey that spoke of spider's web and bird's nest and the lacing of branches.

When the music stopped, the women tied off the ends of their threads. The weaving they had created was a beautiful work of many colors.

Normally, there would be a ceremony of removing and burning the old one, but the flood had taken last spring's weaving, so the women simply hung the new tapestry. The bold design hanging in its proper place on the west wall of the square made things feel right again. Mother Goddess would bless our grain fields and the women's bellies with children. At least, so I was taught. I still had not the first glimpse of her. Perhaps the little fat stone goddess in the temple wall alcove was only a receptacle for the Goddess, like the moon and stars. I could understand that some force brought the seasons, but that force did not appear to care what we did. I could not discern any actions on our part that caused the clouds to choose a perfect rain for crops instead of a flood. I held my doubts to myself, and Noah had not breathed a word of my blasphemy.

One morning of summer's second moon in my fourteenth summer, I awoke and helped Savta prepare food. After we ate, Tubal went to hunt. When he left, Savta said, "Na'amah, I need you to grind barley today. I'm going to visit Adah."

Happy to have time alone, I first went to bathe, using a place where the river flowed into a side pool. Since the flood, I avoided water that churned or moved fast, but a daily bath was my habit.

I dried with lamb's wool and returned to the house, running my fingers through my wet hair to smooth out the tangles. Settling cross-legged on the floor, I opened a jar of barley and dipped some out into a quern. Bennu waddled over to see what I was doing. He tried to climb onto the edge of the quern, but I shooed him away before his weight could spill the grain.

"Hello?"

I started at Yanner's voice, surprised I had not heard his tread. Bennu had distracted me. I turned to see him in the opening to our house, pulling aside the skins. The set of his shoulders meant he was unhappy about something.

"Enter," I said. "No one here but me."

"I thought I'd get to go on the hunt today," He squatted by the fire pit, picked up a kindling stick and snapped it in two.

Now I understood what was bothering him.

"I heard a hive," I said, sharing the news I had been saving. This captured his interest. Honey was a prized find, both for medicine and sweetening food and beer.

"Where?" A thread of excitement weaved into his voice. Finding honey was almost like hunting.

"I do not know yet, but I heard them a moon- cycle ago in the glen by my mother's grave." Our tribe did not bury the dead under the houses like they did in other villages. Perhaps because our ancestors came from a different land, far to the south in Eden, and we brought different customs.

The glen was a place I liked to go, the rare times that were my own. Those opportunities had become even rarer after the flood. I did more than my turn watching the herds, but I did not mind that at all. I lifted Bennu, who had snuck back and put a claw on the saddle quern, spilling the grain. "Bennu!" He was unaffected by my scolding, pecking at the grain. I put him on my shoulder and carefully recovered all the partly-ground meal I could. Without fear of Savta's disapproval, I put the quern aside, knowing the procurement of a pot of honey would more than compensate for less barley meal ground that day.

"Why didn't you tell me before?" Yanner's beautiful face was alight. I cast my gaze down, uncomfortable with looking at him, but smiling at the memory of my glimpse. I could look at the memory, because it was frozen, and I did not feel anxious trying to understand all the different movements that danced across his face.

If I swallowed my discomfort and watched faces, I would get stuck. Other things did that. Sometimes, especially if I were tired, the visual aspects of sound crowded into my mind, and I could become lost watching them. Branches swaying in a crosswind or a waterfall could do the same thing. It was hard to get unstuck and stop staring.

"Na'amah," he said impatiently. "Why didn't you tell me about the bees?"

I pulled my attention back to him, but kept my gaze on his toes. He had knobby toe knuckles. "It was too soon. They needed time to settle and make honey."

"Are they ready now?"

"I think so."

"Good. I'll get the smoker."

I nodded. "Meet me in the clearing at my mother's grave."

He jogged off and I went to the spot, adding a brown rock with red flecks that I had found by the river to the pile that marked her bones. The protective red ochre, the blood of Earth, had long ago washed away from the other stones there and, though I had never seen the evil spirits that seek to steal the dead from their families, I was not certain enough that they did not exist to leave my mother at risk. I made certain the stones were in the order I liked and then sat beside them, closing my eyes to listen.

At first, there were too many distracting sounds, but I put them aside one by one, searching for the subtle undertone of an active hive that wove in the air like Savta's fine stitching.

Yanner's footsteps alerted me, and I opened my eyes, putting my fist to my mouth to remind him not to speak and break my concentration. He bore everything we would need.

I stood and closed my eyes again. This was a matter of trusting my instincts more than my mind. I did not really think about where I was going, just let my feet take little steps, following the gold thread of sound. Yanner's job was to keep me from running into a ditch or a tree. Bennu, on my shoulder, never disturbed me during bee hunting. Yanner said he looked as intense as I did.

After a while, I realized I had steadily made choices that moved me south. The sound was not much louder, so I moved that way without the tedious circling. Then I stopped again to determine the volume. More intense. The gold in the thread was a deeper hue. Good. I smiled at Yanner.

"How do you do that?" he whispered.

"Hush."

I led him deeper into the trees, losing the sound several times and then finding it again. The start and end of hive tracking were the hardest parts, the first because it was so faint, the end because it was loud.

"I hear it now," Yanner said. "That way." He pointed over my shoulder.

I moved a few steps in the direction he indicated. "No." I redirected us. "This way."

With a sigh, he followed, and we found the hive in a tree hollow.

I sank onto the ground, lying back on a patch of ferns, and Bennu exchanged his perch on my shoulder for a walk on my stomach. The intense concentration bee hunting required exhausted me, and I was glad to let Yanner do his part in starting the fire that would send smoke up into the hollow and lull the bees into a stupor. Then he would cut out a section of the comb, careful not to disturb the queen. Most people just stole the whole thing and crushed it to strain out the honey, but I would not let Yanner do that. It was not because bees were sacred to the Goddess; it was because the hive would recover in a moon-cycle or so, and we would mark our trail and come again for more treasure.

I was pleased with myself.

Bennu also seemed happy. He waddled up to my chest and regarded me with a tilted head, opening his mouth as though to speak his mind. Then, spotting something I could not see, he bent forward and nibbled at my eyebrow.

Chapter Eight

The following day, I was restless, though Yanner and I would have the night watch on the north hill, and I should have stayed home or found a place to sleep until then. Instead, I took Bennu and my sling to my practice spot beside the mounded earth and stones that covered my mother's body.

Each morning when I went to the river to bathe, I searched for stones. Round ones about half the size of my fist were best for the sling. Sometimes I found a special one, not necessarily round, but interesting in color, texture, or shape. I would save that one. There was one in my pouch now with silver sparkles in it. I added it to the collection of stones that marked my mother's burial mound. Did she know I did this, seeking a connection with her? The Elders say the ancestors speak with the wind's whisper, but I never heard a word from my mother, and I had very good hearing.

I removed the rest of my stones and laid them in a line on the ground to practice stooping and loading in case I ran out of stones in my pouch. Yanner taught me this way to practice.

Tubal mocked my prowess with the sling, as he mocked everything I did. He was right that I was awkward at new tasks, but I loved my work, and a good shepherd must be proficient with a sling. The sheep depended on me. So I practiced whenever I could. Today was a good day; I hit my target, a large tree stump, almost every swing.

When I was tired, I lay on my back in a sunlit grass patch. Bennu perched in a nearby tree. I could see glimpses of his beautiful white tail and crest through the leaves of a beech that swayed in a gentle breeze. He would warn if any threat approached. He saw as well as I could hear. No snake would slither close or bear wander near without warning, as long as he stood guard.

The same wind waved the yellow flowers that towered above me, their skins luminous with cupped sunlight. Scents of earth and onion grass drifted into my nostrils, and so many sounds—birds conversing, a clicking from Bennu, the rustle of grass, a dog barking in the distance, and there, beneath the other sound, the hum of the beehive Yanner and I had found. I drifted into its subtle vibration and the sweet, furred arms of sleep.

The harsh, throaty croak of a heron woke me to a sky deep into dusk. I called a cranky Bennu to my shoulder and took him home before running out to the north hill.

Yanner and I had spent many seasons on that hill together when it was our turn to take a night watch. The hill afforded a clear view of the herds and the forest's edge. That was how we became friends. Since he now had completed the manhood rites, he would not normally have tended the herd like a child, but the flood had decimated us, and everyone did several tasks, whatever the tribe needed.

Yanner resented it.

"You're late," he greeted me. He sat just outside the entrance of a small cave where he had already built up the fire. It was first watch's responsibility to feed the fire from the pile of dried dung gathered by the younger children. Yanner had hated that task, but I never minded. It was important work, not just to feed the fire, but because it kept the sheep from getting sick. In the past, I would have apologized for being late, but my belly hurt and I was in a foul mood. Perhaps I had eaten too many dates dipped in goat's milk.

"I fell asleep," I said.

He sighed. "Sorry to snap at you. I'm tired."

I sat next to him. "Me too."

"I wish things would go back to the way they were." He did not have to say he meant how things were before the waters washed everything away, including his brothers and younger sister. It was the first time I remember hearing something from another's mouth that echoed my own feelings. I knew Yanner's mind was not damaged like mine, but I wondered if perhaps others sometimes felt the same as I did. The thought gave me comfort. Maybe I was not so different.

Yanner put his hand on my back. "It's been hard for everyone."

His tone was that of a kindly older brother, which annoyed me. His hand stayed on my back. "Where's that old bird?"

"Bennu gets cranky if I keep him awake, so I did not bring him."

"I don't think he likes me."

"He does not like many people," I said. "Only me and Savta and Noah."

Yanner scowled. "Why did your father allow you to be betrothed to such an old man?"

"He is not that old," I said, shifting to find a comfortable spot.

"Almost as old as your father."

"One-Eye is going to give birth tonight," I said, wanting to change the subject. One-Eye really had both her eyes, but a black mark partially circled one. I gave names to most of the sheep. Many of the other children could not tell one from the other, which seemed stupid to me. They were very different from each other, not only in appearance, but in habits. I could know by touch if they were nervous or calm. This trick did not work with people. People are more difficult to understand than sheep.

"How do you know she is going to birth tonight? How do you know such things?" Yanner asked, not questioning my pronouncement. I was rarely wrong.

54

"The way she holds her back legs and head," I said. "And she has an inward look in her eye. Her body is speaking to her."

Yanner's attention for One-Eye waned quickly. He took a piece of sharp obsidian from his pouch and stroked the smooth, shiny surface. "I've had to start shaving," he said, trying to sound casual, but I heard the note of pride in his voice. "Do you prefer men clean-shaven or with beards?"

"You are too young for a beard," I said. "I would not like it on you."

He smiled and began to play with my hair. "Your hair is smooth as water," he said.

I closed my eyes, lulled by the soft pull on my scalp. It was soothing, like when Bennu groomed my hair, but exciting at the same time. As an infant, the press of my nurse-mother's breast against my cheek evoked a deep calm, but at ten moons, I began avoiding touches. They made my skin prickle. I hid under the sheepskins and furs when Savta got out the oil, but now that I was almost a woman, I liked it. Touches did not feel prickly anymore, as long as they were not sudden.

When his hand found its way to the back of my neck, it sent chills down my spine and covered my legs with bumps like a plucked fowl. I flinched a bit and laughed. He smiled at me and pulled me closer. "For warmth," he said, and I did not disagree, even though the night was not that cool. The press of his side against me made my heartbeat quicken. His hand stayed on my neck stroking gently. Something melted in my belly. I had never felt like this. I was liquid.

With a gasp, I pulled away from him and pulled my dress from my thighs. His green eyes widened. "What are you doing, Na'amah?"

There was no mistaking the stain on my leg, even in the dimming light. "My blood," I said, stunned that my womanhood was upon me.

He drew away. "Oh." Confusion or distaste furrowed his brows. "It's bad fortune for a Hunter to touch—" He stopped, scrambling to his feet. "Should I tell your Savta?"

I felt light-headed. My womanhood. I was only fifteen summers, too young. Most were sixteen or even seventeen before their first blood. I would never be a girl again. Change swirled around me like a storm's breath.

His words sunk into my awareness. No, I did not want Yanner announcing my first blood to Savta or anyone else. I stared at him. He had backed away a step, as if readying to flee. "If you tell anyone," I said, "I will wipe your face with my woman's blood while you nap on the hillside."

With satisfaction, I saw he paled. Then he straightened his shoulders. "It's woman's business, anyway. Who cares?" He left me then, even though he should not have. At least a pair should watch together during the night. I wondered if I should find an adult to tell, but I could not abandon One-Eye.

I rose slowly, almost doubled over with a sudden stab of pain in my belly. What was so eagerly awaited about this? While I waited for the pain to stop, I ground my teeth in annoyance. My leg was sticky with blood.

I hated being dirty. Savta fussed about my use of water for washing that we needed for cooking or drinking. "Go swim in that pond off the river you're so fond of," she would direct, and so I did, even in winter, taking sheepskins to wrap in and running back to the house to keep warm.

Here there was only a spring on the other side of the hill. I waddled in that direction, trying to keep my legs wide and my dress away from getting further stained. Without doubt, I looked like a drunk or a bear cub balancing on two legs, and I was glad Yanner had abandoned me.

My path took me through the herd, and I stopped to pluck fluffs of undercoat stuck to the grass and bushes until I had several handfuls. At the stream, I cleaned myself, pulled and rolled the wool on my thigh into strings. Then I tied one end to a stone and twirled it until I had a couple of thread lengths from the wool. They were thick and uneven and would have earned me an exasperated look from Savta, but they were strong. I moistened the remainder of the wool enough to make it stick together like a swath of felt. Removing my cord belt, I fastened it back around my waist, under my dress, and tied the strings from the felt pad to it. It felt strange, and my bone knife would be awkward to reach, requiring me to lift my dress. With such an arrangement, I would also have to carry my sling and bag of stones, but it was worth the inconvenience. Proud of my ingenuity and new womanhood, I started back.

The moment I topped the hill, I froze and dropped to my belly, heedless of its complaints. The tall grass almost hid the shape at the herd's edge, but the twitch of tail that had caught my attention was unmistakable. A long, shuddering breath made its way through me.

Tiger.

Tigers rarely approached, but the flood had altered habits and terrain for many creatures. What was the beast waiting for? The wind blew toward it, so neither the dogs nor the sheep had scented it. It was close enough to have its pick of prey.

Then I realized what it was waiting for.

One-Eye had decided to give birth. In the time it had taken me to clean myself and make the felt, the lamb had worked itself partially out. Head and forelegs were visible, I noted with approval. No need to reach inside and turn it.

The tiger too must have approved. A newborn lamb would be a tasty morsel and a helpless one.

I did not know what to do. What were my choices? I could call the dogs. They were effective at protecting the sheep from most predators, including cheetahs, but they were outmatched by a tiger. They would harass it, perhaps draw it off or anger it enough that one or more dogs would die. We could not afford to lose any herder dogs. Not now.

I clinched my bag of round stones, carefully selected from the river bed for their uniformity of size and shape. I could try to drive it off, as long as my stones lasted, but at this distance my efforts would not be much more than an annoyance at best and more likely, I would miss him entirely.

Wisdom said to run to the cave and blow the ram's horn,

alerting other shepherds and the dogs. I had left the horn, so I could have both hands to hold my skirt from my legs. Foolish.

If I ran for the cave, the lamb would die and maybe the ewe, and possibly dogs, but I would be safe. It was the only reasonable thing to do. One-Eye gave a soft bleat. The lamb was almost out. I should be there helping her. Anger wove into the fear and my reasoning. One-Eye was my responsibility, and the lamb she had carried for moons was not going to be a tiger's meal.

I stood and dropped a stone into my sling, whirling it above my head and moved slowly toward One-Eye, screaming with all the breath of my lungs. Sheep scattered in all directions, bleating in confusion. One-Eye's head rose, and she looked at me in consternation, but she was in the throes of labor and did not try to rise.

At first, nothing moved in the tall grass where the tiger crouched. I walked right toward it. I knew better than to run, because that would elicit the tiger's instinct to attack. I was counting on the loud noise and the confusion of my approach to convince it to seek another target. Even if it went for another of the sheep, at least its prey would have an opportunity to flee.

The dogs, not understanding what I was doing, were trying to herd the fleeing sheep. I did not signal the danger whistle or the come-in shout. I kept screaming, though my throat was dry and scratchy. As loud as I was, I did not think other herders would hear me, as I was in the dip between hills and they do not hear as well as I do.

My scream died in my throat when the tiger stood, tail whipping in agitation. A magnificent creature, rippling with power and grace, he took my breath.

We stood facing each other, the bloody lamb between us, struggling to enter the world.

I knew I must make my choice now. My arm was wearying. Either I had to drop the sling or send the stone. An almost imperceptible tightening in the tiger's haunches decided which. I let instinct choose the timing to release the knotted end of the rope, keeping the other in my grasp. The stone flew. If it hit anywhere, there was a chance of startling the beast into retreat, but if I missed, I was dead.

I stared, realizing I had missed.

The creature did not move through the length of the entire breath I dragged into my lungs. Then, to my astonishment, the tiger collapsed onto its side.

With disbelief, I ran to it, hiking my dress to get to my blade. The animal lay on its side, massive paws almost the size of my head splayed. My stone had struck its left eye and imbedded into the brain. The body twitched. It still breathed. I sawed through the skin with my knife, slitting its throat.

Blood musk, thick and salty gushed into my nostrils. Spotted Dog and Grey Dog appeared, whining and nosing the limp creature with concern to assure it was not a threat.

With trembling hands, I helped One-Eye birth her lamb, watched her lick it clean and helped it find its mother's teats. Neither she nor One-Eye seemed concerned about the dead tiger nearby. Blood was part of the birth smell.

When the lamb, which I named, Fortune, was safely suckling, I went to the tiger's side, running my hand in wonder over its marvelous coat and regretting that life no longer pulsed in such a splendid creature's body.

With the suddenness of a blow, all the fear I should have felt while stalking the tiger slammed through me. I squatted on my heels and rocked to shut it out.

After a while, Grey Dog's worried tongue on my cheek brought me back to the world. I opened my eyes. The dead animal would attract coyotes or wolves. On unsteady legs, I rose and headed up the hillside to the cave. Somehow, I would find the strength to blow the ram's horn for help.

Chapter Nine

The village buzzed like a hive with news of my kill. We received the choicest parts of the meat, and the skin was given to Tubal, as head-of-house. If I were a boy, he would present it to me in a ceremony honoring me. To keep it for himself would make him appear ungenerous and bring dishonor. He threw it at me with a scowl. "I've never seen such a lucky stone throw," he said. "Don't count on it ever happening again."

I did not understand why my brother hated me.

The tiger skin made me sad, remembering the magnificent creature it had been, but the skin was beautiful, and Savta showed me how to soften and stretch it.

Several women in the village came to celebrate my coming of age, including my mother's marriage-sister, Aunt Adah, who brought a lovely red ribbon. It was a happy time. No men were allowed in our hut. Savta braided my hair with the ribbon. We feasted on a newly killed goat and barley beer, and I was the focus of attention for the first time in my life. I received a fine linen dress also from my aunt. It felt like a cloud on my skin. Savta produced a set of fleece shoulder pads to protect me from Bennu's talons and gave me a necklace of white shells.

To my surprise, the Elder Mariah came to our house. Savta greeted her and led her to me. "Elder, this is my granddaughter, Na'amah."

I stood of course. Elder Mariah was one of our three elders

and represented the Goddess. Somewhere to the west of us was a holy cave where the Goddess' Priestess lived. She had sent Mariah to us.

Mariah was a tall woman who carried herself straight as a cedar tree. She wore her silver-streaked brown hair tied in many small braids, beaded with tiny shells and dyed seeds. Her high cheekbones and arched brows added to the dignity of the red-dyed staff and white robes she always wore.

"Na'amah," she said, greeting me with a smile. "Congratulations and happiness on your womanhood."

"Thank you," I replied, glancing at her face and then studying her sandals.

"She is very shy," Mariah remarked to Savta, "for a woman who has killed a tiger."

Savta did not try to explain me, even to Elder Mariah. My father often acted embarrassed about me, and Tubal refused to be seen with me, but Savta gave no excuses or explanations. She smiled her lopsided smile. "My granddaughter is special."

Mariah studied me for a moment. "She is very beautiful. I've noticed her on market days. I'm sure many young men will want to wed her."

"She is already betrothed to Noah," Savta said proudly.

"Noah, the boat maker?"

"Yes." Mariah nodded. "He is a good man." She turned to me. "You will be happy with such a man."

"I will," I said. "He will let me be with the sheep."

A clear laugh like water spilling over stones escaped her lips. She pulled a copper bracelet from her wrist and put it on mine, still smiling. "I like the sheep too."

I knew this was truth because she kept all the sheep and goat lineages in her mind. If a dispute arose about who owned what ewe, Mariah would settle it. She was a wise woman.

"How can the Goddess be Virgin and Mother at the same time?" I asked, deciding to take advantage of her knowledge.

One of Mariah's brows rose.

Savta shook her head, but did not rebuke me, other than

61

to say, "You should request to ask such a question, Na'amah."

I nodded, still looking at Mariah's sandals. "May I ask a question, Elder?"

Stealing a glance from my eye's corner, I saw her mouth twitch in a way that reminded me of Savta. "I believe you already have." Then she surprised me. "You remind me of my daughter."

I wondered if she meant my behavior reminded her of her daughter or how I looked. Was it that I asked a question without permission or some feature of my face? I would have asked her, but I worried that I was only to be allowed one question, and I did not want to waste it. I did, however, want to know if she had a daughter like me. No one in our village was like me, but Mariah had not come from our tribe. The Priestess had sent her to be our Elder. I curled my lower lip between my teeth, something I did when I was practicing patience. If the waiting got too hard, sometimes I bit down a little to keep from speaking. Mariah had still not said if I could ask the question.

"Ask your question again, Na'amah," she said kindly.

Relieved, I blurted, "How can the Goddess be Virgin and Mother at the same time?"

"That is a good question and can be answered many ways." She paused. "This is one way: I am a woman, an old woman. My daughter has daughters. It is obvious that I am a mother. That is easily understood, true?"

"Yes," I said, listening with great care. Perhaps she would tell me something that would open my eyes to see the Goddess where I never had before.

"Before I became a mother, I was a virgin, a girl. I knew youth and strength."

I thought of Noah saying, *In my mind, I am young. I race up these hills as I imagine you do.*

"My skin was as smooth as yours," Mariah continued, "my belly as tight, my breasts as proud."

I imagined her as a girl with mischief in her eyes and no grey dulling her hair.

"Time has no dominion over our true selves," she said. "That

62

youth is me, as much as what you see before you." She held forward her wrinkled hands. "My outside is so." Then, both hands rose to her chest, like leaves born by a sudden breeze. "Inside, I am still that youth. I am still that virgin. Every woman is, as much as every woman is a mother."

"Even those who have not born a child?" I asked.

"We are not mothers merely because a baby has grown between our hips. If you have ever cared for anyone, ever given of yourself, in time, in efforts, you are a mother."

"So every woman is the Goddess?" I blurted.

Her face went very still, and she turned to Savta. "Those who have whispered your granddaughter is slow of mind are very wrong."

"She is special," Savta said again under her breath, so no one but Mariah and I could hear.

Mariah tilted her head. "The Goddess is the earth and the earth is the Goddess, Na'amah."

With another smile and a kiss of luck on my head, she left.

"Do you realize what an honor that was?" Aunt Adah said, coming over to us, her hands on her wide hips. "I don't recall an Elder speaking to me on my celebration day!"

I spun the bracelet on my slender wrist, feeling very much a woman.

My tiger skin was still drying or they would have had me sit on it. I was pressed to tell the story of my encounter with the beast, which was then endlessly discussed as an omen of significance. Did the Goddess not ride a tiger to war and sit down with lions? Did this mean the Goddess favored our tribe?

Savta was quiet during most of this, but later as she and I sat alone in our own hut, she spun wool and said, "It's a sign."

"What is a sign?" I asked, for we had not been speaking. The glow of my welcome to the community of womanhood had faded when I sat at the loom and found that I still could not imitate Savta's deft fingers.

"Your dominion over the tiger, of course. That is an obvious sign."

I kept disturbing the waft threads, and the weights at the bottom would swing, bumping the others and tangling the threads. Disgusted, I looped the thread on the thin piece of wood carved at the frame's edge for that purpose and went to Bennu to regain my composure. Gently, I scratched his head with my finger. He fluffed his feathers in pleasure.

I broke off a small piece of the honey-nut pastry Savta had made and gave him a bit. Bennu loved treats, especially those made with honey.

"What is it a sign of, Savta?" I asked absently.

"Of Mother Goddess' favor. I told you when you were young, don't you remember?"

I remembered, but it never made much sense. "Maybe Mother Goddess let me kill the tiger because she was looking out for the birthing ewe. I do not know why you think I am anything special, Savta." I felt cross. "I wish you would stop saying it."

That was when she told me why she thought the Goddess had marked me. "When you were born," she said slowly, "I rubbed the salt on you for long life, wrapped you in birthing felt, and laid you aside to tend to your mother's body." For a moment, Savta's eyes glimmered with unshed tears. "My poor Zillah."

She sighed. "When I turned back to you—"

Savta paused and took a deep breath, her hands stilling the spindle and her eyes glazed with memory. "You were covered by them."

I frowned. "What? Ants?" I shuddered.

"No." She leaned toward me. "Bees."

I felt my brows rise in surprise. "Bees?" Why would bees be on a baby?

"A swarm," Savta said, her eyes lost in the memory. "The queen bee landed on you and the swarm followed. You made no sound, and I panicked, thinking they had smothered you. I didn't know what to do. I was afraid trying to get them off would agitate them, and they might sting you. That many stings would kill a newborn."

"What did you do?"

"I took a cloth and pushed them away from your nostrils as slowly as I could, trying not to disturb them. You were still, but I felt your breath on my palm, so I knew you were alive. At first, I feared you would cry and squirm, then I realized the Goddess had you under her protection. You never stirred or cried out, and I waited until the queen bee decided to move on. You opened your eyes and yawned."

Savta connected a piece of pulled wool to the one she had spun, overlapping the raw ends. Then she gave the weighted spindle a twist, starting its turning again.

"Did anyone else see the bees on me?" I asked.

"No, I was alone. The other women had gone and your father left you with me, disappointed you weren't a boy. "Mother Goddess gave the sign to me alone, and I understood her intent that it be a secret."

I had no memory of this, but I understood the awe in her voice. A queen bee was a powerful symbol of the Mother Goddess. For a moment, I wondered if the Goddess truly had marked me. Bees and a tiger. I had never heard of bees alighting on a living creature, though I had seen them resting on branches in their search to find a new colony home. Most likely, it was just a strange happening, and I had not moved simply because I was asleep. It was not enough to make me believe in unseen gods who seem capricious and inscrutable with their favors and displeasures.

If I were a goddess, I would let myself be seen and would be clear what I wanted. I would not need people to worship and praise me. What good did that do?

Of course, I did not share these thoughts, even with Savta. Not because I thought she would turn me over to the Elders' judgment, but because I had no desire to challenge the beliefs that were as much a part of her life as breathing and loving me. The wonder was that I did not share them. I knew of no one who did not fear the gods. Why was I different?

Chapter Ten

When harvest time came for the wheat, everyone went to the fields, even those of Hunter Clan. The men used obsidian wedges to sharpen fine edges on the stone blades and cut down the wheat shafts with steady, slicing swings.

Shafts fell with their dusky-gold burden and lay in piles on the ground like a game of sticks. The women and children who were not watching the herds winnowed the grain, tossing it into the air for the wind to separate. I would rather have been in the hills, but Savta insisted I come to the harvest. I think she wanted Noah to see that his future wife could work hard. I pouted. Why did Savta want to get rid of me? How could she keep Tubal's house without me? She was very old. Who would fetch water and wood for the fire?

As soon as I could, Yanner and I escaped to the hills to inspect my sheep. It was a good thing we did, because the dogs had gotten into a fight with a leopard and it mauled a young dog. Yanner killed the injured dog and we took it home to cook. It always made me sad to lose a dog. They were faithful beasts, who did not stint in their love for humans or their duty with the herds, but we did not want to waste the meat, and leaving the carcass would attract more predators.

When I was not doing chores or guarding the sheep, I

went to watch Noah work on our house, which he planned to construct near his own house in a clearing far apart from the village, surrounded by a wood of beech, oak and maples. The way he coaxed wood to his bidding fascinated me, and I was insistent on having a house that would float. I think Noah understood if he wanted me, he had to build this, despite the jesting the idea engendered from others, but he never gave any sign of resenting his task.

Although the winter rains of this year had not flooded the river's banks, they had turned everything into a muddy morass for many days, and the last winters had been colder than anyone ever remembered. The weather was changing. I knew that in my bones, as well as I knew when my bleeding time was near. I did not like change, but it was stupid not to be prepared for it.

My house was nothing like what I imagined. Noah had decided to build it out of wood—cedar. I was doubtful that anything as heavy as tree trunks would stay afloat with the burden of a house on it, but Noah assured me it would. I was amazed that he could amass so many logs in such a short time and none of them seemed to come from nearby.

With a grin, he admitted his secret. "I steal them from a beaver dam in an arm of the river. The beavers make excellent logs far quicker than I could cut down timber with my tools." He indicated the sharpened stone implements lying about in apparent disorder, though I noticed he knew where each one lay when he wanted it in his hand.

"I float the logs downstream and use the ox to pull them up this creek." He pointed to a small gully. "I have an idea about how to build this wooden house over that little creek that feeds from the river. That way, I only have to lift the logs out of the water and lay them across the top."

"How will they stay together?"

He smiled. "I'll cut grooves in the wood to wedge the ropes and lash them together."

I frowned. Tar pitch would soak into bound reeds and seal it. A coating might help keep the wood from rotting, but I did not believe it would seal the spaces between the logs. Water found its way through the smallest cracks, and I did not want my house to sink.

As if he saw my thoughts, Noah said, "Don't worry, when the logs get wet they expand, and when the rope gets wet, it tightens. No water will come through."

I brightened. "That is wonderful. I have never thought much about boats."

"I can't claim to have invented such an arrangement, but I have given some thought to expanding on the idea. I don't think anyone has ever tried to make a boat into a house. I'm going to peg some of the logs on the base and make support poles, then lash more logs to make the sides."

I frowned again. Walls were made of plastered mud. I had never heard of walls made of logs.

"Like this," he said, stripping off several twigs from one of the logs that lay nearby. He placed them side by side and then stood them on edge, holding them together with his fingers. "This will be the walls of the house."

I considered it, and then smiled. "If it tips over, it will float on its side as easily as its bottom."

Noah laughed—his great booming sky laugh. I liked the sound.

"I hadn't thought of it that way," he said and reached both hands to pinch my ears lightly. "You have a sharp mind between those ears. You will be a good boat maker's wife."

That pleased me. "How can I help?"

He considered. "I'll need to make a lot of rope to lash the wood together."

"I do not know how to make rope. Is it like spinning?"

"More like weaving. I'll use bark strips of red cedar. They won't rot when they get wet." He reached into a basket and held up a strip of bark.

"That's too stiff to weave with," I said, frowning.

"We'll soak them to make them pliant, and then braid them together for strength. I'll show you, but first, I have a little something for you."

Noah dusted his hands and hunted among his tools for a moment, as though not certain where he had put something, but I thought his movements unconvincing. With a glance at me, no doubt to see if I were properly anticipating the present, he drew out a small wooden object and laid it in my hand.

A puff of breath escaped my mouth. It was a carving no larger than the size of my thumb, made of white wood. A small horse, its knees tucked under it, looking over its shoulder. Noah knew I admired the wild creatures. In the winter after the flood, the Hunters had taken many in an attempt to spare our sheep and goatherds from utter devastation. I thought they were beautiful, and when they grazed with the herd, I did not let the dogs run them off right away, as I should, but watched them. I thought them smarter than the sheep and wondered what it would be like to sit on their broad backs. They ran with a speed that the dogs could not match.

I cradled the tiny horse in my palm. The wood was smooth with oil. I wondered how Noah's huge hands had managed the tiny details of the eyes and the lines of muscle with his big hands. "Thank you," I remembered to say.

Bennu flew to a perch in a nearby tree. His wing had long since grown out enough to allow him to fly distances. He always returned, so I did not worry he would disappear. He looked down at us and said as clearly as a person, "Na'amah."

Startled, Noah and I both looked up at him. He cocked his head, but said nothing more. My mouth had dropped open, and I had to think to close it. Noah and I looked at each other to confirm we had heard what we thought we had heard.

Another man might have taken such a thing to mean a god inhabited Bennu's body, but Noah huffed and said, "The bird seller claimed he could talk, but I thought it was nonsense."

I pondered all the times Bennu had said what sounded like words or phrases. "I think he has been talking all this time, but in the language of the south."

Noah nodded. "If the seller wasn't giving us a load of ox

dung, the bird came from the River People. That's a land south of the Salt Sea. I wonder what he's been trying to say."

"Na'amah," Bennu pronounced again and ruffled his feathers, pleased with himself.

I laughed, delighted, and Noah smiled. "It's good to hear you laugh; you're so serious most of the time." His blue eyes were full of me. I took in his bared, muscled arms, the breadth of his shoulders and strong set to his jaw, my gaze wandering back up for a quick glance at his eyes. I had made my commitment when he promised to build me a floating house. It was a good decision, I thought. I was a wise woman.

"Bennu's stand washed away in the flood," I said.

"I'll build him another." Noah spread his arms wide and smiled to match the gesture. "No, I'll build him his own room. Why not? All I have to do is lash more logs together and keep the beavers busy. A room all for Bennu."

I clapped my hands. "With branches for him to climb?"

Noah chuckled. "With branches."

I was happy. It was a good thing to have a house of one's own design. I would know every finger breath of it, how the wood fit together, which lashings were made by my hands. A sudden thought formed in my mind. "How many rooms can I have?"

Noah looked thoughtful and then shrugged. "As many as you wish, my beloved. The way I'm building, we can expand. Are you thinking of bargaining my tools or sheep for more birds?" His eyes held a gleam like sun-sparks on water.

I sat straighter, understanding he was teasing me and proud to catch the joke. "Certainly not, but a woman of my wealth should have a room to cook in, a room to spin in, and a room to sleep in."

A belly laugh roared up from him. "You will keep me building this boat-house for the rest of my life! How about a room for each of our children?"

For the first time, the idea of bearing children did not sicken me. The prospect of spending my life with this man felt right, and I turned the thought over repeatedly, examining it in awe and thankfulness. I wanted to hold his child to my chest and drink the pleasure such a gift would bring him.

Chapter Eleven

In my fifteenth summer, I sat in Noah's work area, watching the boat-house I had ordered as my bride price take shape, log by log. How could I know that before I could ever step foot into it, unimaginable events lay in my path?

"Well," an edged voice behind me said, "how is the floating house coming along, boat maker?"

Yanner had grown over the past several moon-cycles. He was almost as tall as Noah, though slender where Noah was broad. He wore a fox tail tied to his cord belt, a sign of his acceptance into Hunter Clan. The Clan's influence had grown since the flood, even though we had seen a harvest. The people feared another flood or disaster where the responsibility of feeding the village would fall onto the hunters' backs. We still had not replenished the numbers of our herds much beyond what we needed for food. We depended on the goats for milk and cheese, and our main source of trade was our fine wool. We needed the meat from the hunters' arrows and spears.

"Be welcome, Yanner," Noah said, but his mouth curved in a frown. He had not missed the mockery in Yanner's question.

Yanner barely glanced at Noah; his gaze was for me. "Na'amah, may I speak to you . . . outside?" I shrugged and moved from my perch on a pile of shaved wood to step outside with him. We moved away from the house into a patch of shade. A breeze off the lake lifted my hair. Yanner reached up to touch a strand. "The sun finds copper hidden in the black." His tone was distracted, but Yanner's words had always flickered with the bright red-oranges of a flame and today they seemed to blaze brighter.

My hands went to my hips and I cocked my head. "What is it, Yanner? You have something burning inside you to speak."

He shook his head, not in denial, but amusement. "I have never been able to hide anything from you. You see into me as readily as you do the sheep, even though you barely look at me."

I kept my gaze steady on his chest, not allowing him to slide away from the subject. "Well?"

Unexpectedly, he grasped both my hands. "Na'amah, I am a man of Hunter Clan now. I've hunted bison in the mountains and brought down deer with my own spear." Pride and fear seemed entangled in his voice. "We have been friends since childhood, but I want to be more than your friend."

I blinked at him.

He plunged on. "I want you to be my wife."

My mouth opened, but speech did not come for several moments. He looked tormented, and I spoke without quite realizing what I said. "Why?"

His gaze darted to the stack of logs behind me, and I turned to see if someone was there, but saw only the wood, waiting for Noah to bind them with rope into walls for our house. Yanner's grip on my hands tightened. His hands were moist. "I want you Na'amah," he breathed hoarsely. "I need you, need to have you."

The rawness of his passion hit me like a blow. My mind whirled with confusion, and I wanted to sit, rock, and hum until it went away, but I knew that was selfish, and I tried to settle myself with deep breaths.

Finally, I shook my head a bit. "You know better than any that my mind is wounded. Why would you want me to wife?"

"I love you, Na'amah. I don't care that you are different. I don't care what anyone says."

"What do they say?" I demanded.

He hesitated, but knew I would persist until I had an answer.

"They say that your children would be like you."

"How like me?"

With a shrug that implied he thought it meant little, he said, "Different."

I knew Savta had given an oath to the Elders that my strangely-shaped baby head was the result of birthing and not a defect that might be passed on to children. If she had not, they would have ordered me put outside the village to die.

A new thought gripped me as tightly as Yanner's hands. What if Savta were wrong or . . . what if she had lied? Would she have done that? I was her last hope of daughter lineage. Daughters were not much valued by the tribe, at least by men, but Savta remembered the days when the Goddess had greater honor than Father God or any of his male forms. How many times had she told me of the Goddess' Cave where her Priestess reigned, a living symbol of Earth Mother's life-giving force? The Priestess and the Daughters dedicated to her were honored by tribes from sea to sea. The Priestess always sent a Daughter to serve as Elder at a tribe's request, as Mariah had been sent to us.

A daughter would have been important to Savta. Perhaps she would have lied to save me. I felt dizzy. "What if I gave my wrongness to my children?"

"I don't care," Yanner said. "You must be mine. I am ill with wanting you."

I stepped back, out of his grasp. "I am promised to Noah. We are to be wed before the end of this moon." Sadness churned in my stomach. When Noah first came to our house and asked for me, I did not want him or children. Now I wanted both, but was it fair to him? He had no children, despite his age, and he clearly wanted them. Would they be . . . wounded, like me?

I sank to the ground right there and pulled my knees to my chest, burying my head against them and rocking. Yanner sat close beside me, his breath in my ear, his body pressed against my side. I could not concentrate on the song with the touch of his flesh.

"He is old, Na'amah. I am young and strong. I am now

Hunter Clan. If the waters come again, I can provide for you. That strange boat he calls a house will never withstand a flood, and even if it did, it would only carry you down the river and be torn apart."

I looked up at him. "Go away," I said. The happiness that had been a bright gold flower in my chest only moments ago had wilted and browned.

Chapter Twelve

I spent more time alone after that, taking the shepherd watches of others when mine were finished. Bleary-eyed, I would stumble home and fall onto my mat, wishing for the first time in my life to be oblivious of the indigo croak of the night heron and the loons' warbling laugh, welcoming the oblivion of sleep.

"What is wrong with you?" Savta asked more than once. "Is it your moon time?"

She knew when my moon time fell, but she asked anyway. Sometimes, she said, young girls' bodies did not keep regular pulse with the moon. Mine did. When the new moon's horn pierced the sky, I prepared bundles of felt and bathed twice as often as normal in my river pool.

Noah also worried about my sudden quiet and failure to seek him out and inspect my boat-home. "Don't you want to come tell me what to do?" he teased. "Besides, I need more rope."

I frowned at him. "You do not need me to do what your hands can do in the dark."

Yanner also came to me, catching me on my way to the hills and once finding me at my bath. "Go away!" I yelled at him, hunkering down in the water.

"I just want to talk to you." He stared at me before averting his gaze and squatting on the bank.

"I will be at the cave at sunset," I said to make him go.

"Who is assigned with you?" he asked.

"Mallet, I think. Now go!" I wondered why he wanted to know. Was he jealous? I sighed. Life had been much less complicated before womanhood.

That night I stirred the small fire in the cave on the North Slope. Mallet was late joining me. The sun had already slipped into the lake, and a full moon glowed red against the horizon. I did not mind. I liked being alone.

A sheep's bleating called me out of the cave, and I scanned the hillside below. I saw nothing but the shifting shadows of the herd. Slowly, the moon rose higher in the night sky, round as a woman's breast, wrapped in a wispy shawl of clouds. On the sky's opposite side, darker clouds brooded in the west, hoarding lightning within them.

Grey Dog appeared out of the shadows, tail wagging. He approached and lay at my feet, rolling over onto his back in submission. I stooped and rubbed his stomach, smiling at the expression of bliss this always produced.

He raised his head at a distant flutter of bat wings and then lowered it. I smiled at him. He knew he should be watching the sheep, not sneaking off for a belly rub. Abruptly, he sprang to his feet with a low growl, facing down the slope, his ruff stiff. I stood, my hand working the sling from my belt.

Shapes formed out of the moonlight. Men.

"Mallet?" I tested the name toward them. No reply.

My heart began to hammer. Raiders. Rumors had wormed their way from the south about a band of warriors who stole women and young men and vanished in the forests. I slipped back into the cave to get the ram's horn, but it was not in its place, something I had not noticed, because it usually hung out of sight behind a curve in the cave wall. Someone had failed to return it to its place. Irritated and frightened, I loosened my stone pouch, fitting one in my sling and went back outside.

Three shapes approached. The rocky ground kept me from recognizing their tread. I could take one and Grey Dog another. If Mallet would get himself up here and maybe another dog or two—, but I knew the odds were against us. Still, I stood straight and pressed my teeth together. I would not die or be taken without a fight. Had I not faced a tiger?

To my surprise, Grey Dog sat, his growl changing into a whine. For a moment, I was confused, and then realized Grey Dog must know the approaching people. "Mallet," I shouted, "you frightened me. For that, you get second watch!" Usually, a stone toss determined who would have to wake before dawn.

Again, no acknowledgement came from the men. Puzzled, I stepped back into the cave shadows, against a wall so I would see their faces in the firelight before they saw me. I looped my sling back on my belt, as there was no room in the small cave for a good whirl, and put my hand on the bone knife instead.

I dropped it to my side when the fire revealed Yanner and my brother, and my brother's friend, Sunnic.

"Na'amah?" Yanner said, trying to peer into the shadows.

"Here" I stepped forward.

All three stopped. "Is something wrong?" I asked. "Where is Mallet?"

Tubal looked around the cave with a contemptuous scowl, perhaps remembering his younger days here. I waited, bewildered at his presence and unwilling to believe my brother would lower himself to take a shepherd watch.

Tubal turned his regard to me and, as usual, it was heavy with disdain. Yanner stepped forward. He stood before the fire, so his face was shadowed, but tension shaped his stance, and he carried himself oddly, as if unsure of his balance. "Na'amah, I have asked Tubal to give you to me as wife."

I stiffened. "Tubal cannot give me as wife. I am already betrothed."

"He is head of your house. It is Hunter Clan law."

The cave wall at my back was cold, the ceiling close. I suddenly wished I had met them outside. The smell of beer thickened the air. Even their stance foreboded danger. Despite the night's chill, sweat tracked a prickly path down my spine.

"Our father agreed to my betrothal to Noah when he was

head-of-house," I said, trying to let anger cover the waver in my voice. "They spit on it. Tubal cannot change that. Only I can, and I will not."

"Please Na'amah." Yanner's pitched his plea low, only for my ears.

"I am sorry, Yanner," I said, suddenly in pity of him. "I like you. We are friends. You are very handsome and many girls turn their heads as you pass. You will find plenty of women eager to be your wife, even one of your wives."

"I don't want another," he said, his voice soaked with misery and slurred with too much beer. "I want only you."

"Na'amah!" Tubal barked. "I am head-of-house. I give you to Yanner."

"My chin lifted. "No."

He smiled and my heart fluttered in fear. "Take your wife, Yanner," my brother said.

I stepped back as Yanner and Sunnic moved in. My back hit the wall. "Stop," I said, drawing my knife. Despite their drinking, they were quick. One grabbed each arm. Sunnic twisted my wrist, making me drop the knife. I fought them, but they were stronger.

"Take her down, Sunnic," Tubal snapped. The words were hard shells on the outside, but inside nested a tangle of worms.

"Uh, not so easy," Sunnic muttered. He was behind me and had my arms pinned, though I struggled with all my strength. He sat suddenly, putting us both on the ground. Then he wrapped a leg around each of mine, forcing them apart and held me atop him. I cried out for help, but I knew no one but the sheep would hear me. Grey Dog growled and then whined, unsure what to do. Tubal kicked him and he ran off, whimpering.

I struggled until I was exhausted, and all I could manage was to pant and glare at Tubal. "You are a true son of Cain," I said.

He knelt beside me and slapped my face. Hard. Tears stung my eyes. "Snake," he responded, a man's ultimate insult to a woman. "You will get what you deserve."

"Why?" I sobbed. "Why do you hate me so? What have I

ever done to you?"

He knelt close. "You lived. You killed our mother and yet you lived. You should have been put out to die, but you live. Men look at you and see your dark-lashed eyes, your full mouth, the curve of your breasts, but I see the brokenness beneath, the serpent that lies in your mind waiting to bite off a manhood."

I could not stop the tears of confusion, of shame . . . of fear. He put a finger on my cheek and caught one. With a slow flick of his tongue, he tasted it. For some reason, this frightened me more than being held pinned on the cave floor with my legs spread apart.

"Your wife is ready for you," Tubal said with the flatness of announcing day had begun.

"I stared at Yanner. Do not do this," I begged.

He hesitated.

"Well, hunter?" Tubal mocked. "Is your spear strong enough? You asked for this. You begged me to help you and here I am helping you, but you must do your part."

Yanner removed his tunic and looked down at me, his hands at the cord of his pants. "I can't while she is looking at me."

My brother laughed. "I anticipated this." He stuffed wads of felt in my ears, threw a thick sheepskin over my head, and tied it. I could see nothing and hear very little. I felt my dress lifted and found the strength to struggle again, but I was helpless in this position.

Sunnic's manhood pressed hard against the small of my back. He kept me pulled tight against him and rocked his hips. I was so accustomed to hearing everything around me, even the smallest noise that the forced silence added to my panic. I heard only my heart's thunderous beating in my ears and muffled voices, and then a hand rubbed between my legs, and I took a sharp breath, realizing it was not a hand.

Pain erupted throughout my body. I screamed, but the thick sheepskin swallowed the sound. The thrusting was hard and quick, forcing the breath from me with every push, so that I had to gasp for air in rhythm to his piercing.

They left me in the cave with my head still covered. I lay in the smothering darkness, wishing to sink into it forever. I could. All I needed to do was not remove the skin, but my hands fumbled of their own accord at the string, and I dragged it aside, taking huge gulps of clean air.

Sound returned to the world. Tubal had cut off my hearing to terrorize me. The smell of blood blended with an unfamiliar, salty odor. Yanner had betrayed me. Anger began to replace shame, straightening my back and lifting my chin. If the Goddess existed, she was my anger, my pain. Men and their god beware.

With no idea how to exact my vengeance, I rolled onto my hands and knees and tried to stand on legs that trembled like pine needles in the wind. At first I just stood, trying to breathe normally, past my fear that they would return. When I could, I stumbled to the creek, desiring only to wash, to be clean again, if ever I could. The cool water soothed my swollen skin and the blood that flowed was less than my moon time, so I thought I would survive.

I would not return to my brother's house. Never. If I had to live by myself in the forest, I would not step over his threshold.

I sat on a rock for a long time watching the moonlit water, until the sun rose over my shoulder. It seemed incredible that another day was born, as if nothing had changed . . . when everything had changed.

Chapter Thirteen

Noah watched me approach with a frown that made his coarse features savage. Without a word, he took me in his arms and held me tightly. Panic erupted in my chest, heaving me back into the darkness with a man's weight on me. I struggled away, panting.

Without a word, he regarded me. I wondered if he would see more than I showed him and if he would turn me away. "Who?" he asked.

I embraced whatever part of the Goddess' anger I could conjure. "Yanner."

His face grew hard, the muscles of his jaw tightening. I did not read faces well, not as well as I could read the movements of animals, because there was so much information in a person's face, and I saw it all at once—the tightness in the forehead, narrowing of eyes, contracting of pupils and nostrils, teeth pressed together. Was it anger, or concentration or fear or derision? I was never sure, and trying to absorb it all was disturbing. But I was sure at that moment—had Yanner stood before us, my gentle Noah would have killed him.

"I will not go back to Tubal's house," I said.

He nodded.

He took my hand, swallowing it in his bear paws. "I take you as wife and beloved."

I trembled, the ground before me dissolving in an image

of a great cliff. Below, water frothed and churned an unknown depth, but there was no other way off the cliff on which I stood. With tight-shut eyes, I put my other hand on his and declared, "I take you as husband . . . and beloved."

Noah treated me with respect and honor. He did not try to touch me, though I could see he wanted to, and it was his right. He satisfied himself with small brushes of his hand, a finger along my cheekbone or a playful tap on my nose and then withdrew before panic could claim me.

I needed time . . . but I was not to have it.

They came the following night, like jackals come to steal the tiger's kill. One held me, stuffing my mouth with felt strips and covering my eyes. I thought they came to take me again, but that was not their aim. Instead, they beat Noah. I heard his muffled cries, the crush of bone. They did not speak, knowing I supposed that I listened. Tears soaked the felt and the hand that held them, not for me, but for Noah. Even in the cave, I had not felt this hopeless.

When they left, I crawled to Noah's side, fear clawing my insides like scavenger birds, ripping shreds from my hope of security and happiness. In the darkness, my hands found his face, expecting blood. There was none, only ragged breathing that told me he lived.

Stumbling from the house, I ran to get Savta, thankful that Tubal had not yet returned home. I had no doubt but that he was carousing with his fellows, celebrating this victory. Savta woke instantly, and I told her Noah was ill, to keep her from asking questions that would delay us. She came with me, bringing her basket of medicines and herbs, and I paused only to grab my tiger skin and my horse carving and coax Bennu to my shoulder.

In the boat-house, after a brief look to make sure Noah was breathing, Savta blew smoldering moss and built up the fire before assessing the damage. Her keen gaze took in the blood and disarray. "Are you hurt?" she asked me.

I could not speak, so I shook my head. She pushed me aside, her expert hands traveling over Noah's body. I pulled my knees to my chest and rocked, but my humming came out more as a keen than song, and I kept my eyes open.

Finally, she leaned back. "Broken knee and ribs," she said. "Perhaps some bleeding inside. They left his face alone."

"Why?"

She shrugged. "Perhaps to make it look as if it could have been an accident."

"Should I get the healer?"

She shook her head. "I know what to do. Chants and prayers can come later."

It was the first time I had ever heard Savta speak so, though she was always practical in her worship. I stared at her.

"It's the Goddess' blessing that transforms the seed into food," Savta said, "but she expects us to plant them and harvest the crops."

"What can I do?" I said.

"Find something to put in his mouth to keep him from biting his tongue." I did as she instructed, using the felt strips that had seen a similar purpose in my mouth. Noah opened his eyes and tried to move. He groaned.

"Lie still," Savta said in a voice not to be disobeyed.

I took his hand.

"No," she said. "He will crush your hand. Let him hold something else. Wood. And I need two stout, straight pieces this long." She spread her hands the width of my waist.

I found the wood, having plenty to choose among, and placed a thick piece in his hand. The other two, Savta placed beside her with strips of cloth she had torn. "Sit on his thigh to hold his leg steady," Savta instructed.

Again, I obeyed. She grasped his lower leg and twisted sharply. Noah screamed.

With quick, deft movements, Savta pressed the sticks along the sides of his legs and secured them with the cloth strips. Then we worked larger strips under him and tied them across his chest.

"It hurts to breathe," he muttered.

"I know," Savta said. "The bandages will help a little, but it must heal on its own."

"And my leg?"

She hesitated. "I've done my best. I'll give you some safflower salve to rub on it for the pain."

He looked at me then. "I'm sorry."

I could not understand why he apologized to me. I had brought this on him. "Why did they hurt you?" I asked, begging for an answer.

Savta was digging through her herbs. "Heat water," she snapped.

My body responded to her voice as it always had, and I was grateful my arms seemed to know how to pour water into the tortoise shell and my legs to bring it to the fire. The poppy drink she prepared would grant relief to Noah, and I wished to drink some as well. Perhaps it would ease the fist that lodged in my chest.

I cradled my husband's head in my hands while Savta spooned the bitter drink into his mouth. When he had swallowed it all, I laid his head carefully back. His gaze found me, those beautiful sky eyes blurred with pain or perhaps the herbs.

"Why?" I asked him. "Why did they do this?"

"Did they pierce you again?" he croaked.

Savta flinched, but said nothing.

"No." It was beyond my understanding. What had they accomplished? "Why did they hurt you?" They were men; he was a man. Somehow, I felt he would know what motivated them.

"I don't know," he muttered, his eyelids slowly settling. He forced them open, but they closed again.

It was the next day that I had my answers.

Chapter Fourteen

Sleep only came to me in small snatches throughout the night, despite the fact that Savta mixed some of the poppy tea with the bearberry she made me drink after learning what happened in the cave. I would wake, my heart racing, sure I heard someone in the house. We would get dogs, I decided. Fierce dogs that we would raise so they would protect us, not run away as Grey Dog had. A tiger would be nice. The laugh that wanted to emerge at such an outrageous thought died in my throat. What could I do? I knew who had done it, though I had not seen their faces.

By morning, I determined Savta and I would go to the Elders. Despite my shame, I would tell them what happened in the cave. Any thinking person should realize the same group of young hunters had hurt Noah. The only reason I could imagine was anger at my disobedience in choosing Noah. But why hurt Noah, instead of me? I hoped Yanner had not been involved; that would crush me beyond even his cruel piercing.

By the time we had risen and tended Noah, however, the Elders came to us. The three stood holding their judgment staffs, flanked by a growing crowd of people. The Elders were not often called, and word spread quickly. Batan was Chief Elder. To his spear-hand side stood Kahor, elected by the Hunter/Warriors and to Batan's left was Mariah, representing the Goddess.

I stood in the threshold of our house, surprised at their

presence and unable to move, until Savta emerged and pushed me aside. She stood straight, despite her many years and the crevices carved into her cheeks. Her thin arms, browned by the sun, were stronger than they appeared. She was a respected woman. I kept silent, trusting her to speak for us far better than I could.

I wondered how the Elders knew what had happened. Did they also know that Tubal and Yanner and their friends, who stood at Kahor's side, were to blame?

"What brings the Elders to this doorway?" Savta asked.

"We will speak to head-of-house," Kahor said, stepping forward. "To settle a claim."

"Noah is head-of-house, but he is injured," Savta said. "I've given him a potion to make him sleep and take his pain."

Kahor did not seem surprised, but Mariah's grey-streaked brows rose.

"I will speak as head-of-house," Savta said.

Kahor frowned.

"There are no sons of Noah," Mariah said, adjusting a copper bracelet that looked similar to the one she had given me on my celebration day, but it had an aged, green color. "It is proper."

With the briefest of nods, Kahor acknowledged Mariah's assessment.

Unease brewed in my stomach. I wanted to shout at them, to make them punish my brother and Yanner and his friends. Tubal stared at me, his tongue flicking to moisten his lips. Yanner's eyes studied the ground, as if he were deciding whether to plant a crop of barley in the spot before his toes. They stood side to side, Yanner's golden hair and skin a sharp contrast with Tubal's darker coloring. Several girls and women stared without trying to hide their pleasure in gazing at both of them. I did not doubt that in those women's eyes neither could be guilty of any wrong. I hoped Mariah would not be so affected.

"Why do you come to Noah's house?" Savta asked.

Batan spoke for the first time. "A claim has been made."

"What claim?" Savta demanded. The patina of age that filmed her eyes did not dim her glare.

"Speak the claim, head of Hunter Clan," Batan directed to Kahor in a tired voice. Batan was as old as Savta.

Kahor's grip tightened on his staff, which was also a spear. "Yanner of the Hunter Clan makes claim of Na'amah, sister of Tubal-Cain, as his wife."

"I am Noah's wife!" I could stand by no longer. "I was oath-promised by my father. We have wed."

"Then it is not a binding joining," Tubal said, stepping forward. "I speak on behalf of Yanner, as clan brother."

My assumptions unraveled before me. The Elders were not here to rule in the matter of Noah's beating or my rape, but to question the validity of my binding to Noah. My throat felt as though I had swallowed a dry wind.

"Were there any witnesses?" Mariah asked.

"I bear witness to the oath-promise," Savta said.

"And the wedding?" Tubal jeered. "Do you claim to bear witness to that as well?"

Batan leaned wearily on his staff. "Hold your tongue, Tubal. It is for the Elders to question."

Tubal's face clouded with fury, but he did not speak.

"Still," Batan said, "it was a just question. Did you witness the wedding?"

Savta hesitated and glanced at me, knowing how lies took me off balance. "No."

With a smirk, Tubal crossed his arms over his chest.

"That alone does not invalidate the marriage, if Noah concurs with their joining," Mariah said, and she turned to Tubal. "Do you have more to offer than the fact that they exchanged vows in privacy?"

"Yes," Tubal said. "I am head-of-house, and I gave Na'amah to Yanner before she spoke vows with Noah . . . if she ever did."

Mariah looked at me. I felt like a netted fish.

"He had no right to give her," Savta said, and added in a mocking tone, "...if he ever did."

My knees buckled and I reached for Savta's arm. She steadied me so I could catch my balance. How grateful I was to her for taking my defense. It could not be an easy choice for her, to side with her granddaughter against her grandson.

"I have witnesses," Tubal said. "Yanner and Sunnic." Sunnic nodded. Yanner finally lifted his head and looked at me, his gaze full of yearning and guilt.

"Sunnic and I," Tubal continued in a flat, even tone, "also witnessed Yanner take his bride."

My hands clinched into fists. "There was no willingness to that taking," I said.

Tubal smiled. "Then you admit the taking?"

I glared at him.

Tubal shrugged and tightened the cords on the net. "According to Hunter Clan laws, it doesn't matter if she was willing or not. I gave her to Yanner and he claimed her. You have all witnessed her admission."

The crowd stirred and people turned to speak and argue with each other. I heard it all as the distant buzz of bees, a noise that had no connection with me.

Kahor raised his judging spear, his jaw set. "Tubal's words follow Hunter Clan law."

Savta appealed to Elder Mariah. "It may be Hunter Clan law, but it cannot be the Goddess' law?"

There was pity in Mariah's eyes. She knew she would be the lone vote on my behalf. "The Goddess sanctioned that law to protect a woman taken against her will," she said, "to give her the option of marriage and to create consequences on the man's part. It is not a tool to force a woman to wed a man who pierced her."

Kahor struck the ground with the spear butt. "Nevertheless, Tubal is head-of-house and therefore Hunter law applies."

"Noah is head-of-house here, and he is not of Hunter Clan," Savta insisted.

Tubal turned to Elder Batan. He looked bored with the whole matter. "Chief Elder," Tubal said, "I offer a solution."

Batan lifted watery eyes to him. "That would be welcome."

"Yanner challenges Noah for Na'amah."

I drew a quick breath, realizing what an idiot I had been. A challenge was the most ancient of methods for resolving disputes. I had never heard of Elders not allowing it.

Batan nodded, obviously happy to have a resolution that would allow him to go back to his house and bed. "Yanner must issue the challenge himself," he said, looking at Yanner.

Yanner still refused to look at me. I felt ill. How could I have loved this man as my friend? There was a time when I would have named him as the only possibility of a mate. Now, if he lay bleeding in the pastures, I would turn my back on him and leave him to die there.

Tubal gave Yanner a sharp blow to his arm. "Speak up, if you still want the snake," he growled under his breath.

Finally, Yanner looked at me. "I still want her," he said. "I challenge Noah, the boat maker, for her."

Batan nodded in satisfaction. "As Chief Elder I grant the challenge."

"Noah cannot fight," I cried. "These same men who claim a challenge came last night and beat him."

"What nonsense," Tubal said. "We were drinking by the river all night."

"That's true," a man cried out. "I heard them. Couldn't sleep."

Snickers and laughs rippled through the crowd.

Mariah raised her oak staff for quiet and turned to me. "Have you any proof of this?"

I fought the urge to drop to my knees and rock. "I heard them," was all I could say.

Mariah looked to Savta. "Were you here?"

"No. Na'amah came to get me after it happened."

Kahor shrugged. "Then there is no proof that she isn't making this charge from air."

"There is the proof of his broken leg," I said through gritted teeth.

"Na'amah does not lie," Savta said.

Tubal spit on the ground, an insult to Mother Goddess, who cajoled the rain from Father God. "More likely he fell off the top of this crazy boat he calls a house."

"Regardless how it happened, Noah is hurt," Mariah said. "There is no justice in a challenge with an injured man."

"If we wait, then the father of any child in Na'amah's belly would be in question," Tubal said. "I demand the challenge fulfilled."

With a shaky hand, Batan raised his own Elder staff. "At tomorrow's dawn, I declare a challenge here—" He hesitated, eyeing the strange structure. "In front of Noah's . . . house."

Chapter Fifteen

Noah slept through the day. Without a word, Savta moved in with us. She cooked a mutton stew with greens and saw that I ate, though I was not hungry. She had me tip tiny amounts of broth into Noah's mouth, while I held his head propped on my lap. I studied his face. What had I brought this gentle, kind man? Only sorrow and pain. And why? What had he seen in me that made him ask to be my mate? I sang to him, his head cradled in my arms.

When dusk softened the day's edges, he opened his eyes. A sea of blood drowned the sky in them. He groaned and then focused on my face above him. "I dreamed Mother Goddess sang to me, but it was you, wasn't it?"

I blinked back tears. "I sang to you."

He started to move and gritted his teeth in pain. When he could speak, he asked with a grim expression, "Did they hurt you?"

"No." I shook my head. There was no point telling him about the challenge. He could do nothing.

With effort, he raised his head and craned to see his leg. "How bad is it?"

"Broken in two places," Savta said.

His face paled. "I am no use to you, Na'amah. I should protect you, and I am nothing but a cripple now."

I did not know what to say. Desperately, I looked to Savta.

"Your job is to rest and get well," she snapped. "Now, drink this." The lines of her jaw said she would accept nothing else from him. She held out a cup with an awful smelling brew. He swallowed it without protest. In a short time, his eyes closed again, but not before he had given my hand a squeeze.

I wanted to scream.

Savta looked at me with sadness, at least that was how I interpreted the twitch at the corners of her eyes, but perhaps it was anger. So much was happening at once on her face. "Tell me," she said.

"What?" I started rocking, Noah's head still in my lap.

"Everything."

I did. I had never been able to lie well and not at all to Savta, or to deny her something she demanded. I told her what had happened in the cave.

Her grey eyes never left me until I finished and then their focus drifted down to her hands, splotched and wrinkled, but strong. "Na'amah, my daughter's daughter," she murmured.

I thought this unhelpful. I knew who I was. What I wanted to know was what to do about the awful situation. "Savta, what will happen tomorrow?"

She sighed. "They will come, and Yanner will demand Noah meet his challenge. It can be a fight to the death if no one concedes."

My stomach tangled into a tighter knot, something I hardly thought possible. My husband, so large and strong, lay like a baby before me, helpless and weak. I had come to him for his protection and now I must protect him.

"Noah cannot fight Yanner," I said.

"Or anyone else," Savta agreed. "He can't even stand and besides, I gave him enough medicine that he will not wake before tomorrow night."

"What are my choices?" When things became complex, this was always a good question to ask.

Savta crossed her arms over her chest and leaned back. "You could do nothing. Yanner would make his demands. Noah would snore through it, and the Elders would declare Noah's claim forfeit. You would go with Yanner."

"Or?"

"Or you could declare a divorce from Noah before the fight and go with Yanner."

"Or?"

"You could go to Yanner and plead with him to recant his challenge."

"Or?"

"I can't think of another 'or.' Can you?"

"I could take my knife and slip it into Yanner's ribs," I said, surprising myself. But when I closed my eyes and remembered his spear ripping me, the surprise drained into a hollow pit of disdain and anger. He had betrayed everything our friendship meant. He deserved my knife. I removed it from my belt and stared at it. The bone was cool in my palm.

Could I do such a thing? I imagined standing over Yanner's bed of grass and furs, watching him sleep, then plunging my blade through his flesh. I had cut enough animals to know what it felt to pierce flesh and muscle. Yanner's eyes would open as his life drained from him. I would lean close and ask, "How does it feel to be pierced?"

As satisfying as this daydream was, it did not solve my problem because I could not do it. I wanted to, but I could not. My hand would tremble and betray me, remembering all the nights we sat together at the cave opening and talked, or huddled together under a bearskin before our fire, or hunted bees.

A sudden weight descended on me and I dropped my head. "I am too weary to think."

Savta laid a hand on my shoulder, a rare gesture of consolation. Savta believed one bore one's burdens with a stiff back.

Chapter Sixteen

The moon rose before I did. I lay for a moment in her cool light, praying, despite my disbelief, to this most brilliant of the Goddess' forms. She watched me through the window Noah had made in the house wall. The hole would give winter's breath an opening, and brought derision from Tubal and Yanner, but layers of skins could seal it, and it made me happy. Also, Bennu liked to perch on the tree branch where he could watch what went on inside and outside the house.

I rose quietly. Owls called from the woods. Noah slept like a hibernating bear. Savta lay on her back snoring softly. With care not to make a sound, I took a deerskin pack and put a clay cup, a tortoise shell bowl and some dried meat into it and rolled the sheepskin I slept on as tightly as I could, wrapping it around the cup and bowl to protect them. I put on the white shell necklace Savta had given me at my womanhood and the copper bracelet Elder Mariah had given me. My bone comb went into the pack and one of the bladder water bags that Noah kept hung on a rail. It was half full. That, I decided was enough weight for me to carry. I needed to travel as lightly as possible. But the sight of the tiny horse Noah had carved for me made my chest cramp, and I worked it into a fold of the blanket.

When I straightened and turned, I almost ran into Savta. She stood between me and the entrance illuminated by moonlight, cradling something I could not make out in her arms. She sniffed. "Here, take this."

"What is it?" I asked, somehow not surprised she had guessed my intent.

"Your tiger skin," she said, stuffing it into my roll. "Take it to the Goddess' Cave. They will understand its meaning."

"The Goddess' Cave?" I had not thought of going there. I had not really thought where I was going, only that I needed to leave.

"You are worthy to be among them, my granddaughter, but I didn't want to give you up." Her eyes gleamed in the moonlight, and she seemed to be trying not to blink.

I looked again at my sleeping husband. My leaving would be painful for him, but how much worse to be a cripple and see me every day in Yanner's hut, knowing I slept in Yanner's bed and bore his children, children that should have been ours? I would not have even a choice to avoid Yanner's arms. He had shown he would be the father of my children regardless of my feelings about it. I knew most women did not choose their husbands, but even Savta understood my decision.

Savta sniffed again. "Go to the Black Lake's edge and follow its shore west until it feeds into a canyon as a snaking river. Continue along the canyon's edge until a cliff halts the river. The Goddess' Cave is inside that cliff. It is a journey of over a moon-cycle to the Goddess' Cave. Her Priestess will protect you, and no man will dare her anger. Custom forbids it, and she has her own warriors to ensure custom is followed."

I nodded, relieved to have a destination and purpose. To dishonor the Goddess would be a curse on the crops and the babies in their mother's wombs . . . or so people believed.

Savta's next words fed hope to my starving soul. "When Noah heals I will send him to you and you can both decide what to do."

"You think he will heal, then?" I asked. Men had died of such wounds.

She shrugged. "It's up to the Goddess. He'll never be the same, but he may walk again."

I grabbed Savta's arm and her eyes widened. I rarely initiated a touch, though I liked to be held tightly...at least, I had before that night in the cave. "Keep him safe," I said. "Keep him in your care and help him heal. I will find the Goddess' Cave and wait for him."

She nodded. "You'd better go. Remember, Yanner and Tubal are Hunter Clan. They will be able to track you until you reach the rocks around the shore. Take care not to leave any prints indicating your direction."

"Well, they will know I have either gone east or west or straight into the Black Lake," I said.

"Then you must stay ahead of them and hide from them. If not, I imagine I will see you again soon enough."

I set my mouth. "You will not see me before Noah is healed."

That was a true prediction, but not for the reason I intended.

Chapter Seventeen

Darkness did not frighten me. In some ways, the night offers a reprieve, a sanctuary from the assault on my senses. I always liked the night watch on my hills. Now, moving through the woods, north of the settlement, I felt like a creature of the night. Perhaps the tiger skin in my pack gave me the right, or so I fancied.

I followed the river, a sleepy Bennu on my shoulder, knowing it would take me to the Black Lake. I wondered about the Salt Sea that cradled our land to the west and south. Some traders called it the Middle Salt Sea and some the Great Salt Sea. The Black Lake's waters were fresh. Would salted water look different?

When I reached the lake, I stood on a rock, my face to the wind that caught and tangled my hair. Bennu sidestepped closer to my cheek and tucked his head under a wing. An amazing thrill coursed through me, as if my true self, suddenly released from the bondage of the mundane, soared on the wind and out over the moon-kissed water.

This was an adventure, I decided, like those had by people in tellers' stories. I laughed into the Lake's breath, putting my sorrows behind me. It was my choice to dwell on them or on my hopes. I chose the latter. My body would heal from its piercing. Noah's leg would bind. He would come get me, and I would have an exciting story to tell our children.

I turned west and stayed as much as possible on the rocks,

careful not to leave an imprint of my feet to give the hunters a way to track me. Of course, they could use the hunting dogs, if they could make them understand they wanted to track a person, not prey, but I was counting on the tide to wash my scent from the rocks.

Throughout the night I traveled, excitement buoying me, so I did not feel tired at all. The more distance I could put between myself and our village, the better would be my chance of reaching the Cave, where belief in the Goddess reigned and I would be protected. What would it be like? Would it be similar to my cave on the north hills or bigger, grander? Yes, the Goddess' Cave would be far bigger, I decided, and people would come every day to offer their best meat and fruit and jewelry to ensure a good harvest and healthy children and all the blessings overseen by Mother Goddess. And, of course, they would welcome me, especially when they heard my story, not the whole thing, but only the part about my brother and Yanner and the beating of my husband. Those women might do more than allow me to wait with them for Noah; they might be so outraged at my story that they would march back to the village and demand justice.

That was the pleasant dream I mused as I walked straight into the waiting grasp of the slavers.

Chapter Eighteen

I was concentrating on where I put my feet and what the women of the Goddess' Cave would be like. Before I knew what I faced, I was taken, trussed hand and foot, and thrown over a hairy, smelly aurochs like a deer carcass.

Behind me, I heard Bennu screeching in indignation and men spitting foreign words with the tone of curses. I craned my head to glimpse one stabbing a knife at Bennu, who fluttered just above him. Blood and white feathers smeared the man's face. My heart gave a lurch of relief when Bennu gave a final shriek and flew away. Was he hurt? *Oh, Bennu, be safe!*

And so, I came to be a captive, draped across an aurochs' back.

Over the past several days, the views from this position changed from the meadows and forest of the Black Lake to the highlands, mountain ridges and valleys, and now a vast, plateau rippled with brown hills and ravines. I knew it was vast because we keep walking over it. Perhaps we were going to Eden, and I would get to see the Serpent's Tree Savta told me about.

For many days, I was carried in this terrible position. I stank and hurt. There was not a piece of me that did not ache, including my heart. I was far away from all I knew and loved— Savta, Bennu, the hills, my dear, stupid sheep, and Noah.

How could the world have turned from joy to disaster in such a short spate of time? Most would blame the gods, looking for how they had offended or failed to honor them. Perhaps I should. Perhaps Father God and Mother Goddess were angry with me for my disbelief and punished me.

For the first time, I wanted to believe for reasons beyond the fact that a slip of tongue could get me thrown in the pit. Believing would give me some measure of comfort, some chance for control. If I was responsible for what happened, I could at least have some hope of changing the future by appeasing those in power. A bubble of laughter worked its way from my aching belly into a pitiful, strangled sound. I had nothing to laugh about except the thought that hanging upside down for many days could produce such musings.

The only thing I could do to take my thoughts from pain was recite my story to myself and listen closely to piece out the meaning of my captors' words. I shut my eyes and listened, trying to hear and see the pattern in their words, which ones they repeated with other words, which were present when the voices ended on a higher tone, indicating a question. At first, it all sounded like a garble of sound, a ball of thread that had tangled so tightly, the beginning and end were lost. After days of nothing else to concentrate on, I began to recognize phrases and then individual word-sounds and tie them to the tones used to speak them.

When I heard a word again, I pulled it from my list, along with its possible meanings, greatly satisfied when I teased a thread clear of the tangle. Perhaps this was easier for me because each word had its own texture and color in my mind, and once I had identified it as a word, I put it in a certain place and could always find it again.

When I was very young, I understood that the sounds I saw and heard were language, but the words entranced me, playing out in my mind in a fascinating cascade of colors and shapes. I spent long periods of time just watching them. Savta would often notice my distraction and bring me back to the world with a tap on my cheek.

By two summers, I learned to keep the visual aspects of sound at bay, not wasting my focus on it unless I wanted to. Now, in the tongue of my people, these images and forms barely intruded, unless I "looked" at them directly.

I had to look at these new words. The individual voices also became known to me and the names that belonged to them. I knew Takunah was the redheaded man who attended to the captives. Rankor was the leader. I called him Foul Temper before I caught his name.

Takunah helped me by pantomiming what he wanted from me and saying the words. I always acted as if I was responding to his gestures, not the words. Every day was the same—I distracted myself from the discomfort with my language game and telling my story and waited for the sweet relief of being off my belly.

As usual, Takunah came for me. He was a tall, wiry man with hair as red as a sunset. I knew his tread as well as I knew the aurochs'. With my sight limited most of the time, my hearing had grown even keener. I heard the mosquito whine before he swiped at his ear to brush it away. He pulled me from the aurochs' back and untied me, leaving the straps that bound my wrists, but releasing my feet. I was grateful, even though my stiff muscles protested.

He was the only one who paid me any attention other than passing remarks from the others. I did not need to know their language to understand those. Takunah appeared to have the least status. Perhaps that was why he had to attend to the captives, but he did not seem to mind. I knew none of the other captives, all of whom were men, except the one other woman I worked with when we made camp. Her name was Inka, and her tribe lived near the shores of the Salt Sea to the south. She spoke enough of my dialect that we could talk.

Takunah untied my hands and waved toward the woods, pantomiming gathering wood. I went, first relieving myself behind a tree. In the beginning, I could hardly accomplish the task, I was so shamed at a man observing this most private of acts, but eventually I stopped thinking about it. Though I knew he could still see me, he would stare off over my head or to the side, and that allowed me the fantasy of some privacy.

When I finished, I started gathering wood. A crunch of underbrush diverted Takunah's attention, and I snatched a furtive glance up into the trees. A small white shape sidled on a high branch. Bennu. I looked quickly away and did not call him to my shoulder, fearful he would find his way into a soup pot.

He was smart enough to catch on and stay out of sight, smart enough, I hoped, not to trust the people who had handled us so roughly. I pulled the pouch at my belt around to hang in front of me, shielding it from Takunah's watchful eyes. It had once held the stones for my sling, but I used it now to hide bits of food. I bent down, pretending to look for a piece of wood and dropped a piece of meat, covering it with leaves. I knew Bennu's bright eyes watched me, and hoped he would remember our game and find it.

I looked for a chance to escape, but was never given one. My thoughts traveled a rut over the same path: Noah could not follow me. Savta thought me headed to the Goddess' cave. Would Yanner or Tubal come after me? Would being wife to Yanner be better than being prisoner to these men? I had not been touched or handled roughly after my first capture, but I did not know what lay ahead and that disturbed me enough to hope for rescue. Perhaps, by the time Tubal's young hunters found me and took me home, Noah's leg would heal quickly, and he could fight for me. That was the hope I clung to, though as each day passed, it seemed more like a dream.

Finally, I was allowed, like Inka, to walk with my hands tied before me. It was not as cold as the heights, but colder and drier than my land beside the Black Lake. I did not like it. I worried about Bennu. He could not survive in cold, and winter was ahead of us.

One day, weary after a long day's travel, I stumbled to where

Inka sat rubbing her ankles.

She looked up and smiled. "Hello, Na'amah. Today was better wasn't it?"

Inka had a way of turning the worst into something bright, which was annoying, but fed the sputtering fire of my spirit.

"Better how?" I grumbled, plopping down beside her.

"It wasn't so warm," she said. "There was a nice breeze." Inka had a different idea of comfortable temperatures than I.

"It was cool enough in the forest." I rubbed the chills from my shoulders.

"True," she said agreeably. Inka was rounder of face and form than I, and her barley-colored hair curled tightly where mine hung straight.

"Sing for me," Inka asked. "It will take our mind off our worries."

"I do not feel like it," I muttered, still in a foul mood.

"Please, Na'amah. Your voice is so lovely."

Inka had a way of flattering me out of my sulk. In the first days, I rocked and sang to myself every night, walling out the terrifying world and all its uncertainty. Now, I just sang quietly for Inka.

We had not long to rest before Takunah came and released our wrists. Days ago, he learned that Inka was the better cook. He set me to the task of mending the rips in the slavers' clothing. We were fortunate in having at least that little freedom. The three men captives never had their bonds removed. Even during the night, they slept with their hands bound behind them.

I settled onto a rock, close to where Inka pulled cooked meat from a deer's haunch to make a stew. "I have studied the night sky," I told Inka, looking over my shoulder to make certain no one could hear me. "We are going southwest." It was not the direction where Eden lay.

Inka nodded. Finished with the meat, she grunted at the effort of cutting a root with the dull knife they allowed her for the task. She licked her fingers. "I think we are retracing the route since they took me captive."

"Have they—? Have they hurt you, Inka?"

"You mean have they pierced me? No."

I asked the question that had been gnawing at me. "Why have they not?"

"It's not because they are gentle people," she assured me.

"How do you know? You do not understand a word of their tongue."

She paused and looked at me. "I just know. It's business. If they're going to sell a woman, they don't want to ruin her."

"Ruin her?"

"Make her pregnant," Inka explained, as if she were speaking of spinning or the right herbs to sprinkle in a dish.

If that were so, the men captives were a different matter. Since they could not get pregnant, they were fair game and most nights one or two of them would be prodded at knife-tip into the bushes to receive the pleasure of our captors. Sometimes, they cried out, and my nails made crescent moon marks on my palms.

I never saw Takunah taking one of the young men aside. Of them all, he seemed the kindest, making sure we ate and drank and had breaks to relieve ourselves. I jerked the horn needle through the skin and fur blanket Takunah had dropped in my lap. Savta would have winced at my work.

I bit my lip. It was the third day of the new moon, and my blood had not flowed. I had dreaded having no beer to dull the cramps or wool to keep the blood from running down my legs, another indignity to add to the rest. But my moon blood had not come. My body was as dependable as the stars in their track over the night sky.

I shivered in the gathering dusk, knowing the only thing this could mean—I was already ruined.

Chapter Nineteen

The days passed slowly. One evening three of the men brought in another captive, a tall woman in skins like a hunter, with copper bracelets on her arms and red ribbons braided into her long hair. She walked proudly, a smear of blood on her arms and neck. I eyed the blood. Four had gone to hunt. Only three returned.

Despite Inka's efforts, the woman refused to speak other than to give her name, Vashti. We thought our tongue might be foreign to her. She was not carried as I was, on the back of an aurochs, but allowed to walk. I thought it was a sign of respect. She kept her eyes ahead and did not deign to look at her captors or us.

The next day we stopped before sunset at a lake. It was small compared to the Black Lake. I could swim across it. When Takunah came to untie me, I turned to look at him, pleading with my eyes. He hesitated and said something in his language that was obviously a question and had the word for "water" and "smell" in it.

I pointed to the lake with my bound hands and then made a washing motion to my face. He grinned and held his nose with his fingers nodding vigorously. I could not help laughing and nodding too.

We were allowed bathing privileges after dinner had been cooked and served, and I had cleaned up all the supplies. To my consternation, our bathing appeared to be an announced event. All but two of the ten slavers gathered at the lake's edge, wooden cups in hand, joking and laughing with one another. Even the three male slaves joined them, though still bound, a strip of braided hide connecting their hands to their hobbled feet, making them have to shuffle in tiny steps.

We stood before them, the three females—Inka, Vashti, and I. Vashti had still not spoken to either of us. She kept to herself, as though we were diseased. We eyed each other and the water. With a scowl at the gawking men, Vashti turned and marched into the water, clothes and all. I laughed nervously and followed her lead, Inka right behind me.

The men howled in good-natured protest at our trick, and I recognized the sound of Takunah's laughter.

Inka shared a small container of oils and salt that were normally applied dry, then scraped and washed off, but we made do. We blocked the men's view for each other so we could remove our clothes and cleanse properly. My belly did not yet show anything. It was wonderful to have clean hair and skin again. Inka and I laughed and giggled, as though we floated inside a bubble, forgetting for a few fragile moments how far we were from homes and loved ones, and that our fates rested in the hands of strangers.

That evening Vashti deigned to speak to us for the first time. "I serve the Goddess," she said, as we sat beside the fire in our wet clothes. "I am a Daughter to the Priestess."

I was unhappy that these men had managed to take someone Savta had assured me was well protected, but Inka's eyes brightened. "Will the Goddess rescue us from these men?"

Vashti stared at her. "I don't think so," she said after a long pause. "I was taken by these men far from the Goddess' Cave. No one will know what happened to me."

Inka sighed and pursed her lips. "Do you speak the tongue of these men?" She kept her eye on our captors. None had ever given an indication that they understood us.

With a shrug of her slender, muscled shoulders, Vashti said,

"I don't speak it well, but I understand some of their speech."

I wondered why Inka had thought to ask the question. As though she could see into my mind, Inka turned to me.

"Mother Goddess' Daughters come from every land, and they learn all the languages of men. Didn't your mother teach you this?"

"My mother died when I was born," I said. I did not add that I had killed her with my misshapen head.

Vashti eyed me thoughtfully. "There is something wrong with you." She left the statement dangling, as if she could not decide whether it should be a question or a statement.

When I was younger, I tried very hard not to be different. I studied how people acted around others and attempted to imitate them. Yanner said I overdid it and made people uncomfortable, so I stopped, relieved, because it made me uncomfortable too.

I knew if I tried to look at Vashti's eyes just the right amount of time to convince her of my sincerity, I would succeed only in confirming her impressions, so I did not try. Inka did not seem to care where I focused my gaze, as long as I listened to tales of her childhood and plans for her future. She wanted a dozen children and had each one's name already determined.

The children who sat with me on shepherd watch or pulled water at my side from the river did not mind me now, though they made fun of me when we were younger. Nor did the women who came to Savta's house to spin and gossip. Noah seemed to appreciate and revel in my oddity, and it apparently only mattered to Yanner that my hair was like water in his hand and my eyes were like dark pools. Only my own brother, Tubal, mocked me and hated me.

Remembering the words he hissed into my ear in the cave, I suddenly realized that most of all, he seemed to hate that I was beautiful. I had not thought much of this odd fact. It made no sense that he resented my beauty; it only meant I would have a high family bride price, which would go to Tubal since father was dead.

"Na'amah?" Inka's throaty voice returned me to the fireside.

"Are you listening?"

"No," I said.

Inka told me what she thought I had missed in my daydreaming. "I asked Vashti if she knew who these men were and where they were taking us."

She had my whole attention now. I looked briefly at Vashti. "Do you?"

She shrugged. "They are called the River People. They come from the south beyond the Middle Salt Sea where they keep the land around their river clear because the river floods without fail in the middle of a burning summer. For three moon-cycles, it soaks into the dry soil and when it retreats, they rush to plant their seeds before it all dries up again. They need slaves to do this. But I think these men also look for something for their king."

"What is a king?" I asked. The word had an odd, sharp shape.

"Their leader. Like an Elder, but he has more power. Whatever he says, they must do."

Inka rested her chin on her palms, as though she were a child listening to a story. "Tell us more."

With a shrug, Vashti said, "I don't know much more, except their children run about naked, and they build their houses from stones."

"Stones?" This was an interesting idea, but since there was no way a stone house could float, I discarded it as an option to share with Noah . . . if I ever saw him again. How could he possibly learn I was in the hands of slavers bound for a distant land? If, I added, his leg ever healed, and if he decided I was worth the trouble of finding. By that time, he would assume I was dead, eaten by some animal, and another woman would catch his eye.

These thoughts cramped my chest, and I pulled my knees to it and rocked, singing softly. I do not know how long I remained like that, but no one stopped me, and eventually I lifted my head to find it was night. The creamy spread of stars overhead told me the moon had not yet claimed her sky. An owl swooped low, chasing small prey in the grass. I knew two slavers stood watch on either end of our camp, though I could not hear them. I tracked their locations by observing the aurochs, which periodically looked up from grazing to check the positions of the men they smelled. Sheep would do the same thing when the dogs were beyond or at the edges of their range of vision. The aurochs' forelegs were hobbled to ensure they did not wander too far away.

I lay back right where I was, between Inka and Vashti. I suspected Inka had thoughtfully moved their bedding while I rocked. I was allowed to sleep on my tiger skin, a fact that seemed a source of amusement among the men, but I feared I would not be able to keep it after I was sold.

"Tell us how you served the Goddess," Inka said, rolling over onto her side to face Vashti.

Vashti sat holding her knees. "I am a messenger for the Priestess. That is what I was doing when I was captured."

"I've always wanted to see the Goddess' Cave," Inka said. "Is it wonderful?"

Vashti grunted. "I was born there. I don't know what is wonderful about it. It's dark all the time. Cold and damp in the winter."

"And only women are allowed, right?"

"Yes."

With a deep sigh, Inka said, "I wouldn't want to stay very long with no men around."

"I see plenty of men," Vashti said. "I asked to be a messenger, so I could see the world and what it was like to be part of it."

"Are you fierce?" Inka asked.

"Do you mock me?"

"Oh, no. I've always heard that the Priestess' messengers were fierce. Did you fight when the River People men found you?"

Vashti's expression grew hard. "Yes, I fought. I killed a man, and the chunky one bears my scars on his arm."

Inka's grey eyes widened. "Really? The bearded one built like a tree stump?"

This broke Vashti's stern mood. She grinned. "Yes, I forget his name."

"Kamukka," I said.

110

Inka sighed, sounding like Savta, which made my heart ache. "How do you remember their names?" she asked. "Their language sounds like one weaving of noise to me."

I shrugged. "I just have to look in the right place and it is all there."

"Na'amah is not only smart, she is fierce too," Inka said with proprietary pride.

Vashti looked at me doubtfully.

"I know she's small, but that tall man, the one that prances around like the leader, he came back wounded after they captured Na'amah."

Vashti gave me a look that seemed one a shepherd might give a ram when reconsidering his decision to make it a wether. I would have told her the marks were from Bennu's talons, but she did not ask. Inka tried to engage more conversation from Vashti, but Vashti grew impatient with her.

Suddenly weary, I closed my eyes, one hand over my womb, and tried to sleep. A muted rainbow of sound drifted to me over the plains—the soft hoot of owls and the rustle of mice in the bunchgrass; the throaty rumble of a leopard; men talking late across the fire.

When sleep finally came, it was full of confusing dreams: Two giants gnawed on the same huge stone, only the stone was a rib bone of Mother Earth. The giants glared at each other, and then began screaming. They dropped the bone between them and grasped each other, wrenching and pushing. I woke with a moan, a tight clinching in my chest. Strange crimson lights danced at my vision's edge and cold pranced up my spine.

"What is it?" Inka asked groggily. "A bad dream?"

At first, I could only gasp for breath. "Fighting giants," I managed.

"What were they fighting over?" she asked, always interested in dreams.

"A stone," I said, distracted by the glimmering lights that still danced in the corner of my vision, and then remembered— "a bone. They fought over a large bone."

"Typical," Vashti grumbled. "Men are always fighting over something. It's the only way they know to get anything. Go back to sleep."

I was too agitated to sleep. "Something is wrong," I said. "Something is going to happen."

Vashti rolled over, turning her back to me. "Something is always going to happen."

Inka, however, sat up and put a hand on my arm. It felt like a hot stick and I jerked away.

"What is wrong?" she asked.

I could not answer. I felt sick, a sick worse than the illness that befell me in the mornings and at other times when my stomach was empty, which seemed all the time lately. The aurochs bellowed. While I was deciding if I was going to vomit, the earth moved. I thought it was my nausea, but Inka gasped.

"Vashti, wake up!" She shook Vashti's shoulder. "Did you feel that?"

Once again, the earth trembled.

"Great Mother!" Vashti said, springing to her feet.

Branches fell from their stack in the fire, catching the dry grass ablaze. The hobbled aurochs snorted and bucked, their eyes ringed with white.

We braced ourselves for the world to come apart. The men on watch raced back into camp and helped dip blankets in the water and smother the fire before it spread. We did not try to help them. After a few moments, the animals settled down and began to graze. I looked around to see that both Vashti and Inka were staring at me.

"Are you still sick?" Vashti asked.

I shook my head.

"She dreamed of giants fighting," Inka whispered, as if this were a secret weapon to hide from our captors.

Vashti snorted, but after that, she seemed to lose her arrogance towards me. Inka, however, wanted to know every dream I had, and she sometimes pronounced its meaning in the middle of our chores. It was obvious to her that the Earth Goddess was angry at our capture. As always, it amazed me how people chose to believe the explanation they preferred. I could think of many reasons for a particular dream. How would I know which one was the true one? Yet Inka never hesitated in her pronouncements and was not disturbed when something contradictory arose. She just waited confidently until the circumstances came around to support them.

I listened for what the River People men thought of the earth's shaking. They made no connection between that event and our capture, but their treatment of us improved, perhaps because we were so far away from our tribes. Over the next moon-cycle, our hands were unbound, except for Vashti. She bore the inconvenience with pride, knowing the River People men considered her dangerous.

I was making progress in understanding the River People men. Vashti shared what she knew, careful not to let them hear us, and soon I was catching inflections that she missed. She was astonished at the speed of my understanding. For the first time, I considered my wounded mind might be good for something more than just finding honey. I was different, but I saw and heard much that was missed by others. When I was able to walk and observe more than my aurochs' hooves and the ground going by, my understanding of the River People men's language grew quickly.

To walk beside the aurochs was a much-preferred way to travel, especially because my breasts were sore, and I had to relieve myself often. I held my water as long as I could, because I did not want anyone to suspect my condition. I walked on the far side of my aurochs, so I could retch into the grass without drawing attention.

"My" aurochs was not always cooperative. The hairy beast acted nervous around me, a fact that made me nervous in turn. Aurochs were temperamental to start with and could be very dangerous, as I had seen often enough. Their long curved horns could easily kill. I liked animals and tried to figure out why this one did not seem to like me.

I was also distressed that I had not seen Bennu for days. Had he abandoned me? There were no trees across this stretch of land for him to hide in, so I was glad he did not show himself, but sad also. The glimpses of him soothed me and made me think of Noah. This sometimes also made my eyes brim. I imagined Noah's distress when he learned I was gone. His bones might have healed by now. Was he making the long trip to the Goddess' Cave? What would he do when he learned I had never been there? I missed watching him working on our boat-house. I missed Savta's sharp tongue and gentle touch. Most of all, I missed my sheep and the hills. I wanted to go home.

After we ate on the morning of the second new moon, Rankor, the leader of our captors, had Takunah inspect us. Vashti was outraged when he told her what he wanted her to do.

"What did he say?" Inka hissed when he left, but I understood. Studying their language helped keep my thoughts from Noah and Savta and Bennu. My understanding of their words now passed Vashti's. This seemed to add to her respect for me.

"What did he want?" Inka demanded again, when Takunah left us that evening. I answered her with a tightness wrapping my chest. "He says we must show him our women's blood."

Inka's paled. "What? Why?"

"To prove we are not pregnant," Vashti replied flatly. "That is apparently important to these beasts."

I shivered, because at that moment Rankor passed by. I was glad Bennu's scars on his face had not healed well and that even his own men had trouble looking directly at him for any length of time. He was escorting poor Panor into the grass again. The man had lost weight and spirit, going about with his gaze downcast and keeping to himself. Rankor did not even bother to shackle him now.

"I will have no blood to show him," I said. My words startled both Inka and Vashti into silence. I turned my head away from the flicker of emotions across their faces.

Inka recovered first. She grasped my hands. "Oh, Na'amah. I don't know what to say. I want to embrace you and congratulate you, but I don't know . . . what will happen."

"Maybe they will release me, since I am 'ruined,'" I said. The bitter words were a strange taste in my mouth.

"I think not," Vashti's voice echoed my own fear.

Turning to her, Inka asked, "Vashti, what will they do?"

Vashti's hands knotted in anger. "They will take her to the grass every night."

I shivered again. I had not forgotten any detail of why my blood would not stain the fleece pads. Vashti's words echoed in my mind: *Every night.* There were ten River People men. How would they decide which . . . or how many would pierce me each night? I wanted to vomit.

Inka looked in the direction that Rankor had taken Panor. We could hear Rankor's grunts. Panor was silent.

My arms found their way over my belly. What would such treatment do to my baby? It was the first time I thought of my pregnancy as something beyond the result of Yanner's piercing. A baby. A baby grew in my womb. A girl. How I knew that was unfathomable, but as clear to me as the fact that my feet ached.

Chapter Twenty

The next day as I walked beside the nervous aurochs, I could think of nothing but my fate when the men discovered my pregnancy. My belly itched. I hated Yanner for what he had done, but it was not my baby's fault. She had done nothing wrong, and suddenly I wanted to hold her and watch her feed at my breast, to braid her hair and teach her the things Savta had taught me. What could I do to keep my secret?

The aurochs turned toward me, lowering his head in a motion that brought his mighty horns to bear for ripping, his eye ringed with white. I stopped and allowed more space between us. Somehow, I offended him, or I frightened him and that caused his aggressive response. Again, I wondered at his behavior.

A hawk shadow streaked the grass in front of me and a rabbit burst into a darting run, bringing an answer. Of course—the aurochs feared me because I smelled like a predator, a tiger in fact. Every night I slept on my tiger skin. I laughed aloud. Inka, walking ahead of me looked over her shoulder and gave me a tentative smile. She would ask me later what had amused me. Inka wanted to know everything. She was also very good at interpreting our captors' emotions and moods, despite her handicap of not understanding their language.

I stepped closer to the aurochs and worked my skin out of his packs. He snorted and broke into a trot. Elated that I was right, I ran after him and stuffed the skin back.

Solving that little mystery lifted my spirits. An idea started to form in my mind. I did not like change. The daily routine of our travel had begun to seem normal. I knew what to expect every day and, though I realized it would not stay this way forever, it was difficult to think of changing everything. Yet, I had to escape to protect myself and my baby. I did not know how I would do it, but I had to.

That evening Takunah brought us fleece pads. "Thank you," I said.

He looked startled. I had never spoken to him before in his language. A smile crossed his angular face. "You are not to mention it," he replied with a nod of his head, giving me the proper response. Then he gave Vashti an approving look. "Teaching them our language will increase their price. Maybe, you will be lucky and all go to the king's household."

Vashti pulled herself to her full height and threw the pad he had given her onto her blanket. "Lucky to be a slave? You are the lucky one."

"I?" he asked with raised eyebrows. Takunah had an easy nature, and Vashti's anger rarely roused him.

"You are fortunate the Goddess has spared you," Vashti said, haughtily, "but her anger will not be contained forever." She pointed at me. "Na'amah is marked by the Earth Mother. That you can't see it is just evidence of your ignorance."

Takunah eyed me. "She is beautiful, but somewhat stupid. Other than that, I see nothing that marks her as favored by the gods."

Vashti lifted her chin. "You remember when the ground shook?"

"Yes, of course."

"Na'amah predicted it."

I gave her a sharp look. That was not exactly what happened.

Takunah laughed. "Is that so? Is she a goddess? Ta-urt, herself, perhaps? Maybe I should fall down and worship her. Is that what you mean? I will go explain to Rankor immediately that we have committed a grievous error."

She turned her back to him, her chin tilted up.

"You do know," Takunah teased, "that Rankor favors you, Tall One. I would not be surprised if he doesn't claim you himself. As for me—" he looked at Inka. "I like the plump one." He laughed again and left us.

"What did he say?" Inka asked, suspiciously. "Why did he laugh at me?"

Vashti crossed her arms over her chest. "He said you were fat."

"Fat?" Inka laid a hand on the small fold over her belly. "I am pleasing and soft. Men prefer that to thin and bony." She glared at Vashti.

"Don't give me that look. I didn't call you fat," Vashti said with a dismissive toss of her head.

I interrupted them. "I have an idea."

They both turned to me. "When your blood starts," I said in a quiet voice, "trade pads with me in the night."

Vashti looked startled. "Why didn't I think of such a simple thing?"

That would purchase me a little more time, but I could not keep my secret more than another moon-cycle or two, and if we were going all the way to the land of the River People, my pregnancy would become visible before we arrived. I had to escape soon.

While I served the night's meal, a roasted roe deer that Inka had prepared, I listened to the conversation among the men.

"We will return now," Rankor was saying.

"Without the king's bird?" another replied. "He will slay us if we do not return it."

"Not if we bring him these slaves. He wishes sons. Three fine women will appease him."

"We came so close. You have the scars to prove it, Rankor."

I wondered if I had understood the word "bird" correctly. Then it struck me. Bennu! Bennu's seller had said he belonged to the king of the River People. The king sent men all this way to find him. Now, I had another concern—that Bennu, if he lived, would show himself and be caught.

"We have traveled far for only a handful of slaves," another said. He was a short man with a thick beard and always scowled at me. All these men, I had decided, belonged to Hunter Clan.

"I thought the bird liked the pretty one we found near the big lake," Rankor said, cutting a hunk from the deer's thigh. "I hoped he would follow her."

Hot grease dripped into the fire with a sharp sizzle.

How had these men missed seeing Bennu in the trees? I often wondered how people did not see things that were plainly there. They seemed to observe only what they expected to see.

I felt Takunah watching me. As far as he knew, I only understood "thank you" in his language and perhaps a few other isolated words. Inka had not even bothered with learning that, and Vashti was at the river we had just crossed, washing clothes. I was careful to keep my face blank no matter what I heard.

"Yes," Rankor mused in a sarcastic tone, two fingers playing with the scars that gouged his right cheek. "The king's bird was not happy with us."

I was glad to confirm those were Bennu's claw marks on Rankor's face. Good. He deserved them. I fingered my neck where Savta's white shell necklace should have been. It had broken when the men attacked me.

"You are right, Kamukka," Takunah said, keeping an eye on me. "We have come far for only three women. One is fat, one arrogant, and one stupid. What gifts we bring our king."

Another man chuckled. "Who cares? They are young and beautiful and fat is in the eye of the beholder." He winked. "I think Takunah has another motive for having us think the plump one is unattractive."

"See there, Takunah," Rankor said, motioning to me with the greasy meat in his hand and somehow grinning at the younger man while he chewed. "So much for your thought that the small one understands us. She didn't react to being called stupid. Any woman who heard such words would react. Women are simple creatures. They like flattery and gifts.

"Besides," he continued, "if they bear healthy sons that do not sicken and die, they will be pleasing gifts to our king."

Now I understood why it was so important that we not be "ruined." We were to be presented to their king in lieu of Bennu. It occurred to me that if Bennu appeared again, I could bargain to capture him and trade him for our release. As much as I loved him, was it right for me to deny Inka and Vashti and those men who were so mistreated a chance for freedom? Bennu would not be hurt. I imagined the king treated his prize bird well.

I studied Rankor's face in my mind, his hard, twitchy eyes. I thought about the way he had broken Panor's spirit in the grass. I could make such a bargain, but such a man would not free us afterward. Takunah might, but Rankor had no honor. He would count himself clever to bring both Bennu and slaves to his king or else, he would just bring Bennu and use or sell us.

I listened to their talk for a while and decided there were too many deities in their land. Every king and tribe apparently had a different one, as did every individual person, and each god and goddess demanded different things. Life was confusing enough.

Kamukka tore the succulent meat from the bone with his yellow teeth. "Can't we capture another woman for us? I am tired of spearing men."

I turned my head aside and bit my lip to keep from flinching.

"As they are no doubt tired of your puny spear," Rankor said, throwing a bone into the fire.

The other men laughed, but Kamukka turned deep scarlet.

Takunah spit out a small bone and changed the subject. "I think we need to go home now and not tarry to find any more wandering girls. If the gods of this land will even allow us to leave it. Did you not feel the earth tremble?"

"Takunah is right," Rankor said, holding his cup for me to fill. "Many things could delay us. Angry gods or villagers. Our boat could be stolen or crushed in a storm."

"Or if we can't find that pass through the south mountains," Kamukka added. "Or that whale we saw could decide to swallow us on our way home. He was bigger than our boat!"

"Whale" was an unfamiliar word, but I understood enough of the context to grasp that it was a very large sea creature. There were strangers who came to Market Day who spoke of fantastical wonders beneath the waves of the vast seas to the south and west of our land. I had experienced enough of water and flooding, and had no desire to see endless churning water that made the Black Lake seem a pond or creatures that could swallow a boat.

Rankor nodded. "It is a long, hot walk home, my friend. Best to keep what we have and bring back women our king will know do not bear other men's seed."

"We don't know for certain they're not already pregnant," another man said when the laughter died.

"We'll know soon," Takunah said. "It's almost the new moon. Women bleed together at the new moon."

It was only a partial truth, but these men seemed content to simplify the complexities of a woman's body as well as her mind. Though I knew girls who giggled over flattery and gifts, it was because they thought the attention sincere, and that they were valued and cherished. Women want to be cherished. I did not think badly of those who were deceived, but of the deceivers.

With that thought, I was surprised to hear the passion in Rankor's voice. "Ta-urt, great mother and goddess of my household," he prayed aloud, "let them all be untouched and protect us."

The other men muttered agreement, and I shivered, having no doubt that the discovery of my pregnancy would make Panor's ill fate my own. Not worthy for the king, Rankor would most likely share me with his men to appease them.

I swallowed. I might survive being taken to the grass over and over, but would my baby? Under normal circumstances, I would not consider running off into the wilderness alone, especially pregnant, but I had no choice.

That night I spoke quietly to Inka and Vashti. I did not tell them about Bennu. I feared they would look for him and alert our captors. I only told them that I had decided I must escape. They tried to talk me from it.

"You will die," Vashti said.

Inka moaned. "They will catch you and beat you,"

"I must do this," I insisted. "I must give my baby a chance."

In the end, they saw I was stubborn and Vashti said, "I will go with you."

"How?" I said. "They keep your hands tied."

"Tell me your plan," Vashti said, "and I will figure it out."

"You're going to both leave me?" Inka wailed softly.

Vashti put her hand on Inka's arm and said with more kindness than I had ever heard from her, "I will bring aid to you, Inka. I am not just a Daughter, but the true blood- daughter of the Priestess. She will send warriors to rescue you, no matter where you are."

Inka sniffed, mollified.

"We need a distraction," I said. "Something that will pull in the men standing watch."

"A fire," Vashti offered, her voice tense with excitement. "That would bring everyone."

I nodded. "Good, but it must look like an accident. I will not have you in trouble for my sake."

Vashti took a deep breath. "Leave this to me. They sleep close to the fire, and the wind blows hard here."

"What can I do?" Inka asked.

"Tomorrow and the next day gather food, water, and a flint and slip it into my pack," I said.

"How will you survive?" Inka asked.

I had given thought to this. "I need a sling."

"Do you think they are just going to hand you a weapon?" Vashti asked with a quiet snort. "Besides, you have to practice a lot before you can hit game with a sling. It's not an easy weapon to learn. I would rather have my spear."

"A sling is easier to hide than a spear," I said. "And I do practice. I killed a tiger with it."

Inka's eyebrows rose. "A tiger?" She put a plump hand over her mouth. "What a wonderful story."

"It is truth."

Vashti gave me a look I could not interpret, but she did not laugh. She touched the skin I sat on. "Is this the tiger you slew?"

I nodded and returned to the subject pressing my mind. "I need a sling," I repeated, ignoring them. "Inka, you must get me one."

"And how am I to do that?"

I took a breath. "Takunah favors you."

She stared at me. "He thinks I'm fat."

"No, he does not. Tell her, Vashti. Tell her the truth."

Inka rounded on Vashti. "Well?"

With a shrug, Vashti said, "Maybe he does. Who can tell what a man thinks?"

"He does, Inka," I said. "He said so, and he always looks longest at you, and when he does, his chest puffs out and the centers of his eyes widen."

She looked at me in astonishment. "You see all that?"

"Yes."

Vashti grunted.

Inka's plump face smoothed, and she was quiet for a moment. "Maybe I can get him to let me take a bowl from his pack. I've seen over his shoulder when he paws through it. I think I've seen a sling in there." She worked her bottom lip with her teeth. "Teach me how to say the words I need."

I nodded. "What words do you need?"

She tapped her teeth with a finger. "Let's start with, 'You are strong and I like you.'"

I almost laughed aloud at the irony. If this worked, women were not the only ones to be led by words. Perhaps I had been unfair to claim men as the deceivers.

It took most of the night for Vashti and me to teach Inka all the words she asked for. Inka did not remember things as well as I did, and we had to practice.

The next morning, I tested Inka's knowledge of the words. To my surprise, she remembered most of them. "I will need the bowl too," I said.

She smiled. "That won't be a problem. I plan to put the sling in the bowl and hold the bowl top against me to hide it. If I can remember all those words, he won't be paying any attention to the bowl."

"Thank you, Inka," I said sincerely. "You are a true friend."

She wiped a tear from her cheek. Will you give me your blessing?" she asked, as if I were someone special.

I hesitated, not knowing what to say.

Vashti looked at me with an odd expression, but did not protest Inka's request, though she was the Priestess' daughter. Finally, I said what I had heard Mariah say, "The Goddess' blessing on you."

A smile bloomed through Inka's tears.

Chapter Twenty-One

We were within sight of a distant, wooded area when all was ready. My pack was full of food, the small cooking pot Inka had filched and, best of all, my own sling. I had begged Inka to get my horse carving, but she told me I was an idiot. Stealing a sling under the nose of a man who favored you was one thing, but Rankor had the horse carving.

Resigned, I fell asleep until Vashti woke me with a shake of my shoulder. "Na'amah, wake! The fire burns."

It took a moment for me to remember what she meant and to interpret the flames that roared near the River People men's bedding.

I had marked which men took the watch and recognized their voices added to the consternation and barked orders of how to quench the fire that burned past the cleared area into the dry grass, lighting the early morning fog with an eerie glow. Unlike the small blaze that the quaking earth had started, this one seemed to have ignited in several places at once—Vashti's work. The wind had breathed life into it and it leapt and roared like an angry beast. Now was my best chance. I rolled my tiger skin inside a thick fleece, one that Inka used for bedding and followed Inka's directions to where I had last seen the black aurochs. I knew the animals would flee the fire, but they could not have moved far hobbled. Their flattened path through the tall grass was easy to follow, even with the lack of moonlight, and I caught up with them.

My aurochs was skittish and would not stand for me. I kept following him, my heart pounding in anticipation of discovery, until he tired of the effort of fighting his hobbles and waited while I fastened my pack on his straps and led him to a rock.

This was where Vashti was supposed to join me. I looked back, trying to see her, but the predawn mist was thick. I secured the soft sheep skin where we could sit on it.

Where was Vashti?

Then I heard the sound of fighting, and Vashti called loudly in my language. "Don't wait. Go! Now!"

With trembling fingers, I untied the aurochs' hobbles, climbed onto the rock and worked my way onto his back. He snorted at this strange arrangement of weight. I tried not to rush him and bent low to seem more as a pack or my own draped body, which he had carried the first days of my capture.

Now the problem was to make him go in the direction I wanted, which was to the trees I had glimpsed the day before, to the south. If we went north, where I really wanted to go, we would leave a trail through the grass too easy to follow. I hoped to part ways with the beast in a forest where my trail would be harder to follow, then when I felt I had lost my pursuers, I would swing back and go home. No, not home. The thought was still a knife stab, not back to Savta or to Noah or to . . . Yanner. No never to Yanner.

If I could get the aurochs to go where I wanted him to go…I wet my lips. That part of my plan rested entirely on my imagination and a feeling that I had solved the mystery of my aurochs' dislike.

Although he had been hard enough to catch, now that he was unshackled and I was astride him, he showed no inclination to move. The other two female aurochs appeared out of the fog into view, and I realized they had followed us. Why had I not anticipated that? My only hope was to move quickly enough to leave them.

Behind us, I heard the shouts of the River People men. "This way!" one cried. They were coming for the animals. I hoped they had not hurt Vashti. Did they realize I was missing?

I worked the tiger skin out and waved it to one side of my aurochs' head. Startled, he turned the other way and broke into a jarring trot. I grabbed his neck, trying to stay on his back. To my horror, we came around in a circle and now headed straight toward the sounds of approaching men.

The three warriors who had come, they thought, to retrieve three hobbled beasts, fanned out to catch us. We came close enough to Takunah for me to see his surprise at realizing I was the bundle atop the escaped animal. He reached out to catch the halter, but my aurochs was having none of it. Either unwilling to give up his freedom or still jumpy from the tiger skin waved under his nose, he turned abruptly and headed out onto the grassland. I let him go, concentrating on holding on and let him put distance between us and our pursuers. I leaned low over his thick neck, as much to lessen the pain in my tender breasts as to hang on.

To my knowledge, no one had ever tried to ride an aurochs. I supposed the idea of doing such a thing entered my head when I was a child watching the wild horses. It apparently had settled there, forgotten in the tangles of my thoughts, until I needed it.

My aurochs slowed and began grazing, chewing the tops off the tall grass. I let him for a moment, trying not to move too much, but aching to get off and find my own way. A warrior can run for many miles, however, and I knew I was valuable property to them. If I tried to escape on foot, the River People men would catch me, and all this, including putting Inka and Vashti at risk, would be for naught.

I needed to turn us the arch of a hand's span south. Light had paled the sky behind us, though night's sharp chill still claimed the air. I held my rolled tiger skin in my right hand, but further away than the first time. He lifted his head, chewing, the white of one eye showing as he considered the movement. A wind shift brought him the scent, and he began to move away. I pulled the skin back to my chest, but we had already moved too far to the left. Shifting the skin to my left hand, I experimented with the distance needed to make him turn. He followed wherever his head went. After a few moments, I was able to put us in the right direction and endured the pounding jolt of his gait until we entered a stand of trees that I had thought edged the grassland. To my disappointment, we found not a forest, but only a few scrubby trees and then more grassland beyond.

These men who followed me were hunters. Though we were beyond their direct sight, they could not fail to follow an aurochs' trail. I could not stop. My daughter's life depended on me.

We traveled this way all of the day, though I could not endure a steady pace faster than his ambling walk and his attempts to keep turning west slowed us greatly. We finally stopped at a small, muddy pond. My beast snuffled the wind before lowering his head and drinking. I was thirsty and needed to relieve myself, but was afraid to dismount. What would stop the aurochs from turning on me or running off? I could hear the River People men behind us now. They took no pains to move silently and occasionally shouted when they had to spread out and someone found the trail in the high grass. They were gaining quickly on us.

I looked down at the aurochs' hooves, barely visible in the gathering dusk. My body ached. My mind mired. The beast lifted his massive head and turned as always to the west. On a sudden impulse, I let him. As long as he did not head right into the spears that followed us, why should I fight him? In fact, a small hope and the vague shape of a plan began to emerge from the tired jumble of my thoughts. I clutched his neck and drummed my heels into his flanks, enduring the sudden pain as he broke into a trot.

His gait grew faster as he realized the tiger smell was not keeping him from his destination. My fear—that he was as weary as I—disappeared as he broke into a lumbering gallop. Strangely, the gait was easier to bear than the jarring trot. After a while, the ache of my back drove me to chance easing tentatively into a sitting position. This was a matter of balance. I was not naturally good at such things, but my life and my baby's life depended on staying atop this creature, and I kept my mind focused on balancing my weight directly over his spine, not risking any kind of distraction. I let him stop and walk when we had put a good distance between us and the camp, but he seemed to have caught a scent that motivated him and, after short rests, he would resume his faster pace. I encouraged a gallop rather than the bone-jarring trot. We stayed on a westward course long after the stars slid from the place where they hid from Father Sun.

The wind's shift brought the bovine scent of my aurochs' goal. He snorted, lifting his nose as if to drink the smell, the large, moist nostrils dilating. Without warning, his sides shook with a bellow he pulled from the deepest recesses of his body. I leaned low and squeezed my aching thighs to keep from falling off. A similar, answering cry came from ahead. I could barely see the dark shapes, but hope throbbed in my veins. A wild herd!

As we closed on them, I shook out the tiger skin, trying to flap my arm without sacrificing my balance. I cried out, making as much noise as my parched throat would muster. I had not dared to pull the water skin from my pack. We entered the herd's edges before the smell reached them. My cries had already started them milling nervously.

I could not say where it started, but suddenly we were part of a massive surge of beasts, merging into a flow that became a stampede. For a moment, I exhilarated at the sheer power I had released. Around me, the musky scent of the herd was almost a force equal to the press of bodies against us and the rumbling noise of countless hooves. I had no further hope of determining our direction. A vast river current took us where it would. My task now was just to stay afloat. I did not want to think about the churning hooves that would pound my flesh into unrecognizable pulp should I fall, but the press of hide around me made me feel more secure, as if I could stand and walk across that expanse of churning backs as easily as I could the ground. I ignored the lure of such a foolish notion, trying to demand my trembling muscles to continue to cling to my aurochs.

When at last we slowed, even my terror could not get a

response from my body. Only fortune or the Goddess' grace on an unbeliever kept me atop my aurochs. A clump of lighter objects ahead seemed to part the herd. I loosened my pack, clasping it under one arm in readiness. When my foot brushed a boulder, I leapt, scrambling to stay in the lee of the rocks while the herd thundered around me. My aurochs disappeared into the dark sea of beasts.

When the last beast passed and the thunder of their hooves muted, I still crouched in my rock shelter, trembling. Weariness pressed on me like the weight of a mountain. I did not think I could go another step, even if I heard the River People men on my trail. I managed to relieve myself, drink, and lay out my skins. Despite my exhaustion, my eyes kept opening at all the sounds I heard or imagined, but finally they closed, and I plummeted into sleep.

Chapter Twenty-Two

The sun's warmth in the lee of the stones woke me. A groan escaped my mouth as I stood. My groin muscles and upper thighs were tight as dried hide. With longing, I thought of my daily bath in the river. I hated being able to smell my own sweat, which now also made me ill, not to mention the stench of aurochs. I liked being alone, but this was different. The urge to rock and sing filled me, but I forced it down. I had to think of my child. She had no one but me.

Throughout the past two moon-cycles as captive of the River People men, I had watched the night sky and knew we moved south. I decided to continue west to the sea and then head north again. As long as I could see the sky, I would not get lost. A laugh escaped my lips at that. I had never been as lost in my life. Or as alone. My hands found my belly. Not alone. I had my child, my baby. "I will name you Sara," I said. "We will find the sea together and go to the Goddess' Cave where you will be born in safety. Then I will get word to Noah and he will come and be your father. We will find a new home."

That was a strange concept—a new home. Home had always been the house by the river and the hills and the sheep and the Black Lake. But the world was larger.

I examined my wounds, unhappy to find blood smears on the rocks. I cleaned them as best I could and hoped rain would wash them away. With cloth scraps Inka had thoughtfully crammed into my bag, I bound my scraped hands.

We walked throughout the day, Sara and I. I took care to leave as little trail as possible for the River People men, not even pausing to gather acorns until I was ready to stop for the night. I hoped the aurochs would stay with the wild herd. That would keep my pursuers off my trail for a long while, maybe long enough to decide I was not worth the effort.

For the first time since realizing I was pregnant, I returned to the worry that had given me misery so long ago— that my child would have a wounded mind like mine. Why had this been absent from my thoughts the last moon-cycle? Perhaps fear for my child's safety had been my first concern. It would not matter what her mind was like if she did not survive.

Now, I gnawed on the thought like a dog that refuses to acknowledge he has stripped every morsel of meat from his bone. I did not want to speak to her of it, but I realized Sara would know something was wrong and it was better to talk about it and assure her it made no difference to me.

"I do not care what you look like or how your mind thinks," I told her. "I will love you and be your mother, and I will not go away like my mother did."

When night fell, I made a small camp beside a stream and ate some of the salted meat and meal cakes Inka had put in my pack. I was delighted to find she had included a piece of sharp obsidian and a small jar of cleaning oil, and I bathed as best I could, washed my dress and hung it to dry, sleeping with nothing but my tiger skin next to my own skin. I wanted to smell of tiger musk. If it frightened an aurochs, it might keep other predators away.

I stayed awake for a long while, listening to the myriad of night sounds swirl around me. In my exhaustion, I felt my mind drifting into a contemplation of their colors. No, I could not afford to become stuck doing that. I needed something in the real world to focus on.

Through the sparse stand of trees, the Goddess, silver-white in her manifestation as moon, struggled from the dark womb of sky. Yes, the moon; I would focus on that. She felt so close and so real, I wondered what she thought of me or if she saw me at all. Alone in a strange land, the desire to believe swept over me. Who was I to spurn the Goddess, when I felt her currents in my own body? I said a prayer that Savta had taught me, just in case, but it seemed wise to nestle deeper against the tiger skin too. I remembered Savta's words—*It's the Goddess' blessing that transforms the seed into food, but she expects us to plant them and harvest the crops.*

Finally, weariness weighed my lids, and I was just drifting into sleep when a fluttering noise woke me. Something battered my face and I gasped, striking out at it. A screech of outrage stopped me. I knew that sound. "Bennu?" In the moonlight, his white feathers were a faint gleam.

Squawking again, he climbed from his position on my stomach up to my chest and nipped my nose in gentle affection. Tears brimmed in my eyes. "Bennu, you found me!"

"Ta-urt be praised," he said clearly in the language of the River People men.

I gasped and then laughed. "I knew you were saying words. I just could not understand them. Good Bennu," I praised in the same language. He tilted his head, stared at me and then repeated, "Good Bennu. Awwk."

I did not know if he understood what he was saying, but it did not matter. Sara and I were not alone anymore. Bennu was there, and his presence made me feel somehow that Noah was with us too. Bennu's hearing was even better than mine, and he would alert me if anything or anyone approached. For the first time since I realized I was pregnant, the knot of anxiety in my chest loosened.

That night I dreamed I stood on a mountain in a place I had never been. Sara, the height of my thigh, stood beside me. Her hair was gold and her eyes green, like her father's. I held her small hand, and the wind tossed our hair. Behind us, a rainbow stained the sky. It was such a vivid dream that I mumbled a prayer to Mother Goddess as soon as I woke. I realized I had kept a small place in my heart open, in case she did exist, and I needed to express my gratitude for the dream and hope of its fulfillment.

The following moon-cycle of days was hard. Bennu shared the food Inka and Vashti had stolen for me, nuts and dried strips of meat. We supplemented what we had with hackberries, wild onager wheat, almonds, and field peas. I picked young thistle and dandelion leaves and other edible plants I recognized as I walked and used the obsidian chip to shape a bone knife to clean the small game my sling brought down. Steppe mice and rabbits were the most numerous prey, both difficult targets, and I missed more often than not. I hated to waste the skins when I did make a kill, but I did not want to take the time to scrape and dry them properly, in case the River People men still followed. For the same reason, I ignored the bigger game, like gazelles and deer. Leaving carcasses like that would not only mark my trail, it would attract predators.

When, however, my foot skins started to wear holes, I did a quick job of scraping a couple of hides. I removed all the fat I could with my knife, and then I wrapped the inner part of the skin around a smooth-barked tree, holding it in both hands and sawing back and forth to remove the stubborn parts of flesh clinging to it. I rolled the hide in a mash solution of the animals' brains and let it soak for a day. The next few days I worked it as I walked. It was stiff when I finished, not the beautiful supple skins that Savta made, but it was the best I could do. I tied them on over the old ones, giving my feet two layers of protection. They needed it, poor things. They were swollen and hurt constantly.

When we emerged from the sparse forest, Sara and I made our way across a strange landscape. The ground became humped and cut with ravines and our progress slowed. I had gone through all the food Inka had stolen for me. I added small snakes to my diet, and filled my water skin at every opportunity. It was much drier here than home.

I missed the company of Inka and Vashti—Inka's easy laugh and even Vashti's sharp tongue. I thought Savta would like them both, but I would never see them again. If Vashti survived whatever trouble she had encountered trying to escape, and if Inka survived the rigors of the journey, the River People men would give them to the king as slaves. This saddened and angered me in turns. It was not fair, but no one ever claimed Father God or Mother Goddess had any concern with justice. I never understood what they were concerned with, though out of respect for Savta and a strong desire to avoid pitting, I kept my opinion as a silent voice in my mind. Only Noah had heard my real thoughts on the subject. He had accepted them, as he accepted me.

I wondered what Ta-urt, the goddess Rankor had called on, was like. Had anyone in the River People's land actually seen her? If I saw a god, I would change all my cynical thoughts and be happy to worship her or him. I wanted someone to be in charge of things. All the chaos of life was disturbing. I liked things in order.

"What about you?" I asked Bennu who rode on my shoulder. "Do you think it good that spring always follows winter? Or would you like a little variety in your seasons?"

For answer, Bennu, tugged on my hair. I stopped to pluck some late, wilted berries and gave one to him. He lifted his talon to grasp it, standing on one leg as easily as I stood on two, and examined it before peeling the skin with his tongue and beak and taking an exploratory bite.

I wore my tiger skin around my shoulders and told myself I had nothing to fear except other tigers, but I saw no tigers or sign of them.

By now, Bennu was accustomed to flying on his own and just coming down occasionally to ride my shoulder. Aside from missing the people I cared about, I did not mind being alone. It s like being in the hills watching the sheep. No people chatter, nly the sheep sounds or the dogs and the wind. Because I saw details that other people missed, I was good at watching the sheep. As I walked through the strange land, I focused on the details of the land. A twisted ankle or broken leg here meant death. I watched the path carefully, taking no risks I did not have to take—making sure of my footing over wet ground or slippery rocks, inspecting the other side of debris before stepping over it. Thankfully, the nausea had vanished for the most part.

When I felt the need to talk to someone, I conversed with my unborn baby, though she was still tiny as a fruit or a bud not ready to unfurl. She listened without criticism. "I thought I did not want children," I confessed to her. "But that was before you. I was selfish. I did not want to be burdened with cleaning after a smelly infant, but I will gladly clean your bottom, if only you will be born healthy."

I edged from a pile of thick brush that might hide a hole. "How is it in my belly, Sara? Dark? Are you frightened? Do you know me as something separate from you or am I part of you, as you are part of me, our heartbeats one?"

I listened very hard for her voice, harder than I had ever listened for the gods' voices, but if my child spoke to me, it was in the language of my body, in the dark rhythm of the blood, asserting her presence, even though she was only a tiny, tucked thing. I came close to belief in Mother Goddess during those days, so marvelous and mysterious was the life inside me, but the Earth Goddess never answered my request to see her or hear her voice, so I focused on Sara and the path my feet traveled.

The moon had completed another cycle and the weather was cooler, especially at night, when we came upon a place stranger than any I had ever seen or heard of. Along the sloping landscape, huge formations of ash-colored rock wrinkled the land. As I approached, they became towering, individual cone structures in colors of cream, grey, and even a pale pink, some pointing like proud manhoods at the sky. Others spread from a high point into wide triangles, like pine cones with precarious rock caps. I stared for a long time at the wonder of it.

Then I realized that people were coming and going into openings in the rocks. I approached with great care, not wanting to be seen and with the wind in my face, so no dogs or other domesticated animals would catch my scent. The River- People men had eroded my trust for strangers.

I found an opening in one of the stones and crawled inside to watch them, lying on a strip of short golden grass. The people wore skins and jewelry of honey or rose-colored stones. I thought about walking amongst them and staying with them to have my baby, until I saw a man strike a woman. He knocked her to her knees and shouted at her. No one paid them any attention.

I slipped away. "This is not the place to bear you, Sara," I whispered. "We will find the Priestess, and she will protect us."

We traveled generally toward the setting sun. My plan was to find the sea and then turn north, following the coast until it butted into the cliffs where Inka said the Goddess' Cave lay. The days were warm, but the night's cold pierced my tiger skin. Bennu slept beneath it, next to me for warmth.

Once we left the hilly terrain, we moved at a good pace, and I lost the hard edge of the fear that the River People men would find me. I did have to rest often because my feet hurt. We skirted the edge of a marshy pasture teeming with birds. I was familiar with them, as the same birds lived near the Black Lake, but I had never seen so many in one area. Storks, plovers, cranes, grebes, kestrels, and geese made a constant cacophony that kept me and Bennu nervous. In the evening, the mosquitoes were so thick, I stopped to pat mud on my cheeks and the back of my neck to soothe their bites and protect my skin.

One evening, a grey heron flew overhead and landed with hardly a sound in a pond. It stood motionless for a while, head tilted, watching the still water, then stalked away through the dappled shadows. It was so graceful, I wanted to stay and watch for him again, but I did not dare. What if I were wrong and the River People men still followed?

At night, the crickets and water frogs pulsed and clacked,

an incessant background to deep owl hoots and throaty night birds. I longed for the quiet of my hills and thought I would never fall asleep, but exhaustion claimed me. Eventually, the night sounds blurred into a background noise I was aware of, but not focused on, like the color of the sky, and I wondered if I could go to sleep without them.

Once, when we had walked all day, Bennu gave me a sharp warning, just as I heard something bulling its way through the rushes. I readied my sling, my heart racing. Whatever it was, it was not small game. I felt Bennu's sharp talons, even through the padding on my shoulder. He took off with a squawk at my signal, and I began my swing circle. The sling cut the air in a familiar whistle that steadied me.

A wild boar stepped into sight, an older male with a shaggy grey-brown coat and large, protruding tusks. Sweat trickled down my back. The odds of a kill were better than they had been with the tiger, but still too long for comfort. If I missed or just wounded him, he could charge and tear out my intestines with those tusks. I kept the sling circling, but backed slowly away. To my great relief, he was more interested in grubbing for food than tearing out my intestines.

When we left the marshes, the few trees that scattered the land began to wear their autumn colors. I worried that I was too thin to support Sara, so I made sure to eat the fat of any animal I killed.

"How far do you think we are from the Salt Sea, Sara? Sometimes I think I smell it on a south wind. Do not worry; we will get there. I promise." I was so tired, I could barely put one foot in front of the other, but I kept going.

One afternoon, I felt so weary, I stopped and stretched out in a nest of warm sunlight, watching a sparrow hawk fly across the sky. Sleep tugged me gently into its currents, and I dreamed I was a honeybee crawling through the vast corridors of a hive. When I woke, but before I opened my eyes, I heard the quiet undertone of humming that meant a hive was near. I listened for a moment. The sound was very near, as if I truly were inside a hive.

Confused, I opened my eyes, startled to see Bennu standing on my chest, his head cocked as though listening. I blinked, trying to understand through the fog of sleep what was reality and what was dream. For a moment, I thought Bennu also heard the bees, and then I realized that he was making the sound himself.

When I sat up, he flew off a short distance and then watched me, lifting a talon to scratch behind his ear. I had heard him mimic many creatures, but never bees. Why would he do that here? Bennu loved honey. Did he hear a hive?

I closed my eyes again and concentrated on listening to the sounds around me. It was difficult after the stress of running from the River People. This kind of listening required discipline and patience to identify layer after layer of sound, like peeling petals from a tight bud to reach the center nectar. Finally, I was rewarded with a faint hum, too faint to be Bennu, and I followed it, using the circles to locate where the sound was louder.

Somewhere in the process, Bennu flew to my shoulder, apparently very interested in what I was doing and perhaps anticipating the reward of a delicious treat. Had he heard the hive and alerted me to the bees by imitating the sound? Or had he just decided to make that noise for some unknown reason, and it was coincidence that there actually was a hive nearby? I would never know the answer to this and might as well believe the Goddess had used Bennu to show me some honey.

I built a fire at the end of the log I eventually found and encouraged smoke to billow into it. The piece of comb I stole was rich, and I had to cut it into pieces to fit into the spare jar Inka had used for the food in my pack. Bennu got his treat, and I was well pleased because honey does not spoil and was a good medicine.

Chapter Twenty Three

Not long after finding the honey, the soil became poorer, supporting only stunted juniper and thorn and scraggly grass that would make poor grazing. I explained to Sara what kinds of grasses were best for sheep. In fact, I told her everything I knew about sheep. She would be born a shepherdess.

The days bled into one another until I could not distinguish them. Only the changes in the moon and my belly made me realize that the Goddess had cycled yet again. Grey- black basalt rock now covered a treeless landscape. One morning I saw a shimmer in the distance which resolved by late afternoon into a lake at the foot of a massive cone-shaped mountain. On a stone that partially protruded from the ground, I found a faded painting. In the center, a few strokes defined an image of several mountain cones with more pointed tops and great swaths of red flames erupting from them. Little stick- men ran with upraised arms from the mountains. I wondered if this portrayed something that had happened in the past. I touched the faint dyes, and it seemed as if I heard the rumble and groans of the earth, the crackle of flames, and people screaming and calling to loved ones. Around the edges of the stone were signs of the Goddess—bulls, triangles, the wavy lines that meant water, moon crescents—many of the symbols Savta had taught me.

This was a holy place.

There was no one around to ask if I could bathe in the water without offending, so I pulled off my clothes and waded into the dark pool, despite the water's chill, which I imagined was due to an underground spring. Bennu ventured to a small eddy to do his own bath ritual, dipping only his head in the water and fluffing out his feathers. I failed to see how this cleaned him, but he seemed satisfied.

After washing, I floated on my back, my belly now a small island rising from the water, the taut skin starred with gleaming droplets and crossed with faint blue vein lines. Quiet cradled me, and I was at peace.

My ears were underwater or I would have had warning. When I turned upright, treading water because the current had drifted me into a deeper patch, I saw him on the bank. For a moment, I forgot what I was doing and slipped under. How could he be here? How had he found me?

I half expected to see no one when I emerged, to find he was just my imagination tricking me, but he still stood there, taller than I remembered, bearded, his golden hair pulled back and tied at his neck, framing the clean lines of his nose and chin. The pelt that marked him Hunter Clan hung at his hip.

"Yanner," I sputtered. Then I could think of nothing else to say.

"Na'amah."

The sound of my name from his lips shattered my astonishment. I wanted to sink under the water again, to hide from the memories that swept me back into them. *Hands grasped my arms, wrenching them back, strong legs wrapped around mine, pulling them apart.* I gasped, as though living it all again.

"Na'amah," he repeated softly. "I will not hurt you."

My glazed vision refocused on this man who had brought me so much pain and now declared he would not hurt me. Anger, fed from some hidden, smoldering fire, flared, melting my fear.

"Yanner, Son of Heptah," I said, making each word bite. "Warrior of the Hunter Clan."

His head dropped.

"Turn," I demanded.

His lips tightened. "I will not turn from the sight of you. You are my wife."

Slowly, as though I were the Goddess herself, I strode from the water, making no attempt to cover myself. Yanner looked at me in surprise. His gaze found my breasts and then moved down to my belly. I thought they would continue down to my womanhood, but they lifted back to my face. This time it was he who gasped.

"Are you with child?" he asked stupidly.

"Yes," I said, bending to pick up my sling and pouch of stones. If he tried to hurt me or Sara, I would kill him.

His brow furrowed. "The father?"

"I was not touched by the River People men," I replied. "The girl-child in my womb is yours," and I added, "but I am Noah's wife."

His hand rose, as though disconnected from his mind, fingers outstretched toward my belly, but he did not touch me.

"I have followed you all these moons," he said, "watched for you when everyone else gave up and returned. I waited for a chance to rescue you."

"I rescued myself," I said.

"You won't survive alone. You need me, Na'amah."

"I am surviving fine." I said.

"You are still more stubborn than Gadem's ox," he said with a hint of the smile I had known all my life tugging at his lips.

A dark cloud dampened the sun's gaze. Tears suddenly filled my eyes. "Why?" I asked. "Why did you force yourself on me?"

The smile vanished as quickly as a snuffed flame. "I wanted—I want you so much, Na'amah. I have for a long time. You fill my mind, my thoughts. My fingers itch to touch you, to hold you." He reached out to me again.

I stepped away, but I did not think I would have to use my weapons, so I bent to retrieve my clothing and turned my back to him. I wiped the tears as I dressed, not wanting him to see them. He did not deserve to see them.

"And my brother?" I asked, my back still to him.

I heard his sigh. "I went to Tubal for help. I knew you were promised to Noah, and I didn't know what to do. He said he loved me as a clan brother and would help, that the laws of the Hunter Clan could override your betrothal. If I . . . took you, we would be married. You would be mine."

"I do not care what the Hunter Clan laws claim," I said. "You have stolen my friend, the Yanner I played with and talked to throughout my childhood, the person I trusted."

"Tubal warned me of this," Yanner said with a catch in his voice.

I spun around to face him. "Did he? And what was my brother's advice?"

Yanner met my glare without guile. "To ignore your anger; that it would disappear over time, and you would learn to be happy as my wife."

"So you did it for my happiness?"

He took a deep breath. "I did it for my own happiness. I hoped for yours." He pulled off the pack at his back and opened it, removing my malachite necklace, the one Noah had given me. He offered it to me, and I took it.

"I found it," he said, "with one of Bennu's feathers between some rocks at the Black Lake's edge. I knew you would never just drop it. Sunnic and I searched for signs of a struggle and found your trail."

My lip curled at Sunnic's name. He had held me atop him in the cave. "Where is Sunnic?"

Yanner frowned. "When we found you with those warriors, I sent him back to get Tubal and others. He hasn't returned."

"Noah would have come if you and your Hunter Clan brethren had not broken his leg," I said bitterly.

Yanner's jaw tightened. "I knew nothing about that until it was done, but what I did was out of love for you. Don't you understand?"

"No," I snapped. "Because of you I am pregnant, running for my life and my child's life in a strange land from men who enslaved me."

"Tubal will find us. He is a better tracker than I am, and I found you."

"My brother will not lift a hand for me, much less travel for moons to rescue me."

"Of course he will."

A sudden wind brushed us.

"Do you hate me, Na'amah?"

I pulled wet hair from my face. "Yes."

He took several breaths without speaking. "I know you always speak honestly. If I did not believe you needed me now, I would ask you to kill me." He nodded at the sling in my hand. "As you did the tiger."

I narrowed my eyes, unwilling to give up any of my anger, but my mouth had gone dry. "Why would you do such a thing?"

"Because I did a great wrong to you, and I cannot bear your hate."

I did not know how to read people, but I had known Yanner all my life and his words had the shape of truth to them. My feelings were so jumbled and confused, I did not know if his remorse changed anything. I wrapped my arms around myself, concentrating on the comfort of pressure. I wanted to sit and rock, but at that moment, the sky darkened and wind howled along the edges of the cliffs behind us. Something struck my shoulder, and I spun around to see who might have thrown a pebble at us. My heart raced, fearing the River People men had found us and hid among the mountain crags.

Another rock struck my head, a bigger one, and suddenly stones were pelting us like rain. With a cry, Yanner lunged at me, forcing me to the ground.

For an awful moment, I thought he was trying to pierce me again, but he yelled, "Lie still!" Around us, dull thuds pattered the ground. Atop me, Yanner's body flinched. We were being stoned, I decided, my heart echoing the thuds.

I did not think much of his strategy. Better to fight or run if there were so many.

We were going to die here, Yanner, myself and Sara.

The thudding stopped as quickly as it had begun, and the sky lightened to a dull grey as wind pushed black clouds onward. With a groan, Yanner rolled to his side to release me. Around us, clear, fist-sized stones littered the ground. I picked one up, startled at its coldness, and realized it was not a stone, but ice.

Yanner, too, was amazed. "Ice?" He picked up a chunk and examined it.

I was still adjusting to the reality that no one had attacked us.

"A sign of Father God's anger?" Yanner asked, his voice edged with awe.

I was in a foul mood, maybe because I was tired and frightened, or the idea of ice falling from the sky disturbed my view of the world, or because I was pregnant, and Savta said a pregnant woman's feelings slosh around like water in a jar. "Why anger?" I asked. "They could just as well be Father God's tears or his necklace broken and spilled to the earth."

As well as he thought he knew me, Yanner did not hear the sarcasm in my words and appeared to be seriously considering what I had said. I did not blame him. It was only the second sarcastic comment of my life. No one, aside from Noah, would understand the joke, and I did not dare explain to Yanner that I did not believe in the gods. He would have thought me to blame for any number of misfortunes, from the flood last autumn to the falling ice and possibly for my own enslavement. Yanner was very keen to please the gods, or at least, Father God.

If Father God did exist, he did not appreciate my wit either, for the wind began to blow with fierce strength. My hair whipped into my eyes, blinding me. Something, a branch torn from a tree, I think, grazed my cheek. That was strange, because there were no trees nearby.

"Shelter!" Yanner yelled, grabbing my arm. He pointed toward a gully with a rocky overhang, and we stumbled toward it, trying to protect our heads from flying debris. I had never experienced a storm like this. The wind's force shoved me sideways and only Yanner's hold kept me on my feet.

We were almost to an outcropping that promised some

protection when I heard a faint squawk. I stopped.

"Come on!" Yanner yelled. "What are you doing?"

"Bennu! I heard him."

"I didn't hear anything," Yanner protested, but he knew my hearing was keener than his, and that I would not leave Bennu in this. He looked around. "I don't see him."

I did not see him either. The wind's force increased. Small sticks and stones battered us. "Bennu!" I yelled.

Another squawk and a flutter of movement several man-lengths away gave me hope, although it could have been a piece of anything thrashed by the wind. I wrenched away from Yanner and crawled, hanging onto large stones anchored in the earth. I kept my belly close to the ground to protect Sara. Debris peppered my skin. Crossing the short distance took all my strength, but I kept going, worried that Bennu might panic and try to fly. I half shut my eyes to keep out the dust. Tears leaked from them.

Finally, I pulled myself close to the place where I thought I had caught the movement. At first, I saw nothing but a mass of sticks and leaves, and then I glimpsed something white and still beneath them.

With a trembling hand, I reached inside and got him. He bit me. More tears flowed as I pulled him to me and tucked him under my tunic. As soon as he was in darkness, pressed against the warmth of my body, he released my finger and quieted.

I turned to make my way back and crawled right into Yanner. Surprised that he had followed me, I tried to shout that I had Bennu, but now the wind's pitch was too loud. It was a vast, orange roar in my mind.

Yanner grasped my arm and pulled me against him, refusing to let the wind have me. At last, we made the alcove in the stone and hunkered in the corner, watching the wind rage.

Chapter Twenty-Four

I woke sometime during the night to the sound of the wind still blowing and realized my head was on Yanner's shoulder and his arm rested over my shoulder. With a quick jerk, I moved away. He moaned and stirred, but did not waken. Scratches covered him, and blood from the worst cuts had soaked through the linen under-tunic on his back.

I considered him. When ice fell from the skies, he had covered me and taken the blows without complaint. In the teeth of what he perceived as Father God's rage, he had not abandoned me, but stayed with me and pulled me to safety. How could I reconcile that with what had happened in the cave? It made my head hurt.

Yanner opened his eyes, startled for a moment, as if he did not remember where he was or why, and then he saw me, and the beautiful smile I knew so well lit his face. "Na'amah, you're all right."

I sniffed. "I am fine, but the flesh is torn on your back." I rummaged in my bag for the clay pot of honey. "Take off your tunic and turn around."

He obeyed or tried to. The blood had dried and stuck to his clothing, so it was painful to remove. I helped him and then spread honey over his wounds. My fingers traveled over the muscled hills and ridges of his back.

"Thank you," he said.

I did not respond. I did not feel like niceties. I felt confused. I wanted him here, yet I did not want him here. He had hurt me badly and yet, he had borne hurt for my sake.

I decided not to think about it and spread some honey over my swollen finger where Bennu had bitten me, the cut on my forehead and my other wounds, which all seemed minor.

Only much later did it occur to me that was the first time I had not reacted to such confusion by rocking and singing to myself or wanting to.

Yanner looked at my belly. "Do you think the baby is all right?"

Maybe that was why he protected me. I carried his child. "She is fine too," I said, a hand covering my belly.

"She?" His brows arched. "How do you know?"

I shrugged.

He smiled again, but it was a thin smile accompanied by a shake of his head. "Why do I even ask such a thing? You are so different from everyone else. You don't know things that others know, yet sometimes what comes from your mouth astonishes me. I think that is why I want you, Na'amah."

"Not because I am beautiful?"

He laughed. "See? Only you would say that." Then his mouth straightened and he looked hard at me. "No, not because you are beautiful."

I looked outside. "The wind has stopped."

"Yes, we should go."

I sighed, knowing that he had followed me for two moons, and I was not going to be rid of him just because he made me feel confused. "I am tired," I complained. "Can we not wait here until dawn?"

"No."

"Why?"

"Because they are following you."

My heart jumped. "The River People men?"

"I don't know who they are. Even when I crawled close to your camp, I couldn't understand what they said."

With a frown, I rubbed my eyes, trying to still the pounding behind them. I had not considered that they would still be pursuing me after all this time. Rankor thought me a stupid woman who was barely worth his effort. I thought he would have given up. It would make much more sense to find another for a slave. Why would he go to the trouble? With sudden perception, I realized he might be insulted and angry at my escape. It was difficult for me to understand, because I would not feel that way. I would think about whether it was worth the effort and decide based on that.

With the insight, I rose to my feet. "I am ready. Let us go."

Evidence of the windstorm's ferocity greeted us for two days. Trees lay on their side, torn from the earth, their roots exposed like a tangle of snakes. Confused at the destruction of their habitat, wildlife appeared almost at our feet, and Yanner did not hesitate to take advantage. We ate well, but he fretted. "We're moving too slowly," he complained as we took a short rest.

I examined the blisters on my feet. "I cannot go any faster. Why do you think they still follow us?"

He scratched his chin, running fingers through his gold beard. "They have trailed you for a long way. I just caught a glimpse of you astride an aurochs in the fog and only realized that you were gone when it cleared, so I watched them. I may not understand their words, but I know when men are hunting a trail. They tracked the aurochs for a time and then lost the trail when it joined a herd. I followed and stumbled on your blood on some boulders."

"How did you know it was mine?"

He shrugged. "I didn't at first, but there were no animal parts lying around, no bones from a kill. Then I saw bird droppings that looked like Bennu's on a rock above you."

So, Bennu had perched on the boulder and kept watch over me while I slept. I wanted to press my cheek against him and remind him what a good, thoughtful bird he was, but he was asleep inside the fleece sling I had made for him, and I worried that, after the trauma of the storm, he might bite me again if I woke him too suddenly.

"I picked up your trail and followed you," Yanner continued. "Unfortunately, the men turned back and must have found the place with blood on the stones as well. When I had the opportunity, I covered some of your spoor and led them south. They took that bait for a time, but I think they realized my trick and returned to the hunt. They found and lost your trail many times, but then it seemed you were on a straight path, and I ran ahead to find you. I caught sight of the pond and knew your love for cleanliness. "

"How did you know I would go straight?"

He grinned. "I know you. Once you set a course, you stay on it. I took a chance, hoping to find a trace here and there to confirm your path. That gave me an advantage and allowed me to find you first. It seemed worth the risk since I had little chance of fighting them all if they did find you first."

"Can they catch us?"

"Depends. They have not traveled fast, returning at day's end to where the slower members of their party camped. I believe they thought to find you quickly or find your remains. If they continue to do that, maybe not." He looked over his shoulder. "But if only a few warriors track us—" He did not finish. He did not need to. Yanner, by himself, might be able to hide his tracks or outdistance them, but with me, his task was difficult, if not impossible.

"What can we do?" I asked in a small voice.

"Keep moving. I don't think we dare retrace your path or try to swing back yet towards home."

"I am not going home."

He looked at me steadily. "I'm not leaving you, Na'amah."

"Which way, then?"

"If we keep moving west, we should come to the Salt Sea. If the shore is rocky, perhaps we can hide our tracks."

"Then which way?" I asked, not bothering to tell him this

150

had been my plan as well.

"North."

"Will they not guess that?"

"They might, but then again, they will wonder if we went south to fool them."

"So, we must depend on luck?"

"No, and neither will they."

"What do you mean?"

"They will split, some north and some south. It's what we did tracking you. Tumni and Balgar went east. Sunnic and I, west." He helped me to my feet. "Where were you going, anyway?"

"Away from you," I said flatly.

His jaw hardened and he said nothing.

Chapter Twenty-Five

The next day, crossing a dusty plain, we found a great mystery.

A settlement, larger than any I had ever imagined, spread out before us, but it was deserted. Mud brick houses nestled against each other, as numerous as trees in a forest. Despite our haste, we could not help exploring some of them. Entrance was gained through the roof, down a ladder and into the cubicle rooms. I recognized a raised area for sleeping, a hearth, and a domed oven much like the ones we used. Yanner was interested in the stone tools and pieces of obsidian made to shape them, but he would not touch anything.

"Their ghosts may haunt this place," he said, casting uneasy glances in the corners.

I had never seen a ghost, much less one haunting anything, so I was not concerned. What would be the point? Still, something had driven these people from their homes. It was one more thing I did not understand, and I added it to the growing mountain of them. I could either make up stories about what I did not understand or acknowledge I did not understand, and hope I would learn more about it later. Yanner preferred the stories.

Most fascinating were the plastered ox and deer skulls and the beautiful, many-colored paintings on the white plastered walls. The goddess symbols were evident here, just like the ones on the rock beside the fire-mountains. One image showed an exploding fire-mountain behind the village. Could that be the reason people abandoned such a marvelous place?

"Why do you suppose that man is pulling a bull's tongue?" I asked, examining another painting.

Yanner moved closer. "I don't know. Maybe they thought drawing such a thing would give them power over the animal."

We explored many rooms, finding a small temple with a recessed alcove very similar to the one in our village. I thought it interesting that we saw no sign of worship dedicated to Father God, no paintings or statues, no temple. I picked up a small statue of Mother Goddess, running my fingers over her protruding belly. "Savta would like this."

"No!" Yanner said, snatching it from my hands. "It is bad luck to take anything from this place. Leave it."

I sighed. "All right, but this would be a good place to sleep the night. I would feel safe in here."

Yanner paled. "No. We can't rest yet. We must move on. The River People men will find us if we don't hurry. They are stubborn men."

I did not think Yanner's determination to leave the settlement before dark was due to the River People men. He refused to allow me any of the turquoise or shells or copper necklace or the beautiful black obsidian mirror I found. Though I did not share it, I understood his fear. Why such an amazing place was deserted was a mystery; Yanner had an imagination that would fill the unknown with terrible scenes.

We climbed the wood ladder back out and made our way from roof to roof. I liked being up high, and decided that since the roof of our boat-house was made of logs, like the sides and bottom, it would hold us just fine. I would have to get Noah to make a hole so we could climb up.

At least one of Yanner's fears was correct.

We traveled west the next day across a river and through a forest of tall, stately cedars with branches that shot straight out from the thick trunks. The smell was wonderful, enveloping us in an invigorating cocoon. Yanner kept trying to start conversations.

"Tell me about your journey, Na'amah. How did you think to ride an aurochs? I couldn't believe it when I saw you astride one."

"The smell," I said.

His brows knotted. "What?"

"That was what made me think I could guide the aurochs." I realized I was so accustomed to being alone that I began in the middle of a thought. Sara understood everything, because she heard my heart. I had to learn anew how to talk to another person.

I tried again. "The aurochs was afraid of the tiger skin's smell, and I thought I could guide it that way."

When it became too dark to walk, Yanner insisted we keep watch through the night, and even though he let me sleep the first part of the night, I was so tired I could not stay awake through the predawn for my watch.

We woke that morning to spears at our throats. Kamukka and Rankor stood over me. Two more men threatened Yanner. "So, Stupid One, Rankor said, kicking my side. "You had assistance in escaping. I thought so."

Despite the pain from his blow, I did not respond or move, not wanting the sharp stone at my throat to slice it open.

"We will camp here until the others catch up. I could use a little rest and"—he glanced meaningfully at Yanner, who lay as still as I—"some amusement."

I knew he meant to take Yanner for his pleasures. Yanner, of course, understood none of this. A voice in my head said that was a fitting thing. Let Yanner see how it felt to be pierced by force. He would crawl to me and beg forgiveness for what he had done. I would hear his cries and laugh.

But I would not laugh. I did not want this to happen to Yanner. Yet I knew no way to prevent it.

Rankor looked back at me and scowled. "Or perhaps I will take you aside, since you are already ruined. Yes, and then I will give you to all my men, before I kill you."

The fear I had run from all these moons had found me. The pain in my side from his kick was not the reason I could not draw breath.

At that moment, a wave of sickness washed over me. It was not the morning nausea that I had experienced, but something much more powerful. Wavering red lights danced in the corners of my eyes, and I suddenly remembered when I had felt this way before. I bit my lip and cried out in the River-People's language.

"Stop! You have angered Ta-urt, your goddess!"

Rankor spun to look at me with surprise. I am not good at reading faces, but had no trouble seeing that rage replaced his astonishment. "What do you know of great Ta-urt, barbarian?"

"I speak for her," I said boldly.

He raised his foot to kick me again.

"No," I said before the blow could land. "Do not hurt my servant. I will prove she is mine." I swallowed hard to keep from vomiting. The gold hum of bees, countless, invisible bees, swarmed over me. They were suffocating me with their humming, their insistence that I do something, be something.... I crawled up through the noise, the confusion, to shout, "I will shake the Earth, herself!"

Nothing happened. The air seemed sucked from the world, and the spear loomed in my blurred sight.

Then I felt it, a stirring beneath me that grew into a shudder. The spearman lost his balance and staggered as the earth convulsed. Rankor took a step toward me. "Blasphemer!" he hissed. "Kill her."

Kamukka hesitated, then drew back the spear to plunge it into my throat.

A great *crack* filled my ears. Kamukka froze. A sharp snap followed, then more snaps and cracks, one after another, cascading like seeds popping in a fire. Men shouted. Only then did I realize one of the great cedars was falling, breaking branches and lesser trees within the reach of its mighty arms. It seemed to fall forever and in every direction.

Like a rabbit, frozen in fear, I could not move. I did not know which way to run if I could have convinced my legs to carry me.

With a resounding *boom*, the massive tree hit the ground, shaking it once more. I swallowed, willing my roiling stomach to calm. In the sudden silence, I saw Kamukka sprawled before me, his severed head partially obscured by a feathered branch of green. Yanner, scratched and bleeding, but whole, pawed his way through more greenery. The rest of us were untouched.

Pale as the moon, Rankor dropped to his knees, staring at me. Bennu chose that moment to land on my shoulder with a frightened squawk and announce, "Na'amah!"

As if the appearance of the king's bird sealed his awe, Rankor prostrated himself. "Great Ta-urt, forgive us. The bird is yours, goddess. We are your servants!"

I swallowed hard to keep from vomiting on him; it seemed hardly to be an act of great Ta-urt.

One by one, the other men with Rankor dropped their spears and lay flat on their stomachs before me. I left them so, noticing for the first time that Yanner was staring at me, openmouthed. I did not speak to him either. I do not lie. Yet, I had just done so, a bigger untruth than I could have even imagined. Too much had changed in my life. I only wanted to be back in my village with Noah and watch the sheep that were my charge. I did not want to be a goddess. Without another word, I sat up, wrapping my arms around my knees and rocked, humming the shepherd's song.

They left me to rock without saying a word. In fact, when I finally looked up, Rankor and his men were still prostrate before me. I had no idea what to do next, but it was obvious that I should not give up being Ta-urt if I did not want trouble. Learning I had tricked him, Rankor would kill me without a qualm or take me for his personal piercing attentions. Neither fate appealed.

"Stand," I said.

Stiffly, the four men rose, their gaze averted.

Rankor stepped forward. "Please, Ta-urt, we knew nothing of your identity. Forgive us!" He threw himself on the ground again.

I wondered how a goddess would respond. She would be haughty, I decided, and unafraid. I was neither, but I must pretend, like the games where children pretended. I would not break the rules, because I was creating the rules.

"Well," I said, "It is proper that you are contrite."

"Please do not shake the earth again," another man said, his gaze still on the ground before him."

I started to promise that I would not, but hesitated. What if the earth shook again? It had already done so twice, and I would have been as frightened as anyone, except it made me sick for some reason. I remembered the dream I had the first time. "Two giants fight in the earth's depths," I said.

"Keep us safe, great Ta-urt," Rankor pleaded.

I decided I did not need to respond, but I was already tired of this game. It was very taxing to lie and made my mind ache. "Take care of the girl, Na'amah, while I choose to live in her."

"Yes, Ta-urt," Rankor said.

"You must guard her from harm and do what she says," I added, just to make sure.

"Yes, Ta-urt," Rankor said again. "Thank you for the privilege of serving you."

"And give me back my horse."

His eyes widened. "Have mercy. I don't understand. Your what, Ta-urt?"

"My horse," I repeated and then realized I had said the word in my own language. I did not know what the word was in his. "The creature with four legs and a long tail that runs across the plain, fleeter than an aurochs."

"A deer?" he ventured.

"No, bigger."

"A camel?"

"What?"

"Does it have a large hump on its back, Sacred One?"

157

"No." My mind was indeed wounded. I did not need to explain what a horse was. "You stole a white carving from me. I want it back."

Relief flooded his voice. "Oh, yes. Forgive me."

While he searched his belongings for the carving Noah gave me, I turned my attention to Yanner, who looked more confused than I had ever seen him. His eyes were still wide, and he did not move. This was power, I realized. I could command Yanner killed or pierced or abandoned. He knew it too, even though he did not understand what had happened. He was afraid, yet, he did not try to run away. He put his trust in me.

After Rankor returned Noah's carving and I had rested, I instructed Rankor to send the third man, whose name was Gossett, back along their trail to bring the other men and the slaves they had captured to me. He obeyed without hesitation, taking off at a run. Perhaps being a goddess was not a bad thing.

Yanner made a fire, glancing at me on occasion, but wisely holding his tongue. Things had changed so quickly, I hardly knew what to do. What if the earth shook again? Would Rankor doubt my story?

Sara was the most important thing. I must keep her safe. The dream of her standing beside me on the mountain was so real, I felt I could close my eyes and touch her cheek and her fine, sunlit hair.

That was when the first pains began. Five moon-cycles were too soon for pain. My heartbeat doubled and a moan escaped my lips. I wished I had paid more attention to the pregnancies of the village women. I wanted to lie down, but I feared to. I was afraid. Sara was afraid.

"Na'amah!" Yanner cried, seeing my face contorted in pain and rushing to me. "What's wrong?"

I clung to his arm, desperate. "My baby . . . our baby is in danger." My eyes pleaded with him to save her, though he had no power to do such a thing.

"How?" he asked.

Another pain stabbed me. Yanner grabbed me as my knees

buckled.

"No," I said, as if lying down would ensure the worst. I began to pace the edges of our campsite. Rankor and the other men watched for a while without a word, assuming, I suppose, that a goddess's behavior was inscrutable. Yanner stayed awake with me throughout the night. I heard none of the sounds that normally impinged on my awareness: the rustle of leaves, the wind, night birds, and hunting animals. Pain racked me.

Yanner matched my stride and covered my shoulders with a blanket. The night stretched into a long, dark tunnel, punctuated by the stars like holes in a dark cave ceiling. I spoke to Sara, silently at first and then aloud, though softly. My words were not for anyone else, but between us. "Do not be afraid," I told her. "My dream will come to be."

How do you know? she whispered, frightened despite my words into finally speaking to me. *Did Mother Goddess send the dream?*

"Yes, she must have. It was so real."

But you do not believe in her.

My daughter-to-be had caught me. For her sake, I had lied, but I could not lie to her because she was part of me. She knew.

I wanted to believe in Mother Goddess. I wanted to plead with her to save my baby, but I had seen many women plead with Mother Goddess to save their born and unborn. Either she was fickle in her answers or only the wind caught their pleas and carried them into nothingness.

Believing in Father God would be of no help. He was uninterested in the affairs of women.

You are afraid, Sara whispered.

"Only for you."

No, you are afraid I will tear you like you tore your mother. Kill you like Coel's baby. Do you push me from your womb so I will not grow too large?

"No!" I screamed and staggered at a lance of pain, grasping a tree bole to stay on my feet. The hard ground called to me like a bed of soft furs. I wanted nothing so badly as to lay on it, to let the earth cradle my aching belly and back. "Sara," I muttered and forced myself upright.

Yanner was beside me, his hands supporting me. "Lie down, Na'amah, please. What good does this pacing about do? I've never seen a woman do that."

"No," I said. "If a woman lies down, she will lose her child."

"Where do you get such a notion?"

I shook my head, which was empty of an answer. Thoughts tangled together like knotted threads. I could not trace one to its beginning or end. My eyes were dry and begged to close. I needed Savta.

"Where is Vashti?" I moaned. "She will know what to do."

"They are coming," Yanner assured me. "Soon."

"I must walk," I insisted. Fear drove me. What if I was expelling my baby because I feared she would kill me, as I had killed my mother? How could I live with that? Or what if the goddess, Ta-urt, was angry at me for impersonating her. Just because I did not believe in her, did not mean she was not real. What did I know? I had the impression in my imperfect understanding of the River People's tongue that Ta-urt was the protector of pregnant woman. I wrapped my hands around my belly. If I had brought her anger on me, Sara would suffer for it.

Grim-faced, Yanner put an arm around me and walked with me. He said nothing when I resumed talking to Sara, and I leaned against him, grateful for his strength. "This is your father," I told my daughter.

I know, she said.

"Noah will be your father too."

I know.

"Fortunate child to have two fathers."

Yes.

Yanner held me tighter. I glanced at him. A tear, luminous in the moonlight, slipped from his eye to trail the contours of his chiseled cheek.

Chapter ⟡ Twenty-Six

Vashti and Inka arrived at dawn with the remaining River-People, their slaves, oxen, and aurochs. A small trail of wet trickled down the inside of my leg. I stopped pacing and stood on trembling legs. "Please, Na'amah. Sit. Lie down," Yanner said, his hoarse chant throughout the moon's journey across the sky.

I shook my head, locking my knees to keep them from betraying me.

Vashti and Inka came at once to my side. I could see they too had not rested, but traveled through the night.

"What do I do?" I asked Vashti.

She took in the situation with only a glance and her lips tightened. "Lie down," she directed.

In relief, I allowed my knees to buckle and sank to the ground, my collapse eased by Yanner's support.

Vaguely, I was aware that they worked furs beneath me. A wet cloth moistened my cracked lips and my face. "Save my baby," I pleaded with Vashti.

"Hush," she said in a comforting tone I had only heard her use once before. Vashti was strong, resolute. She did not believe in giving comfort. I did not want comfort. I wanted Sara standing by my side, the wind caressing her hair, life bright in her beryl eyes.

Vashti pulled up my dress and wiped the inside of my thigh. I heard Inka's sharp intake of breath and knew much blood stained my leg and the cloth. The pain grew worse. How could giving birth to a child who was so small cause so much pain?

Mother!

It was her last cry.

I remembered little of what followed. Numbness wrapped my heart in a thick fog, and I barely recalled watching Yanner and Takunah digging the small hole that would hold my daughter. For a stone, I took the malachite necklace that Noah had given me when I was ill and laid it on the mound of raw dirt. Vashti took one of the red ribbons from her hair and wove it around the stone to protect Sara's spirit.

Inka told me later that I insisted on traveling to the Goddess' Cave, though I did not remember saying it. To her amazement, the River-People men instantly gave up their plans and obeyed my desire. As soon as Vashti said I could travel, they followed her guidance, and we resumed the journey I had begun so long ago.

I only moved one foot and then the other, hearing nothing but the vast silence where my daughter's voice had been. Where had she gone? I could not believe she was no more than words on the wind. How could that be?

I accepted comfort from no one. One by one, they gave up trying to give it, merely taking turns walking beside me. Even Bennu's presence made no difference.

We traveled slowly, deferring to my weakness. When I stopped, everyone stopped. Under Rankor's orders, I was fed first, given the choicest pieces of dried fruit or meat. Vashti, from her knowledge of the River-People's language and Yanner's description of what happened, was able to piece together that I had predicted the earth moving, which convinced the River-People that one of their many goddesses possessed me.

I did not speak. I had nothing to say.

We continued west, coming to a waterfall. Normally, the noise of the churning water would have made me anxious, but the numbness that wrapped me kept that discomfort at bay. The sound had multiple layers of color—whites and blues. Part of me wanted to remain there and just watch the sound swirl through my mind. But I did not protest when we moved on.

The beauty offered by the land we traveled was little solace for me. Inka tried to rouse me, pointing to a hillside ridge where a breeze upturned the dark green olive tree leaves, exposing their silver undersides in ripples of light. I saw only the ancient, gnarled trunks bent and twisted, battered like my spirit. The River-People men took their spears and beat the trees' branches to get them to release their prized fruit. Inka, as chief cook, was delighted.

"Savta uses olive oil to treat wounds and bruises," I noted, trying to show some interest for her sake. "It is good for healing the goats' bruised heads after mating season."

She blinked. "Oh. I did not know that."

Once we came to a place that stirred me from my dreary thoughts. Winter had begun to show its teeth, and I was always cold, despite the furs wrapping me. I carried poor Bennu under all the layers between my breasts. I did not want to lose him too.

We trudged on, until one day we stopped for some reason. "This is the "Place of Healing," Vashti said. "Its waters will take some of your sorrow."

I lifted my gaze from the ground. Before me, rising abruptly from the plains, loomed a white-crusted cliff that cradled concentric layers of basins. At first, I thought the scalloped pools held frozen waterfalls dusted in snow, but, despite the chill, columns of steamy mist rose from them.

Vashti took me and Inka apart from the men and showed us how to climb to the terraces. It was, indeed, a marvel. Not snow or ice, but some kind of mineral frosted the cliff and basins. Occasional yellow, red, or green streaked the pristine white. Behind us rose the shadowy blue-grey of mountains. Vashti gave a blessing and offered thanks to Mother Goddess, then, away from the sight of the men, we disrobed and entered the water.

For the first time in moon-cycles, I was truly warm. Heat soaked into me like a balm. Bennu stalked happily along the white rocks, plucking tiny creatures, invisible to our eyes, from crevices.

We stayed near the place for two days. It did not replace the deep hole in my heart, but I felt more like a person than a disembodied spirit when we continued our journey, turning north.

"What happened when I escaped on the aurochs?" I asked Inka, remembering that I knew nothing of what had happened after Vashti yelled at me to go. The fog had been too thick for me to see her.

"Vashti fought two River-People men to keep them from stopping you," Inka said with pride. "She killed one of them, Zelick, the one with the funny ears."

"Yes, I remember him. I was glad Vashti was alive and chastised myself for not thinking to ask about her. "Were the men angry at her?"

"They were more impressed than angry, and they kept her hands tied behind her again. It was very inconvenient, until Takunah asked her to give her word that she would not try to escape when she was untied."

"She agreed to that?"

"Yes. She told me her word bound her more than the ropes. It made things easier for us."

"I am glad you are both all right," I said. She put her arms around me and hugged me tightly, and we both cried.

Chapter Twenty-Seven

It took two full moon-cycles of weary travel through hills, then onto the plateau again, more hills and mountains, a deep gorge and more mountains, until we came to a piece of the Salt Sea—only a cove, Vashti told us. The water was calm, an intense aqua and cobalt. We made camp and watched the sun set into it. "Isn't it beautiful?," Inka asked.

I nodded. The sea-sky of painted colors reminded me of my view in the hills above the Black Lake and made me homesick.

The next morning we followed the long curve of coast until we reached a stretch of rock and patchy grass that overlooked the gently lapping waves of the cobalt sea. Vashti led us north to a place where the ground ended in an abrupt drop, plunging into a long, jagged cliff that bridged a narrow canyon of dark grey water. The water wound north beyond our sight. Without thinking about it, I knew almost sixty men would have to stand on the shoulders of their fellows to reach the river below. The water's churning unease pulled me with an invisible tether toward the edge. Eddies whirled into circular pools with black eyes that stared up at me, calling me into their oblivion. Still muffled from the world by a patina of numbness, I stepped toward the edge until I felt Yanner's hand tighten on my shoulder. He said nothing, only held his biting grip, until I moved back.

"That leads to your Black Lake," Vashti said, pointing northward where the river dimmed into the distance. She shifted her finger to indicate a settlement on the right bank. "And there is my birth village."

We could see the shape of houses, and figures moving that were surely people.

"So where is this cave of your goddess?" Takunah grunted.

"We are standing on it," Vashti said, lowering her finger to the ground beneath us and sweeping her hand out to encompass the land-bridge.

I looked down at my feet in surprise. The Goddess's Cave lay inside this promontory. It held back the river below on the north and the much higher Salt Sea on the south. We stood on a rise, and I could see that the section of the promontory closest to us was a maze of rocks and boulders. Beyond it, going toward the setting sun, the land-bridge flattened into a grassy plateau that joined the land beyond.

"You cannot enter the Goddess' Cave," Vashti continued to Takunah. "I will take you to the village where you can wait for us."

We walked along the cliff. Yanner took care to keep between me and the edge, until the land met the canyon wall that ran along the eastern side of the river. From there, I looked back at where we had stood and could see signs of a trail that snaked from the top down the cliff and disappeared into a large, dark opening about half way down. The people in the village lived within sight of the Goddess' Cave. Despite my earlier fascination with the long drop into the water, I shuddered now at the thought of having to travel that path to reach my destination.

When we came to the settlement, we entered unchallenged. Houses stood back-to-back on a clearing and various fires belched flames. I saw many of the activities I would have seen in my village—people engaged in building, cooking, tanning hides; making tools of stone, bone, and copper; beating the softened material into tools, or ornaments. The River People men watched in amazement. "We have traded for such pieces," Takunah said, "but have never seen them made."

"It doesn't appear so difficult," Manuk huffed, stopping to

examine a hunk of copper the color of sunset. "Our people could do this."

The villagers spoke to Vashti, but largely ignored us. They seemed accustomed to foreigners and strangers. Even their dogs did not bark at us.

We passed a field where lithe women trained in combat. Vashti's mouth curved in a rare smile. "I spent many moon-cycles on that field."

Even Yanner was impressed. "I have heard stories of the Goddess' women warriors."

Vashti raised her chin. "We learn our skill to protect ourselves and the Priestess." She leveled a steady gaze at Rankor. "Many people come here to honor the Goddess. They see the richness of our copper works. It is good for them to see also that we are not helpless."

People recognized Vashti with respectful nods. She led the men to a clearing on the far side of the village. "Stay here," she commanded and repeated, "Men are not allowed to enter the Goddess' Cave." Rankor frowned and looked to me, but I kept my gaze down, aware of the weariness that I wore like a heavy robe across my shoulders.

"Are you ready?" Vashti asked me.

I nodded. Vashti never treated me as divine, even in front of the River People men. I did not care how she treated me. I did not care if I ate or not. I had fallen back into the emptiness. I only craved sleep. Sleep was a welcome oblivion, and I bedded early and rose late. It was a wonder it only took two moon-cycles to reach the Cave.

Inka and I followed Vashti back through the village onto the plateau that rose between the two bodies of water. There was a trail through the rocks and boulder and out onto the flatter grassy section. From there, we made our way down the narrow, winding path I had spotted in the cliff side. It was not as fearsome as I had assumed. Large stones fisted out of the ground on either sides of the trail, and their presence kept me from feeling the pull of that call toward the edge. Wind chilled the air in the cliff's shadow. Vashti twisted her hair in one hand to keep it from her face, but I let mine whip. She pointed to storks' nests in the cliff rocks. "The Goddess blesses their nesting places."

I nodded. Stork nests were never molested, even if the birds built them in an inconvenient place.

Inside the dark entrance that was perhaps halfway down the cliff face, women in white wool met us. Out of the wind, I put Bennu on my shoulder. The women made much of him, but he was not in a temper to be friendly.

"Oh," said one with freckles sprinkled across her upturned nose, "I've never seen anything so beautiful. Like a cloud." She reached up to stroke him, but Bennu hissed a warning and opened his beak.

"He is cold," I said. "If there is a place he can stay warm, he will relax and let you touch him."

Vashti spoke with them, and they escorted us into a cave. Bennu puffed his feathers in an attempt to put a layer of insulation between him and the damp chill. A shiver coursed down my back with a sense of something more; something I could not identify.

Vashti had explained that the women here worshiped the Mother Goddess and served her by mating with men who came from near and far as supplicants to her blessing. Messengers like Vashti carried any sons born to them to the villages. Daughters belonged to the Goddess and remained here. It was a system that satisfied all, as the villagers prized boy children and the girls were raised with the status of Daughters. Some, when they showed wisdom and maturity, the Priestess sent to be Elders or Advisors, depending on the tribes' customs.

We moved deeper into the cavern, our path lit by burning brands. The women showed us into a small room. Furs lay thick on the floor around a stone pit where a fire burned. Water dripped somewhere, the sound in equal tempo to my sluggish heartbeat. I put Bennu on a stone near the fire and sank into a ball on a fur, falling instantly asleep.

Chapter Twenty-Eight

I do not know how long I slept, but Inka woke me with a steaming cup of broth. I let her talk me into sipping it, wanting only to return to the embrace of sleep, but she insisted I wake up.

"The Priestess is coming to talk with you," Inka said. "Let me at least comb your hair."

I sat still while she worked the wind tangles from my hair, conscious for the first time of how stiff and sore I was and how dirty. With longing, I thought of the hot steamy basins where we had soaked. I had never bathed in hot water before, and I wondered if there was a way to do it at home. Perhaps if Noah built a wooden vat, and we carried hot water to it— I sighed. In the winter, it would all be cold before we had enough water.

"Talk to me," Inka said.

I did not feel like talking, but I did not want to hurt Inka who was trying so hard to help me heal. I asked the first thing that rose to my mind. "Are the River People men still there?"

"Yes. . . ."

I heard the hesitation in her voice. "What?"

"Nothing." Inka bent her head over a tangle, as if she needed to concentrate on it.

"You asked me to talk, so I am talking. What has happened?"

With a sigh, she bit her plump lip. "Panor is dead."

A needle of sorrow pierced me, though I thought my heart immune to more pain. "How?"

"He went to the cliff and leaped to the rocks below."

"But I forbade Rankor to touch him again," I protested. My mind offered the image of Panor, pale and thin, standing in the wind, high on the rocky precipice looking down at the water swirling against it. Perhaps I had given him release from Rankor's hands, but I could not liberate him from the shame that lived inside him.

"I offered prayers that Mother Earth would accept his spirit," Inka said.

I nodded, wishing I could pray for Panor too and for my Sara with any hope that gods would hear my plea.

Before Inka finished with my hair, a tall woman, taller even than Vashti, strode into the room. Red embroidery decorated the hem of her white woolen gown, and she wore a shawl, also fringed in red, the color of power and protection, of blood, of life. I had no doubt this was Mother Goddess' Priestess.

She sat across from me on a flat stone. After a long moment of silence, she said, "My daughter, Vashti, has told me about you. I am sorry for your loss."

I stared at the fine, fleece-lined lambskin that covered her feet.

"Na'amah," the Priestess said gently.

Hearing my name startled me, but I did not move.

"Your name is justified, child. You are very lovely." She paused. "But I wonder how deep your roots go."

"What do you mean?" I asked with a stir of curiosity. This was not the conversation I expected.

"Beautiful pines perfume the air with their scent, but their roots are shallow, and they fall in a strong wind. In contrast, the olive tree is withered and twisted, yet its roots are deep. Storms or fire can batter or scorch it, but it survives for countless seasons, through many generations of man. Do you understand what I am saying?"

"You are asking if I am a pine tree or an olive tree," I replied.

The Priestess smiled. "You are different, but not slow-witted. Which tree are you?"

I shrugged. "I do not know."

After a long moment of silence, the Priestess reached out and touched my chin with a finger, lifting my head. She stared into my eyes as though measuring the depths of my roots. "Vashti believes you are the Special One."

Astonished, I stared back at her for a heartbeat before dropping my gaze in unease.

More silence wedged between us, until she sighed, making my heart ache anew for Savta. "We have waited ten generations for the Special One. We will not waste the Goddess' gift on another who claims what she is not."

This puzzled me because I had not claimed anything. "I do not know anything about your Special One."

Creases appeared in her forehead. "So, why are you here?"

I searched for the images that would explain to her and to me why I was here, running through the series of happenings that began when Tubal brought Yanner to the cave on our hillside to make me Yanner's wife. No, it really began after that, when I chose to flee the village, rather than have Yanner fight a wounded Noah for me. If I had not fled, Sara would still sleep in my womb. Surely, from that decision, all that followed had forced her prematurely from me. It was my fault she was gone.

I said none of this. What I said was, "Savta sent me."

The Priestess blinked, perhaps surprised by the simplicity of my answer.

The sternness in her tone softened. "What tribe are you from, child?"

"The Tribe of First Man. My people settled beside the Deer River that flows into the Black Lake."

"Are you the wife of a man named Noah?"

My mouth dropped, my attention returning briefly to her face. "How do you know that?"

"He came here seeking you. He camps not far from the village."

A knot formed in my throat. Noah had come for me and waited all this time. Savta had told him where she sent me, as she promised. I stood. "Tell me where he is," I said. "I want to go to him."

She held out her palm. "Wait."

Again, silence vibrated between us, punctuated by the steady drip of water.

"I will send a messenger to your Noah to tell him you are safe here and to wait for you."

I considered this. "Why?" Savta had sent me here to give Noah time to heal, and he had healed or he would not be here.

Leaning forward, the Priestess said. "Has anyone ever told you that you were special in any way?"

It was my turn to blink. I did not think she meant that Rankor thought I was his goddess, Ta-urt. I saw Savta leaning toward me the day we celebrated my womanhood to speak the secret she had kept since my birth. "Bees," I said.

"Bees?"

"Savta said I was special because a swarm of bees settled on me when I was born."

Quick intakes of breath from the other women startled me, and I suddenly recalled Savta's warning that speaking this would be dangerous. I bit my lip. I kept a secret as badly as I told a lie.

"Do you remember this?" the Priestess asked.

I shook my head. "No."

"What else?"

I shrugged.

"Tell her about the tiger," Vashti prompted.

All the women looked at me expectantly. I felt awkward talking about the incident; it made a natural thing seem portentous.

"I killed a tiger," I said. "A fortunate aim."

"On the day of her first blood," Vashti added pointedly.

The women attending the Priestess whispered. I heard the phrase, "Tiger Lady," pass among them.

"There is a third thing," the Priestess announced. It was not a question.

I shifted uncomfortably. "The earth tremors?" It came out

a squeak.

"Tell me." Her gaze fastened on me like a serpent eying prey. My mouth went dry. This was dangerous, just as Savta said, although I sensed for a different reason than Savta meant by her warning. I did not have the strength to face it. I squatted, reaching my arms around my knees and rocked back and forth, closing my eyes.

After a while, I felt better and opened them. Everyone, including the Priestess was in the same position. That had only happened when the River People thought I was Ta- urt. People usually move away and leave me when I rock, unless they know me well. Yanner, Noah, and Savta might wait for me like this, but strangers had never done so.

I wanted to rock some more, but I knew they would not go away and would just continue to wait for me. Lying was not a good option, as I did not understand why Savta warned me, and a lie might make everything worse. Vashti and Inka had witnessed one incident and Yanner another, which he had told to both women and anyone else who would listen . . . several times.

Well, if I were to be thrown in a pit, so be it. "I get ill before the earth shakes," I said.

"Ill?" The Priestess' brow furrowed. That apparently was not what she expected me to say. Maybe she thought I would claim the Goddess spoke to me.

"Yes," I replied, glad to make it sound less significant.

"I want to vomit."

Chapter Twenty-Nine

The Priestess left me alone for three days with only Vashti and Inka to keep me company. Vashti led me to a clear pool inside the cavern, and she and Inka helped me bathe. I suppose I needed help. I still felt separated from the world, a sea creature curled in a chambered shell, emerging only when grief or distractions roused me from my slumber. The steady, silver stir of the river against the cliff became a background song, like the frog croaks and night birds of the marshland.

"You will have more children, my friend," Inka said. "Many more."

I thought about that. Would other children fill the hole in my heart for Sara? I could not imagine it.

"Why will the Priestess not let me go to Noah?" I asked Vashti. The question made her smooth the white dress she now wore, an odd, fidgety behavior for her. Vashti normally kept her dignity wrapped around her like thread around a spindle.

"The Priestess is fasting," she said.

"I want to leave. Why am I a prisoner?"

Vashti's head darted up. "You aren't a prisoner."

"Then why can I not go?"

"That is not for me to say. Please Na'amah. This is the third day. She will come tonight and tell you, and it will be your choice."

"My choice to what?"

She only smoothed her dress again in answer.

Two young women dressed in white came and helped me from the bath. They rubbed lavender-scented olive oil into my skin, but they could not erase the tension that knotted my chest and belly. The soft white linen in which they dressed me only made me think what a fine birth wrap it would have made for Sara. My hair was too thick to loop properly through the small copper circlet, so we waited in silence until a Daughter found a larger one. Finally, Vashti pronounced me ready. I had stopped asking her for what, because she would not answer.

I followed her, flanked by the two girls who had rubbed me with oil. Inka trailed behind. Lavender was a calming scent, but I felt danger with every step.

Vashti, carrying an oil-soaked torch, led us down into the belly of the cliff, so deep, I knew we were far below the level of the sea that pushed the stone walls. In fact, the sound of water grew louder as we descended. When the narrow tunnel opened up into a vast cavern, I was unprepared and stopped to stare.

Vast jagged spires rose throughout, like inverted black icicles, many the height of the cone towers in the strange landscape that Sara and I had seen before coming to the marshland. The walls gleamed with moisture, reflecting light from more torches wedged between the rocks, more torches than I could count. They glimmered against the darkness like stars. Below us, a deep crevasse split the entire cavern.

I glanced at Inka, whose mouth had dropped open in astonishment. Even through the weight of my despair, I felt the glory of the place.

Before me, Vashti turned. "This is Earth Mother's heart."

Despite my own doubts, a chill danced down my spine. The Goddess had many names. Earth Mother was one. I remembered the others—Virgin, Lover, and Blood-seeker. It was the last that worried me.

"Only those who serve are privileged to see this, and no man treads here."

"Why are we here?" I asked.

"The Priestess waits below," Vashti replied. "She will answer."

Vashti's words only intensified my understanding that neither Inka nor I should be here. I wondered if the crevasse served as a pit. The Earth Mother accepted the dead into her embrace but, despite her aspect as Blood-seeker, she usually seemed satisfied with symbolic offerings of the first grains. It was Father God who demanded blood to still his tempers. Still, my feet were in no hurry to follow Vashti.

We made our way carefully down a path that wound between spires. As we descended, I sensed the vastness of the vault above us, but none of the many burning torches revealed anything about the ceiling. It was a silent weight of dark above me.

When we came to a stone bridge that arched across the ravine, I balked. Below, water careened and churned around boulders. Nothing could have terrified me more. I saw through childhood's eyes the flood water pouring through the village, carrying away livestock and children. Quiet water did not frighten me, but this was different.

Vashti, thinking curiosity or wonder stopped me, opened her palm to indicate the water. "It flows from beneath the river and disappears down a crack in the earth. No one knows where it goes. Perhaps to the Salt Sea or perhaps it returns to the river." She indicated a net suspended below the bridge. "Our main source of food, other than harvest offerings, comes from this channel."

She started across the bridge. My feet remained pressed into the solid ground. She turned. "It is quite safe, Na'amah. Generations of priestesses have used it."

On the far side was a flat area surrounding a raised stone.

The Priestess stood before it, flanked by two other women. Vashti stepped back and reached for my hand. "Come, the Priestess waits."

My feet grew roots. I shook my head.

"Na'amah, you must."

I just looked at her. Images raced through my head, while I struggled to find the words to match them. Her tone tightened.

Vashti had never had much patience with me.

"You cannot keep the Priestess waiting like this because of some silly fear." I would not look at her.

At my side, Inka put a gentle hand on my shoulder. "Maybe if you close your eyes, you wouldn't see the drop," she offered.

I sat where I was and hugged my knees to my chest.

Vashti groaned.

I tried to shut out the water's rush with an old song Savta liked to sing while she spun.

It was always difficult to tell the flow of time. I sang the same songs over and over, so that did not help me judge. I just rocked until I felt better. This time, however, Inka's voice in my ear stopped me. "It's all right, Na'amah. You don't have to cross the water."

I opened my eyes to see the Priestess standing before me. She had come across the bridge to me. She was regarding me with impassive assessment, except for a slight tremor of her brows.

"Na'amah of the tribe of First Man," she said.

I looked at my hands knotted over my knees. They bore scratches from my travels and a small white scar where Bennu had bitten me. The faint patina of lavender oil on my skin gleamed in the fire light.

When I did not look at her, the Priestess took a deep breath. "For three days I have fasted and sought the Goddess' will. She has spoken clearly to me that you are the Special One we have awaited for many generations."

A tiny red salamander poked its head from between two rocks, catching my attention.

Enraged, Vashti snapped, "How can you be so disrespectful to the Priestess, Na'amah? You are a woman, not a child. Stand up and look at her!"

The Priestess put out a hand, palm flat to Vashti, and Vashti stepped back. "There is no need to defend my honor, Vashti, my daughter. Any grace I have is a gift of the Goddess, and she has anointed this woman, not long out of childhood, to be her mouth, to speak to those who serve her. The Goddess as Earth

Mother is troubled. Her time is not our time. Our lives are but the brief season of a butterfly to her, so she has waited for generations for this one."

I did not know what she was talking about.

To my surprise, the Priestess stepped forward and squatted, so she was eye-to-eye with me. "Na'amah, this is not a thing for you to accept or deny. It simply is. Do you understand?" I focused on her neck to keep from looking at her face, but I felt the intensity of her gaze.

"No," I said.

She sat back, putting a little space between us. "Do you know the story of First Woman?" she asked.

I nodded, looking down at the smooth rock I sat on and relaxing a bit in anticipation of a story. "Savta told me."

"So you know that First Woman understood things that First Man did not."

"Savta said First Woman spoke in a secret language."

This time the Priestess nodded. "Yes, that is one of the stories."

This caught my interest. I loved stories. "What are the other ones?"

"There is one told from Priestess to Priestess since the first days. The true story." She paused and took both my hands in hers. "Na'amah, you have no reason to trust me, but I ask it of you. I asked you to trust me as a mother to a daughter."

Her words yanked a cord that knotted my heart. *Mother to daughter.* Sometimes I woke in the night, afraid I was back in that tight, dark tunnel—all I knew of my mother. I had only the stories Savta told me. Tubal was old enough to remember her, but he said I was not worthy of knowing about her, since I had killed her. Perhaps the emptiness that lived in the space of my mother was what bound me so tightly to my unborn daughter.

I looked briefly at the Priestess' face. Muscles around her eyes and mouth released, smoothing her face, and I realized she had been afraid, afraid of my mistrust.

"We have felt the earth's rumblings," she said, "and know

that the Goddess is trying to speak to us, but we are too deaf to hear anything but her distress. We don't know what to do, how to guide the people." She looked away. "I have been tempted many times to admonish those tribes who have turned from honoring Mother Goddess. I want to claim that they are the cause of her anger, but that is my own anger speaking. I do not know if it is truth." She tightened her grasp on my hands. "We must have truth."

This was something I understood. My respect for the Priestess rose. Why could not everyone seek truth instead of insisting on complicating the world?

"What do you want me to do?" I asked.

"I can't even tell you unless you become a Priestess, my inheritor."

Vashti stiffened at these words.

"I cannot be Priestess," I said at once.

"Why not?"

"Because I am Noah's wife."

"Women leave their husbands and tribe to serve the Goddess," she answered.

"I am not sure I even believe in Mother Goddess," I blurted.

Vashti's body grew even more rigid and the other women murmured to each other. I cast a nervous glance at the ravine's edge. Why did I not simply throw myself into a pit?

The Priestess' hand rose again, bringing instant silence. "How can you not believe in the Mother Earth in whose belly you sit?"

I took one of my hands from hers and placed a palm on the stone beside me. "I believe in this stone, enough to sit on it."

"But how did it come into being, what force breathes through the stones, the trees? What buds a flower into bloom and brings seeds to fruition? What takes death into itself to produce life?"

This sounded very much like Noah's questions. "I do not know. You tell me the Goddess, but how do I know that is so? Stories? I want truth."

She jerked as if I had struck her and then, slowly, a smile curved her lips. "Your journey for truth has brought you here."

I was not convinced of that. I was here because this was where Savta said to go. At least, that was why I thought I was here. My revelation about the origins of my bond with Sara meant that truths did not always float on the surface of things.

The Priestess released my hand and stood. "It does not matter what you believe, Na'amah. The Goddess has chosen you. I ask not for your belief, but for your trust. I do not ask that you forsake your life to be Priestess. If your truth-journey brings you here again, that is well, if not--" She shrugged. "The Goddess' ways are not for me to fathom."

I considered this. She could not tell me the secret story unless I became a Priestess, but there was no obligation on my part to being the Priestess. I did not have to stay here. I could go to Noah and go home.

"What must I do?" I asked again.

The Priestess pulled down the sleeve of her dress, exposing her shoulder and a small triangular scar. Then she indicated the fire that burned atop the flat stone. "Allow the Goddess' mark."

I looked across the bridge. "I do not want to go over there."

"That is not necessary," she said. "Do you agree then?"

I wanted to go home. I wanted to know the true story of First Woman, and I felt fairly certain that no one would pit a Priestess. So, I agreed.

She laid a hand on my head. "You have already been cleansed."

At her signal, an older woman plucked a stick from the fire and crossed the bridge to us. The thin, glowing end of the stick approached. I could not pry my attention from it as it moved closer and closer.

When it was a hand's breath from me, I saw it was a finely worked copper piece, a triangle, fitted into the end of the stick. Vashti and another woman grasped my left arm and pulled down the loose sleeve, baring my shoulder. I had just enough time to realize I had agreed to be burned, when the pain hit. I cried out.

Before I had the presence of mind to jerk away, the Daughter withdrew the brand and applied a cooling salve to the wound.

"Leave us," the Priestess said. All of the women withdrew. With a sigh, the Priestess found a nearby stone that was smooth enough to sit on. "I know it hurts. That will pass."

I wiped at my tears, wishing for Savta's comforting arms. She always held me when I brought her a scrape or cut, rocking me in her arms and singing to me until I stopped crying. She did not sing anymore, because her voice cracked.

"Tell me the true story," I sniffed, wanting my reward for enduring the pain.

The Priestess looked at her hands and began. "In the beginning was the Wisdom, the Mother who gave birth to all."

I knew this. Savta had told it often. I said the next words. "And from Mother Goddess' womb came her son, her lover—Father God. And then First Woman and First Man and all living things."

Nodding, the Priestess continued, "First Woman had understanding because of the Goddess' gift to her, a special sensitivity to the earth's voice. A berry that grew on a vine only in a certain tree in Eden could augment that gift. That is why the serpent is sacred to us and a symbol of wisdom, because the vine that wrapped the tree grew thick as a serpent."

"I never heard that part," I said.

"First Woman discovered the fruit. Although it was bitter, she found herself returning every day for a taste. Once, she had too many berries. She stretched out onto the ground, feeling the earth's pulse, and the Goddess spoke to her."

"What did she say?" I asked.

"She warned that Father God planned to scorch Eden and make it a desert."

"What did First Woman do?"

"She warned First Man, who tried to eat the berries himself, but only grew terribly ill."

Was this what Savta's story meant by First Man learning fear when he tried to fathom Mother Goddess' secrets?

"Together with their families," the Priestess continued, "they fled Eden, which is now a barren wasteland. But before she left,

First Woman gathered as many of the berries as she could. They ripened in her pouch and fermented. She sealed the drink in clay containers, which were passed down the generations through her daughters with a warning that it be tasted only in times of dire need by those chosen by the Goddess."

As I have said, I was damaged, but not stupid. I saw where this was going. "You want me to drink this sour beer that has been stored away so long?"

"It isn't beer; it's wine."

"Wine? I have never heard of wine."

"It's not fermented from grain like beer, but from a fruit with sap from the terebinth tree to keep it from souring. We have only the last bit of it left. I ask you to consider it. I believe the need is great, but it is not an act to take lightly. Two Priestesses who tried in my lifetime have died. The longer it ages, the more potent it becomes.

"You do not have to decide now. Stay with us a few more days and think about it.

"I do not need to think about it," I said. "I do not want to drink poison. I want to find Noah and go home."

Vashti, Inka and another woman escorted me to the clearing where Noah waited. My thoughts had been preoccupied with this meeting. Excitement mixed with anxiety made my heart flutter.

He stood beside the fire in the midst of the River- People's camp. I broke away from the stately walk of my escorts and ran to him. He folded me into his arms and held me as tightly as I had hoped. All my fears drained from me in the strength of his embrace, the solid comfort of his chest against my cheek. He lifted me from the ground and held me in the air, as if I were a child.

Finally, I muttered. "Put me down, Noah."

Gently, he lowered me back to the ground, but kept me pressed against him. "You are not angry with me?" I mumbled into his chest.

"I'm furious," he said. "But right now, I just want to weep with joy. Later, I'll beat you."

I knew he was not serious, but I replied, "You cannot beat me. I am a Priestess."

That made him laugh. "So I was told." He tugged gently on my ears, his reminder that he was pleased with me.

It was good to hear that deep laugh again, but then he stiffened against me, and I turned to see Yanner standing on the fire's far side. The setting sun turned his hair gold. He stood silent and still, waiting.

Gently, Noah took my shoulders and moved me aside. "Do we fight?" he asked. "Or are you just a jackal sneaking into my house at night to cripple me?"

Yanner's face revealed nothing.

He had changed. Six moons ago, every emotion would have played across his features. My own thoughts danced like wind-battered wheat, brushing from one side to the other. I saw in rapid succession Yanner protecting me with his body from the sky's ice-tears; Yanner guiding me through the wind storm; walking beside me through the night while I paced to escape the pain and fear of miscarriage.

I looked at Noah, a man as solid as a tree, nearly as old as my father, kind and gentle, a man who respected me and loved me just as I was.

In that moment, my heart tore in two.

Then Yanner said, "We do not fight, Noah. I ask forgiveness for your injury. Though I was not present, it was done in my name and it was a cowardly act." He took a deep breath. "Na'amah wishes to be your wife. I relinquish any claim to her, here before the Goddess' servants."

In the utter silence that followed, Noah stared at him, his eyes stones.

5521 BCE

PART II

Chapter Thirty

I had two reasons to fear Noah's bed:

The first was pain, pain that was not just an image in my head. My entire body remembered it and shrank at the thought of a man's body on mine. Noah, especially, was a large man, and I a small woman. Would I suffocate? Would my flesh tear?

Also, after losing my Sara, I had no desire to have another child or try to have one. What if I lost her again? Or if Noah did not get the son he longed for?

Too much had happened. I wanted the familiar back and yet nothing was the same. I could not return to my father's house and would not, anyway.

Inka had chosen to come with me, along with Takunah. They found their own home in the village, but I saw her every day. That was a good thing, because Inka was now familiar, and I never had a real friend other than Yanner.

While I was still a goddess, I told Rankor to release all the slaves he had taken and return to the River People with a warning to stay on their side of the sea or risk my displeasure. I proclaimed that I would dry up their great river, which they depended on for survival. It seemed a fitting threat for a goddess, since Father God had scorched Eden. This made Rankor's entire face whiten to match Bennu's scars on his cheek, and he swore an oath on Ta-urt's name he would obey.

So, because of all my fears, when we returned home, I sat

on the floor of our boat-house and rocked for a very long time.

"Come here," Noah said, when I finally looked up.

He towered over me, though he sat on a large flat stone across the room. It was a strange room with a floor of wood. Noah had stripped the bark from the logs and covered it with pitch and then another layer of thin planks. He had built it as he had planned over a shallow gully with a stream that branched from the river.

"Come," Noah repeated.

"I do not want to," I said.

I heard the sorrow in his voice. "Na'amah, my Little Bird. I will not hurt you. Ever."

He had never called me anything but Na'amah. "Little Bird?" I echoed.

"Because to hold you I must be so careful not to crush you, yet I must hold tightly enough that you do not fly away."

This spoke directly to one of my fears, so I smiled though I kept my gaze on the floor, concentrating on a whirl in the wood. The center was darker and had a small space missing. "If I am a little bird, you are a big bear."

He chuckled. "Won't the Bird trust the Bear and come only to nestle against his furry chest?"

I wanted to keep looking at the pattern in the wood, but he tempted me. I loved the soft hairs of his chest and the strength of him when he wrapped me in his arms. The pressure soothed me.

Awkwardly, because my legs protested at unfolding from a long-held position, I stood and walked to him. He did as he promised and took me in his arms to hold. To my surprise, he began to rock with me, as though I were a child. I closed my eyes and let my fears seep from me, the way my hair, wet from the river, dried in the sun's warmth.

He choked softly, but kept his grip tight. At first, I thought he was in pain, then realized my neck was wet, and that he wept.

I said nothing, only stretched my arms as far around him as I could. This could not have been satisfactory, as I could exert little pressure to comfort him, but after a while, he muttered in my ear. "Promise me that you will not fly away again, Little Bird."

"Why would I go away? Yanner has given up his rights to call me wife."

Noah's tone stiffened. "Did he harm you again after he found you?"

"No. You know I do not like lies, Noah. Why do you ask me the same question over and over? Your mind is not wounded."

He gave a little snort of laughter.

"Answer my question, please," I said. "Why do you keep asking me this?"

"I suppose I want an excuse to choke the life from him."

I felt the blood drain from my face. "Promise me you will not do that."

"Why is his wellbeing a concern to you . . . after what he did?"

I did not like his tone. "Yanner is still my friend."

"I don't understand that."

"We share so many memories and he protected me and— It is difficult to explain; I am confused." I twisted my hands.

"So am I." He did not seem happy with this. We were silent for a while, until he said, "Very well. I will not kill Yanner, if you will not run away."

This seemed a reasonable bargain to me. I pulled away from him and stood, spit on my hand and held it out to him.

He laughed and did the same, grasping my hand in his huge paw-like one.

Chapter Thirty-One

Noah did not pressure me to come to his bed. He knew my interest in animals and brought me a fine puppy from Dawn's line. I named him Brindle because his coat was the color of dark wood sap stirred into grey. His eyes were bright and warm and his little body was a bundle of pure love. Bennu was furious at the attention I gave him and tried to bite his tail, but Brindle was always wagging it so fast that Bennu could not get hold of it.

Brindle was clumsier than I was, which delighted me. His feet were too big for his little round body, and he was always stumbling over them. He did not seem to mind.

Noah was impressed with how quickly I trained him to go outside to relieve himself. It was not hard. Anyone who paid attention could tell when he needed to go and just take him outside. Soon, he understood that was the place for such things.

Bennu was not so good at understanding this. Sometimes when he puffed his feathers a certain way, I knew what was next, but I could not get to him fast enough to move him. Noah made me a little wooden tool to scoop up Bennu's droppings. He stayed inside a lot after Brindle came. I think it was jealousy more than the cold that kept him near me.

At first, I was happy mending Noah's clothes and doing wife chores under Savta's direction. I had her, Bennu, and Brindle for company, but I missed the hills. Noah was afraid to let me go alone. In fact, children were not permitted to watch the herds anymore out of fear that more slavers would come.

"Things have changed," Savta said as she milked Balky, our goat. Savta lived with us, which made it seem more like home.

I leaned into the scraper, shaving off a layer of fat under a beaver skin. I did not fret at the task, as I had when young. I appreciated having good tools, remembering my poor efforts at making foot coverings when I escaped from the River People men.

The beaver was a gift from Tubal, dropped whole at our doorstep, of course. My brother spoke very little to me, which was fine. I never knew what to say to him when he taunted me, which he took care not to do in Noah's presence.

"Which things have changed, Savta?" I asked. "There are so many."

She snorted. "You are right. Nothing has been as it was since the flood and your abduction. Some things are worse; some are better."

"I like living here better," I said. "But I wish I could go back to watching the sheep."

"We all miss the things we did as a child, Na'amah, but you are a woman now."

"I do not like being a woman."

She pursed her lips in the manner I always suspected might stifle a laugh. When I was little, I did not like people laughing at me. I do not mind so much now, at least not Savta, Inka, or Noah. Unlike Tubal's mocking, their laughter seemed to be in delight, so I was glad to please them, though I did not do it on purpose.

As if my thoughts had called her, Inka appeared with a basket of grain. "For beer," she said, setting it down beside the doorway. "Takunah is a fine farmer. He has learned everything he could about our methods and thinks them superior to those in his land."

Savta frowned. She liked Inka, but had not forgiven Takunah for stealing me.

"What is superior about what we do?" she asked with

suspicion, not willing to give in to flattery.

"Our wheat plants hold their seeds tighter, so they aren't spread until they're harvested. In his land, he says, the seeds fall out at the slightest touch."

Savta snorted. "We've grown our wheat like that for generations. These River People must be idiots."

"Yes," I agreed with a straight face, planning to tell a truth that would surely sound outrageous. I had determined that jokes contained an element of surprise, though surprise was not always funny. "I've heard Takunah say River People farmers train little hairy men with long tails to pick their fruit."

Savta stared at me.

I smirked, proud of myself. Takunah had indeed said that. I did not know if it was true, but the thought had made me laugh. "Sit, Inka," I said, enjoying the sight of Savta speechless. Had I accomplished a joke?

"Sit Inka," Bennu repeated from the elaborate perch Noah had made him.

Inka laughed then, but more at the double invitation, I thought, than my joke. "I will then." She settled cross-legged across from me, which Brindle took as an invitation and promptly invaded her lap, trying to lick her face. He was growing. She rubbed his black ears and studied the house. "I see Noah is working on another section to his project."

"Yes, he is building a room for Savta, and then he promised me we could have a hole in the roof like the houses I saw in the south."

"I never heard of such a thing," Inka said, "but Takunah says he's seen it in his travels. Takunah has seen many things."

"Indeed, he is wiser than any of us," Savta said, an edge to her voice, "I don't know how he bears staying here with such backward people."

"He says his people are backward compared to us, and he is here because he loves Inka," I said, "and Inka is here because she loves me."

Savta glared at me. Inka blushed and looked down, touching

her belly.

"Are you pregnant yet?" I asked her. I knew they tried almost every night, and the sliver of new moon had pierced the sky several days ago.

"Not yet." Disappointment frosted the simple words.

"Did you try my suggestions?" Savta asked.

"Yes, all of them."

My brows lifted. "At the same time?"

Inka laughed. She stopped, looked at me, and then burst into harder laughter. Tears ran down her cheeks.

I did not understand why my joke had failed, but a simple question amused her so greatly.

"Na'amah, you always lift my heart," she said when she could talk. "No, that would have been quite a night."

Even Savta was chuckling.

"What about you, Na'amah?" Inka asked. "Have you been to Noah's bed yet?"

Of course I had. I slept with him every night, but I knew that was not what she meant. She wanted to know if Noah had pierced me, and if I had hope of a child. I shook my head, not wanting to talk about it.

"Na'amah, I know you pine for your lost baby—"

"Her name was Sara," I said.

"It is bad luck to name one who was never born."

"She was born," I said stubbornly.

Savta pulled the goat's teat a last time. "Her spirit returned to Mother Goddess. She will come again."

"Yes," Inka agreed. "She will. Maybe as someone else's child."

"She is *my* child," I said fiercely, dropping the stone knife and turning away from her.

I left, walking the longer way to the river. When I got there, I squatted on the bank and washed the animal fat from my hands and arms. As I stared down at my hands, tears dripped into the river's flow. The ache in my chest seemed a knife wound that would never heal. When the tears finally stopped, I felt empty. I did not even have the will to rock or sing to distract myself. All

I could do was stare at the water, caught by its movement and the patterns of light and froth that played on its surface. I rose and stepped into it. The cold that embraced my ankles seemed a murmur of welcome. I stepped deeper, to my thighs, feeling the current's soft tug.

Tubal said the river had taken our father during the flood. I wondered if I let it take me, if I would see my father again. Or, if I would find Sara. Maybe she waited for me somewhere in the mists of death.

If I just released my knees and let the water cover me, it would take all my sadness; sweep it away. . . .

"Na'amah!"

I did not need to turn to see who called me, knowing the voice as well as my own.

"Come back," Yanner said. "This is not the season to swim in the river. You know better."

I did not move, unable to take my gaze from the play of light on the water's surface. The current tugged. Another step and the river would take the choice from me. He made no sound entering the water. I was aware of him only when he put his hands on my shoulders and turned me around to face him, pulling me onto his chest. He held me, and I cried again, great sobs that shook my body. I felt as if a hand had reached into my soul and ripped up the roots of my being.

He kept me pinned to him, then when I sagged, he swept me into his arms and strode back to the shore, laying me gently on a bank of grass. I looked up at him, my senses so dulled I was able to meet his eyes. They gleamed like still water.

"Sara," I said, my voice so soft I did not know how he would hear it.

But he did. He blinked and tears rolled down the beautiful angle of his cheek. He nodded. "I know."

"She was your child too," I said. I reached for his hand. "Give her back to me." I meant that not as a plea for him to lie with me, but to grab her from the Earth Mother's arms and return her to mine.

He choked and could not speak for a moment. This time, he was the one who could not meet my gaze. He stared at the distant trees. "You are Noah's wife," he said finally, still not looking at me.

I released his hand, closing my eyes.

With tenderness, he brushed the hair from my face. The touch of his hand stirred a distant desire for life in me, but I kept my eyes shut, unwilling to deal with any sensation but that of his hand on my skin.

"I am no longer Hunter Clan," he said after a long silence.

I took a breath. "Why?"

"When we returned, I found no joy in it. I always thought I hated watching the sheep, but that is what I do now."

It was no longer a child's task, since the River People men had stolen me, but I was surprised. All Yanner ever wanted to do was belong to Hunter Clan.

"How is One-Eye?" I asked, opening my eyes.

"She is fine."

"And her lamb?"

"All grown. In fact, I think she is pregnant, but she's acting strange. I wish you would come look at her."

I was silent. I knew Noah would be very angry if I did such a thing.

"I promise I will not touch you," Yanner said, his voice hoarse. "I will be on the hill before our cave tonight."

Chapter Thirty-Two

That night thunder rumbled in the heavens. "Father God is restless," Noah said, holding a small fruit up to Bennu. Bennu regarded it from the high perch and made his way down the intricate branches Noah had built him toward the offering. With great patience, Noah waited until Bennu was close enough to grasp the fruit with a talon. Expertly, Bennu split the skin and used his agile tongue in concert with his beak to peel it.

"The greedy thing never says 'thank you,'" Savta noted. "Seems you could teach it to say that."

Noah smiled. "You are the one here all day." By which he meant if Savta said 'thank you' enough, Bennu might pick it up. Noah and Savta often bantered, but I knew they cared about each other. Savta had been pleased from the beginning that he wished to have me as wife. She was happy that anyone wanted me with my strange ways.

She turned her back to us every night, hoping, I knew, that we would conceive a child, a great grandchild for her, before she died. I did not want to think about Savta dying. I knew she would, but it was a truth I did not want to hold close.

Though we did most of the summer cooking in Noah's old house, he had surmounted the challenge of building a fire pit on a wooden floor by placing it on layers of sand, hardened clay and flat stones. As the night chilled, the fire's heat warmed the stones and clay and the room better than the oven in our old house ever did. Savta moved her bedding close, claiming the heat helped her aching bones. Bennu too, I had noticed, moved to the end of his perch closest to the hearth. Though it did not get as cold here as it did on the plateau, he did not like the cold at all.

From our bed, I watched Noah put the last bit of wood on the fire and turn to me, as he always did, with hope in his azure eyes. As always, I turned away. With a sigh, he bent over and kissed the top of my head, sliding into the furs beside me. Brindle curled at our feet.

I closed my eyes, but I heard my heart beating. Every sound grew louder, until it felt as if the night crowded into our house.

When, at last, Noah's breathing changed and a soft snore escaped Savta's lips, I slipped from the pallet, wrapped a fur around me, and tied on my foot coverings.

For a moment, I watched Noah, his big paw of a hand reached out to the spot where I had been, his rough face smoothed in sleep. It was almost as still as a memory-image.

This was a good man. He provided for me, sheltered me, waited for me. What had I done to deserve that? Why could I not give him what he wanted most—a son?

The hills called me. I felt their pull like invisible arms reaching out to me. The walls of our house were suddenly the walls of the pit in the village. My spirit felt dried like a fruit left in the sun, a small wrinkled version of itself.

In the dim light from the smoldering fire, I saw Brindle lift his head to watch me, alert to my every movement. He was not going to be left out. When I slipped outside, he was at my heels, bounding about, delighted at the idea of a midnight romp.

Grateful that the wind had pushed the storm aside and the moon was high enough to provide light, though she was not even half full, I made my way along the path to the river and followed it downstream before turning for the hills. When the strain in my calves told me I was climbing, a strange peace mixed with exhilaration settled over me. My lungs pulled in the sweet night air. My spirit soared into the canopy of night sky. The stars burned a bright ache in my throat.

When we reached the edge of the grazing fields, Spotted Dog on patrol came to inspect us, greeting me as if I had never been gone and paying little attention to Brindle's worshipful puppy adoration. Then he moved on. He knew his job.

The scent of sheep thickened, a smell that loosened a cascade of memory-images. I heard a snort, a foot stomp, a bleat. I wanted to run and hug the first sheep I saw, but that would have frightened the herd.

Beside me, I heard a small whine from Brindle and realized he had never seen an entire herd of anything. He pressed against my leg, and I felt the tension in his little body. He did not know whether to run, to chase, or to stand and protect me. I scooped him up and gave him a reassuring squeeze. He licked my cheek.

When I put him down, he seemed to understand that a more subdued nature was called for or perhaps it had been bred into him, but he stayed at my heels as I walked through the herd, greeting old friends and taking note of the new ones. I found One-Eye, who looked well and recognized me with a bleat. Her daughter, Fortune, was close, clear-eyed, and healthy. I saw nothing wrong with her and no indication that she was pregnant, as Yanner reported.

When I had inspected them all, I made my way up the slope. Yanner sat outside the cave in the place we had watched the sheep together so many nights. He did not move when I approached and sat beside him. Brindle sniffed him over, decided he was all right, but not terribly playful, and went off to explore the cave.

An awkward silence hung between us as if the intimacy of our previous encounter was a thing that, if touched, would shatter . . . or shatter us.

"One-Eye's lamb looks fine to me," I said.

"Good," he muttered. "I wasn't sure."

"But Nosey is lame and Hot Head has a skin infection that needs to be treated, and you should isolate Tangle Horn. His breathing is ragged and his eyes are filmy."

Yanner was quiet for a moment, absorbing this. "I saw none of that," he said. "I thought I was doing well just making sure they were all there and protecting them from hyenas and wolves."

"That is important too," I said.

We sat together without speaking, watching over the sheep.

Near dawn, as we approached the boat-house, Brindle seemed as excited to be coming home as he had been to leave. Clouds rolled in again and the wind picked up, whipping my loose hair into tangles. Lightning speared the sky, and the clouds that now obscured the moon and stars released a sudden, drenching rain.

Noah was tending the fire when I entered. I froze, water dripping from my soaked hair and clothes, pooling on the wooden floor. He looked from me to Brindle.

"Perhaps I can make a hole in the floor so you don't have to go out in the rain."

That seemed a stupid thing to do to a boat-house.

"I'm teasing, Na'amah," he said.

"Oh."

I realized he must have just wakened and thought I had gone out to relieve myself. "Where's Savta?" I asked, noting her empty bed.

"She went to your Aunt Adah's. Jabel came out to report she was sick." Behind him, Bennu scratched the back of his head with a talon and yawned.

I continued to stand where I was.

Noah frowned. "Come, get out of those soaked clothes. Aren't you cold?"

I took a step toward the fire and let my fur drop to the floor. He picked up a wool blanket and started toward me.

I went to the hills," I said, pulling my gaze from the flames' tangle to him.

My words arrested his step. He stared at me, his gruff face paling. A few silvering hairs in his beard gleamed in the firelight. Instead of dropping my gaze to the floor, I focused on a spot just above his head, keeping my chin lifted. I heard Noah's breath tighten, felt my own pulse in my ears, and the silent shifting of the world, opening a chasm between us.

Oblivious, Brindle shook, spraying water onto the fire and our legs.

Into the long silence, Noah said, "Yanner?"

In that word, I heard an ache deep as the pain of losing his wife and child. He thought he was losing me too.

I wanted one, but a lie would not come to my lips. I had claimed once to be a goddess to save my life, but I could not lie to save Noah pain. I did not understand myself.

"Yes, Yanner was there," I said. "He asked me to look at One-Eye's lamb."

"In the middle of the night?"

"Yes."

"Go to him then, Na'amah, if that is what you want. I release you from our marriage."

Startled, my mouth opened, but nothing would come out.

Noah turned his back on me, a formal symbol of a divorce. I was falling into the chasm. Were those my choices, then—the chasm or the walls of the pit?

Images of the future flashed before me: Savta and I returning to my father's house and begging Tubal to take us back. Or, going to Yanner and asking him to take me as his wife. I felt certain he would. I was bound to Yanner in ways that stretched to our childhood . . . and even what had happened in our cave. He understood me, understood what losing Sara meant to me, and what the hills and the sheep meant to me. He loved me.

But I continued to fall into that chasm. If I hit the bottom, I felt I would break apart. I was Noah's wife.

"Hear me, husband," I said. I had never called him "husband" before. I saw the muscles stiffen along his back.

"Will you hear me?" I asked. "You know I will not lie to you."

Slowly, he turned to face me, his face etched into stone, except for a tiny twitch beneath his left eye. He held rage and sorrow within him, locked away. I looked aside.

Never had I wanted more to squat and rock away this

confusion in my chest. But that was a child's response. I was a woman, and I had to face this.

"I did not go to Yanner," I said, forcing myself to look into his eyes. I held them as long as I could before letting them drop. Long enough to see doubt misted them.

He did not speak, but his silence gave me the courage to go on. "I went to the *hills*."

"I don't understand," Noah said gruffly, the muscles in his face as tight as the fists clenched by his sides.

"Yanner was there." I tried to piece out the difference to myself as I spoke. I saw Yanner waiting for me and the sheep. How could I explain what I felt, what I needed?

"I need the hills," I said. "Not Yanner, though he is my friend."

"The friend who pierced you against your will?"

"Yes."

"You feel no desire for him?"

In my mind, Yanner stood in a stream when we ran from the River People men, the sun gleaming off the smooth muscles of his body and the wheat-gold of his hair. To answer Noah's question would only hurt him further. I could not try to reason with him that he might feel desire for another attractive woman and yet not go to her arms. I had always answered direct questions directly, but this time, I did not.

"Yanner is a beautiful man, but he is not my husband. I want to lie only with my husband."

Noah turned and paced the room. Brindle whined and went to curl in Savta's empty pallet, watching him nervously. "That is a revelation," he said. "You have not wanted to lie with me. I have waited patiently for you. I thought I understood why you were afraid, but now I think maybe it was not fear, but desire for another."

"No," I said. "It was not desire for another."

He stopped then and looked at me, his anger wanting to disbelieve me, but his mind knowing I told him truth. "What is it then, Na'amah? I do not understand."

"I was afraid," I said, taking a deep breath. "I am afraid," I corrected. "I am afraid of . . . losing who I am." He stared at me, but I knew he was trying, and I plunged on, not really sure what I meant either. "I am not good at sewing or cooking. I will be clumsy and rotten at making babies. But I am good with sheep."

I was relieved that he did not laugh. He waited for me to find the words.

"I know the sheep better than anyone. I understand them. I make a difference to the village and our people because more sheep live and are healthy when I am watching them. And I need the air of the hills to breathe right."

I stopped talking. I wished I had better words. How could he understand with such poor ones? But I did not have any more.

We stood facing each other, and I began to tremble. Whether from the cold or my agony, I did not know. Noah still held the blanket in his hands. He stepped toward me. "Take off your clothes."

I obeyed him, standing naked and wet before him. He came forward and wrapped me in the blanket. "I have caged you, Little Bird," he said, "and I didn't realize it. I thought you wanted to be my wife."

"I do," I said miserably.

He hesitated. "Yes, I believe you, but you are not like most women who are eager to take on a household and children and leave the hills behind. I hear you, Na'amah. I have kept you from what you love and from doing what is meaningful to you."

I felt tears welling in my eyes. My heart ached, not with sorrow, but joy that he did understand.

"When you were hurt," he said, dragging the words up slowly, "I was not there to protect you. I could not fight for you when Yanner came to claim you. I could only limp to the land's edge to wait for you."

He had waited for me. He left everything he knew to come and wait for me. Everyone. Not that Noah liked people very much. That was why he lived apart from the village. He said it was so he could be close to the trees, but I knew that was only part of the truth.

"I only ask that you not go to the hills at night. I want you beside me at night."

I nodded.

"I thought I had lost you again." His voice cracked. He swept my wet hair over my ears with his fingers, his thumbs tracing the lines of my cheekbones. A shiver ran through me. He bent down and touched his lips to my forehead, moved to my nose, and then my lips. His beard prickled, but I was keenly aware of the softness of his mouth. He drew back slightly and whispered. "I want you, Na'amah, my Little Bird . . . my wife."

"I am afraid," I said, still trembling. "But I want you too, my husband." I let the blanket fall off my shoulders to the floor.

Noah pressed me to his chest, holding me tightly. He knew this calmed me, but I did not want to be calm. I pushed back and reached up to grasp his beard, pulling his lips down again to mine.

His kiss was still gentle, but more urgent. I felt his manhood press my stomach. He picked me up in his arms, as Yanner had done in the river, and took me to our bed.

His hands moved slowly over my wet body, giving me time to absorb and adjust to the sensations. He lingered on my nipples, already hard from the chill. Then he took one into his mouth and my back arched at the sensation. He slipped his hand down my hips, his thumb stroking the inside of my thigh and then a feather touch between my thighs. I heard myself moan softly. This was far different from what had happened in the cave. Perhaps I would not be as bad at this as I was at sewing.

Chapter Thirty-Three

I made my way down the hills full of my secret, my emotions bouncing between wonder, awe, and disappointment.

Inka met me on the way to the boat-house. "I was coming for a visit," she said, offering me a skein of warm beer. I drank from it eagerly. The wind had been unusually dry on the hills. Normally, the air was moist from its journey over the Black Lake and a light rain customarily fell every few days. We had not had anything like the flood of my childhood again, but Noah continued to expand the boat-house. Savta had a room of her own, and we had a section to store grain and walnuts. Noah and I now slept in a smaller room built on the roof. I loved being able to look out at the trees, level with the branches.

Brindle bounded out of the grass to greet Inka and then dived back into it on the path's far side. He had grown almost to my thigh. He was my shadow, as was Bennu, who perched on my shoulder and nibbled my ear.

"Inka, I am pregnant," I said.

The hesitation before Inka's pronouncement of joy made me remember that she had been trying far longer than I. "Mother Goddess is good," she said. "Your child shall be like my own."

"That would be a fine thing. It is a boy."

She looked at my belly, which was as flat as ever. "How do you know?"

"I would know if it were Sara," I said. I had listened for her voice. Inka gave me a strange look and turned to walk beside me.

"Does Noah know?"

I shook my head. "Not yet. I will wait another moon- cycle to be sure.

Inka stopped and took my hands. "Na'amah, this one you will have. I know it."

"It will help that I am not carried upside down over the mountains on an aurochs' back."

She laughed. "Yes, that should help a great deal." She noted the purple stains and scratches on my hands. "What have you been into?"

I opened my bag of berries. My eye had gone for the dark fat ones buried in a nest of thorns, their skin gleaming with swallowed sun, and my skin had paid the price. "Try some. The sun has sweetened them."

Never one to turn down food, Inka dug into the berries.

"What is that on *your* hands?" I asked.

With a smile, my friend scoped a handful of berries into her mouth and then held up her wide hands, stained orange from red and yellow ochre paints. "Your Aunt Adah is teaching me her pottery techniques. I thought my village made superior pots, but her work is much finer." She sighed. "I don't think I'll ever be as good, but I enjoy trying. I like it as much as cooking."

I smiled. "Well, you had better not stop doing that or Takunah might have to eat my cooking."

Inka rolled her eyes. "That would be a disaster!" She shook her head. "You should sit with me in the workshop and try it. It feels good to work the wet clay into a shape that will serve someone's need, and I'd wager you would have a steady hand to paint the protection symbols."

With a wry smile, I held up my hands. "These are best used at determining the depth of a ewe's coat or starting her first milk or helping a lamb from the womb. They have never been skillful at much else, but I am glad you found something that gives you purpose. Is Takunah still happy working in the fields?"

"Yes."

"What does he do in the winter moons?"

One of her stained hands covered her mouth, and her eyes sparkled. "He 'works' at trying to impregnate me."

Startled, I looked at her, and then we both began laughing. With a disgusted screech, Bennu flew off my shoulder into a tree. We laughed so hard, we had to sit down right there in the path. A touch of sorrow threaded the mirth, an irony that she, who wanted to have enough children to fill a river valley, had none, and I, who had wanted none, was now with child.

Laughter with a friend is better than a salve.

We walked back together, eating the berries.

"When Takunah isn't in the fields . . . or me," Inka said with a mischievous grin, he is talking politics. He loves rumors and news."

"Does he tell them to you?"

"Oh yes. And I tell him everything I hear from the market or the other women."

"You are a fine match. I do not pay any attention to those things. What is happening?"

"Well you should. Your brother is in the heart of things."

"What things?"

"Things that would make Vashti angry, that's what. I can't believe you haven't heard."

"Stop teasing and tell me!"

"Tubal has been sowing seeds about how Father God demands to be the only god."

I sighed. "He has said that for a long while."

"I know, but now people are listening to him. He says that was the reason for the flood seasons ago and why the raiders came and stole you."

"Ridiculous," I said.

"How do you know?"

"How does *he* know? What makes him the messenger of Father God?"

Inka shrugged. "He just claims to be, and many people are starting to believe him."

"Just talk."

"No, it's not. Not since Mariah was found dead."

"What? Elder Mariah?"

"Noah didn't tell you?"

I shook my head.

Inka's hands found her ample hips. "I came out earlier with the news, but you were gone."

"I have been in the hills. Did Mariah die in her sleep?" I asked hopefully, somehow knowing this was not so.

"No. Takunah found her in a ravine with a broken neck. Tubal says it was Father God's judgment."

I bit my lip, remembering how she had visited me on my celebration day and given me the copper bracelet I still wore. "How coincidental that the only elder representing the Priestess fell in a ravine she has crossed countless times. That leaves old Batan and Kahor, head of Hunter Clan, as Elders."

"You don't think the Priestess will send a replacement?" Inka asked.

"So she can fall into another ditch?"

Inka hesitated. "I don't think Mariah fell either, but no one is challenging Tubal."

"If I were Elder Kahor, I would not turn my back to Tubal on a hunt," I said.

With a nervous look over her shoulder, Inka placed an orange-stained hand on my arm. "Be careful what you say, my friend, even if he is your brother."

I snorted. "Tubal hates me more than any other. Nothing I can say will make it worse."

Inka's grip tightened.

"All right," I conceded, "I will be careful what I say and to whom."

Later, when Inka and I sat outside the boat-house in the shade of the oak tree to catch the evening breeze, a man I had never seen walked up. He was dressed in the skins of a herder, my nose decided. A trail of geese marked the sky behind him. He stared for a long time at the house and shook his head. "I would have sworn an oath by Father God that I was being led by the nose, but the story is true. Will this house truly float?"

At that moment, Noah returned from a day cutting wood. "It'd better," he said with a hearty chuckle, dropping his pile onto a stack, "or my wife will divorce me."

I started to protest and then realized this was a joke. I understood many jokes now, but I still had to think about them.

"Did you come to see our boat-house?" Noah asked.

With a wry grin, the man replied, "No, actually I came to speak with Noah's wife."

Noah cocked his head. "I am Noah of the tribe of First Man, and this is my wife, Na'amah, and her friend, Inka."

"I am Samaben," he said. "My settlement is to the southeast."

"Be welcome, guest," Noah said. "Sit."

I rose. "A cool beer?"

His thick grey brows lifted. "Cool? How do you manage that in this heat?"

I smiled proudly. "As you see, our boat-house sits over a ditch which runs with a stream from the river. Noah dug it out under the house, so the water is deeper. We hang a jar over the side into the pool. It keeps our beer cool even in summer, and if the smoke-house is full, we can suspend meat and keep it fresh or at least edible for a few moon-cycles."

"What an excellent idea!"

I beamed and went to fetch a cup. The idea had been mine, occurring to me after Noah joked about cutting a hole in the boat-house's bottom for Brindle and me to relieve ourselves.

When I had attended to our guest and discussed weather topics to their death, Samaben turned to me. "Word has spread about your treatment for sheep rash. It is ruining the coats on our flocks. I traveled here to ask if you could aid us."

Surprised, I glanced at Noah, who nodded encouragement. "Of course, I will help," I said. "It is a simple recipe. Linseed and flax oil with yellow powder mixed in honey. I will give you a jar to take with you."

"The tribe of First Man is generous."

While I rooted in our stores for a clay jar of salve, I overheard their conversation.

"Your wife is a most beautiful and kind woman. You are very fortunate."

"I agree," Noah said, with an undertone of amusement. He knew I could hear every word.

"Is she always so shy with strangers?"

I sighed. This was the usual interpretation for my downcast gaze. I hoped Noah would not try to explain my wounded mind.

"Yes," he said simply.

My heart filled with love for him. I never for a moment regretted being his wife. I was the fortunate one.

"Are the berries ripe on your hills?" Inka asked, changing the subject.

"Oh yes, the dry moon-cycle has ripened them early."

I groaned quietly. Back to the weather.

When I told my husband I was carrying a child, his joy matched the day we were reunited at the camp near the Goddess' Cave. He swept me into his arms and twirled me around.

"I am dizzy!" I cried.

"So am I," he laughed and set me down before him, tweaking my ears. "Never have the gods so blessed a man. It is a blessing to have you as wife, Na'amah. Twice so to have a child."

"A son," I said.

He paused and then slid his hands down to my shoulders to keep me squarely before him, though my gaze stayed on his chest. "Wife, I am grateful for a healthy child, son or daughter."

His happiness melted some of my sorrow that Sara had not returned to me.

With that news, Noah decided to add to the boat-house yet again. He talked about a third level with windows for the breeze and was afraid it would be too top-heavy without a wider base. He seemed contented when he worked on it, which he did whenever he was not making a boat or wooden implement for someone.

As the days passed, other people came to ask for advice on sheep and goat ailments and behaviors, although I think they often used that as an excuse to gawk at our boat-house. Visitors began to bring offerings—a couple of hares, a boar loin, a well-made tool or clay pot. Samaben brought a fine, white linen shawl on his next visit. It felt like a cloud on my shoulders. Sometimes I wore only it to bed and let Noah unwind it. We inevitably had an interesting night when I did that, even though my belly was rounding. I teased him that he was eager for another son to keep the one growing there company. He agreed and rewarded me with his deep, wonderful laugh.

Chapter Thirty-Four

As I grew heavier, I could not make the climb to the hills or stay in the cold wind, and I chaffed at having to sit still. It made my back ache. I went for short walks and helped Savta. There was always plenty to do, but I had never been a great help at chores requiring skillful work with my hands. And I missed seeing Yanner and the hills and the sheep.

I was picking bits of grass from a pile of wool when a boy of about eleven summers appeared at our door. Savta looked up sharply. "Is someone ill?"

He panted, unable to speak until he caught his breath and shook his head. After a moment, he managed, "The Elders meet at the village center and ask for Noah's wife."

A chill traced my spine. Was Tubal behind this? I had no reason for my fear, but recognizing that did not banish it.

Savta waved him out. "Wait for us outside. We'll come in a few moments. She's heavy with child. Let her prepare."

The boy disappeared and Savta turned to me. "What have you done, Na'amah?"

It did not help the knot in my stomach that she was worried too.

I searched through the arrangement of mind-images from the last several days, which had passed with the same monotony as the ones before that, broken only by Noah's presence and Inka's visits. Winter was coming, and no one had come even for salve or advice.

Savta did not hurry me; she knew how my mind worked. Finally, I said, "I have done nothing to call myself to the Elders' attention."

With a grunt, she climbed to her feet. "Put on your tiger robe. It's chilly out."

The tiger skin was not that warm, and I eyed one of the thick sheepskins, but I did not feel like arguing. The long walk to the village square would warm me. I went to the storage room where I kept it, grunting with the effort of leaning over my bulging belly to pick it up. At once, my hands knew the difference in its weight, and I let it unroll. The outside remained the same, a beautiful orange skin with deep black stripes, but thick, brown fleece now lined the inside. I held it to my chest and returned to the main room, tears brimming in my eyes. Everything made me cry lately. It was annoying.

"Savta, what have you done?"

She gave me her crooked smile, looking very pleased with herself. "It should keep you and the baby warm."

I eyed the finely-worked stitching. "This is a treasure I will pass to my daughter." With a gasp, I realized what I had said, and the tears brimmed over.

Savta's smile vanished. "Only the Goddess knows if you bear a boy or a girl child. And this will not be the only one you have, judging from all the noise above me in the night."

My sobs turned into a giggle and then a laugh. My emotions changed with the breeze. Savta said it was normal and not to be concerned about it.

Sniffing, I wrapped the tiger skin around my shoulders, relishing the soft inner fleece against my skin. Bennu was happy to be left inside in the warmth, but Brindle rose to follow us. He moved more sedately now, but his coat was still shiny and supple.

"Let's go see what the Elders want then," Savta said with a cheerful lilt to her voice.

That only returned the worry to my stomach. Savta was never cheerful. Inka was cheerful, which made Savta crankier, though she did not protest Inka's frequent visits and always sent her home with her favorite treat—goat cheese and date wraps.

Outside, Savta gave the boy a wheat cake and asked him to carry a message to Noah explaining where we were going. Our home was the farthest one from the village and neither of us moved very quickly, much to Brindle's disgust. The sun was low when we arrived, and Noah had beaten us there. A small sound of relief escaped my lips when I saw his wild hair and shoulders tower above the crowd in the square.

I had not been to the village since my return. Inka shopped at the market for us. All the differences shouted at me. There was no weaving on the lodge wall. It looked empty without the bright colors honoring the Goddess. Bits of garbage littered the area, something that Elder Mariah would never have allowed. Worst, another pit was being dug beside the first one. Brindle pressed against my thigh, as he had the first time he encountered a herd of sheep. The sights and smells of market day had never bothered me as a child, although I did not like all the noise or the press of people, but this was different. Men and women milled in groups like frightened flocks. I saw Takunah and Inka and remembered my promise to her that I would watch what I said.

The same boy who had brought the summons appeared and led me forward. The crowd parted before us, and Noah gave me a reassuring nod. I knew he liked crowds no better than I.

I was glad to see that the Goddess' image still stood in the alcove of her temple in silent acknowledgment, or perhaps fear of angering her to the point where the crops failed. Midway between Father God's temple and the bare western wall where the spring weaving had hung all my life, Elders Batan and Kahor stood on two large, flat-topped stones. Tubal kept close at Kahor's elbow, identifying himself as a powerful person of Hunter-Clan. My brother's dark eyes feasted on me as if he were the tiger and I a lamb. I dropped my gaze to the ground and concentrated over the hill of my belly on where I put my feet.

"Perhaps they want to hear from your own mouth the experiences with the River People raiders," Savta said.

That was a hopeful thought, but the presence of the pits loomed behind me, even though I could not see them. Could someone have told the Elders that I questioned the gods' existence? Perhaps disbelief in the Goddess would not doom me now but, according to Inka, the Elders punished severely any criticism of Father God. Tubal's influence on Kahor had grown with my brother's leadership among the young men, and old Batan rarely stood against Kahor.

I halted before the stones.

To my surprise, it was Elder Batan who spoke. He leaned against his staff, his watery eyes staring at me. With a start, I realized he was only a little more than a handful of summers older than Noah, and my heart twisted. I did not want to think about living without Noah.

Batan cleared his throat with a scratchy sound. "Na'amah, daughter of Lamech of First Man's tribe and wife of Noah of First Man's tribe, a claim has been made. You are called to give witness."

With a swallow, I gave the formal reply, "For what am I called, Elder?"

"Zett claims a ewe of a ewe out of his ewe has given birth. Nathan also claims them, saying the original ewe was his. All of the shepherds have been questioned and none can answer."

Relief poured over me like a welcome summer rain. I was not being judged for angering the gods with my disbelief. I glanced at Yanner, because both men's sheep were in the flock Yanner watched. He shrugged, a wry twist to his mouth.

"How could she remember such a thing?" Noah asked, a defensive edge to his voice.

"Have you the sheep?" I asked.

Batan waved at the boy who had brought the message to us, and he and two other lads went behind one of the huts and returned leading seven adult sheep, the last with a lamb hurrying behind her.

I recognized at once One-Eye and her grown baby. I went to One-Eye and laid a hand on her. "This sheep belongs to Zett,"

I said and then went to the next. "And this is the lamb I saved from the tiger. She is out of One-Eye." Several people muttered, remembering the story and telling it to anyone nearby who did not remember.

Moving through the sheep, I placed a hand on a large brown ewe. "This is the offspring of One Eye's lamb, and it also belongs to Zett."

"How can you take her word?" Nathan shouted. "Everyone knows her mind is addled."

"A valid point," Tubal said to Kahor.

Without responding, I moved to the darker ewe. "She is out of the long-haired ewe there." I pointed. "They both belong to Mather."

"That is right," Mather shouted. "They are mine. My mark is under her tail. The girl knows her sheep!"

"And this last one does not belong to the north hills at all. I have seen it in the south pastures, but I do not know who owns her."

"Right again," a voice I did not recognize called out. "She's mine, out of a long line going back to my great grandfather."

I ran my fingers through the thick coat of the last sheep. "This girl belongs to Nathan. I have not been to the hills in the last moon," I said, my hand on my own prominent belly, "but she was pregnant the last I saw her."

"I think that was the one who lost her lamb a few days ago," Yanner said. "I can't keep up with who owns what ewe. I just watch them to make sure nothing happens the dogs can't handle." He turned to Batan and Kahor. "As I gave witness, Na'amah knows each one, their lineage, anything that's been wrong with them, everything about them. She's amazing."

Noah scowled at him. I suppose he did not like Yanner saying I was amazing. I did not feel amazing. To me it was strange that Yanner could not remember such obvious things.

Kahor nodded and spoke quietly to Batan. It made me nervous that Tubal stood close, obviously privy to their consultation, as if were an Elder.

"It is our judgment that the lamb belongs to Zett," Elder Batan said. "It is also our judgment that ownership was no mistake on Nathan's part and that he sought to steal Zett's ewe."

Two men of Hunter Clan stepped beside Nathan, whose face had paled. Kahor raised his staff, a sign he spoke tribal law. "Any adult ram, other than those marked for breeding, belongs to the tribe for those who hunger. Ewe lambs belong to the family who owns the ewe. Death is the punishment for stealing." He brought the staff down onto the stone with a *thunk*.

I watched in horror as men made Nathan strip and stand naked before the new pit. He looked at his wife with an expression that burned itself into my mind. I was not sure if it was sorrow, anger, or despair or a combination of all, but I will never forget it. They moved back to give him the opportunity to step into the pit on his own, but at the last moment, he spun and tried to run. They caught him, and he struggled and cried out. "No! She is wrong! The ewe was mine. I can tell you the line of her ancestry. Who will care for my wife and children? No! Please!"

The men threw him into the pit, where he did not stop screaming. His wife ran to the edge. I thought she would call comfort to him, but to my surprise, she spit. Her words were low, not meant for anyone besides her husband to hear, but I did.

"You have met an end that is worthy of you, and I am glad you are untangled from my hair and my life." She stepped back, scooped up a child onto one ample hip, another tailing with one small hand grasped onto her skirt.

Chapter Thirty-Five

"Is he all right?" I panted, holding Inka's hands so tightly, I thought her pudgy fingers would squeeze off in my palms. The miscarriage had hurt, but nothing like this. How could my baby live through such torture? "Am I dying?"

"Everything is fine, Na'amah," Savta's voice from between my legs reassured me.

I was so thankful she was there and Inka too. I leaned back onto her and my Aunt Adah, who both supported me as I squatted on the birthing stones. They were stones that Savta had carried to births since long before I was born.

Such pain . . . Goddess, please make it stop!

"Your story, Na'amah," Savta reminded me. "Breathe in and out, then say a line."

I could not remember when I told her about my story. *Breathe.* Did I tell her? I could never keep secrets from Savta. I would believe it if she told me Mother Goddess whispered in her ears.

Oh no, I could not say that. We were not supposed to mention Mother Goddess anymore. They must not throw me in the pit now. I had a baby inside me, trying with all his might to be born. He would need his mother. "Hurry," I panted to the baby. "Hurry."

"Breathe slowly, Na'amah," Savta said sternly. "Breathe first and then say a line."

How did she know?
Breathe.
I could not remember any of my story.
Breathe.
It was hard enough to remember to breathe, which was why Savta kept reminding me. A pain ripped through me. "Oh, Mother Goddess, help me!"

No one burst into the house to haul me off to the pit for screaming for the Goddess as loud as I could, and the Goddess did not seem to mind my sudden piety during childbirth. My first son, Shem, was born a wrinkled, blood-splotched, healthy mess with a set of lungs that made my outcries seem paltry. When Savta cleaned him and placed him in my arms with his cord still attached to me, I looked down at him and cried.

Inka cried too. I was not sure if her tears flowed from happiness or sorrow for her womb's emptiness. Maybe a mixture of both.

Savta cut the cord and went to show it to Noah, as was the custom of our tribe. Shem's eyes were a cloudy blue. I knew babies' eyes change and hoped he would have his father's sky eyes. His hair was blacker than mine, black as a bee's stripe. I marveled at the tiny, perfect fingers and toes and especially the ears, carved with such grace on his little head.

When Savta returned, she helped me show Shem my nipple's purpose. It is very important for lambs to have their mother's first-milk. If the first-milk is too thick to flow properly, they can sicken and usually die. "What if my milk is too thick?" I asked in sudden panic.

Savta made a clucking sound in her throat. "Your milk is fine. Look at him go."

I did not need to look. I felt it. Such an odd sensation, more than a relief for my swollen breast. Not the same feeling as when Noah took my nipple in his mouth, but satisfying on some deep level that connected this baby to me.

"Let him go as long as he wants," Savta said.

"Am I too young for good milk? What if I do not have enough?" Why had I not thought of these questions before?

She laughed. "Too young? Why do you ask such a thing?"

"A younger ewe produces less milk and her first-milk is not as rich."

"Women are not sheep, Na'amah. If he's still hungry when he finishes one breast, give him the other teat. You've been roughing your nipples like I told you?"

"Noah has."

She laughed louder. "Then you're ready for anything this one can do."

I remembered those words many times in the following moon-cycles. They were not truth.

Chapter Thirty-Six

Tubal came, as custom dictated, to see my son. My brother had married a young girl from another settlement, but no child swelled her belly yet, so my Shem was heir to head-of- house. Tubal's wife was slender and dark, like me, but taller. She smiled at me and my gaze slid downward. I pitied her.

Tubal stepped forward and pointed to me as if I were one of the ewes he had inherited from our father. "This is Na'amah," he said, giving her more status by introducing me to her, though I was a nursing mother and thus had status above her. Not that I cared a wasp's tit about status. It was just Tubal's attempt to wound me.

With a flush that stained her throat in blotches, she came forward and laid a couple of clay bowls beside me. My gifts, I supposed. Even to my untrained eyes, they appeared clumsily made. Dana stared at my baby. "May I hold him?" she asked.

My arms tightened around Shem, and I shook my head. "He's too young yet. Later, when he's stronger." It was custom to keep an infant isolated from any but immediate family in the first moon-cycle. Besides, Tubal was an influential man, now. The birth had taken place in our isolated boat-house. What if Tubal took my baby and claimed it was his? Was that Hunter Clan law too? If not, he might proclaim it to be. I would scratch his face if he tried. Inka would fight too, though Vashti would have been more useful. Vashti would have a knife or two on her.

Tubal's wife stepped back with empty arms.

"So, what is my new sister's name?" I asked, relieved that the threat I feared was just in my mind. Still, I wished I had not insisted Noah go to the beaver dam for more logs and that he take Brindle with him. He had been hovering over the baby and me, and so had Brindle. I thought we could all use the space.

My gaze stayed on Shem's face. For some reason, I could look directly at my baby. It was as odd a sensation as his mouth suckling my nipple. I could not get enough of looking at him.

Obviously embarrassed that Tubal had not even bothered to give me her name, she coughed and then said, "I am Dana of the South Lake Clan."

Savta had left to tend to someone with a stomach pain, but Inka, who came every day since I had Shem, squatted beside the fire and removed a pot of grass tea. "Inka," I said, "this is my brother's wife, Dana." By naming Inka first, I returned Tubal's insult.

His fists clenched into stones at his side. "I wish to talk to Na'amah alone," he said, his voice low as a tiger's growl.

Immediately, Dana slipped outside.

Inka hesitated.

"It is my right to speak to my sister alone. I am head of her clan," Tubal said.

"Go," I said, convinced he was not here to steal my baby and not wanting him to strike Inka.

She came to my side and bent over, as if to inspect the baby, and whispered in a very low voice, knowing my good ears would hear, "Have you noticed the bruise on her cheek?"

Of course I had, though Dana attempted to cover it with her hair. "It is all right," I repeated. Tubal would not dare hurt me while I nursed his heir. Besides, he had never threatened me, except that night in the cave when he had slapped me and called me a snake waiting to bite off a manhood. It was a strange and hateful thing to say and made no sense. Why would I want to do such a thing?

"I'll be just outside," she whispered, patting the baby.

When we were alone. Tubal eyed my baby and said, "Well, Ugly One, you've finally done something useful. Its head looks normal, not like yours did."

I kept my gaze on Shem nestled at my breast. Tubal stared too, with a strange fire in his eyes. "You have not bothered to see me since I returned from the raiders," I said, wanting to change the subject. "If you are such a great leader, why have you not asked me about them? Do you not care about protecting the people?"

He stiffened. "I spoke to Yanner."

"Yanner does not speak their language. I do."

"I don't believe you learned their language in a few moons. Maybe you can say some words, like that stupid bird."

Bennu, who sat on one of the intricate branches of his perch leaned forward and tilted his head, as if listening very closely.

I shrugged. "Believe what you want."

Tubal moved closer, squatting beside me. I smelled his scent, the musky-salt smell of a man who has drunk a lot of beer. "I don't need to know anything you observed from under their man-spears," he said.

"They did not pierce me," I replied coldly.

He frowned. "Why not? Did they find you ugly? Perhaps their women have more meat on them or larger breasts?" His hand moved toward my exposed breast and then stopped.

"Do not touch me." Outrage spilled into my voice and gave me words that were normally slow to form. "I am Noah's wife!"

"You should have been Yanner's wife," he said. "I was head of your house and clan, and you disobeyed me when you ran away."

Furious, I felt tears fill my eyes. "Why do you hate me so much?"

He ignored the question, but leaned even closer. "I will tell you a secret, Stupid One. It was not Yanner who pierced you that night in the hills."

I almost choked on my indrawn breath.

"It was my manhood you felt rammed into you. My hands at your breasts. Mine."

I could not exhale. Memories engulfed me like a fog sliding down the mountain. I saw only darkness. Sounds, usually so clear and sharp were muffled though the thick sheepskin tied over my head and stuffed into my ears. The only sensations left to me were touch— the ache of my arms and legs spread apart as Sunnic held me atop him; the pressure on my chest and hips, crushing me against Sunnic; and then pain between my legs where I had never had pain before, a ripping inside me, plunging over and over.

There was something more, a scent that wormed its way inside the bag, the musk of a man's sweat—a man who had drunk a lot of beer. For the first time I realized it was not Yanner's scent. It was Tubal's. *My brother.*

"I could do it again," he said, his breathy voice a scrape from his chest. "Right here. Now. I could take you here in Noah's stupid boat-house."

"Noah would kill you," I rasped, more frightened than I had been when strange warriors captured me.

In a swift movement, he covered my mouth with one hand and pinched the nipple of my breast. I yelped, but his hand muffled the sound.

My free hand flew reflexively toward his face. He caught it, his hand encircling my wrist. For the second time in my life, I hated being small and being a woman. Or if I had to be a woman, I wanted to be like Vashti, who would have cut Tubal's throat, even with a nursing baby in one arm.

Tubal ran a rough finger over Shem's head. "Cry out and I will snap his neck in an instant."

It was harder to breathe than when I had given birth. My heart beat like a flailing bird. I believed he would do such a thing. A man who would pierce his own sister would not hesitate to kill an infant, even his own kin. I would not risk Shem's life.

Tears of frustration and fear spilled from my eyes. I could not fight him.

All my life I had struggled to find words to express the images in my mind, but at that moment when I needed words more than

I ever had, there was not even an image.

Tubal stroked the breast where Shem fed, softly this time, as if it were the coat of a prize ewe-lamb. I did not need to look to know his manhood was hard as a tree limb. Words stumbled from my mouth.

"You cannot do this."

He smiled, his hand slipping to Shem's throat. Snapping his tiny neck would be a small effort. "Why can't I?" He spoke the question casually, as though the conversation were something of minor interest. His thumb caressed the baby's cheek, sliding down to the ring of my nipple where he suckled.

"This is against all laws, even Hunter Clan's," I said. "They will pit you. For this and for what you did to me in the cave."

"Who would believe you? I have Sunnic's complete loyalty and Yanner would doom himself if he spoke. Sunnic and I would both swear it was his deed, as he, himself, claimed publicly. Or have you forgotten?"

I had not forgotten. Yanner had claimed so, before many witnesses.

Tubal reached down and slid his hand under my lambskin dress. I flinched at his touch, pressing my thighs together, and he furrowed his brows in disapproval, his other hand moving back to Shem's tiny neck.

I froze.

Choking on every desperate word, I asked, "What will stop the Elders from believing what you do here?"

"My wife will say anything I tell her to," he whispered.

I gasped as his fingers forced their way between my thighs and intruded into me. I was still swollen and tender from giving birth. I wanted to twist away from him, sick and frightened at what he was doing and what he wanted to do, but more afraid for Shem. I kept searching for words to distract and delay him.

"I will bleed."

"Not unusual, I understand, so soon after giving birth."

If only Inka would return—

A horrid image immediately replaced the thought: Inka in a

ditch, her neck twisted at an impossible angle. Then I imagined Dana swearing that Inka had left soon after they stepped from the boat-house. I reversed my wish. Let Inka not return.

The only thing left to me was to plead, but instinct warned me that was what he wanted. He would get pleasure from my frantic appeals and my pain. He had come when he knew Noah was away, and he had the excuse of custom and his wife as a witness against anything Inka might say. This was not something inspired by beer or impulse. He had planned this, perhaps for a long time. There was nothing to stop him.

His fingers pushed deeper into my tender opening. Throughout my childhood of enduring the torments of his scorn, I had never hated him. I hated him now. If my bone knife had been in my hand, I would have plunged it into him.

"You are worth nothing besides this," he said, leaning closer, his beer breath rank in my nostrils.

With an odd clarity, I suddenly understood. Gritting my teeth against the pain, I made myself look at his face so close to mine and spat.

He recoiled, pulling his hand from me, and in the instant before he could react, I struck him with my knowledge, hoping I was not wrong, for I had just enraged him.

"All these seasons," I said, "you have despised me only to cover your *desire*. You are the deformed one, not me."

He hesitated, wiping the spit from his cheek with the back of a hand. "Fool," he said. "Liar. You mean nothing to me." I knew by the timber of his voice and the twitch of his cheek that he was the liar. How had I missed what now seemed so plain? I who missed nothing?

"What a shame it must have been," I said, "to want your sister as a lover. What a blow to your Hunter Clan pride that while other boys chased village girls, your damaged sibling made your little spear rise."

He looked as if I had taken a hot stick, reddened from the coals, and plunged it into his gut. Shaking, he rose. "You are not even worth piercing," he said, anger dripping from his voice, but

225

I knew my words had defeated his manhood. Now, he would hate me more than ever for seeing a truth that he had run from for so long, he believed his own lies about it.

His hand found the handle of the knife at his waist.

I tried not to clutch Shem too hard. The danger of being pierced might have passed, but that did not mean my baby or I were safe.

Bennu sidestepped toward us on his branch, as the white knife cleared Tubal's belt and gleamed in the firelight, a tooth hungry for my flesh. It had feasted on much in its time . . . perhaps not only animal flesh.

He took a step toward us. The last thing I could do for Shem was to try to protect him with my body, but I was unable to move, trapped in the horror that held me in its fist. I could not look at Tubal, only the knife. His ragged breathing joined mine and filled my ears like a storm wind building from grey to black, shadowing the world.

Never had the familiar sound of my husband's uneven tread or his booming voice calling my name filled me with such joy. Tubal's arm dropped. He slid the knife back into his belt, visibly struggling for control of himself. His gaze darted to me. "If you speak of this, I will slip into your house one night, slit your throat and the baby's."

Noah entered the house, limping. Sweat ran from him, and I realized that Inka had gone to get him, understanding she could do little to help me herself. Noah must have run all the way on his bad knee to get home so quickly. His face gave no indication of the pain I knew he felt. The knee that had been shattered had healed, but not without knots of bone that ached almost constantly.

Brindle stood beside him, the thick ruff of fur around his neck stiff. He smelled the fear.

"Tubal," Noah said without politeness, a stone-headed axe dangling in his hand. "What do you want in my house?"

My husband was aging, but he was still a large man with a steady hand and solid muscles from the endless felling of trees, chopping and shaping wood. Tubal was younger and quicker, but Noah was an imposing sight, and Tubal had not missed the axe.

"I came to visit my first-nephew, the heir to my house," Tubal said.

Noah studied my face. I was light-headed and knew I must be pale. "You are brother to my wife and head of her clan," my husband said coldly, "but I ask you to leave my house."

With a shrug meant to be a casual gesture but was to my eyes, laden with tension, Tubal turned and left.

Chapter ✦ Thirty-Seven

When Tubal left our house, a long moment hung between us, as if Noah sensed our lives balanced on an edge he could not see, and he feared to move lest we fall into the unknown.

I had already fallen, so I spoke first. "It was Tubal who pierced me in the cave, not Yanner."

He looked dumbstruck. Finally, a response tumbled from his lips. "Your *brother*?"

I understood his incredulity. I still reeled with it myself, but I believed it.

Without warning, another shock hit me and I whispered, "Sara was Tubal's child." The wrongness of that pierced deeper than anything he had done to my flesh. I closed my eyes, seeing Sara as I had in my dream, her gold hair and summer-grass green eyes, her mouth curved in a smile that was unmistakably Yanner's. It had been a dream, just a dream. She had not lived. She had never spoken to me. I made it all up out of longing. I was a fool.

In that moment, despair tore into me like the cut of winter ice. I realized then that since my miscarriage, I had kept a tiny flame of hope burning in some deep corner of my being. A hope that she would return, my child, my Sara, lost to the darkness of death before she had taken life's first breath.

Vaguely, I heard the axe drop to the wooden floor and wondered through the fog of my pain if my husband would despise me for lying with my brother, even though Tubal had forced me. The Elders would pit Tubal for such a thing, and I would not escape his fate. Tribal law would declare me forever unclean.

I did not need a law to feel unclean.

The pressure of Noah's arms startled me. He held me tightly in a side embrace, so he would not crush Shem. Brindle's wet tongue bathed my cheek. Shem stirred in his sleep, his tiny mouth groping for my breast. As if Bennu, too, sensed my need, he left his perch with a squawk and flutter of wings and landed on my head.

I burst into tears.

Inka finally arrived, breathing hard, her hands clasping her side. Bennu had moved to my shoulder. Brindle curled at my feet. Shem slept, and my tears had dried.

"Is Tubal gone?" she panted.

I glared at her and she lowered her voice, knowing Shem did not like loud noises.

Inka eyed me and said, "What did that son-of-a-jackal do to you?"

Still in Noah's embrace, my thoughts whirled with images of the future. In one, I swallowed what had happened and what I had learned, and I lived in fear. In another, Tubal learned that I had told, and he killed Shem. Neither was acceptable. I glanced at my friend and my husband and made my decision.

Inka's knees weakened when I told them. She paled and sat right where she was. She had known what happened to me in the cave, but liked Yanner nevertheless. She found romance in the story, since the handsome young man had come to rescue me from the River People men. Even Inka, however, could find no bright side to this story.

"I will kill him," Noah said, close to my ear. I shuddered. Despite his size, Noah was a gentle man. Rarely did anger spark his eyes or an ill-meant word escape his lips.

"No," I said. "The Elders would have you in the pit, and Shem would have no father."

He reached a hand to the baby, nestled against my breast. His fist was bigger than Shem's head. With one thick finger, calloused and sun-browned, he lightly brushed the tiny cheek. Noah's face, normally calm, pinched with conflict. I dropped my gaze back to Shem.

"In my tribe," Inka said slowly, "the woman would also be killed . . . and her child. It is said the child's blood would be poisoned."

"It is the same here." I grasped Noah's sleeve. "Promise me, husband, you will not murder my brother."

In that moment, I realized that I had never been as neutral in my feelings about Tubal as I imagined myself to be. Buried beneath my careful habit of ignoring him, lay hurt that he looked on me with disgust and loathing. Now I understood. The root of that disgust grew in himself, at the desire he had always harbored toward me. He made me a scorned object, blamed me for our mother's death, rejected me as his sister . . . because he hated himself.

Understanding my brother did not mean that I loved him or forgave him. I would never do either. But giving my husband permission to kill him would be the same as if the knife were in my hands. I would not do that, and not just because it might plunge us all into the pit. The murder that stained Tubal-Cain's name would not be on my hands or my children's.

"Swear it to me, Noah," I insisted.

"I will not let him touch you again," Noah said, refusing to look at me, his gaze on Shem.

Inka rose on unsteady legs. "Na'amah, Noah, let us help." She too looked at the sleeping baby. "I have no children of my own. You have no sisters. Let me be aunt to yours. Let me live here with you. Takunah can grow his barley here. The land is good. I can help Na'amah and Savta, who is getting too old to be burdened with work."

"Na'amah?" Noah said, after a moment's pause, deferring to

me. "I think it would be a good thing, but it is your household."

Noah was head-of-house, but the home was mine. I almost laughed. Inka and Takunah's presence would offer us some protection. Noah would not have to stop his work. Besides, I had left to Savta the responsibility of managing a home to run off to the hills. Yet, I could not give up my hills without choking something crucial to me, something I could not name or even see in my mind.

"I would love this," I said. "You are most welcome, my friend, but this is Savta's home as much as mine."

"What are we talking about?" Savta said crossly, ducking under the skins of the doorway and entering. "Two people are ill in the village with some fever I have never seen. I've been up with them all night. One has died."

We were silent in respect for the death and Savta's efforts.

"Well?" She straightened, one hand clutching the hip that ached.

"Inka has offered to come live with us and help raise Shem," Noah said.

Savta's teeth, those she had left, poked out her lower lip. "Do you think I'm too old to take care of a baby?"

"No, of course not," Inka said quickly. "But your healing skills are needed by many people and your spinning is the best I've ever seen. I could just help free you to do those things."

"Humph," Savta grunted, but I knew she was mollified. "What about that skinny husband of yours?" she demanded. "He know anything about this?"

Inka smiled, her head cocked at a saucy angle. "Not yet, but he will agree."

"I've been thinking anyway about a third floor for Na'amah and me," Noah said, one hand thoughtfully pulling at his beard. "We like sleeping up high."

"Makes her think she's in the hills, I suppose," Savta said with a sigh at my peculiarities.

"When it's finished," Noah continued, nodding at Inka, "you and Takunah can have the room we are in now."

Inka shook her head in amazement. "There has never been a house like this, Noah. People speak of it, even far away."

Savta's other hand found her hip too, but for a different reason. "As if we had food to feed all the people who come to gape at it." She sounded annoyed, but I knew guests pleased her. Besides, they usually brought offerings with them.

"So, Savta?" I asked. "What do you think?"

"Doesn't matter what I think. It's not my household."

"Your feelings on this are important to Na'amah and to me, Savta," Inka said.

I played with the curl of dark hair on Shem's head, wishing he would wake up and relieve the pressure in my other breast. How soon, I marveled, did small things pull us into their grasp. A short while ago, I had been in fear of my life and Shem's.

"Well," Savta said. "I guess I'm going to die soon and someone will need to take care of everything." She stomped off to her room.

Inka grinned. She knew as well as I, this was as close to an invitation as Savta would give.

Chapter Thirty-Eight

The days were full of Shem, and the excitement of Inka and Takunah moving in. As she predicted, her husband came willingly. He adored his wife, despite her childlessness. This vaulted him in my eyes. We had all forgiven him for stealing us. That seemed a distant memory, though I could recall every detail.

The house rhythm changed with their presence and the presence of a baby. Everything revolved around him. He was passed from hand to hand, which he accepted with a gurgling laugh, busy trying to stuff his chubby fist into his mouth. Savta gave me herb teas to help the swelling in my body.

No one spoke of Tubal, but I was never alone. Either Takunah or Noah was with me or within shouting distance. Takunah did his planting near the boat-house where there were fewer trees about. Noah fashioned stout sticks for both of them. Takunah already had a planting stick with a bone attachment that Noah had made for him, but Takunah was very particular about using it only to dig holes for the seeds. Before spring planting, he wiped Inka's moon blood on the bone hoe for the Goddess' blessing.

Noah's staff was stouter, and he used it to lessen the weight on his knee as he walked. Takunah had no ailment, but said it was useful in inspecting the brush or barley stalks for snakes. I knew both staffs served a different purpose.

Noah also insisted that Brindle stay with me. Bennu ignored Shem, but Brindle looked after my son. If anyone put the baby down, even for a moment, Brindle padded over to inspect him, shoving his cold nose into his face and giving him a loving, wet bath. This made me laugh, but irritated Savta. "I just bathed him," she would yell and chase Brindle away.

"So now he is twice clean," I said, glad for the distraction, as I was fumbling with trying to spin.

Inka, who was gradually taking over cooking duties, grinned, but knew better than to laugh aloud. She always treated Savta with respect, even when Savta's temper broke, deferring to her knowledge of herbs and seasonings and asking her opinion. This wisdom gave Savta the illusion of being in charge of things, something I had never claimed, even though it was my household. Inka's skills awed me, and I understood why she never doubted Takunah would agree to whatever she wanted.

Unfortunately, though I saw what Inka did, I was unable to change my nature and continued to speak whatever popped into my mind.

I was grateful for all of them, but after a moon-cycle, I began to fret. The spring sun on my face and the tease of breeze made me long for the hills. I worried about the ewes I knew were pregnant and whether Yanner needed me to help manage the randy rams.

We were all surprised when Batan, the Chief Elder, arrived. He walked with a staff too, but it was obvious he used it as much for support as to show his status as Chief Elder. He was Savta's age, but where Savta always walked straight as a sapling, a curve to Batan's back made me think of a turtle. Grey streaked his lank hair, and lines buried into his face like the humpy creases of the Great Plateau.

He spent a long time walking around the boat-house and talking to Noah about its construction. He insisted on going as far as he could into the ditch to inspect the bottom, which Noah kept well sealed to protect it from the creek bed when it rose.

"Amazing," Batan said when he had settled inside with a bowl of cool beer and one of Inka's barley cakes sweetened with honey. "People have talked for seasons of how your boat-house has grown. I can't imagine why I haven't come back to see it." He chewed slowly, moving the food around in his mouth to encounter the few yellow teeth residing there. "Tubal always insisted it wasn't much of anything, but he was wrong. Just amazing."

Noah shifted, uncomfortable with praise. "Thank you, Elder."

"Although," Batan continued with a frankness that endeared me. "I can't imagine what use it has."

With a grin, Noah replied, "Nor I. Aside from giving us lots of rooms and privacy one normally doesn't have."

"Ah," Batan said, his watery eyes gleaming. "That, I understand." He winked at Savta, who snorted. Now that Inka and Takunah slept directly overhead, her complaints about noise had increased. Takunah never gave up trying to put a child in Inka's womb, not even saving his seed for her most fertile times, a fact which greatly annoyed Savta who had trouble sleeping soundly.

Batan took another bite of Inka's cakes and nodded enthusiastically. "My wife should come take lessons," he said. "Na'amah, did you make these?"

"Inka did," I said crossly, trying to unite the ends of a broken thread.

"Well, Inka, thank you."

She beamed. It was not often one had a personal visit from an Elder, and she was leaning forward, wanting to catch every scrap of gossip and information she could. Batan, however, was not ready for serious conversation.

"Your crops look better than anyone else's," he complimented Takunah.

Takunah grinned. He had let the hair grow beneath his nose, like a red roof over his mouth. Inka had giggled about it, saying it made his kisses tickle. "Thank you, Elder."

"I hear you feed your plants fish."

"Yes, actually, I do. I mash fish parts and bones that we don't eat and spread it on my crops. It is something my people learned to do. Our great river floods seasonally and leaves fish and silt behind for our fields. The crops thrive on it. Unlike my homeland, more than enough rain falls here, so we've no need to irrigate, but the land gets hungry after growing a crop."

"Interesting. Mariah would have been fascinated and made everyone copy your methods." My gaze flicked to his face. His eyes grew distant. He must have thought much of the woman who had served as Elder with him, and I wondered if he believed her death might not have been an accident. The thread in my fingers broke again. Disgusted, I let it drop, feeling useless.

"This beer is excellent," Batan said. Savta gave a satisfied nod. Her beer making was one thing she refused to allow Inka to touch.

Now that he had warmed everyone to him, Batan gave me a long glance and then turned to Noah. "I am honored to visit your house," he said, "but tribal business brings me."

Noah put down his bowl of beer and waited.

From his elaborate perch of branches, Bennu cocked his head and opened his beak, wagging his tongue as though exploring a sound. "Na'amah!" He fluffed his feathers, pleased with himself.

Startled, Batan looked at the bird. "Father God!" he said. "The bird speaks!"

"Only a few words," Noah reassured him.

"Well," Batan brought his sheepskin tighter over his shoulders, despite the warm weather. He needed more substance over his bones. Their outline pushed against his flesh. What would happen when he died? Would the tribe elect another to take his place? Since before Savta could remember, three Elders had governed, one chosen for age and wisdom, one the head of Hunter Clan, and one a representative of the Priestess and Mother Goddess. Since Mariah died, there were only two. When Batan followed her to the Great Unknown, Kahor was old enough to take the place of eldest. My heart sank when I thought of who stood as next in line to represent Hunter Clan—Tubal.

"Well," Batan said, "the bird is right. I did come because of Na'amah."

Noah's hands tightened around his bowl. A deer barked in the distance.

"I have done nothing wrong." The words escaped my mouth before I thought.

"No one has said you have," Batan said.

I flinched. Tubal had probably told him I was an unpredictable idiot, and I had just confirmed it.

Inka flashed me a look of warning.

I picked up Shem, who was thrashing his hands and feet and rocked him in my arms. The movement calmed me as much as him.

"Your knowledge of the sheep was very impressive in the matter of Zett and Nathan's dispute," Batan said. "Since we lost Elder Mariah, no one has been able to keep the livestock lineage."

"Daughters of the Priestess are trained for that," I said.

Inka rolled her eyes, exasperated with me. Go ahead, her look said, be pitted, but Savta nodded in silent agreement.

"Tradition has always dictated that a Daughter serve as an Elder," Batan acknowledged, his voice weighted with sadness and caution. "That has changed."

"So you don't want Na'amah to be an Elder," Savta snapped.

Inka and Takunah stared at her. Laughter at such a thought broke from my mouth, drawing everyone to turn shocked faces to me. But Savta was unperturbed and continued the mending she had taken up.

After a moment, Batan regained his composure and a smile tightened his thin mouth. "That is somewhat of an awkward part to this. We're not asking Na'amah to be an Elder—" "Just to have the duties of one," Savta finished his sentence and jabbed her curved bone needle through a fine, soft lambskin wrap she was working on for Shem. I watched the tendon thread dip and climb through the skin. Tendon thread was best for skins, though too thick for wool. That was something I would have taught Sara. . . .

I forced my mind from the image of Sara sitting beside me, watching me sew, and concentrated on what Batan had said. Although I had not thought about it for a long time, the irony of the situation did not escape me. I did have the qualifications to be Elder for the tribe and bore a mark for proof. No one other than Inka and Noah knew this, and I needed to keep it so. It was now a death mark.

Batan ran a finger around the rim of his clay bowl, one Inka had crafted. I bit my lip. Everyone had skills—Inka cooked, Savta sewed, Noah worked with wood, and Takunah with his crops. I was awkward at everything. What could I do? I could hear honeybees. I knew all the stars, and I knew sheep. I knew from the texture of wool whether the creature was healthy or ill and what its general ancestry was. I knew when the herds were uneasy or just looking for fresh pastures. I knew which sheep were best to start when a herd needed to be moved and which were better left to follow. I knew how to reach inside a ewe when she was giving birth and make sure the lamb was turned properly and how to cull the rams. Next to sheep, I knew very little about people.

"I am old," Batan said, unexpectedly. "I cannot stand against those who want change."

Savta's mouth tightened. "Mother Goddess is not a force to disappear with men's whims."

Inka paled and Noah's hand tightened on his staff, though he sat. Savta continued to sew.

Batan looked at her. "This truth cannot be spoken outside the walls of this house, Leah."

I was surprised to hear her name on his lips. All my life, I had never heard anyone call her anything but Savta, Grandmother. She and Batan had been children together, of course. It was difficult to think of Savta as a child. She had always been old.

A smile whispered like a fleeting breeze across his mouth and he turned to me. "Na'amah, your honest tongue is a gift from your Savta."

I was astounded. Everyone always attributed my bluntness to my wounded mind. The fact that I was like Savta was a new thought, and I was not sure what to do with it.

"Will you take up the task, Na'amah?" Batan addressed me directly. "It is a burden without the benefits of being Elder, but it is needed. It is for the tribe."

"I will," I said.

"What will be required of her?" Noah asked, his hands still on his staff.

Batan rubbed his chin. "I see no reason the shepherds can't come here with their reports."

"Some," I said, excitement stirring in me, "but I must visit the herds to learn all the sheep and goats and inspect them."

"Of course." Batan nodded, but Noah shifted in agitation. "She can't go roaming around the hills alone."

I glanced at him in surprise. I had done so all my life. Then I remembered—Tubal.

"Tubal thought the same," Batan agreed. "It is a shame that we should have to worry about raiders, but the world has changed. He has offered to share the duty of accompanying her."

"No." The word sprang from my mouth.

Batan turned to me politely, waiting for my reasons.

Lies were difficult for me. Trying to tell them was like walking through a wall of thorns. I had no idea what to say.

Noah's hands had tightened again on the staff. He was too full of emotions to speak wisely, and Savta did not know what had happened the day Tubal visited me. I did not know if Inka had taken Takunah into her confidence or not.

Relief poured into me when Inka said with great casualness, "It's a brother-sister thing. They aren't getting along."

"Never did," Savta added with a keen look at Noah. Her old eyes saw much.

"I'll go with her," Noah said.

Savta gave a quiet snort, and for the first time I realized I often made the same sound. Why had I never realized that? She said, "Not with your knee, you're not. You take a quarter of a day just to get back and forth from your beaver dam. All the lambs would be ewes and rams before you got to them."

Inka's elbow found Takunah's ribs. "Uh, I can go," he muttered, "when I don't have to tend my crops."

"I'm sure there will be others who will volunteer," Batan said. No doubt. Several would volunteer at Tubal's prompting. I did not want him knowing my path or schedule so he could trap me alone.

"Yanner," Noah said.

Everyone but Batan stared at him. Noah cleared his throat as though a piece of honey cake had lodged there. "Yanner is young and knows something of sheep. Someone else can take his herd."

I could not believe I was hearing this.

"And he was Hunter Clan before he decided to herd," Noah added. "He can protect her . . . from raiders or beasts."

I caught my breath. My husband's love and concern for me went deeper than jealousies. I bent my head over Shem to hide the tear that carved a path down my cheek.

"This is a good idea," Batan said, unaware of all the currents that had swept through the room in the short span of his visit.

Chapter Thirty-Nine

"I do not want Yanner's foot in my house," Noah had said. And so, Takunah escorted me to the north hill. Inka had combed my hair into a single, thick braid, and I had my knife and sling. Shem rode in a different kind of sling across my chest, shielded from the sun beneath the fine linen. He waved chubby arms, his blue eyes bright at the world, trying to absorb every shift of light and every sound that came to his ears. I was happy to share my hills with him. Brindle was thrilled to be out of the house and dashed off exploring everything, as if he had not run this path all his life.

Yanner stood waiting for us outside our cave. A soft golden beard curled his chin. His green eyes followed my every move. Brindle went to him in greeting, and Yanner stooped to stroke his head. Takunah handed him an oak staff. "Noah made this for you."

Yanner took it without moving his gaze from me. "Give him my thanks."

Takunah clearly wished to return to his barley field. He was proud of his crops. "It's still early," he said, eyeing the pink horizon. "You should have plenty of time. I'll return at sunset."

"Thank you, Takunah," I said, my gaze on Yanner's knees. I was remembering how the pearled water gleamed on his bare skin and the muscles of his chest and, oddly, his hand on my hair the night we sat together under the stars, the last night of

T.K. Thorne

my childhood.

We stood, facing each other unmoving, wrapped in our memories, even after Takunah left. A melee of colors wove mine, like the women's offering to Mother Goddess at Spring Rites. Unlike my husband, an unchanging steadiness in my life, this man spawned extremes that churned, unnamed, in me. I knew that no matter what happened in my life, I would always be bound in some way to him.

"May I hold him?" Yanner asked, his gaze on Shem.

I was unprepared for the hope in his voice. It drained the anger that had flamed since Tubal told me what had really happened in the cave. I lifted Shem from his sling and offered him.

Yanner held him as if he were a fragile bowl.

"He will not break," I said.

With a quick smile, Yanner shifted him closer and sat on a flat rock. "He has your hair."

"And Noah's eyes."

"Yes." The simple word trembled between us.

"Why did you not tell me the truth?" I asked.

Startled, he pulled his gaze from Shem's face. "What truth?"

I pointed behind him to the cave set in the hillside. "About what happened that night."

He paled and then flushed. "I've already begged your forgiveness. What else can I do?"

"Tell me the truth from your own mouth."

"What more is there to say?"

I took a deep breath. "Tubal told me."

Yanner leaned against a large stone, holding Shem against his chest. "What did he say?" His voice was little more than a whisper.

"He told me that you did not pierce me. That he did."

Yanner said nothing.

"Why did you let me believe it was you? That I bore your child?" My voice wavered. I tried not to think about Sara.

Finally, he looked up. "Na'amah." His voice was thick. "I

242

loved you so much, but I couldn't . . . do it. I couldn't take you like that, by force, even to have you as my wife."

"It was Tubal's idea from the beginning, was it not?" Yanner looked at the ground. "He said it was the best thing if I invoked Hunter Law, and that you would be thankful later. He said there were things about Noah that I didn't know, that he would abuse you and didn't care about you. We drank beer and he talked and talked in my ear until it did sound like the thing to do. He said we had to do it that night, while I was convinced."

"Did you know I would be alone?"

Yanner frowned. "No, I guess I thought— I don't know what I thought. Why were you alone?"

"Mallet was supposed to join me. He never appeared."

"Not—?" he choked and cleared his throat. "Not even . . . afterwards?"

"No."

"A coincidence?" he asked.

"No."

"I don't understand."

Oddly, I felt none of the terror that usually flooded me when I thought about that night. "Why did you not pierce me, Yanner? Was that not the plan?"

He swallowed. "Yes, that was the plan."

"But when you could not do it, Tubal did it for you, being the true friend that he is."

Yanner dropped his head. "It was wrong, Na'amah, but he did it for me. I couldn't tell you. I was so ashamed, and then when you were pregnant, I was afraid for your life if anyone knew."

"He did not do it for you, Yanner. Do you still not understand? He filled your ears with talk of how I would never be yours unless you claimed me in the Hunter way. Tubal arranged that I would be alone, and that you would be drunk and desperate enough to agree to such a plan. He also arranged to bring a bag stuffed with lamb's wool to put over my head. I thought he meant to terrorize me, but it was so I would not see or hear what happened."

"What are you saying?" Yanner croaked. "That Tubal planned to pierce his . . . sister?"

I said nothing, giving him time to absorb it, to rearrange what had happened in his memories, to see that I was right.

"I can't believe such a thing," he said.

"Tubal came to the house 'to see his nephew,'" I said, "only a few days after Shem's birth."

Yanner was staring at me.

"He told Inka and his wife to leave us alone. He knew Noah was away, working at the beaver dam."

Yanner stood. "Did he hurt you?"

"He tried. Inka ran to get Noah, and he returned too quickly for Tubal to carry out what he planned, but he threatened to kill my baby if I told."

"Oh, Na'amah." A world of sorrow weighed his words. "What a fool I have been."

Chapter Forty

Yanner accompanied me on inspections of the various herds, both sheep and goats. The bison herds we occasionally saw in the valleys were wild and hunted for meat. No one tried to keep up with them, although hunters captured some of the young ones and castrated them for oxen. I had no trouble learning all of the sheep and goats and who owned each. By the time winter arrived, Shem had grown too heavy for me to carry easily, and I welcomed the respite at our fireside. My body had responded to the exercise of climbing my beloved hills and breathing the clear air. I felt strong and well, which was a good thing since, at eight moons, Shem required constant watching. He was crawling and curious about everything.

I was not disappointed in Brindle's clumsy sheep skills. His lack of exposure to older working dogs when young resulted in him being slow to understand what to do, but he was a wonder with Shem, watching him constantly. When Shem crawled too close to the fire, Brindle was the first to respond, putting his body between the flames and "his" baby.

Shem, in turn, was delighted by Brindle and laughed whenever he saw the dog or could touch him, grabbing his nose or fur. Brindle's tail would wave in patient pleasure at the attention, even though it was obviously sometimes painful.

Balky, our house-goat, had some patience with Shem, until he grasped her udders as he had seen us do. She knocked him away with her hind leg and broke several pieces of Inka's pottery in her dash to escape him. Bennu was a different matter and stayed out of Shem's reach.

I kept Shem at my breast, but even so, that winter Noah quickened another child in me. I told Inka and Savta before Noah.

"Perhaps this will be a daughter," Inka said.

"Perhaps," I agreed, but I knew it was another son. Despite understanding that Sara had been Tubal's child, I believed I would know if she returned. I could not offer a reason for this. If I believed in the gods, I would have said Mother Goddess whispered it to me, but I still had seen no evidence of her. Perhaps it is just my stubbornness or perhaps my wounded mind did not think like others.

"How do you explain the miracle that quickens in you?" Noah asked one night when we lay together. The second new moon had not brought my blood, and I told him I was pregnant. He laid his big head on my belly with a joyful sigh. "How do you explain this, if you do not believe in the gods?"

He was still the only person with whom I would discuss such things. I knew no one in our house would report me to the Elders, but Savta would have blackened my ears with chastisement. Inka's faith was simple and unquestioning, and not concerned with reason. Takunah still worshipped his own gods, though he gave honor to ours. He had long ago given up the idea that I was divine, much to my relief.

"I cannot explain it," I said, running my fingers across the scar on his jaw. "I am in awe of the mysteries and the magnitude of what I do not know."

"Then how can you dispute the gods' existence?"

"I do not so much dispute it, as I am unconvinced they are as the stories say," I said. The soft grunting and moans below us made me smile. Takunah and Inka had not given up the idea of children of their own.

I moved my hand to Noah's head, playing with his thinning hair. "If the gods exist, and if they control everything the way people claim, why do they not give Inka a child? What evil has she ever done to earn their disdain?"

"I don't know," Noah said. "I just know I am blessed to have you and Shem and this little unborn one."

"You are blessed and Inka is cursed? There is no reason to that. If the gods exist, they care nothing about us," I said.

"That is a frightening thought." He kissed my belly and sat up.

I pulled aside the skins covering our window and looked out into the night at the vast empty sky where stars had not yet emerged. "Yes," I agreed. "It is."

Winter passed slowly and my belly began to round. Savta was sour about more mouths to feed, but Inka was delighted. She was still barren. Playing with Shem lightened her spirit, so I was glad to let her. Shem loved her. Shem loved everyone and everything, including creatures great and small. He would watch insects for long periods, fascinated by their journey across the wooden floor. He cried if someone stepped on one. I kept him on my breast, but he started to eat moistened grains and grew fast.

"See those big feet on him?" Savta said, pointing a bony finger. "He's going to be as tall as Noah."

For all her gruffness, she allowed Shem to get away with mischief she never allowed from me, and gave him cloth knots soaked in honey when she thought I was not looking.

As large as it was, the house felt crowded and I missed my hills . . . and Yanner. I often thought of him and it occurred to me that I did not even know where he lived. Was he still at his friend's house? In all our conversations, it had never arisen.

Our winters were mild compared to those in the mountains or the Great Plateau, but the wind off the Black Lake worked through the skins covering the windows, and this season brought a dusting of snow. To entertain us, Takunah told tales of his country and the hot desert, while we busied ourselves cooking the cured meats with Savta's stores of dried herbs, or twisting the mounds of wool into thread, the thread into slender ropes. Some of the ropes were used for Noah's work on the boat house, some were sold at market and some we used to make nets. Each section was set high above the fire to dry. If it did not dry immediately, it would be ruined. I was better at ropes than threads, so that was my job.

Noah and Takunah fished in the river or hunted for fresh meat when our stores grew low, though one of them was always with me. They did well and we only took a ram from Noah's herd when we had to.

I loved the snow, the way it muffled sound in an odd way and augmented others, but I grew restless for spring. When it finally came, I spent every moment I could outside, hungry for the touch of the sun on my face, the sight of snow flowers and the songs of returning birds.

Chapter Forty-One

We were never sure what brought the bear. Savta thought he smelled my honey. Noah believed it was the fresh deer kill he had hung in a tree. I thought the beast was sick.

Noah's knee hurt, and he was at home, being grouchy. Takunah had used the excuse that he needed to inspect the ground in his field to leave the boat-house. I was washing clothes in the little creek a short distance from where the gurgling water ran under our house. At that point, the banks were shallow, and I could see the yard. Shem was playing outside, stumbling on awkward legs after a butterfly, his chubby hands reaching for the promise that kept fluttering away before his fingers could close around it.

I heard it first, even before Brindle, who was sleeping in a patch of sun. That low moan of distress was unmistakable, but it did not occur to me that it would approach us. Bears, like wolves and most wild creatures, avoided humans.

I decided the deerskin leggings needed another rinse. They were Noah's and had not received a cleaning all winter. I did not blame Brindle for keeping her distance.

Something made me turn at the same time Brindle woke and alerted. A large black bear stood on all fours at the edge of the house. Inka's back was to the bear. She was hanging the clothes I had already washed to dry on a rope tied to the house and one of the trees that grew nearby.

Shem had seen the bear. My heart sank like a stone in my chest. Predictably, Shem headed straight for the new furry playmate.

Brindle acted before I could, racing silently toward Shem. I dropped Noah's leggings and scrambled up the shallow bank, a scream frozen in my throat. I was too far away.

Brindle moved faster than I thought capable for a dog his size. He was moving so fast, he did not stop in front of Shem, as I thought he might. Instead, his momentum carried him with a flurry of teeth and growls straight into the bear.

With one swipe of claw, the bear tossed Brindle aside, ripping his side. The trapped scream in my throat escaped. Inka had turned as Brindle launched into the bear, and she added her cry to mine.

Shem sat where he was and began to wail. Before either Inka or I could reach him, Noah came out, his staff in hand, but the bear was now between him and Shem, headed for the tender, unprotected morsel. Noah chased after and brought his staff in a mighty two-handed blow across its rump.

Annoyed, the bear turned and rose on its hind legs.

Inka tripped, sprawling on the ground.

I do not know how I covered the distance to Shem. Time seemed to stop, only returning as I snatched him to my chest. We were now behind the bear, which was advancing on Noah. Inka, dirt smeared across her face from her fall was beside me, but I did not know what to do or where to go. We backed away.

Noah struck again. With an awful sound in its throat, the bear lunged, taking Noah's staff in its massive jaws. The stout wood splintered as the creature shook its head.

Ears flat, it huffed and slapped the ground. I knew it was readying to charge. "Back away!" I yelled at Noah. "Do not look at it!" To an animal, direct eye contact was a challenge. In its normal habitat, such a display might make the bear back down, but this one was enraged and now hurt. It would attack my husband, kill him, and then turn on us. I knew I should run, but I could not abandon Noah.

I shoved Shem into Inka's arms. "Run," I snapped and paused just long enough to be sure she did.

With trembling fingers, I reached for my sling. It took two attempts to put a stone in the cradle. Why had I not continued my practice?

I could see the bear's profile now, its lower lip stuck out in aggression. Noah backed toward the house, casting his gaze down. The bear advanced after him. I could hear the grunts deep in its chest as the whirling sling sliced the air over my head.

When I released it, I knew it would miss its mark. It went too high and *thunked* loudly against the boat-house.

The bear hesitated, assessing the sound's meaning, and I fumbled for another stone. This one hit the shaggy winter hide, hard enough to turn the bear around in rage to face this new aggravation. There were no more stones near me.

Below the creature's small, wild eyes, its mouth gaped wide. One tooth was notched and yellowed.

Death covered the distance to me in three lumbering, measured strides. I heard Noah scream my name from the far end of a long tunnel. My attention centered on the foam that frothed around the huge teeth.

The bear hit me with such force, I could not tell where he struck me. My whole body ached as I flew backwards, landing hard on my back, the breath knocked from me. I could not move or breathe. The black blur followed, straddling me for the kill.

The next moments left me confused. I did not understand why I was still alive, why my throat and guts were not ripped out. I gasped, sucking air into my shocked lungs. It took several breaths to realize the bear lay beside me, a spear wedged deep behind its front leg.

I recognized the pattern of swirl in the wood of the spear. Noah had shaped that wood into a staff, but Yanner had attached the double row of sharp flints to its end, turning it into a spear. It had found its way straight and true to the bear's heart.

The next moment in my memory was of Noah pulling me from the bear's carcass and holding me in his arms, his whole body shaking. Another odd thing—I should have been the one trembling. A kick inside my belly reminded me that I was not the only survivor. Gratefully, I drank sweet air that I thought I would never taste again.

"Na'amah!"

I knew that voice well.

Yanner stood a few paces from us, his face ashen, dark circles under his green eyes. "Is she—?"

Slowly Noah turned to him. I did not know what to expect. He tried to speak, but had to stop and clear his throat. "Thank you," he said finally.

Yanner just stared at us.

"Yes," I said. "I am all right. The baby is all right."

Yanner tottered on an edge. I knew he wanted to touch me, hold me like Noah did, assuring himself by that contact that I was alive.

His arms still around me, Noah said gruffly, "How did you happen to be close enough?"

Yanner looked straight into his eyes. "I have been close enough since . . . I learned what Tubal had done. What happened to Na'amah was my fault. I bear the burden for it."

Noah stared at him for a long time. No one spoke.

Finally, my husband said, "Where do you stay?"

With a shrug, Yanner said, "I sleep in the woods. In different places."

"You've been watching us?" A rumble of anger grazed Noah's voice.

"Yes, but only outside your house. I was watching for Tubal."

"We never leave Na'amah alone," Noah snapped, as if he thought Yanner accused him of not protecting me.

"Tubal is not afraid to come at night with others . . . as you know."

Tension hummed between the two men. I loved both, I realized. If one killed the other, how would I bear it?

Noah stroked his chin for a moment. "I need someone to help me work on this house and Simeon's boat needs repair."

Chapter Forty-Two

That was how it began—a time of peace and happiness for which I thanked the Goddess. I sometimes forgot I did not believe in her.

After the bear attack, Yanner carried Brindle into the house and laid him before Savta. She sniffed and gave me a prickly look that said her skills were not for animals. She always let me know her displeasure when I used her herbs and salves for the sheep or goats or other animals that neighbors sometimes brought.

But she gave only one additional sniff, glancing at Shem's tear-stained face as he watched from Inka's arms, one fist stuffed in his mouth for comfort. "Get me some water and the honey salve," Savta snapped, and got to work on Brindle's gaping wound.

Shem twisted out of Inka's grasp when Savta began to stitch and toddled over to where Brindle lay stretched on a deerskin. Brindle seemed to know we were trying to help him and bore the pain with the dignity animals seem to possess. Perhaps they also do not feel pain like people.

Despite the hands that snatched at him, Shem insisted on going to Brindle's side. He plopped on the floor beside the big dog and took one paw in both hands. He sat like that the entire time Savta stitched. Brindle did not move.

"Will he live?" I asked, echoing the concern on Shem's little face.

She shrugged. "Sometimes they do; sometimes they don't. The Goddess decides." She glared at Yanner, as though daring him to challenge her mention of the Goddess.

Yanner said nothing.

"Well," Savta said, wiping her hands. "You all look as if you were starving. Inka, is that stew ready? Did you add the safflower and hackberry seeds?"

Even the ever-hungry Inka looked startled that anyone would think of eating after such events. "Yes, I did. It's ready."

"Good. These men need to eat and then do something about that bear in our front yard if we don't want tigers and jackals crawling all over us in our beds tonight."

Savta turned the extraordinary into just another task. It calmed us all and we did as she directed. Somehow, it seemed natural for Yanner to follow Savta's instructions after the meal to take from the stores of furs and sheepskins and make his bed in her room. He fell asleep in moments.

"Looks like he hasn't shut his eyes in days," Savta complained, as if it were our fault.

Noah said nothing, but stayed within sight of the house the rest of the day.

When Takunah returned from the market, Inka told him what happened, and he helped Noah butcher the bear carcass, skinning it and cutting the meat into edible portions, which we would dry and later seal with melted fat to preserve. Rather than hang it in nets in the trees, which only kept some predators away, Noah had portioned off a small room in his old house for the purpose, keeping a constant fire burning. We stored grain and dried grass in plastered square bins along the other side of the partition to get Balky and Long Tail through the winter. Noah had made a tiny opening at the roof for a vent. It was hot, even in winter, and if the river water was too icy for even me to bathe, I would go into the room and strip, letting the sweat cleanse me, then scraping my skin with hyssop and pine needles.

Noah would always bury his nose in my neck when I crawled into bed after such a session, declaring me fresh as a tree. This would elicit a laugh and an effort on my part to deliver a playful punch, which rarely landed, as he was ready for it.

The dark circles under Yanner's eyes left his face, and he seemed happy, ready with a smile or laugh, the way I remembered him in our childhood, but sometimes I caught an aching look in his eyes when he thought I did not notice him watching me. When our hands touched sharing some task, it felt as though the skin burned where we had made contact. I was always aware of him, in a way that was different from my general awareness of everything around me.

We spent many days in the hills inspecting the herds and offering advice when asked. More shepherds were asking, and I found a level of respect I had never known. In fact, Inka told me, the tribe was proud to have me and bragged on me to visitors, much to Tubal's annoyance.

I took up practicing with my sling again, trying to compensate for my pregnancy when I grew larger. Yanner asked permission of Noah to touch my stomach, and I believe when he pressed his hands on my rounded belly, his joy equaled Noah's.

My second son, Ham, was born, to my great relief, with less pain and trauma than Shem. He entered the world with no hair at all, to Shem's delight. Shem would stand beside us for as long as we would let him, stroking Ham's smooth head, looking down on his brother with proprietary wonder.

Tubal did not come to visit.

Chapter Forty-Three

It was the fifth moon-cycle of Ham's life that brought Vashti to our door. She was as I remembered her, tall and strongly built, but a few fine lines had etched themselves around her mouth and eyes.

"Na'amah," she said, relief in her voice.

Inka and I stood at once, Inka faster because I had Ham at my breast. Inka rushed to her and embraced her.

"Vashti, what are you doing? Have you come to visit us? I am married—to Takunah, can you believe it? Na'amah has two children now, both boys. Oh, you must be so tired and here I am babbling."

"Yes, come in and sit," I said, shifting Ham to my hip to embrace her.

Savta came in from the meat room. It was only harvest season, but she got cold easily and spent a lot of time in there, "aging with the meat," she said.

"A visitor?" she asked.

"Savta, it's Vashti, the Priestess' daughter," Inka said. "The one who was with us when we were captured. You remember, we've told you about her many times."

"Yes, of course I remember," Savta snapped and turned to Vashti. "Be welcome in our humble home, Daughter. You honor us."

Vashti looked around at the large wooden room. "This is

hardly humble in any sense. I'd heard tale of this boat-house, but didn't believe it. What a wonder."

"Inka, surely we have some beer for our guest? And food?"

While Inka hurried to gather food and drink, Vashti, at Savta's insistence, sat on the bear skin, near the fire, normally Savta's spot.

Noah, Yanner, and Takunah entered, bringing the smell of men who had worked hard. Savta wrinkled her nose.

"We have an honored guest," she said. "Go bathe."

"I've smelled men before," Vashti said with a grin. " I need a bath myself." She eyed Takunah. "Although, it might be the righting of an old wrong to watch this one strip and bathe."

Takunah appeared startled at her bold words and then looked closer. "Vashti? Is that you?"

"Yes, it's me, slaver." She turned her head with a considering gaze to Inka and then back to him. "So, Takunah, you went fishing, and the fish ate you."

Takunah laughed. "That is so." He sat. "It is a fine thing to see you again."

We ate and drank barley beer into the night, talking about our memories and sharing what had happened in our lives.

"You are still so beautiful, Na'amah," Vashti said. It was not like her to give compliments, but she had consumed more beer than any woman I had ever seen.

"It's the pomegranate seeds," Savta said. "I've made her eat them every day since her first-born." She sat up straighter. "What do you think has kept me around so long, eh?" She chuckled. "I've outlived all my sisters . . . and a few nieces, for that matter." She had drunk a little too much beer herself, I decided. "An excellent medicine," she continued, leaning closer as if to tell Vashti a secret. "Pomegranate's the thing for children's worms too. Take that back to the Priestess, my dear."

Everyone laughed, except Noah, who had remained quiet. Worry etched grooves into his face, deepened by the firelight's shadows. Finally, he spoke. "You are welcome in our house, Vashti, for as long as you wish to stay."

"Thank you," Vashti nodded, her cheeks rosy from the beer. "I am fortunate to learn such gems at your Savta's feet."

This caused peals of laughter from Inka and Takunah. Noah did not smile. "I must warn you, if you don't know, that this tribe does not give open worship to the Goddess."

The mood instantly sobered. "Some have not forgotten her," Savta said bitterly.

Vashti put down her cup. "The Priestess knows this, husband of Na'amah."

"Is it friendship only that brings you, then?" Noah asked.

With a sigh, Vashti cast her gaze down and then back at Noah's face. "I wish it were so, but you are correct."

Silence fell into the hole that, only moments before, laughter and smiles had filled. Something twisted in my stomach, and I held the sleeping Ham closer.

"The Priestess is dying," Vashti said, her gaze fixed on me.

Noah's face tightened. Yanner, as though sensing a threat, half rose.

"We are sorry," Inka said.

"Will you take her place?" Savta asked. "There must be a Priestess."

Vashti continued to look at me, and the knot in my gut traveled up into my throat. "When my mother dies, Na'amah will be the Priestess."

No one spoke. Memory-images flashed in my mind: Mother Goddess' Priestess squatting before me in the great cavern, her voice low, pitched only for my ears. *Na'amah, this is not a thing for you to accept or deny. It simply is. Do you understand?*

The mark on my shoulder burned as if it had just met the hot copper triangle. My mouth went dry.

Savta made a choking noise and to my surprise began to cry softly. Everyone turned to her. Savta never cried. Even when the bear almost killed me, she had simply barked orders to everyone.

"I knew it," she said and blew her nose on a scrap of woven grass. "Since the bees came, I knew she was special. Marked by the Goddess, but I didn't dream this—"

"Bees?" Yanner echoed. "What are you talking about?" He turned to me, the firelight catching the gold in his hair. He wore it tied at his neck to keep it out of the way while he worked with Noah, cutting trees and hauling wood. His body had grown more muscular with the work, his face changing from the gentle curves of boyhood. On the rare occasions I went to market, Yanner at my side, my keen hearing caught gossip I was not supposed to overhear:

"It isn't fair. Why does she get a husband *and* Yanner? Men take two wives. It's not proper for a woman to do so."

"Yanner is so smitten, he won't take a wife."

"Did you know he lives with them? Noah is twice her age. I wonder if he shares their bed."

Yanner's voice yanked me back into the present. "What does she mean, Na'amah?" "What is this about bees and the Priestess?"

I had told Noah about the Priestess' mark that he could not have helped but see. No one else, not even Inka, knew all that had happened in the Goddess' cavern.

"Show them," Vashti commanded.

For the first time since Tubal had come unwanted into my house, I wanted to rock and shut out the world. I had put that behind me when I bore children. Shutting out the world meant not seeing my baby toddling toward the fire or a ditch or not hearing him scream because he fell or was hungry.

I laid the sleeping Ham beside me on a sheepskin and drew down the side of my sleeve, exposing my shoulder and putting my life in the hands of those who sat in our boat- house. I did not know what Tubal would do with such knowledge, and I did not want to learn.

"I don't understand," Yanner said. "Who burned you?"

"The Priestess." Vashti sat straight, as she always had, but tension hummed in the tightness of her muscles. "It is Mother Goddess' mark."

"I cannot go," I said.

"Have you felt the tremors here?" Vashti asked.

What I felt was the blood draining from my face. "No."

"My mother believes they are getting stronger," Vashti continued. "She is certain that the Goddess still tries to speak to us. She begs you to come and say the words the Goddess wishes to give us."

I remembered the Priestess wanted me to drink a wine made from berries that had grown in Eden, a drink that had killed two Priestesses.

Shem waddled over to present a cricket he had captured and sat in my lap, as though to claim me. I played with his hair, twining a soft curl around my finger. "No," I said. "I will not leave my family."

Vashti leaned forward, "Na'amah, do this *for* your family, for everyone's family."

I did not believe in Mother Goddess. That the earth trembled was a fact, but the earth shook in stories that stretched back to the beginning of time. People wove meaning into the tale, like the outlandish ones about Mother Goddess forming a woman from clay and Father God breathing spirit into her nostrils. Who could believe such a thing? I looked at Savta, Yanner, and Noah. Well, perhaps many people believed it, but I did not. The day I saw a piece of clay come to life, I would believe Mother Goddess had something to say that she could not make people hear unless they drank poison.

I pulled Shem closer to me, my mouth set in a firm line. I did not like disappointing my friend, who had come a long way to ask me to do something. Once, she had fought two men to give me freedom, but I had also freed her, so we were even. "I am not going to be the Priestess," I said, "and I am not leaving my home to—" Almost too late, I remembered my oath not to speak about the secret rite.

"I knew you were special," Savta said, as if she had only heard the part she wanted to hear. "I knew you were marked by the Goddess. I told you so."

I did not want to be special or to be marked. I only wanted to live with Noah, Yanner, Inka, and Savta in our boat-house, to watch my sheep and to watch my children grow into youths and then men. I wanted everything to remain as it was, and for Vashti to go back to her cave and her mother.

Chapter Forty-Four

When Vashti did go, it seemed the Goddess's spirit left Savta, leaving an old, bent body where my strong grandmother had been. The harvest season turned to winter, the bitterest I had ever known. Harsh wind blew across the Black Lake, icing the trees.

The noises of the house stilled. Shem stayed beside me, watching with an unnatural patience, sensing the wrong that permeated everyone's thoughts. Only Ham acted normal, crying when he was hungry or wet.

Savta stayed in the hot room, shivering despite the pile of furs and skins we wrapped around her or the broths we insisted she eat. She did not want to eat.

"My time has come," she said one evening when I brought her dinner. Her voice was weak, almost a whisper. "I have stayed far longer than was my right."

"No." I stared at her face, coppered by the sun, as if the discomfort it brought me would somehow pay the price for additional moments of her life. It made no sense, but I did it. I focused on the line of her mouth where it dipped on one side.

"Na'amah," she sighed, and the sound left an ache in my bones like a fever. What if this were the last time I would hear it?

"Sing for me, child," Savta said. "I want to hear your sweet voice."

I did not think I could get any sound out of my clogged

throat other than a sob, but I managed to get through her favorite about Mother Goddess and the bee queen.

Inka knelt on her other side. Inka found joy in everything—even wash day, but sadness weighed her shoulders and the edges of her eyes.

I was not sad; I was afraid.

Savta took my hand, her skin brittle and thin as a dried leaf. The wind moaned around the house. She spoke to Inka first. "You have been a daughter to me." Her other hand trembled across the distance between them and settled on Inka's belly. "May the Goddess bring life to your womb."

Tears gleamed in Inka's brown eyes. "You have been a mother to me. Any children I bear will know of your kindness and strength, and I will teach this also to your granddaughter's children and their children, if I live so long."

"Go now," Savta said with a weak nod. "Watch Shem and Ham. Those men have no sense with babies. They wouldn't notice if Shem climbed into the fire until he started screaming."

A smile flickered across Inka's lips and she rose, hesitated as if she wanted to say something else, but then tightened her mouth and left us alone.

"Why did you send Inka away?" I asked.

"I had family things to say."

The chill that resided between my shoulder blades ate its way down my spine. "What things?" My voice sounded distant, as though someone else spoke the words.

Her hand tightened briefly on mine. "I want to tell you about your brother."

I did not want to hear it. "Do you want some soup?"

"No. I want to tell you what I've never told anyone."

I was silent. I had never told her that Tubal, not Yanner, had pierced me in the cave, nor about what really happened during my brother's visit after Shem was born. I only told her that Tubal had threatened me.

"I need a sip of water," she said.

She had taken so little to drink the past few days and nothing to eat, so I was glad to hear that. I supported her head and held the cup to her lips. It was her favorite cup, the one that Aunt Adah had made her, with a playful face on one side of the rosy pink clay. Savta only wet her lips and lay back, resting her shaking hand again in mine.

"Tubal is wrong to abandon the Goddess," she said.

I shrugged. "Many follow him."

"It is great foolishness. Even if she is generous with her blessing and allows the crops to grow and women to bear, without her in their hearts, men will be like fruit without seeds, sterile in their arrogance and pride."

"I know this." I may have had doubts that the Goddess existed in the way Savta believed, but male and female spirit danced entwined. That was a truth as obvious as the need to draw breath.

"Tubal's childhood was more difficult than you can imagine," Savta said, as though explaining his foolishness. "While your mother, my Zillah, lived, she protected him, but when she died—"

"Protected him from what?"

She sighed again, and this time I heard a rasp in her chest that frightened me more than the tiger's growl the night my womanhood came on me in the hills. "Do not talk, Savta," I said hastily.

For a moment, her face tensed with indignation. "I will," she said and her agitation stirred a chain of coughing. I did not protest further, not wishing to disturb her more.

Her gaze sought the far wall where her herbs hung to dry. We had used more than half the stock during the winter, but most of the wall pegs still held fine nets of dried rosemary, sage, mint, lavender and dozens more. In the summer, Yanner and I picked them on our way home from the hills. They did not smell much after they dried, but when we first hung them, they filled the hot room with a delightful cornucopia of scent, especially the hyssop that covered the decay of the aging meat.

"Na'amah," Savta said irritably. "Pay attention."

I realized I had let my thoughts wander, perhaps to keep from acknowledging what was happening.

"After your mother died," Savta said, "your father . . . hurt Tubal."

My brows tightened. "Hurt him? How?" Knowing the time left with her ran through my fingers like water, I forced myself to look at her face.

As if it were suddenly as hard for her to look at mine, she pulled her gaze from me to the herbs. "Your father hurt him the same way that Yanner hurt you in the cave."

The air I pulled into my chest burned. I could not speak for several breaths, trying not to see the images that flashed in my mind. "But he was only six summers when I was born!"

She said nothing, giving me time to absorb this.

There was not enough time in the world.

An old image rose in my mind—Savta bent over a lap of mending, trying to keep the large bruise covering half her face from sight. "I remember a time," I choked. "I think I was five summers. You said you fell into the river and hit your head against a stone." I bit my lip. "It was not a stone, was it?

"No," she said. "It was not. I tried to protect Tubal. I failed."

I heard the old anguish in her voice.

My throat felt full of dust, like Takunah's desert. With a trembling hand, I lifted the cup with the laughing face to my lips, but I could not drink. "If our mother had kept Lamech"—I could not name him 'Father'—"from hurting Tubal, and I killed our mother, it is no wonder my brother hated me."

"He hated," Savta said, "and he loved."

I did not believe Tubal loved me. How could I?

"Forgive him," Savta said. "I tell you this so you can forgive your brother."

She did not know what she asked of me. Yet I found mind-images of Tubal as a boy, seeing with a different judgment the shadows that lurked in his eyes. I had always thought he looked shifty and unreliable, but now I realized he was haunted and frightened and had no one to trust, for no one could help him.

If he had ever spoken of what happened, he would have joined his father in the pit for such an abomination. Yet, at the same time, I saw him leaning over me, one hand on Shem's tiny throat and the other pushed inside me. I saw the hate and lust that burned in him.

My resolve to look at Savta's face broke, and my gaze dropped to her hand, brown-splotched and ridged with veins. The hand that had spun countless threads of wool, mended clothes, scraped furs, made beer, cooked meals, cleaned babies, and comforted children.

It lay cold in mine.

I looked back to her face, and realized I did not have to force a lie to my lips and assure her I forgave my brother.

She was gone.

We buried Savta next to my mother. The ground was too hard to bury her deeply, so we gathered stones to cover her and keep the jackals from digging up her body. I doubted the gods, but I did not doubt Savta's spirit. One moment it had lived in her, and the next her body was empty. She had melted into the air and I breathed her, mixing her with my own spirit and those of countless others who had trod this earth before me. I would live so in my children and their children through time that stretched so far, I could only dimly conceive of it. This thought made me tremble with awe in the brief moment I could hold it, but it was too much to carry, and I let it go, replacing it with the sharp sting of grief.

Noah could only offer me the comfort of his arms.

5521 BCE

PART III

Chapter Forty-Five

For fourteen winters, I did not add to my story. I was just busy living every day, but when I decided to return to it, I remembered all the words and their order.

A green patina stained the copper bracelet Elder Mariah gave me so long ago. Noah's knee hurt, and his back, as well, especially when the weather was damp. He no longer built boats or expanded the boat-house. Its fame had spread farther than we knew the world existed. People still came to gawk at it, travelers with different shades of skin, and many brought gifts of food or items made in their own land.

One such offering, a finely-made copper sickle, so sharp it would cut skin, thrilled Takunah. The copper blade fitted tightly into a wooden handle with a hard resin unlike the older one that only used a flint inset. He said it would make harvesting grains and grass for winter a pleasure. Indeed, he cut so much hay that we needed Savta's entire old room to store it, and we took in several goats to keep them fat and give milk through the winter. We were very wealthy.

Shem and Ham were fifteen and fourteen summers old and had grown tall. Ham was the shorter; he was heavier and slower than Shem. Shem had my love for animals. He began bringing them to me as soon as his chubby little hands could hold something. First, it was insects, then a wounded chipmunk, a baby raccoon, even a deer. He had a way with the dogs that the shepherds admired.

Ham preferred to sit at the teller's feet in the market and hear stories. He pried them from every traveler who came to see the boat-house. Under their father's eye, the boys worked hard. They kept the house's bottom sealed with pitch against the constant dampness of the stream that ran below, and they repaired what time and weather broke or peeled.

Yanner continued to accompany me on herd inspections. People came to us for questions about healing too. Though Savta never formally taught me her skills, I learned more than I thought by listening to her and asking for salves to heal animals, and I was able to help some of them.

I bore another son, Ja'peth, who had celebrated his twelfth summer. Ja'peth was a joy, always trying to please. I was one season shy of thirty-two, an old woman. To live as long as Savta had was a rarity. Unless she gave such a gift to me, my remaining days were numbered, though I felt well and strong. It was good that I had borne all my children. Three was enough. Three healthy sons were a blessing that would bring joy to any woman's heart.

Noah saw deeper into my heart than I.

One evening we sat outside the opening to our sleeping room. This floor was the roof of the second layer.

I liked to sit on the edge and look out over the forest to the hills, especially in the mornings when fog covered the lowlands and wrapped the hills in skirts of mist. At night, my beloved stars spangled the sky and when it was clear, I came out to speak to them. That night, Noah joined me, lowering himself with a painful grunt beside me.

"Do you ever wonder what they are?" he asked, looking up into the sky.

"Every time I see them. They will not be shy tonight because there is no moon. I think I can just reach up and grasp a handful to take inside and light our room."

He laughed. "When I was small, my father lifted me onto his shoulders. He told me to reach as far as I could, grab a handful and then swallow them without looking. If I opened my hand to look, they would fly away, he said."

"And did you?"

"What?"

"Swallow the stars?"

"Of course." "What did they taste like?"

"Like ice that isn't cold."

"You make me laugh."

"That is a good thing," he said, reaching over to pull a piece of hair from my cheek, "since I am too old to do much else."

I knew what he meant. For the past five winters, he had fretted because his manhood had decided it was not interested in fathering any more children. It was not that important to me. Noah held me and stroked my hair and any other part that needed attention. "You are good for plenty," I teased.

He put an arm around me and said softly, "I can't give you Sara."

Hearing her name shook me. I had not heard or spoken it in so long. It felt like someone had reached inside me and wrenched my insides. The strength of my reaction surprised me. "We have three fine sons." My voice trembled.

"Yes. Three fine sons. A man could not ask more of Mother Goddess."

Since Savta's death and the revelation of my status as Priestess, Noah acknowledged the Goddess openly, despite the fact that Tubal railed against her on market days and most people of our tribe spoke only of Father God . . . or maybe Noah acknowledged her because of Tubal's ranting. Maybe that was Noah's way of confronting him, since he had promised me not to kill him. Men were strange creatures.

He pulled me to him. "I love my sons, but I wanted to return your lost child to you."

I swallowed. "Why do you speak of it now," I asked, "when there is no hope?"

He took my hand. "I have thought of this for a long time, and I can only bring myself to say it once." He took a deep breath. "If . . . you were to lie with Yanner and bear another child, I would not be displeased."

My heart raced. I felt certain he could feel my pulse throb in the hand he held. I could not speak for awe of this man's love for me or for the way my breath caught at the thought of going to Yanner's arms after all this time.

"I . . . I will think about it," I said finally.

He pulled me down beside him, so we lay on the deck looking up at the stars strewn across the vast darkness. They did indeed look within reach, but I knew they were not. They were children of the moon, casting fragments of her light with aloof indifference.

We never spoke of Sara again.

Yanner and I were hunting honey when I heard Shem's call. An urgency in it made me grab Yanner's arm.

"Something is wrong!" I gasped.

He was used to me hearing things before he did. Black Dog, a third generation puppy fathered by Brindle, accompanied us. Brindle had spent his last days like Savta in the hot room, too old and stiff to follow us any distance. He died last winter, surrounded by his family. Even Noah had not been able to hide his tears as Brindle's old eyes clouded, and he made the effort to thump his tail one last time.

"What is it?" Yanner asked.

"Shem."

"Where?"

Black Dog's ears pricked. I watched him for a clue to the direction of the cries, as he was better than I at discerning the source of a sound. He stared toward the hills.

This way, I said, gathering the linen skirt to free my legs. Yanner followed at an easy jog. His presence always added a keenness to my senses. Noah was my rock and shelter, the ground from which I grew. Yanner was fire and wind.

I had told him nothing about Noah's offer. I did not trust that we could lie together only to create a child. The two men who meant so much to me had grown into close friends. I treasured that, perhaps more than they did, and despite Noah's words, I did not want to risk destroying it.

"Mother!" Shem's cry was close now, and I thought it held more excitement than fear or hurt, so I slowed my pace. I was not young any longer, my hips a bit wider, my breasts not so eager to point, though I am still beautiful, or so Noah tells me.

"Mother, Yanner!" Shem cried, running toward us down the path that led to the hills.

I stopped and let him come to us. "What is it?"

My suspicions were confirmed when he reached us, dark eyes shining with excitement. He caught his breath. "Come see it. You have to help."

Yanner rolled his eyes. "What kind of animal is it, Shem?"

"A horse," he said between breaths.

"A horse?" My interest pricked. "How? Where?"

He turned and led us to a clearing where a foal stood on wobbly legs near the body of its dam. The young creature was still wet from birth. Its mother must have died before she was able to lick the poor baby's coat.

"We have to help her," Shem said, his anxious eyes on me.

Yanner knelt beside the prone mare, running his hands over her. "I can't tell what killed her. It wasn't a predator." His gaze lifted to the hills and the forests. "But one will be along soon to claim the meat."

I went to the filly, trusting Shem's keen eye to make the discernment of sex. She was unafraid, too young to know there was anything to fear in this new world. She would learn soon if we left her.

Yanner knelt beside me. "Inka would make a fine stew of this tender meat." Both Shem and I stared at him in outrage. He laughed at us. "I'm joking. I know you both better than that."

"How do we get her home?" Shem asked. "She can't walk all that way, even if she would follow us."

"And what do we do with her once we are there?" I said. "She needs milk to survive."

"Grumpy can nurse her," Yanner said.

Grumpy was our milk-goat, Balky's replacement. I sighed, but Shem knew I would try my best to save the animal he adopted. I always did.

Yanner removed the bag he carried and handed it to Shem. To our surprise, Yanner dropped to his hands and knees and crawled beneath the foal, gathered her legs in both arms and stood, hoisting her onto his shoulders. He held the foal's long legs in an attempt to still her panic.

Shem moved to the foal's head and breathed gently into her nostrils, a method I had taught him to calm frightened sheep. She stopped struggling and gave a snort, as if accepting the fact that the world was new to her and who was she to question whether being hoisted into the air by a strange smelling, two-legged creature was normal.

The long walk home was pleasant. The sun warmed my shoulders and the air was light in my nostrils. Shem danced around us, excited about the foal, until I handed him a bowl from Yanner's pack and made him go look for berries.

"Is she heavy?" I asked Yanner when Shem was out of hearing distance.

"Yes."

"Is there some way I can help carry her?"

"Not that I can think of." He grunted and shifted the weight a bit. The foal's eyes were half closed.

"She is weak from hunger." I stroked her still-wet flank. "I do not know if Grumpy's milk will save her. We need first- milk."

"Today is market day. When we get back, I'll go and see if anyone has a goat that's just given birth."

"It does not have to be a goat," I said. "A sheep or ox will do as well, though a goat is best."

We walked in silence for a while and then Yanner said, "Are you happy, Na'amah?"

The question startled me, and I stumbled over a rock embedded in the ground. "What?"

"Are you happy?"

I glanced at him. He was in earnest. I thought about it for

a moment before answering, realizing that other meanings lay
beneath the question.

What should I say? Images flashed in a jumble. In younger
days, I simply spoke truth, and truth was simple. But this
question was not what it seemed. Yanner really asked something
unspoken between us. I knew I could say words that would
change our lives. I could tell him that I wanted to go away
and live with him as my husband. He would do it. We would
betray Noah, abandon my children and be miserable with guilt,
but we would cling to each other with the mystery that flamed
between us.

I could say those words.

Was it a lie then to say I was happy? I thought of my children,
of Noah's strong arms around me, his gentle spirit. I saw us lying
on the deck together watching the stars. He was old now, but
I still wanted to be with him, to be his help-mate. I had given
my oath to be so while we lived. To abandon him would make
me someone I was not, a stranger to myself.

"I am happy," I said.

We did not talk about it again.

Yanner brought home a ewe whose lamb was stillborn and
the foal thrived on her milk. Shem named her Fleet. I wondered
if a horse could be tamed, or if she would revert to her wild
nature when she was grown, the way the baby fox had done.
The raccoon still returned at night to ramble through the house
and tease a disgruntled Bennu.

As she grew, Fleet's rambunctious behavior made us laugh.
She snorted and bucked, constantly trying to get Grumpy to
play with her. The goats ignored her; the sheep ran from her,
but Black Dog, who was still young, adored her and engaged
in chase games. Black Dog was supposed to be watching the
few sheep we now kept near the house, but he could not resist
chasing Fleet. Though she would have complained the loudest,
I thought Savta would have enjoyed watching them. It saddened

me too that she had not seen her great grandsons grow into the fine men they were becoming.

Shem worked with Fleet daily, determined to tame her. "What good is that wild animal?" Takunah said. "She will eat all my winter hay, and we can't even cook her." He glared at me.

"Leave him alone," I said. "If an aurochs can be tamed, why not a horse?" An aurochs was the one animal that was not to be found in or around our boat-house. I had no desire ever to see another.

Fleet was three springs old when the rumblings began. The animals and I knew a quake was coming at the same time, and the people I lived with understood when I clutched my belly and my eyes unfocused with nausea, they needed to make sure pottery was not at risk of breaking. I believed the earth's rumbles affected me because of my sensitivity to sound, as if I heard something pitched so low or high that my ears did not know how to hear it. I thought this because red stars wobbled at the edges of my vision, accompanying the nausea that warned of a bad tremor.

Bennu was also a good alarm. He would move about restlessly and make strange, ducking motions. The tremors became an accepted part of life, more an annoyance than anything to fear, but Inka, who kept up with gossip and news, told me that Tubal was using them to speak out against those who followed the Goddess.

Old Batan had died. Kahor had become Chief Elder, and Tubal had become Elder and head of Hunter Clan. Only those of my generation remembered the days when the Priestess had sent an elder to represent Mother Goddess. Though other tribes still maintained that practice, still more had begun to heed Tubal's words and turn from her worship.

"You should hear him, Na'amah," Inka said, as we sat in the shade of a twisted black pine and picked clean a pile of wool. "He doesn't just talk, his face reddens, and his eyes gleam. Everyone stops what they are doing to listen to him."

"I do not care what he does as long as he leaves me and my family alone."

"Well, people are listening to him. He says Father God is angry at us."

"Why?" I asked, despite my wish to avoid speaking of my brother.

"He says Father God is angry at the Goddess and anyone who gives honor to her, even if it is just in their thoughts."

"Their thoughts?"

"Yes. He says Father God can see their thoughts, and he is angry. He used that to have Mather pitted."

"Mather? He was killed because Tubal claimed he *thought* honor to the Goddess?"

"Yes." She leaned closer, even though there was no one within hearing distance of us and I, of course, would hear even a whisper. "I think it had more to do with Mather gathering a following against Tubal."

I shut my eyes, but that did not dim the image that stayed before them—Nathan struggling naked before the open, freshly dug pit, crying out his innocence and my error in naming the ownership of a ewe. I was not wrong about the ewe, but I saw that pit yawning before him, as if I had opened it in the earth myself.

Chapter Forty-Six

I never thought Shem would look at a woman with the same devotion as his animals, but he did, one of Elizcim's three daughters. Of course, the other boys were not to be outdone, and they convinced Noah to make an arrangement for the remaining two sisters. The three marriages took place together. It was a wonderful day.

My joy was compounded by the fact that they all wished to live in the boat-house. For moon-cycles before the weddings, Shem, Ham, and Ja'peth had worked to build more rooms. The second level now had four rooms, as everyone wanted an upper sleeping room. I was glad we had the third level, the very top for Noah and me. The boat-house was grander than ever.

I was glad. If our sons had taken their brides to their own houses, we would have been left with a very large, very empty house, for all its fame. My sons' wives eagerly took on the duties of the household under Inka's supervision, allowing me more time in the hills.

The only thing that marred my life was Yanner. A sense of wrongness had hovered over me for days, and he had hardly spoken to me. "What is it?" I asked him.

"Nothing."

"It is not nothing."

"Nothing is wrong," he insisted.

"I know you better than I know myself. Talk to me."

"There's no point in talking about anything."

It struck me how selfish and foolish I had been. In my vanity, I believed Yanner stayed with me out of love, but how could he love me? I gave him nothing.

I finished putting salve on the wound of the ewe he held and wiped my hands on the grass. Glancing at his face—a face I knew so well—I forced words from my mouth that I did not want to speak. "I release you, Yanner."

"From what?" he asked gruffly.

It took longer than usual for me to find the rest of what I needed to say, but he was accustomed to the wait. With a swipe at the strand of hair a sudden wind tore free, I said, "I release you from being at my side as if your own life did not matter."

"This is my life."

I shook my head. Storm clouds gathered overhead, casting us in shadow. "Your life has been driven by guilt. It is wrong. You should have a wife, children. Instead, you have . . . nothing." I had allowed it. Now guilt swallowed me.

He turned away, and the world tilted. He would go. He would leave me. I forced an image of Noah into my mind. My children were grown now. They did not need me, but Noah did.

"I don't stay with you because of guilt, Na'amah," he said, his back to me.

I did not believe him, but I wanted to.

That was the moment that the earth ripped apart.

It gave me only a brief warning, a red haze over my vision, and more dizziness than nausea, before the shaking began. The tremor grew stronger. Sheep bawled and scrambled in panic. Dogs barked. Black Dog howled, as though in pain. Just beyond us, a crack opened in the ground, breaking off turfs of grass and tumbling rocks aside. The ground on one side of the crack sank the depth of my hand to my elbow.

It stopped as abruptly as it had begun.

My heart did not. It continued to gallop.

I realized Yanner's arms were around me and wondered whether my heart raced from fear or something else.

"Home," I said. What if something worse had happened there? We hurried back.

All was well. They had only felt a stronger-than-usual tremor. For the first time in my life, I did not want to go to the hills. Yanner encouraged me, thinking I needed to face my fear, but he did not understand. The feeling of wrongness did not subside. It grew.

The animals felt it. Bennu was in constant agitation, stretching his head and flapping his wings, as if he needed to fly away. The goats and sheep milled like waves chopping the shore. Fleet pawed and showed the whites in her eyes for no reason.

No one else seemed to take particular notice. I grew inured to the sickness, though spurts of dizziness hit me at odd times. I felt compelled to do something, but I did not know what. One morning I left the house and went into the forest. Black Dog stayed beside me, abandoning his usual practice of exploring ahead. Yanner followed me out of habit and perhaps concern.

The wrongness there was immediately apparent. I stopped.

"What is it?" Yanner asked.

I glanced at him in amazement. "You do not hear it?"

He shook his head, a slight smile on his face. He was used to not hearing what I did. "No, what?"

I took a deep breath. "Silence."

For once, it took him longer to reply than I. Finally, he said, "I don't hear anything."

I squatted and buried my head in Black Dog's ruff, needing the touch of him. "Exactly. No birds. Nothing."

"What does it mean?"

"It means they are gone."

"Who?"

"The birds. They've gone."

He stared at me and then around, searching for some sign of life. Deep beneath us, the earth trembled.

It was hard to catch my breath. "Something terrible is going to happen."

He said nothing; his breathing filled the space of silence in the world.

Then, finally, he asked, "What should we do?"

His question fell on me, a burden so heavy, I sank to my knees. Why would he ask me such a thing?

My vision clouded with memory-images. Before me, the Priestess sat on her heels in the Goddess' Cave, her gaze intent on me. *You are the Special One we have awaited for many generations. The Goddess has chosen you.*

Savta looked up from her sewing. *You are a special girl, Na'amah. . . . Mother Goddess gave the sign to me.*

And proud Vashti, daughter of the Priestess: *The Priestess is dying. . . . She begs you to come and speak the words the Goddess wishes to give us.*

The old scar on my shoulder burned, and I put my hand there, shaken. Silence filled my ears like doom. "I must go," I said.

Confused, Yanner sat on his heels beside me. "Where?"

"To the Goddess' Cave."

"Why?"

I almost told him the truth, but the words caught in my throat. Yanner would stop me if I told him I was going to the Goddess' Cave to drink poison.

"I think," I said carefully, "that I can learn what is happening."

Chapter Forty-Seven

Noah was not pleased. "I don't understand," he said, limping across the upper deck. "You don't even believe in the Goddess."

Wind rustled my hair. "I do not know what I believe anymore, but I know in my bones that something terrible is going to happen, and I must go learn what."

"If it's about the tremors, that doesn't make sense. The earth has been shaking since I was born and nothing comes of it."

"This is different." I took a breath. "The birds have fled."

"What?"

"It is true. Go to the forest and see if you hear any."

In the end, he let me go. He wanted to come, but he could not walk that far with his bad knee. "Yanner and Shem will go with you."

I nodded. "I leave in the morning."

Inka insisted on coming too. Takunah stayed to oversee the planting. When I woke, Yanner and Shem had packed Fleet. She stamped and tossed her head, but let Shem lead her. "She'll be faster than the ox, Mother. I've been working with her."

I was about to say no, but the word "fast" resonated with my need. "All right, but do not leave her untied for a moment."

Sede, Shem's bride, ran out for one last kiss. Yanner grinned at them, glanced at me and then away.

I had braided my hair for the journey and taken only what I could carry. I knew the trip would take over a moon cycle each way. The tiny horse Noah had carved for me so long ago hung from my neck, and the fleece-lined tiger skin was rolled tight for my bed. It was not the most practical item for that purpose, but I wanted it with me.

Noah took me in his arms. "Come back to me, Little Bird," he whispered. "Life is not worth living without you."

"I will," I promised, my head nestled against his chest. His beard scratched my neck. I wanted to stay there where I could hear his heart beat. What if something happened to him before I returned?

We traveled west along the Black Lake. I saw none of the birds that normally wheeled the sky and dove for fish or floated out on the lake like old women sitting around for a gossip. But the Black Lake lapped the shore as it had done since time began, and when we reached the western edge, its child, the Black River, twined around bends and boulders in a journey to the great cliff wall that separated it from the Salt Sea.

Spells of dizziness assaulted me at unexpected times, sometime followed by a tremor, sometimes not. It felt worse when the ground did not shake, as if something boiled with no escape from the earth's bowels.

Inka tried to keep up my spirits, but I was in a dark mood. I wanted to be alone and yet feared to be. In some ways, it reminded me of my first trek to the Goddess' Cave after I lost Sara. I wondered if that memory lurked somewhere in my mind and tried to pull me down into it, or if it had more to do with the terrible thing I felt looming over us like a boulder about to topple. I believed when it fell, it would start an avalanche. What kind of fool was I to think I could stop that? What was I doing?

When we finally reached the Goddess' Cave, dark clouds hung low, and the wind blew hot and thick with moisture, but it did not rain. We came upon the cliff from the east, never seeing the azure coast that had been our approach so many seasons ago. I recognized the trail down the jagged cliff wall to the Goddess' Cave.

Yanner and Shem chose to camp in sight of the cliff, wanting to be close to the Goddess' Cave. Inka climbed the rocky trail with me. I knew we were watched and was not surprised when two women dressed as warriors barred our path.

"Who are you?" one demanded, placing the tip of a spear in my belly.

"I am Na'amah."

The woman flinched at my name and stared at me. I watched the ground at her feet, aware of every movement she made. If she did not believe me, she might kill me.

Slowly, I lifted my hand and pulled down my sleeve, revealing the mark.

The woman dropped her spear point. "Priestess," she breathed, "you have returned at last."

"Who is head here?" I asked.

"You are."

That startled me, even though I should have expected it. That meant Vashti's mother was dead. "I mean, who before I came?"

"Vashti, daughter of our beloved Priestess, Aruru."

Aruru. I had never heard Vashti name her mother or call her anything but Priestess. "Please, take us to Vashti."

We followed her into the caverns set high on the cliff overlooking the snaking river. It was just as I remembered.

The woman who led us must have whispered to one of the women she passed, because Vashti came to greet us. She wore the fine white linen robes and a necklace of tiny white shells and carried her mother's red-dyed staff. She was older, but still possessed a strong beauty.

"Na'amah!" She greeted me with her arms outstretched. "You have come." Tears filled her eyes.

I was confused. This was not like Vashti. Vashti, the warrior, did not cry. She greeted Inka with warmth. "It is so good to see you both, but especially to welcome you home, Priestess."

"I do not intend to stay," I said.

Vashti looked as if I had struck her across the face. "Then why did you come?"

"Something terrible is going to happen," I said.

"So my mother warned seasons ago." Vashti seemed to take this as a long-accepted fact.

"I have come to drink—" I looked at the women who had gathered at arm's distance around us. "I have come to learn what the Goddess is trying to say."

Vashti's face was grim. "It may be too late."

Her words sucked the air from my chest, leaving a tight emptiness. She spoke truth.

"Still," I said, "I must try."

Chapter Forty-Eight

Under Vashti's instructions, I fasted for three days, only drinking water that Vashti said came from a sacred pool in the cavern's heart. The night of the third day, two silent young women bathed me, much as had happened on my former visit. They anointed me with lavender oil, dressed me in white linen and, and escorted me into the great chamber. Vashti met me at the edge of the stone bridge I had once refused to cross. An image of the water that churned far below made me hesitate, but I could not afford to heed my fears. I focused on the stony ground to keep from looking down and put one foot in front of the other. Weak from fasting, my legs wobbled.

Nausea churned in my stomach and the ground shook, tumbling loose a stone almost from under my feet. We both lost our balance and fell as the earth continued to shake. I could not distinguish the fear in my own body from the bridge's tremble.

"Mother Goddess, protect us!" Vashti muttered.

We crawled the rest of the way across the bridge, even though the ground had stilled. No one waited for us on the far side. A small wooden bowl sat in a depression on a raised stone. Vashti stood, but I preferred to stay close to the ground.

With great care, she took the bowl in both hands and brought it to me. Carvings of a snake with a woman's head wound the outside. "This is very old," she said. "The serpent is a symbol of wisdom because she possesses the secret of immortality, shedding her skin to go from an old life to a new. This cup was hewn of the Tree of Wisdom and the juice in it from the fruit of a vine that wrapped the tree like a serpent. "This is the last of it." Her hands trembled.

"Drink," she said, her voice changing into a soft singsong. "Become the Goddess—Mother, Virgin, Lover, and Blood-seeker."

I thought of Elder Mariah's words to me on my Womanhood Celebration Day. I had asked her how the Goddess could be Virgin and Mother simultaneously, a concept that seemed contradictory to me. *The earth is the Goddess, and the Goddess is the earth*, she had said. Suddenly, this was clear. The earth was constantly Virgin, renewing herself with each uncurling spring leaf, with each newborn creature. She was Mother, giving birth to all new life; she was Lover, offering petal and nectar to bees, painting the bold or subtle passions of color, sound, and smell that enticed and seduced. I thought of the tiger I had killed, of ivory teeth bared in the moonlight, muscle and sinew tight with longing for blood and flesh, the hunger of every creature that required death from another to live. She was Blood-seeker. Yes, the Goddess, the Wisdom, was all these things.

I took the bowl and looked at the thick, black contents. "It stinks."

Vashti smiled. "It does."

"How much do I drink?"

Her smile faded. "I don't know."

"Your mother, Aruru, told me two others had died drinking this."

Vashti nodded, her gaze on my face. "The Earth Mother's gifts are both life and death. They are the same— death and decay begets life, and life begets death."

A swirl of images danced rapidly through my mind: Shem in my arms, still splotched with my body's blood; Noah's eyes filled with me and hope of me; Yanner's despair marked in the slope of his shoulders as we sheltered from the ice storm.

I did not want to leave this world or the people I loved. The

Na'amah who had been here before, suffering from the loss of her first child could not have done this. I remembered everything, yet I knew only vaguely that young woman-girl I had been, as one knows a distant kin. Who was she? Who was I?

I raised the bowl to my lips and drank it all.

The thick liquid snaked like fire down my throat. I gagged at the bitter taste and my nostrils burned. Vashti did not allow me to remain there, but coaxed me to my feet. Dizzy, I stood, leaning against her. "We must go to the sacred pool," she said. She led me to the far side of the raised stone where I was surprised to see a steep path spiraling downward. Burning brands wedged into crevices lit the way. She had to support me as we made our way around the cone of rock. With each step, I seemed lighter, less connected to my feet. I only knew they were there because I could see them moving forward one at a time. I watched them in fascination.

I do not know how long it took to reach the bottom. Time seemed oddly stretched, as when the bear charged me. We could have fallen from the pinnacle of rock, and I would have lived a lifetime before hitting the stone floor. The river surged beside us, calmer here. "We believe it flows beneath the earth and into the Great Salt Sea," Vashti told me, seeing my attention fixed on the water.

I stumbled and she caught me. Inka appeared and helped support me—my dear friend who now looked like one of the plump stone incarnations of the Goddess that Yanner and I had found among the roof-house settlement. Inka gave me the warm smile that had buoyed me through the hardest times of my life. I had insisted that she be with me. Vashti would not allow her to be present at the altar stone, but assured me she would be at my side afterward. She had kept her word, and it was a good thing because my legs would not work right. My mouth and tongue were thick and swollen. Was I dying? The thought did not frighten me as I supposed it would.

We came to a place where a stream from the river diverged into a still pool. Pots of burning oil edged the rough oval, reflecting in the dark water like stars.

Vashti and Inka removed my clothing and lowered me into the cool liquid. They stood on either side as I floated on my back, holding me, though the water took most of my weight.

I left my body.

I slipped from it, not with the effort of a snake shedding its skin, but as easily as I had stepped from the linen dress. Like a leaf caught in smoke, I floated up, looking down at my naked form in the pool between my friends. From above, I saw my body convulse. Vashti held my head, but did not try to restrain me, letting the water cushion my jerky movements.

They held the Priestess. No, I was the Priestess. My thoughts confused me, so I stopped thinking.

At once, I drifted higher, connected only by a shadowy, silver tether to my body. Up, I floated, past the altar stone where I had drunk from the ancient tree's fruit; up to the arched dome of the cavern's ceiling, between the stabbing teeth that hung there. Then, without pause, I slipped through the stone ceiling, into the starry night.

Was I really in the sky or only in a strange dream induced by the poison? I could not tell. I had no skin to feel the night's kiss and test reality. Directly below me lay the surface of the bridge of land through which I had emerged, a grassy plain that grew rockier toward its eastern end. The north edge plunged down into the massive cliff that halted the river's journey through a long gorge.

Higher.

On the south side of the land-bridge, the Great Salt Sea gleamed like a dark sward, cut by countless slivers of white foam, stirred by the earth's shaking to slam into the cliff's side. That side of the cliff was only a man's height above the ocean. Spray glistened the edge of the rock-and-grass plateau that divided the sea and the river.

Up.

The Salt Sea was vast, but far to the west it joined another sea that filled the horizon. Takunah had told us stories, but I did not really believe that anything could be so huge. I felt tiny, insignificant, a whisper on the wind. I fell up . . . into the spangled star-path of the night sky. Glory was the only name I could give it.

In that moment, my hearing awoke. It had never been so keen. I heard the stars crackling, as though they spoke to one another; I heard the sea gnawing the land. I gasped in joy and then pain as the sounds grew louder, and felt a sharp tug on my tether.

I woke in the pool, every part of my skin not in the water covered with sweat. Walls of sound battered me from all sides. "Please," I whimpered, "cover my ears."

They allowed me to sink far enough that the water covered my ears. Vashti remained at my head, while Inka held me at my waist. The instant my ears dipped below the water, the clamor quieted. Silence buffered me from the world.

I sank into it, grateful, and again left my body, lured by muffled sounds that wormed into the silence.

This time I floated down into the water, slipping out into a current that went through me without force, out into the river that flowed along the cavern floor and then dipped into a subterranean passage.

I was the water. I flowed over and around stone, pulled by an elemental force, pushed by the weight behind me.

From the darkness, I spewed into the depths of the Great Salt Sea, somewhere beyond the breakers, into a world of shifting shadows. I flowed, following the ocean's bed along a well-grooved water path.

Down.

A sound that drew me, still faint, grew slightly louder. It was distant, elusive. I followed it like bee-hum. The tether binding me to my body thinned, stretching. Time stretched with it. I had no past, no future. I was aware of myself only in that I sought something. I did not feel the water sliding by or cold or heat or movement, but I knew I moved downward.

At last, the sound grew louder, and I saw indistinct shapes, great creatures suspended in the murky darkness who regarded me with round black eyes. A memory-image drifted slowly to my mind's surface—the River People men talking around the fire, a word for a creature large enough to eat a boat—*whale*. Yes. Whale-song was what I heard, I decided with the conviction of a dreamer. Whale-song woven on the depth's loom, had drawn me here.

The haunting cries were alien and magnificent. They began as deep blue vibrations and rose into mournful calls that stirred primeval, nameless emotions. I could not understand them with my mind, so I let the sound be my blood. I did not try to understand . . . and so understood.

Their cries gave voice to the Mother Goddess's pain deep in her belly, the grinding of mighty forces building to the point where release was inevitable and imminent. The whales heard the earth's ache and gave warning with songs sung in the long ago...and the now.

Below us, the sea floor lurched and bulged into a mountain. Far below, a wound opened in the earth, exposing a line of luminous crimson like blooded light, then it darkened and water roiled, boiling to the surface.

In an instant, I was snatched back to my body, as if the distance I had traveled did not exist. My eyes opened, perceiving an expanse above me and tiny flickers of light surrounding me. I thought they were stars, and that I floated again in the heavens, until I blinked, and realized they were the little burning oil pots.

"Na'amah?" a voice said. "Are you back with us?"

I searched for a mouth to speak and found only a dry, thick place. Briefly, my gaze focused on Vashti and Inka standing over me, their faces creased with concern. "What did the Goddess say?" Vashti asked quickly. "Did she speak to you?"

"I do not know if it was she," I said. My head was still in the water and my own voice seemed as far away as theirs. I closed my eyes, drifting. Random thoughts brushed the surface of my mind like cavorting butterflies.

"Na'amah!" Vashti said sharply. "The Goddess has many

names. What name did she give you? Tell us!"

Her question did not make sense to me. I grasped Inka's hand and forced my eyes open, finding Vashti's face. "Send out messengers," I rasped. "Tell people to go as far as they can from the sea and rivers—" I hesitated, thinking of the flood of my childhood, then adding, "and lakes."

"What will happen?" Vashti asked.

"Inka," I said, clinching her hand in desperation. "Go. Take Shem and go warn the village. Take Noah and my sons to the mountains. Hurry."

"Tell us what will happen," Vashti repeated.

"The Goddess cannot keep what is inside her belly," I said, fighting against the darkness that pulled me down into it. "She will spew it out."

Vashti leaned close. "What is in her belly?"

I summoned all my strength to make my swollen lips whisper the answer to her question.

"Death."

Chapter Forty-Nine

When I opened my eyes again, they burned. A crusty film cratered my lips, and my body responded reluctantly, as if I had aged many seasons. Uncertain where I was, I tried to roll over, and pain lanced my elbows and knees.

Poison, I remembered. I drank poison. Why had I done such a stupid thing? My mind, as sluggish as my body, failed to give an answer.

I must have fallen asleep again, because the next time I woke, Vashti sat beside me, moistening my face with a wet cloth. For several moments, I lay still, keenly aware of life pulsing through me, the subtle throbbing of my heart, the sounds of other people, of water dripping somewhere. I had not expected to be alive. I wondered if eating those mushrooms Tubal gave me long ago had taught my body how to resist poison. Then I remembered and panic slapped me. "Inka?" I croaked, trying to sit up. "Did she go to warn them?"

Gently, but with firmness, Vashti pushed me back down. "Yes, she and your son did as you instructed, and I sent out messengers days ago to other tribes. All but two of the Daughters are spreading your warning."

"Days ago?"

"Yes. You have fought hard for your life, my friend."

I remembered what the earth held and it seemed a useless effort. "You must leave here, Vashti."

"I will not leave the Goddess' Cave," Vashti said with such finality, I did not try to persuade her. I did not have the strength. Exhausted, I fell again into the darkness.

A deep rumbling woke me out of a dream that I lay in the bottom of a boat, looking up into Noah's sky eyes.

Furs tangled my feet. Red edged my vision. I must have rolled or been tossed off the pallet in my sleep. The rumble grew louder and shook the ground with more violence than I had ever experienced. I expected the cave walls to collapse, and I curled into a ball until the world stilled again.

Vashti entered the room. "Na'amah," she said, then amended, "Priestess, Please come with me."

"Where?"

"To the surface of the land-bridge. There is another opening higher in the cliff wall. It is a shorter distance from here."

I wished my mind would clear. Higher ground . . . to be safer? Something niggled in the back of my thoughts. "Inka is gone?"

"Yes, she is gone."

"What about Yanner? Did he go with her?"

Vashti hesitated. "No, he did not."

"Where is he?"

"He waits for you near the cliff."

"Bring him," I said.

"That is not possible. No man may enter the Goddess' Cave."

"I am the Priestess, am I not?"

My strong, valiant friend fell to her knees. "Yes, you are Priestess."

"Then do as I say and bring him. I am not moving from here unless you do."

Vashti took three long breaths before getting to her feet and stepping behind an opening. I heard her voice rise in command and then she returned. We waited. Vashti helped me relieve myself in a corner bowl and combed my hair, as though nothing unusual was happening. Then I practiced walking. Vashti stayed close, supporting me through the dizziness and nausea that might have been from the poison or the earth's silent screaming. The ground shook twice before Yanner came, but the cavern walls held their place.

When Yanner arrived, he strode quickly to me, his face pale with worry, and I knew he wanted to grasp me to him. I wanted nothing more than to feel his arms around me, but Vashti stepped between us, handing Yanner a pack he slung over a shoulder. "Hurry," she said. "Follow me."

We did as she bid. Yanner put an arm around my shoulders and helped me walk. I was weak. At the threshold, two Daughters in white waited. What are your names?" I asked. They were the same young women who had helped me bathe and prepare for the visions, and I had not known their names. It seemed an important thing to know when the world was ending.

"Dianna."

"Rani."

"Follow us," I told them.

We climbed the trail outside the caverns, dodging tumbling rocks, as the ground continued to shudder sporadically. Storm clouds gathered overhead, casting us in dark shadow, but it did not rain. My hands bloodied pulling myself over stones torn from positions they had occupied ages beyond counting.

As we reached the grass plateau at the promontory's top, the cliff groaned and shook, sending us to our knees. Nausea churned inside me and crimson blurred my vision.

From the direction of the far cliff face that jutted over the Salt Sea, a seam opened in the earth, running toward us in a jagged line that sought a path through dirt and rock as water seeks a sloping course. It traveled beneath the knees of one of the Daughters, Dianna, dividing our party.

For a heartbeat, nothing more happened. Then, with sharp cracks and the groan of straining forces that reminded me of the massive cedar's fall, the earth's rent widened into a gouge that swallowed Dianna.

"Sister!" Vashti yelled, reaching out, though she had no hope of stopping Dianna's fall. The widening crack carried Vashti away from us. My mind reeled as the landscaped changed in a single breath. I do not deal well with change, and I froze, wanting to return to my childhood and rock until the world righted itself.

When the ground stilled, Dianna lay motionless at the bottom, beyond our reach. Vashti stared down at her twisted body. I saw I was not the only one stunned and unable to move.

Yanner, Rani and I were now separated from Vashti by the ravine between us; we on the western side, she on the east. Wind whipped our hair and clothes with the furry of a storm, but still no rain spilled from the sky. Yanner recovered first, climbing tentatively to his feet. He looked for a way around the divide, but the fissure appeared to stretch the entire width of the promontory.

Perhaps some vibration or internal instinct warned us, because we turned as one toward the Salt Sea. I was usually the first to notice a detail out of the ordinary, and I pointed at the long smudge above the horizon. It grew as we stared, as though we watched an artist thickening a brush stroke. "What is that?" Yanner asked, squinting into the south wind.

Vashti turned back toward us and stretched her hand over the chasm that lay between her and us, beckoning. "Hurry, the sea comes! There is shelter on this side."

Yanner eyed the crevasse. He and Rani could jump it, but I was still weak from the poison.

"Go on," I said.

He ignored me, his gaze searching the length of the chasm. The dark line on the horizon grew bolder. "I think we can climb down to there," he said, pointing at a narrow ledge a man's length below the ground. It projected out, making a shorter jump to the other side. The wall there presented a steep, but possible climb to the far side where Vashti waited.

"Come," Yanner said, having to shout in the rising wind. "You can do it. It's not far." He leapt down and helped us find footholds, first Rani, and then me. "Don't look down. Stay close to the wall."

Obediently, we hugged the side of the cliff. If the earth shook, we were lost. I made minute gains, fighting the unsteadiness in my grip and balance.

Yanner jumped across the chasm, followed by Rani, who hiked her robe and climbed on her own to the plateau. Yanner waited for me on the ledge across the chasm. Above, Rani and Vashti watched anxiously. I stood on my ledge, leaning back against the rock wall, a solid presence that I knew was only an illusion. It could change shape at any moment and toss me after Dianna. My whole body trembled with anxiety. I knew I should not look down, but the bottom pulled my gaze.

"Jump!" Yanner insisted.

I could not.

A shudder racked the cliff, dislodging me and sending me staggering toward the rim.

"Jump!" Yanner cried again.

Panic flooded my chest, thundering my heart. My feet scrambled against the cliff. I pushed with all my strength, trying to turn a fall into a leap and angle myself toward Yanner.

He caught my arms behind my elbows, dragging me up and over the edge, and we staggered backward onto the far wall. I did not think I could move again, but Yanner took my hands and placed them on each stone, moved my foot into a crevice, and pushed.

I concentrated on each movement, trying to apply the same concentration to this task as when I rocked to shut out the world. I focused on the muscles in my arms and legs, willing strength into them.

"Hurry," Vashti yelled again. She and Rani reached down for me and helped me over the edge and up onto the promontory. Yanner pulled himself up and stood. I followed his gaze out over the Salt Sea. The ridgeline in the sea had grown into a massive wall, looming larger as it rushed towards us with a hiss, filling my mind with the image of a coiling green serpent preparing to strike. Already several times our height, it grew higher as it approached the strangely calm shoreline.

Vashti and Rani tried to pull me toward an alcove of rock that faced to the west and would offer a refuge. Dizziness forced me to lean against Yanner, and then my legs gave way. "I cannot,"

I muttered, my ears full of the green hiss. Yanner snatched me into his arms and ran.

Over his shoulder, I watched the water mountain approach, gathering marbled swirls of green-grey, feeding an insatiable hunger, until it towered over us, a living creature of foam, seaweed, and flotsam. Even the wind changed directions, sucked into the wave. For a long moment, the water beast paused, surveying its prey.

Then, as it breached the line of rocky shore, an edge curled over into a majestic arc of white foam that rippled down its length. Like a knapper's strike, the wave's blow against the promontory widened the crack already broken by the earth's writhing.

The air was salt and spray. The earth groaned as it split. Stumbling, Yanner ducked into the rocky recess, Vashti and Rani just behind, as the surge of water raced toward us. We backed into the alcove as far as we could go, wedging into crevices and hanging onto each other. Through the wide entrance, we watched, helpless, as a roiling mass of water and foam churned boulders and chunks of earth with the same disregard as wind scatters autumn leaves. I clung to Yanner, unable to breathe. Cold water swept into our alcove, rising quickly to our knees and then chests. I managed a gasp of air before it swept over my head, plunging me into a world of dark chaos. My body lost the anchor of the earth's pull, but Yanner's arm kept me close. Tendrils of my hair feathered my face and neck. All was muffled darkness.

Without warning, the water suddenly receded, sucked backwards as though an even larger beast devoured it. Yanner worked us out of the narrow opening where he had wedged us, and we stepped out onto the promontory.

Only then did we see the second towering wall of water that had hidden behind the first. Yanner grabbed me and spun me around, trying to shield me, but my vision blurred crimson, and the earth convulsed in a mighty heave, spilling us to the ground in the lee of our shelter.

Less than a stone's throw before us, the fault line that now split the promontory ripped apart. Chunks of stone and earth the size of an entire village tumbled into the chasm.

Before I could absorb what was happening, a white roar encased me. Above us, the towering wave curled along its length, as its brother had, and smashed with unreserved fury into the broken land. I buried my head under my arms. Wind and spray battered us, but we were not swept away.

Cautiously, I lifted my head from my arms. The water's force had channeled into the chasm that only moments before was the Goddess' Cave.

The Salt Sea followed the wave's path, gushing through the crevice and over the cliff into the river below with a thunder that filled my body. It was difficult to believe what I was seeing. The barrier that had stood for all time between the river and the Great Salt Sea was forever breached.

I remembered my vision when I had floated in the sky, and knew the Black Lake could not hold the vast sea. My mind locked on the cataract, caught in the water's froth and tumble. Yanner turned me away, and only then did I realize he had been yelling my name. I blinked and returned to the world.

This time when I looked at the water, it did not capture me. I could think. A nervous glance over my shoulder confirmed that there were no more water walls coming at us or even smudges on the horizon. My stomach had calmed, bringing hope that the earth would not shake again, at least not for a while.

Only then did I realize blood trickled down my leg where a stone outcropping had cut me. It did not seem worth staunching.

My gaze returned to the sea rushing through the passage. How long before the new sea drowned the valley I thought so vast? Over time, the flow would eat away at the land-bridge, widening the fissure even further. The Black Lake and its rivers would swell and swell and go seeking new land to cover.

Fear clutched my heart again, but not for myself.

"Yanner, take me home."

Chapter ✦ Fifty

Lightning lanced the sky throughout our journey back, but the clouds held their grey bellies, and the land was drier than I had ever seen it. We traveled east along the route we had come. The sound of the cataract behind us made talking difficult. It was an intense, yellow light in my mind and made my head throb. As the days passed, the bulging shoreline overflowed its banks and crept slowly toward us, forcing us to adjust our path.

My gut gnawed with frustration at our pace and lack of supplies. Yanner had left Fleet and our pack at the now deserted village. We had not found Fleet there and assumed the villagers or women warriors had taken him to carry their packs.

As we put distance between the rent in the rock cliffs, the constant thunder of rushing water muted. Long after Yanner ceased to hear it, however, the sound still rumbled in my chest.

We were able to travel some of the way without stopping to hunt, living on the provisions that Vashti had scrounged together for us and placed in the pack she had given Yanner. Little remained of the Goddess' Cave when we left, and I knew the sea would continue to chew it away. Vashti had refused to leave with us. Rani stayed with her. I did not know what they would do or what would happen to them.

At first Yanner had to carry me parts of the day, but gradually I regained some of my strength. After half a moon- cycle, we found Fleet. She apparently had broken free and headed home.

Her rope had tangled in branches, forcing her to a halt. I had no idea how long she had been caught, but it could not have been too long, or some predator would have found her. She neighed in relief at seeing us. A few of our provisions were still strapped on her. "I don't like to handle her," Yanner confessed, so I kept your things packed there."

"A blessing you did," I said, stroking Fleet and speaking softly to calm her. A thought came to me as I rubbed her sweaty neck.

"Yanner, when I escaped from the men of the River- People, I rode an aurochs."

"Yes, I remember," he said, testing the straps on Fleet's far side.

"I think Fleet would let me on her back."

His head jerked up. "Are you moon-crazed?"

"Well, she trusts us, and she carries weight on her back. Why not?"

"Well, because . . . because—" he floundered.

"I am afraid we will not get back in time," I said quickly to reinforce my position. "What if no one believed Inka? Who would believe such a thing?"

"The fishermen will see the lake is rising," Yanner said. "They will feel the ground shake."

"The ground has been shaking for a long time, and they do not know why the Black Lake rises. They may think it is just raining somewhere. They will not realize that nothing can stop it. I must get there as quickly as I can."

Yanner stared at me.

"You can move faster without me," I pressed. "If I ride, you will not be far behind, but if we continue at my pace, it may be too late."

"It's too dangerous."

I laughed. "Yanner, you are not thinking well. The water will drown everyone if they do not believe and leave. We cannot let that happen. You can ride ahead, if you wish."

He shook his head. "I'm not leaving you behind."

"Then I must."

Reluctantly, Yanner agreed. I gave him my tiger skin and we divided the meager amount of provisions we had. "I will be home in less than a handful of days," I said confidently.

Yanner shook his head. "I will find you on the trail with a broken neck."

I shuddered, remembering Elder Mariah.

Fleet was more curious than afraid when I climbed onto her back. I tied provisions onto my own back. We left a rope around her belly behind her front legs, and I wedged my feet beneath it and took the rope's end that looped around her nose and behind her ears. With a snort, Fleet craned her neck to sniff my foot and then shook herself as if I were a fly she needed to dislodge. I almost fell off before we had moved a step, but I grabbed a handful of her mane and stayed on, forcing a smile for Yanner.

After a moment, realizing no one held her, Fleet took a tentative step and then another. I was counting on her desire to go home. I did not try to use the tiger skin to guide her, as I had the aurochs. She had never been skittish of the tiger skin, possibly because she had associated the smell with me since she was a foal, or maybe it had lost much of the scent after all these seasons. To counter the lurch of her movement, I squeezed my legs tighter around her belly.

This was a mistake. Startled, or perhaps trying to escape the pressure, she broke into a trot. My teeth clattered together and every bone in my body shouted in protest. Too late, I remembered how painful the wild aurochs ride had been. I clung tighter, determined after all my protestations not to fall off within sight of Yanner. In response to my clench, Fleet broke into a gallop, which was faster than the aurochs', but easier to ride than the jarring trot. It was fortunate there were not many trees on this stretch of land, or Yanner's prediction would have proved true very quickly. I leaned forward to put my weight closer to her, hoping it would stabilize my balance. Again, Fleet increased our speed. I could do nothing but try to stay on until she tired. Without the ropes holding my legs, I would have fallen a dozen times. I realized, however, that if I did lose my balance enough to fall, regardless of the ropes, I might be dragged. I would not survive that.

At last, Fleet tired and her pace became a fast walk. My trembling legs could not hold their clench against her sides, but that turned out to be good, because she slowed even more. I rode all day, jumping off only to relieve myself or to drink from a stream. Fleet snatched at grass or leaves, and I ate from the store of the dried meat Yanner had saved for me. I had to find a stone to mount her again. Many times I breathed a thank you to Shem for his work with her, because she stood very still whenever I did this.

We rode this way for several days. Yanner could have covered the same distance on foot as we did at a walk, but I, still weak from my ordeal in the Goddess' Cave, could not have. I was terribly sore and had to force myself to climb back on Fleet each morning. I learned to guide her a bit by pulling her head in the direction I wanted her to move. It took constant attention to anticipate which way I needed to go in time to make sure the rope was on the needed side. Then I realized I could tie the end behind her chin and pull either way at a moment's notice. It was a great improvement. In general, however, I let her find the way, confident that we were headed home, even though I couldn't see the stars.

Grey clouds continued to gather, blocking them at night and the sun in the day. I had never seen so many days of such without rain. At last, I reached a familiar river. I had to cross it here, knowing this was the shallowest part. Even so, it was far wider than I had ever seen it, and the waters churned. My heart pounded at the sight of the current. As always, when I saw rushing water, images from the flood of my youth returned—bodies swirling like flotsam against Noah's thighs. I thought it odd that memory images of my childhood had more power over me than the violence of the water wall which I had experienced so much more recently. The mind was strange.

Deliberately, I found a quiet eddy and bathed, washing the sweat and horsehair from my sore thighs. I did not know if water held a spirit or not, but I spoke to the river, asking that we be friends so she would allow me safe passage across her. I cupped water in my hands to drink, but spewed it out.

Salt.

Normally, this river flowed into the Black Lake, but the volume of water pouring through the breach at the Goddess' Cave had reversed the river's flow. The Black Lake was becoming the Black Sea. Fear struck me anew with the brackish taste, but it was fear for my family and stronger than my terror of the rushing water. I led Fleet through the shallowest spot I could find, but even so, we both quickly lost contact with the ground. The current swept us aside like a passing thought. I kept hold of the rope, but my weary legs did not respond as I ordered them to, and several times I went under. The poison and exhaustion of my journey had taken its toll on me.

Desperately, I hauled myself along the rope, concentrating on moving one hand over the other, until I came close enough to grab Fleet's mane and let her pull me. When we reached the far side, I did not have the strength to maintain my hold, and the rope slid from my raw hands. I crawled as far from the water as I could and collapsed.

When I opened my eyes, I lay still, momentarily confused by the size of a honeybee that crawled along my arm, so close I could see the dark lines in the transparent, saffron wings and the fine, golden hairs that furred its body. It moved hesitantly on jointed legs, the large, dark eyes full of mystery. I could kill it with a slap of my hand.

Despite my haste, I watched it until it took wing. Savta would say it was a message from Mother Goddess, but I saw it only as a honeybee. I granted its life a reprieve. There was enough death to come.

The river had crept up behind me and risen to my thighs. Shaken, I forced myself to stand and headed home. Fleet had abandoned me and I was on my own. The village lay between me and the boat-house. I hoped to find it empty, hoped Inka and Shem had made it back, and Inka had spread the message to flee. Surely, Noah had heeded me and left with our children and their families, but I had to make certain.

When I reached the village it was not deserted, but fewer people than I ever remembered were about. The pottery workshop was empty and to my dismay, Mother Goddess' temple lay in ruins, the small goddess that had watched over the village center every day of my life strewn in pieces.

The low-hanging clouds had darkened, sending the afternoon into gloom. A man nearby turned his head. I recognized Sunnic in the square and turned to slip away, but he saw me and cut me off. "Na'amah, the troublemaker, herself. Where are you going?" he said loudly, his hand rough on my arm. Then he looked up and called over another of Tubal's friends. "Here, come take her other arm. She's wily, for all her size."

I did not struggle. I was too tired and there was no point in it. They brought me before the raised stone and sent another man to bring the Elders, only two now—Kahor, head of Hunter Clan, and Tubal. A crowd gathered. They were not happy with me.

"My brother and his family left because of you," one man yelled in anger.

Others spoke up with similar complaints.

Another said, "What if she is right? The river's flow has reversed and it's rising faster than I've ever seen it, though we've not had a drop of rain!"

Kahor and Tubal stepped up onto the flat stone. Kahor struck it with his spear-staff and the crowd quieted, though still muttering among themselves.

"Step forward, Na'amah, wife of Noah," Kahor said. You are called to judgment."

Both men released me, but stood near. I stepped forward. "I have traveled far. I wish bread and water first, as is my right."

Kahor nodded. "It is your right." He lifted his hand and someone brought me a hunk of dried bread and a skin of water. No one spoke while I ate and drank. I made it last as long as I could, trying to garner my strength and my thoughts. Finally, I could draw it out no longer. I returned the water skin empty and faced my judges.

"You are accused," Tubal said, "of spreading fear in the name of one who is not worshiped by this tribe."

I knew speaking ill or disbelief would incur tribal judgment, as they would believe my words might bring impotence or disaster, but I did not understand why people believed Tubal that Father God wished to dominate or eradicate the Goddess. The Father God I had learned about at Savta's knee had never been jealous of the Goddess. Father Sky embraced the earth and sea. How could the sky exist without the earth, or the earth without sky? I was taught they needed and balanced each other; and my tribe had always respected strangers' gods . . . until Tubal twisted things.

I looked around. Men, women, and children stood watching. Most I had known all my life or were related to people I knew. They were doomed if I did not make my case, yet making it would doom me. I had not even considered this possibility and yet, how could I not have foreseen it?

A young girl I had never seen slipped to my side and tugged on my dress. "Are you Na'amah? The Tiger Lady?"

Aghast, her mother snatched her away.

"Tiger Lady?" I echoed.

"You live in the boat," the girl said over her shoulder. "My aunt told me."

"Hush, Lily," the older woman snapped, but looked up with defiance at Tubal.

I made the connection then. It was said that the Goddess, in her form of mountain deity, rode a tiger to show her strength. Telling children stories about a "Tiger Lady" was a secret way to teach reverence for Mother Goddess when it was unlawful to speak her name. I hardly qualified as an embodiment of the Goddess, but I realized that I might have an influence with those who kept the Goddess in their hearts. I had to try to give them a chance to survive.

"I am the Tiger Lady," I said loudly, a lie as bold as when I had claimed to be the River People's goddess. "And I have come from the Goddess' cave. Earth Mother spoke to me and warned me that a great flood comes. She cannot hold what strains to escape her belly." That was truth.

I took a deep breath. "You have heard her tremble with the effort. Flee to the mountains. Take your families and your possessions and go!"

Tubal's face flushed a deep crimson, and his knuckles whitened where he gripped his staff. He stepped forward. "Liar! Blasphemer! It is Father God who is angry, angry at those who challenge his supremacy. Like you!" He pointed his staff at me. The point held a single piece of flint, sharpened to a fine edge.

A confused muttering spread through the crowd, then someone shouted. "Pit her! She's a strange one. No wonder Father God is angry."

Another cried, "No! Who will keep track of the herd lineages?"

"I've known her since she was a child," an old woman cried. "Knew her mother and Savta. She's done nothing wrong."

"You would risk Father God's anger?" Tubal shouted. "You would let us all die because of your stubbornness and ignorance?"

At that moment, the earth shook, sending many, including me, to their knees. Dust clouded the air. Tubal used the staff to keep his balance. My vision clouded. The quake's timing sealed my fate.

"Do you still doubt?" Tubal cried. "Father God has spoken. Na'amah, wife of Noah, is condemned to the pit."

"Na'amah, *sister* of Tubal," I said, raising my head to look at him.

His eyes were frosted beyond the reach of claims of family blood . . . or mercy.

Kahor stamped his staff. "Let it be so."

I tried not to tremble as they stripped me of clothing. Some might still believe, I told myself, so I must clothe myself with the Goddess' dignity.

"Look,"—my keen ears heard a whispered voice— "that mark on her shoulder. It's the mark of the Priestess." I closed my eyes and thought of the little girl who had named me Tiger Lady. For her sake, I must appear brave. Maybe her mother or aunt would still think to follow my words, even after I was thrown in the pit . . . even when I was dead. Besides, to act otherwise would not help me.

Sunnic and another man took me to the edge of the older pit, the one that had been in the village square all my life. Sunnic moved his hand so that it briefly cradled my bare breast. "I haven't forgotten," he whispered, "how it felt to hold you against me that night in the cave."

I stiffened, but could not think of anything to say. His efforts to demean me seemed absurd when the next steps would bring a slow death. The bread and water I had consumed would only make me suffer longer.

The pit drew closer, though I had no memory of moving toward it. The hole loomed, a dark, hungry mouth. Sunnic stopped at the edge. My breath came in shallow pants. I could no longer pretend to be brave.

I did not have to. Without another word, Sunnic pushed me.

Instinctively, I put out my hands to protect my head, but was not prepared for the force of the impact. My stunned body forgot how to breathe. I decided to cheat my judges of a lingering death, but after a long moment, I gasped and gulped. Air and life filled my lungs, heedless that they were not wanted.

Everything hurt. I must have broken all my bones and was certain I would not be able to move, but after several breaths, I pushed myself from the ground's embrace. Bruised clouds still blanketed the sky. As was custom, no one came to speak to me or even look in the pit. I no longer existed to the tribe. They would not hear my cries or pleas.

When my vision adjusted to the shadows, I realized that I was not alone. With no apparent fear of me, a rat picked flesh from a bone in the corner, a human bone, one of many. I scrambled as far from it as I could and sat, huddled against the dirt wall, shivering from the cold and my fear. For the first time since I had birthed a child, I grasped my knees and rocked, a song struggling out between sobs. It was a shepherd's song, a simple one that had brought comfort when children mocked me or adults lost patience waiting for me to speak.

My hills, my home,
Mother mountain's bone,
Beneath the eagles' searing cry.
Here, I lie.

My hills, my home,
Green grass; grey stone
Beneath the stark, star-sky.
Where I will one day lie.

In the darkness behind my eyes, I saw the brown sheep grazing the lush, spring meadows. Father God finished his sun journey across the sky, touching the Black Lake. His light pooled the hollows between hills with an orange haze that suspended time, like a breath never exhaled.

I found a small peace and fell asleep.

The next morning I awoke with dust in my mouth, though the air was sticky with moisture, pricking sweat along my brow. Above, the sky still hovered, bloated clouds dark and swollen. At least, the rat had disappeared through one of the several small holes that pocketed the walls.

The day passed slowly. I rocked and dreamed, and hoped Noah, Inka, Takunah and my children had escaped what was to come, and that Yanner would make it to the mountains. I did not sing any more. My throat was raw with thirst. I began to wonder if any of the bones were sharp enough to use to cut myself. It would only hurt for a short while. I put my head in my hands and wept, pitying myself, even though it wasted my body's moisture.

Chapter Fifty-One

That night I watched for the moon to rise, but the heavy clouds blocked her light. No stars to swallow tonight. I prayed for Mother Goddess to sweep me into her night sky, where the spray of stars netted the darkness. I prayed for her to take me where the great sea creatures hung in the shifting, watery shadows and sang of the earth's beginning and end. I hoped my death would reveal such marvels that Eden's poison had held. I wanted the gods to be real. I wanted to see them and ask them why they were destroying the world.

I slept only fitfully through the night. The next day hunger gnawed at my belly, a fierce beast, but one matched and then overcome by thirst. I dozed and dreamed of cutting Fleet's throat and drinking her blood. Would that initiate me into Hunter Clan? My thinking grew wobbly. I was not sure what was real and what was only in my mind or my memories.

I did not want to prolong my death, but thirst drove me to take one of the bones, a broken leg bone, and dig in the deepest corner of the pit, where the ground seemed cooler. I dug up to my elbow before finding moisture. My heart beat faster. All I could think of was the taste of water on my cracked, swollen lips. The ground was softer now, and I scraped deeper, until I had to rest. I closed my eyes for what I thought was only a moment, but realized when I opened them again that the sun had moved a fist's distance across the sky.

Water had seeped into my hole, enough to cup in one hand. I savored it. It gave me strength to dig deeper, but the water refused to fill my well any faster. Finally, exhausted, I stopped digging and resigned myself to wait. That seemed to be the only meaning left to my life—waiting for a tiny amount of dirty water to collect in a hole.

That night I had almost drifted off when I heard voices, angry voices. Yanner! My heart leapt. He must have run day and night to be here. Hope rose in me. I did not want to die in this awful place, but what could he do? The elders had passed judgment. Voices grew loud enough that I could hear the words.

"What have you done with her?" Yanner demanded.

"She was pitted," my brother said calmly. "Come and see for yourself."

After a few moments, the sudden light of a torch blinded me, and I put up a hand to shield my eyes.

"Why?" Yanner said. "She came to warn you. Don't you understand? A terrible flood is coming. The Great Salt Sea is pouring into the Black Lake. I've seen it."

"That was the same lie she told," Tubal said. "Do you also claim this to be a message from the Mother Goddess?"

"Do not, Yanner!" I called. My voice cracked. "He will pit you too."

Yanner hesitated. I could see him now, behind the flicker of the brand Sunnic held. "You've made a mistake, Tubal. She's no threat to you. For the sake of our childhood, let her go."

"That's not possible. It was the elders' judgment. Besides, if the calamity you claim is truly coming, it doesn't matter how she dies, does it?"

"Please, Tubal. Get her out of there, and we'll go away. I promise. I'll take her away, and she'll never speak a word about the Goddess to any of the tribe."

"You always wanted her, didn't you?" Tubal said, stepping closer. "I tried to give her to you when we were young, when we were Hunter Clan together, but you couldn't do what was necessary. I had to do it for you."

I heard the dry scrape of Sunnic's laugh.

"You did nothing for me," Yanner replied, his voice low. There was no more pleading in it.

"Well, I will do this for you. I will give you Na'amah once again."

Lightning veined the sky.

In the sudden, intense light I saw Sunnic, behind Yanner, draw back his hand. It held a rock.

"Yanner!" I yelled in warning, though my parched lips split with the effort. With a Hunter's instinct, Yanner ducked under the blow. Now I could only see what the flickering torch revealed. Sunnic swung again, but Yanner blocked it with his arm and twisted, taking Sunnic down. I lost sight of them as they rolled from the pit's edge. The torch light disappeared, gutted, I assumed, by their bodies.

Darkness.

Illuminated in a flash of lightning, they appeared again. A knife hovered over them, but I could not see who held it. They moved closer to the edge, clinging to one another.

Darkness again.

Lightning: Sunnic was astride Yanner. They wrestled for control of the knife. Thunder rumbled.

Darkness.

Someone groaned. Blood-smell sank down to me, a tangy, cloying scent I knew well.

In the next burst of light Yanner pushed Sunnic's body aside and rolled to his knees to stand, but Tubal's staff met his head with a dull thwack, spraying blood. The blow carried Yanner over the edge, into the pit.

"No!" I screamed and stumbled to his side. His head bled. I tore his linen tunic to press against the wound, though it might have been a kinder fate to let him bleed than face what the pit offered. The blow had hit him in the back of his head. If it had struck him on the side, it would have surely killed him.

I glared up at Tubal, who I sensed stood above us, wrapped in foreboding silence and darkness.

"Savta asked me to forgive you," I managed in a hoarse croak. "But I never will. Never."

"It's your own fault," he said coldly. "It always was. If you had been put out to die, as you should have been, none of this would have happened."

He turned away. I could not see him, but I heard the uneven footsteps I knew so well.

With trembling fingers, I pulled Yanner's water skin from his waist and drank, savoring the sensation in my mouth and throat, then I cradled Yanner's head in my lap, rocking him as though he were my child. After a few moments, I adjusted enough to the darkness to see that he opened his eyes. I choked back tears. "You are alive," I gasped.

He sat up and put both hands to his head. "I have a terrible headache."

My sob turned into a halting laugh.

One hand dropped to his bare chest. "That was my best tunic."

I hiccupped. "You are trying to make me laugh," I accused. "Like when we were children."

With tentative tenderness, he touched my cheek. "Is that such a terrible thing?"

I took a breath. "It is my fault you are here. You could have escaped to the mountains."

"I would never leave you."

I started to cry again.

"No," he said, taking my head gently in his hands, his thumbs brushing away the tears. He was so close, I felt his breath on my lashes. My heart stuttered. I did not move. I could not.

"Na'amah," he said, a world of longing in the word. "Look at me."

My breath came in shallow pants. I lifted my gaze to his as light pierced the sky. Even in the white glare, his eyes were shadowed, but I knew their color of spring grass as well as I knew every line of his face and mouth, the slope of his shoulders, the shape of his chest. I closed my eyes. We did not need to speak of the fire that burned between us.

We were going to die, here in the pit or drowned in the gods' rage or indifference, but Yanner held the small distance between us. "I would not dishonor Noah," he said, his voice a deep rasp.

I took another gulp of air, as though I were already drowning and closed the space between us. His arms encircled me. My cheek lay against his. I tasted the salt of his skin and forgot my belly's hunger. We both trembled. "Noah has blessed this," I whispered.

That was when the rains began.

The sky released its hoarded burden in large, warm drops, as Yanner's mouth found mine. Thunder shuddered through us and lightning stabbed with intermittent light. Like the sky, we had held back what we felt for so long—now we held back nothing. The eager, dry ground quickly soaked. Naked, I lay back in the wet earth, reborn as Savta's story of Mother Goddess shaping First Woman out of mud. I was that primeval woman, created by the Goddess, and I was the Goddess, creator.

It was dawn and still raining when I awoke, wrapped in Yanner's arms. I lay still, absorbing the sensation of the rain's patter on my skin, his leg's weight on my thigh, and the rise of my chest that lifted his arm with each breath. The golden hairs along the solid length of his chest appeared with the same clarity as the bee that had visited my arm. In that moment, I did not care that we were going to die. Death comes to everyone, and no one can predict the time. I was at peace to be in his arms, even at the bottom of a mud-filled hole.

Yanner stirred and rolled to his side, brushing a filthy strand of hair from my eyes. He smiled and kissed my forehead. "Beloved," he whispered. "I can die now."

A shiver ran through me at how close our thoughts matched.

"Well," a voice above us said. "I see you have finally taken what I gave you."

Tubal stood at the pit's edge in the gusting rain. Yanner

reached for the soaked remains of his tunic and helped me into it. I trembled, suddenly aware that the air was much colder.

"Are you chilled, Ugly One?" Tubal taunted in the same tone he had used when we were young. He tossed a bundle into the pit. "I think you dropped this, Yanner."

"My tiger skin," I said in surprise. I wanted to untie it, but hesitated. Why would Tubal do me a kindness?

Yanner and I got to our feet, and he reached first for it. I started to speak my question and then shrugged, my teeth chattering. He unrolled it, keeping the fleece side down, out of the rain, so it was dry and warm when he pulled it around me. He tied it with the cords Savta had cleverly sewn into it.

Tubal hefted his staff, the staff of a Hunter Clan Elder, which meant it was a spear.

"Good," he said. "You will die as Tiger Lady."

"That makes no sense," I said, my heart hammering, despite my recent peace with death. "What difference does it make how I die?"

"Because," Yanner answered for Tubal, his eyes narrowing, "the rivers have flooded and the waters of the Black Lake creep toward us. Because he is afraid the people will see you were right, and they will come to pull you out of the pit and listen to you."

I stared at Tubal. "And you would no longer be the voice of Father God," I finished. "That is why you will kill me, is it not, my brother?"

Tubal's hand tightened on the raised spear, but he said nothing.

"You will stain our family again with your sister's blood, Tubal-Cain." I glared at him, because I could do nothing else.

"So be it." Tubal's arm drew back farther, slowly, as if he moved under water. I saw the muscles of his arm tense, heard the short grunt of effort as the spear flew from his hand. Tubal was Hunter Clan. He would not miss.

As my hands rose to shield my heart, Yanner leaped between me and the spear's strike. The flint-edged blade pierced him through the chest with such force the tip emerged through his back.

He crumpled at my feet.

I stared down at him, unable to comprehend what had happened, even though it had occurred right before me. I stood numbly in the pit—cold, pelted by rain, wrapped in my tiger skin and Yanner's torn tunic.

My knees buckled and I sank onto them in the mud, reaching for Yanner. He turned and groaned, the sound piercing me like a spear through my own heart.

"Na'amah," he whispered, his hand groping for mine. I grasped it in both of mine, tightly to make certain he would feel it, would know I was beside him.

"Yanner," I gasped, my tears mixing with the sky's. "I am here. You are not alone."

I heard the same rattle in his chest that had marked Savta's last moment. His eyes were bright, but they focused just beyond me. His lips parted, but no sound emerged. His body arched with the effort to speak, his grip crushing my hand.

"Live," he whispered.

The strength faded from his hand. His eyes dulled, as Savta's had, replaced with a glaze that meant his spirit had gone where hers had gone, that I must now find him in the brush of wind on my cheek, in the cold light of stars, the warmth of sun. I did not want him that way. I wanted his arms, his smile, the way he looked at me as if I were sun and stars and wind.

I lifted my head. Tubal stood at the pit's edge with clenched fists. I thought he might jump down into the pit to strangle me with his hands.

A wave of nausea racked me. I thought it was from shock and horror, but the earth began to tremble. Red lined my vision. The ground shook harder and harder. I turned aside and retched, though there was nothing in my stomach.

Beside Yanner's still form, a miniature ravine opened with a loud, sucking pop, drawing puddles of rainwater into it. With a violent jerk, the crack widened, and Yanner's body slipped halfway into the muddy hole. I reached for him, not ready for

316

the earth to take him. His body should be washed and wrapped in the skin of the bear he had killed. My hand found his cold fingers, but another violent tremor threw me back against the wall and the hole widened, claiming Yanner.

My heart followed him into Mother Earth.

Another wave of nausea assaulted me, and I leaned against the slick wall. With a deep rumble, the hole that had swallowed Yanner deepened, the crevice racing to the wall where Tubal stood, splitting it apart beneath him. Lightning flashed as Tubal wavered and fell into the pit. I thought the gaping maw would take him, too, but he managed to cling to a boulder exposed by the ripped earth.

In the rapid flashes of light, I watched, more afraid of him than the black hollow in the earth, as he worked his way toward me on the eroding mud. He made it to an outcrop right beneath me and reached up. I pressed as far from him as I could, but I had nowhere to go. He grabbed my ankle and glared up at me.

"When I fall, you will too," he said.

I caught a sob in my throat, fighting nausea and the fear of being pulled over the edge with him. I remembered Dianna's twisted body. Even in the lightning flashes, I could not see the bottom of this crevice. My hands fumbled for something to hit him. A bone lay just beyond my reach, but if I tried to lunge for it or struggle with him, he would pull me down. How far would we fall into darkness? What waited for us?

I was more terrified than when I drank poison. Perhaps that was stupid, but I had chosen that possibility of death, and it would have been a death with a purpose. Tubal was choosing this one for me. I wanted to live. Yanner gave his life for me to live.

"Why do you hate me so?" I gasped.

Mud streaked his face like black tears. "You took everything away," he snarled.

"It was not my fault that Mother died. I was an infant trying to be born. I wanted life."

Hatred burned in his eyes. "It began when you were born."

I remembered what Savta had told me and realized what

he meant. I, who saw everything, had failed to see what was before me or perhaps I had seen through a child's eyes and not understood. "Tubal," I said with genuine regret. "I am sorry that Father hurt you. I did not know. Why did you not run away?"

Bitterness threaded his reply. "Stupid child that I was, I thought I had to protect you."

Surprised, I asked, "What do you mean?" A spasm rippled inside my stomach, and the earth shook yet again. Crimson sparks danced in the corner of my vision. His grip on my ankle tightened, but he kept his feet, craning over his shoulder at the yawning chasm behind him. "If our father did not have me to hurt," he snapped, "do you think he would have kept his hands from you?"

I drew a sharp breath. It had never occurred to me.

"That was the price," Tubal said, each word forced through clenched teeth, "so he would not touch you."

Tears ran down my cheeks with the rain. Finally, I understood his hate for me, and why Savta said it was mixed with love.

"Tubal," I managed. "That day when it flooded and you went with Father—he did not die from an accident, did he?"

Thunder bellowed in our ears. Into the silence that followed, he said, "I killed him. I grabbed a branch that floated by, hit him with it as hard as I could and watched the water sweep his body away."

I had no blame for him. I felt as I had when I drifted through the ceiling of the Goddess' Cave, more spirit than flesh. In that moment, nothing existed but us. Our eyes locked with a calm of purpose untouched by the fury that swirled around us or the unease that usually came with looking at a person's face. I moved away from the wall and squatted at the edge of my small ledge, covering his hand with mine, but not trying to force it off my ankle. "I forgive you, my brother."

He made a quiet, animal noise.

I extended a hand. "Climb up here with me." I believed my own ledge was also doomed, but we could stand on it together as long as we could.

318

A deep rumble warned us. Multiple flashes of lightning blanched the world. Beneath Tubal, his footing began to slide away. Again, he tightened his grip and I held my breath, preparing to be snatched over the edge with him. He stood now on one foot, all that was left him, one hand grasping the bit of earth beneath me, and the other, my ankle. The support for his remaining foot dissolved, leaving him hanging by one hand.

He looked at my extended hand and then up at my face. With his next breath, he released the ledge...and me. A flash of hard, white light illuminated him as he fell. He was still gazing at me. The thunder that followed knocked me back against the wall.

I buried my head in my hands.

Chapter Fifty-Two

Huddled against the mud and rain, I watched the narrow ledge of mud, the space that held my life, slowly erode from the pouring rain and tremors. Never had I felt so isolated and alone. I had fought for my life, but I was not sure I wanted to live. Part of me did, because I clung to the wall, my heart pounding, unable to think beyond the image of falling into oblivion.

"Na'amah?"

At first, I thought I was dreaming that Yanner called me, so well did I know that voice. Then I realized the sound had the timber and color of wood, knotted and whorled, and worn smooth by skilled hands. It was Noah's voice. I looked up. In a flash of lightning, I saw him on his belly at the pit's edge.

"Stay where you are," he said.

I almost laughed. Where did he think I could go? Another tremor tore away a piece of my ledge, and the laugh froze in my mouth.

I looked up again, wanting to see Noah's face before I died, but he was gone. Instead, something dark and long was sliding over the pit's rim. "Hurry," I heard my husband's voice, "but be careful. We can't trust the ground."

The long object tipped over the edge and fell right beside me, one end still at the top of the pit's edge. It was a tree trunk with most of the branches shortened to make a ladder.

"Are you hurt?" Noah shouted. "We can come get you."

"No," I said, although I was still very sore from my fall. "I can climb."

It was difficult to climb with both care and speed. I knew if the ledge went, the log would tumble over and I with it, but Mother Goddess or luck allowed me to reach the top.

Noah grasped me and pulled me out, holding me tightly and saying my name repeatedly. I wanted to stay there in the haven of his arms. All three of my sons crowded around us. My heart swelled with love and pride in them.

"Mother, are you hurt? We were so worried about you," Shem said.

Ham, loving his stories even at such a moment, added, "Inka found out just this morning that they threw you in the pit. We've been working on this tree. None of the beaver logs would work, so we had to cut one down."

Ja'peth put a hand on my shoulder. "We worked all day to get this tree here."

"Fleet dragged it," Shem said with pride in his voice. "She came home."

"My sons," I sobbed and turned to embrace them all. Then shock and sorrow and exhaustion hit me, and I wavered. Noah scooped me into his arms. "What about your knee?" I said into his ear, not minding the scratch of his beard. "I can walk."

"Hush, woman."

"Yanner," I said, beginning to cry again. "Yanner is dead."

His grip around me tightened. "Hush."

I barely remembered getting to the boat-house. Shem took me from Noah, carrying me the entire way. The sky remained overcast, and rain continued to fall, but the darkness lightened from black to grey, enough to announce the morning.

Our boat-house rested over the channel on a small roll of ground. Water had already flowed over the creek banks, rising even as we watched, and we had to wade to the house. Noah carried me inside and laid me on a pile of furs. Inka rushed to me, her face pale.

"Did you warn people?" I demanded, sitting up and grabbing her arm. "Why did you not flee to the mountains?"

"Yes, I warned them, Na'amah. Your brother's wife and child went. They will be safe. Many people left."

I lay back down. "Then it was worth it."

"Of course it was. And Vashti sent messengers out everywhere. People will survive because of what you did. Now you must rest."

The entire house creaked and groaned.

Ja'peth said, "I guess we're about to see if this thing will float."

"It smells in here," I said, starting to slip over the edge of consciousness into my exhaustion.

"You didn't think Shem would let us leave his animals outside, did you?" Inka teased, though worry pinched her eyes. "Didn't you notice the sheep and goats? All his creatures are here, even the snake." She wrinkled her upper lip. "And look, there is a horse in here too."

"Of course I noticed," I mumbled. "I notice everything."

Chapter Fifty-Three

While I wait for Bennu to return, I am finishing my story. I hope Bennu will find his way back before he wearies. His wings, I remind myself, are large and strong. He has returned twice when I thought he was lost.

Noah finds me and Black Dog on the upper deck of our house, as a shaft of sunlight pours through a crack in the sodden gray heavens, the first sign in many days that the rains might stop. "How do you feel?"

"Better." The turbulence had made me ill for several days. "I feel best out here."

He nods. "Just don't go too close to the edge. I should have built a rail."

"Well, when we find land, you can build one."

"What will be the need then?"

"You think I will live in a regular house now? What if there is another flood?" I put a hand in Black Dog's ruff to hide its tremor.

Noah tucks me under one arm. "Look."

I follow where he points.

"Do you see the colors Father God paints on the sky?"

"The rainbow?"

"Yes. It's a promise he won't flood the earth again."

I snort. "Is that so?"

"Yes, of course it is so."

I lay my head on his still-broad chest, amused that he would try to comfort me with such silliness. "I would rather wedge this house on some mountain peak than trust in a beam of colored light."

He looks east. "There must be mountains somewhere."

I peer cautiously over the roof's edge into the murky, swirling water. "Perhaps they lie beneath us." I feel his shudder in reaction to my words, and I do not blame him, though we think the purple shadows on the eastern horizon are mountains. As far as we know, everything that had existed— villages, fields, and even perhaps my dear hills, now lies beneath the water. We have no idea how deep it is or where we are. We could be adrift on the Great Salt Sea.

How many made it to the mountains? I cannot stop seeing mind-images of people caught in the rising flood— climbing trees to escape, thinking the waters would recede when the rain stopped, not knowing, or not believing, that the Salt Sea poured into the Black Lake, and it would never recede. I see children clinging to their mothers, men and women grasping at wood or debris—all the memories of my childhood terror and many that I had not actually seen, but imagine too clearly.

Old as I am, I curl into Noah's arms when the images crowd my mind, clamoring and burning my eyes, and let him rock me. He even tries to sing and that makes us both laugh.

I try to think how fortunate we are to live, to have our family and dearest friends with us, and to believe that there will be a future.

A flutter of white above us catches my eye. I point to the top section of our boat-house, our bedroom we now share with several of Shem's creatures that do not mix well with the sheep, goats, or Fleet. Some wild animals have clamored aboard and we care for them as well as we can. Fortunately, no tigers or aurochs.

Noah turns to see Bennu settling on the roof. "What is that he's got?"

Bennu launches off the roof and flutters down to us. I extend my arm to give him a wider choice of perch and to discourage him from landing on my head. He alights between my shoulder and elbow and sidles up my arm to settle on my shoulder, dropping a piece of branch into my lap.

I lift his offering with a smile. The leaves are dark green on top and silver on the bottom. An olive bough. If any tree could survive, it would be an olive tree, whose roots run deep. My heart lifts. "This is a much better sign than your rainbow. The water is receding somewhere close enough for Bennu to reach land."

A very welcome sign. We cannot live like this many more days. Every bowl and pot has gone into service to catch rainwater. We have slaughtered all but four of the goats and three sheep for meat, and Noah began to disassemble parts of the upper deck for firewood. The animals are restless. Even the dogs are short-tempered. Over the years Shem has acquired many animals with stories like Fleet's, parentless and needing his protection. Keeping them all from hurting themselves or each other is exhausting work, not to mention trying to maintain a clean house. It amazes me what can come out of an animal, even when there is very little going in the other end.

"If we live through this, what a tale we will have for our grandchildren," Noah says.

I hook a piece of hair that has escaped my braid over an ear. "We need to charge one of our sons to tell the story."

"Ham," Noah says at once. "He loves stories. You can tell him yours, the one you've been keeping since you were taken by the River People."

"He will get it all wrong," I complain. "I've heard him story-telling to Ja'peth. He twists the tales, changing things and putting in extra, even to Savta's stories—those handed down since the time of First Man."

"Would you rather leave it to Ja'peth or Shem?"

I sigh. "You are right. Shem's mind is full of his animals, and Ja'peth could not remember his own name if his wife did not repeat it every other breath."

"This is a story unlike any other." Noah takes a deep breath and spreads his hands. "How can you not believe in the gods after this?"

"I believe—" I say, gazing out at the rainbow glazing the sky with fragile color.

Noah huffs in surprise. "I didn't think you would ever believe in anything you couldn't see or touch or smell." "I do see," I said, trying to sort out my thoughts. "I do feel and smell and know, but I cannot contain it with a name."

The smile I catch on his face is one of amusement and respect. He waits for more, patient, as always.

"Everything," I tried again, "every stone, every bird, every plant seems to have a purpose, a secret self, beyond itself and yet . . . the purpose is itself."

Still, he waits, as if I am not finished. Perhaps I am not. I should know better words, I who have trod the depths of sky and sea.

Or perhaps I delude myself and the berry's juice only enhanced my hearing and spun an extraordinary dream. Perhaps so, and if so, did Mother Goddess or Father God send the dream?

Always with the whys. I smile at Savta's voice in my memory.

I do not know where truth lies. It is difficult not to believe that the earth is alive or that some hand strews the stars across the sky. Elder Mariah's words still dance in my mind— *The Goddess is the earth and the earth is the Goddess.* I still do not know if Mother Goddess or Father God or some Unknown God exists or cares what we do, but I do know awe at the world, at all that I know and the more that I do not. I know a deep gratitude that I am a part of such a mystery . . . and that will have to do.

"Maybe all the gods are true gods," I say, only partly in jest and partly because I can say anything I wish to him.

"Maybe," Noah agrees, his thick, gray brows almost touching. "The people who came to see our boat-house worshipped gods I'd never heard of. I would not have believed there were so many, but I do not see any reason for us to judge which ones are real and which are not."

"Then again," I say, "maybe all of them are really only one."

"Well, that is an interesting idea." He tugs my ears. "I am

glad I wed you, Little Bird, not because you are beautiful, but because you are full of interesting thoughts."

I smile at him, take his hands from my ears, and place them on my belly. "That is not all I am full of."

Startled, he stares at me before his sun-stained face brightens. "Is it—?"

I nod before he can finish. "Yes."

I will miss Yanner for the rest of my life. This ache for him that burns a hole in my heart can never be filled, but he has given me the most precious of gifts. I know we will survive, because one day I will stand on a hillside with my daughter. Her hair, like honey held to the sun, will catch in the wind, and she will look up at me with eyes the color of spring grass.

I cannot explain how I can be so certain, but Noah does not dispute my truths. I am his wife, and he, after all, is my husband.

For the next three millennia, the goddess reigned
as the primary deity in the Middle East.

Postcript

Although *Noah's Wife* is a work of fiction, there is scientific evidence to support the theory that a great flood nearly wiped out a relatively advanced civilization living along the shores of a fresh water lake we now know as the Black Sea. Marine geologists William Ryan and Walter Pitman proposed this theory and cited significant geological and archeological evidence in their book, *Noah's Flood, The New Scientific Discoveries About the Event that Changed History* (Simon & Schuster, 1998). This theory is supported by the exciting explorations of Paul Ballard, the famous adventurer who discovered the sunken *Titanic*. Ballard has found evidence of the remains of a civilization hundreds of feet beneath the Black Sea, corroborating previous radiocarbon dating and paleontological evidence from shells and sediment. From these sources, the date of the flood was set at approximately 5500 BCE. Further research around this time period established the setting for this novel, which takes place in Anatolia, current day Turkey. Stories about a flood are found in almost every civilization on earth, the oldest written one being the Mesopotamian epic poem, *Gilgamesh*. Many scholars believe that the Genesis tale "borrows" from this much older work.

According to geologists Ryan and Pitman, the Black Sea flood of 5500 B.C.E. reversed the flow of the Tigris and Euphrates rivers, no doubt flooding the flat southern plains of modern day Iraq. The book of Genesis states that Abraham came from Ur, an ancient city in that area. Perhaps he brought with him the tale of Gilgamesh.

Noah's wife is barely mentioned and not directly named in the Genesis story, however, some Hebrew scholars believe a later section giving the genealogy of a woman named "Na'amah" refers to Noah's wife. I drew on the Biblical story primarily for the names and relationships of Noah and his family. From there, the tale is my own.

Evidence supports the primacy of the goddess religion for thousands of years in the Levant and especially in Anatolia. Small statuettes of female deities are the oldest physical evidence of human worship. Similarly, excavation at one of the world's most ancient sites of civilization, Çatalhöyük, has uncovered a society that primarily worshiped a goddess. Michael Balter explores this fascinating dig in *The Goddess and the Bull: Çatalhöyük —An Archaeological Journey to the Dawn of Civilization* (Simon & Schuster, 2005).

The goddess, the Earth/Sea Mother, was absorbed into the pantheon of later cultures, such as the Hittites. Gradually her powers were usurped and eventually repressed by a patriarchal interpretation of history and worship, which culminated in the compilation of the Hebrew Bible (11th to 6th Century B.C.E.). Even so, modern archeological evidence exists that she played a significant part in early Hebrew culture. Raphael Patai (*The Hebrew Goddess*, Wayne State University Press, 1990) and Merlyn Stone (*When God was a Woman,* Harcourt/Harcourt Brace, 1976), among others, have documented her influence and prominence and her reappearance in many guises and forms throughout history.

For thousands of years, societies in the Black Sea area were transitioning from hunter-gatherer/herder to agricultural cultures. I take responsibility for using the concepts of Father God and Mother Goddess to represent the possible conflict this engendered and to foreshadow the eventual clash of religious views. Father God (storm god) as the predominant deity does not appear to have taken permanent root in the area until sometime near the end of the 3rd millennium and into the 2nd.

In *Noah's Wife*, I made Na'amah an Asperger savant. The term "Asperger Syndrome" (AS) or "Asperger's" was, of course, unknown in ancient times, but there is no reason to believe that the syndrome did not exist. Most experts put it on the high-functioning end of the autism spectrum, although there is some disagreement about whether it is a form of autism or an independent developmental syndrome. AS and autism, in general, exist on a spectrum. Individuals' experiences and symptoms vary along that continuum.

Many persons with Asperger's are highly intelligent. Some have extraordinary recall and obsessive knowledge about areas that capture their interest. Na'amah's obsessive interest was sheep. While savant skills are not universally present in persons with AS, they do occur and can include prodigious memory and/ or skills with numbers and math. Some have heightened sensory perceptions and some experience synesthesia, a condition where one type of stimulation evokes the sensation of another. For Na'amah, the hearing of a sound produced color and sometimes shape visualizations, and she had savant abilities of memory recall.

I took literary license to extend Na'amah's sensitivity to sound to include the infrasound, low frequency vibrations below the audible range. Infrasound has been known to cause symptoms of nausea, discomfort, and wavering in the peripheral vision. It is theorized that infrasound is produced prior to earthquakes, and that this might be the explanation as to why some animals seem able to predict major quakes.

It was also my speculation that the discomfort many persons with this condition feel when looking at another person's face is related to an overload of information, as some persons with autism and AS do not seem to have the ability to screen or synthesize information as neurotypical people do. On the flip side, this may give persons with AS the ability to notice details that others do not.

Research has identified a cluster of genes that may be

responsible for autism and AS. When the genes express in one way, a person may be severely handicapped. Expressed in another way, the result may be creativity or even genius. There is some evidence that Einstein and Hemingway, for example, had AS. It is possible that we all have some degree of this condition/abilities. Perhaps these gene clusters are part of nature's exploration of survival characteristics. If so, we should be respectful of that and very careful about genetically "curing" it, as we might be curing the human race of creativity.

Any historical errors are mine. I do not have Asperger's and therefore have relied on information from those who do and from researchers (with the exceptions noted) but take responsibility for any missteps there, as well.

Glossary for *Noah's Wife*

Adah Lamech's former wife; Na'amah's "aunt"
Aruru Priestess of the goddess
Aurochs ancient bovine, cattle ancestor
Batan chief elder, tribe of First Man
Bennu Na'amah's bird
Elizcim father of three sisters who married Noah's children
Ham Noah's second son; married Ne'ela
Inka Na'amah's friend
Jabel Na'amah's uncle
Ja'peth Noah's youngest son
Kahor elder representing Hunter Clan
Kamukka River People warrior
Lamech Na'amah's father
Mariah elder representing Mother Goddess
Na'amah Noah's wife, tribe of First Man
Natan villager, tribe of First Man
Noah boat maker, tribe of First Man
Panor male captive of River People
Rankor leader of River People
River People pre-dynastic Egyptians
Sara Na'amah's daughter
Savta grandmother (specifically, Na'amah's grandmother)
Selkeit Scorpion goddess; watches over bearing women
Shem Noah's first son; married Sede
Sunnic Tubal's friend
Takunah River People warrior
Ta-urt goddess of the River People
Tubal Na'amah's brother
Vashti Daughter of the Goddess
Yanner Na'amah's childhood friend
Zett villager, tribe of First Man

About the Author

T.K. Thorne is a retired police captain in Birmingham, Alabama, USA. She holds a master's degree in Social Work from the University of Alabama and currently works as the executive director of the business improvement district in downtown Birmingham. Her writing has won awards for poetry, fiction, and screenplays. *Noah's Wife* is her debut novel. She lives on a mountain in northeast Alabama with a family that includes several horses, dogs, and cats (but no aurochs or tigers).

The author invites you to her website for
book club questions, speaking events, newsletters and more.
www.TKThorne.com

Author's next work is

Angel's at the Gate
the Story of Lot's Wife

CPSIA information can be obtained at www.ICGtesting.com
Printed in the USA
LVOW062044260712

291630LV00001B/4/P